The Roommate

The Roommate

♡ ♡ ♡

ROSIE DANAN

JOVE
NEW YORK

A JOVE BOOK
Published by Berkley
An imprint of Penguin Random House LLC
penguinrandomhouse.com

Library of Congress Cataloging-in-Publication Data

Names: Danan, Rosie, author.
Title: The roommate / Rosie Danan.
Description: First edition. | New York: Jove, 2020.
Identifiers: LCCN 2019059078 | ISBN 9780593101605 (trade paperback) |
ISBN 9780593101612 (ebook)
Subjects: GSAFD: Love stories.
Classification: LCC PS3604.A4745 R66 2020 | DDC 813/.6—dc23
LC record available at https://lccn.loc.gov/2019059078

First Edition: September 2020

Printed in the United States of America
1 3 5 7 9 10 8 6 4 2

Cover art by Vasya Kolotusha
Cover design by Colleen Reinhart
Book design by Alison Cnockaert

For Micah Benson.

You're the reason my characters get the love they deserve.

chapter one

♡ ♡ ♡

W HEN THE MAN of her dreams ran a hand across his devastatingly handsome face and said, "I have to tell you something, and I don't want you to freak out," Clara Wheaton considered, for the first time, the alarming possibility that she could get dumped by someone she'd never managed to date.

She cursed her wicked ancestors as she glared at the pineapple-scented air freshener hanging from the rearview mirror of Everett Bloom's Jeep Wrangler.

No matter how many lines she'd fed her mother's friends back in Greenwich about "pursuing fresh career opportunities," she'd moved across the country because part of her believed she stood a chance at winning Everett's heart after fourteen years of pining.

"I rented my room out for the summer," he said, the words both gentle and firm, the way someone might confess to a child that Santa wasn't real.

"You . . . rented your room?" Clara's response came slowly, comprehension dawning with each syllable. "The one you offered me two weeks ago?" If he hadn't been driving, and her mother hadn't made her memorize the etiquette of Emily Post in her adolescence, she might have lunged at him.

She'd broken the lease on her apartment in Manhattan, left behind her friends and family, and turned down a curatorial internship at the Guggenheim. All for . . . nothing?

Even compared to generations of storied Wheaton family scandals, surely this nosedive into misadventure could claim a land speed record.

The palm trees they passed along the freeway mocked her, a hallmark of the Hollywood happy ending slipping between her fingers.

She hadn't even unpacked her suitcases . . . an undigested airport pretzel still floated somewhere below her diaphragm. How could Everett already be saying good-bye?

"No, hey wait, no. I didn't rent *your* room." His signature lazy smile—the same one she'd fallen for the moment his family moved in next door all those years ago—dropped back into place. "I rented the master. The band got an offer to go on tour last minute. Nothing too wild, but we're opening for a blues band outside Santa Fe with this crazy cool sound, and Trent bought a sick van to haul the equipment . . ."

His careless words sent her straight back to high school. How many times after his social standing skyrocketed in tenth grade had Everett canceled plans with her in favor of band practice? How many times since then had he looked over her shoulder instead of into her eyes when she tried to talk to him?

No one would believe she'd earned two advanced degrees from Ivy League institutions only to end up this stupid.

"Who rented the room?" Clara interrupted his detailed description of the tour van's vintage fenders.

"What? Oh, the room. Don't worry. He's this super nice guy. Josh something. Found him on the Internet a few days ago. Very chill." He waved a hand in her general direction. "You're gonna love him."

She closed her eyes so he wouldn't see them roll toward the sunroof.

No matter how many times she considered the lengths she would go to in her quest to finally win Everett Bloom's affection, she'd never imagined this.

He turned the car onto a street proudly sporting a rainbow crosswalk. "Listen, I'll drop you off and give you my keys and stuff, but then I gotta head right out. We're supposed to be in New Mexico by Friday." The last traces of apology ebbed with his words.

Clara watched his fingers, the ones she'd often imagined running through her hair in a tender caress, resume their furious beat on the steering wheel. She searched for any trace of her childhood best friend underneath his aloof veneer and came up short.

Pain burned beneath her breastbone. Somewhere in her bloodline, a Wheaton had crossed Fate, cursing his descendants to pay the price. That was the only explanation for why, the one and only time Clara had taken a leap of faith, she'd landed with a spectacular belly flop.

She dragged a deep breath into her lungs. There had to be a way to salvage this whole thing.

"How long will you be gone?" If there was one thing she'd learned from her ne'er-do-well family, it was damage control.

"Hard to say." Everett pulled the Jeep up to a Spanish-style rancher in desperate need of a new coat of paint. "At least three months. We've got tour dates through August."

"Are you sure you can't wait a few days to leave?" She hated the note of pleading that bled into her question. "I don't know anyone else in Los Angeles."

A face from the past, blurry through the lens of adolescent memory, flashed through her mind before she pushed it away. "I don't have a job here yet. Hell, I don't even have a car." She tried to laugh, to lighten the mood, but what came out sounded more like a grunt.

Everett frowned. "I'm sorry, Cee. I know I promised to help you get settled, but this is a huge break for the band. You get that, right?" He reached over and squeezed her hand. "Look, this doesn't have to change the plan we made. Everything I said over the phone is still true. This move, California, getting out from under your mother's thumb . . . It'll all be good for you."

He held his palm out for a high five in a long-familiar gesture. They might as well have been back in homeroom cramming for the SATs. Reluctantly, she completed the unspoken request.

"L.A. is summer vacation from real life. Relax and have fun. I'll be back before you know it."

Fun? She wanted to scream. Fun was a luxury for people with less to lose, but like generations of Wheaton women before her, Clara resigned herself to silent fuming instead of confrontation.

If a friend had told her a week ago that they planned to move across the country and give up a better life than most people could lay claim to for a shot with a guy—even a particularly handsome guy—Clara would have invested significant energy into trying to stop them. *That's insane*, she might have said. It's always easy when the shoe is on the other foot. No one from Greenwich knew the consequences of an ill-conceived impulse better than a Wheaton. Unfortunately, like grain alcohol, unrequited love grows more potent with time.

Everett unloaded her bags from the back of the Wrangler and hugged her—too tight and too fast to provide much comfort. "I'll call you from the road in a couple of days to make sure you're settled." He fumbled with his key ring.

Clara stared at her own hand with detachment as he pressed the small piece of metal into her palm. The urge to run, primal and nonsensical, sang under her skin.

She had two choices. She could call a cab, book a seat on the next flight back to JFK, and try to rebuild her old life, piece by piece.

Or she could stay.

Stay in this city she didn't know, live with a man she'd never met, without a job or friends, without the clout her family name commanded on the East Coast.

The Greenwich gossip hounds would salivate over her disgrace. She could already picture the headline. *No Longer "In Bloom," Careful Clara Shacks Up with Stranger.*

Not this time. She straightened her shoulders, smoothed her shirt, and ran her tongue over her teeth to ward off rogue lipstick. You only got one chance to make a first impression.

The heavy thump of Everett's car stereo pounded in her ears as he pulled out, but Clara didn't turn to watch him drive away.

Paint peeled back from the faded door when she pressed her palm against it. *Damn.* The society pages were going to have a field day with this one.

Bracing herself, Clara entered her new home the way soldiers enter enemy territory: with light footsteps, eyes mapping the terrain, and elbows tucked tight against her body.

Plush carpet muted her heeled sandals as she surveyed the living room. Without rose-colored glasses crafted by over a decade of repressed lust, the space left much to be desired.

She ran a fingertip through the blanket of dust coating a bookcase in the corner. An odor of decay wafted from abandoned take-out containers littering the coffee table. Clara tried to inhale through her mouth.

Underneath her foot, something crunched. Kicking up her heel, she identified the remains of a potato chip.

Despite the stench and the mess, the little house radiated a retro coziness that stood in direct contrast to both her family's sprawling colonial in Connecticut and the cramped Morningside Heights walk-up she'd rented near campus.

The faded wallpaper exuded kitschy charm, fighting for her affection, but she couldn't shake the crushing weight of her disappointment. Clara wiped off the seat of the sofa before sitting down.

"So this is how it feels to be well and truly fucked."

"I get that a lot," said a low voice behind her.

Clara sprang to her feet so fast she stumbled. "Oh . . . um . . . Hello." She scrambled to stand behind her massive wheeled suitcase, creating a fifty-pound shield between her and the man standing in the doorway separating the kitchen and the living room.

He leaned against the door frame. "I don't suppose you're robbing me?"

When Clara frowned in confusion, he gestured to her ensemble.

She lowered her chin and scrutinized the sleeveless black turtleneck and matching skinny jeans she'd picked out that morning. Some time in her midtwenties, she'd traded the Argyle and houndstooth of her youth for a closet full of well-tailored monotone basics. Unfortunately, it seemed black clothing, while widely considered slimming and chic in New York City, was the preferred attire of home intruders in Los Angeles.

"Er . . . no." Clara tugged at her collar, glad, in retrospect, that she'd suffered the indignity of touching up her makeup in the tiny airplane bathroom while one of her fellow passengers pounded on the door. "I'm Clara Wheaton," she said when silence lingered.

"Josh." He closed the distance between them, offering her a handshake. "Nice to meet you."

When their hands came together, she inspected his fingernails as a bellwether for his personal hygiene habits. Neat and trim. *Thank goodness.*

After five seconds, Josh raised an eyebrow and Clara released his hand with a sheepish smile.

Despite his impressive height and the fact that his shoulders had filled most of the door frame, she didn't find him intimidating. His rumpled clothes and the mop of overgrown blond curls suggested he'd just rolled out of bed. Striking dark brows should have cast him as surly, but the rest of his face resisted brooding.

He was cute but not quite handsome. Not like Everett, whose mere presence still made her speech falter after all these years. Clara accepted this small form of mercy from the universe. She'd always found it impossible to talk to handsome men.

"Nice to meet you," she echoed, adding, "Please don't murder or molest me," as an afterthought.

"You got it." He raised both hands in a helpless gesture. "So . . . I guess that means we'll be living together?"

"For the time being." At least long enough for her to develop a contingency plan.

Josh peered into the open door of the bathroom. "Where's Everett? He didn't stick around to get you settled?"

Clara's shoulders crept toward her ears. "The band needed to get on the road right away."

"Pretty crazy, huh? Them getting invited to tour last minute?"

"Yeah." She fought to keep the bitterness out of her voice. "Wild."

"Worked out for me, though. I couldn't believe the lowball rent Everett asked for on a place this nice."

Clara decided not to mention that Everett had inherited the house, free and clear, from his grandfather and likely only charged enough to cover the taxes. She massaged her temples, trying to ward off a monstrous headache. Whether it came from stress, jet lag, or dying dreams, she couldn't say.

The longer she stood in this house, the more real the nightmare became. She sat back down on the couch when her vision swam.

"Hey, are you okay?" Her new roommate came to kneel in front of her, the way adults do when they want to speak to a small child. Clara glanced away from where his thighs strained the seams of his jeans.

He had a spattering of freckles across the bridge of his nose. She focused on the one at the very center and spoke to it. "I'm fine. Just reckoning with the consequences of a multigenerational family curse. Pretend I'm not here."

You'd think decades of old money and carefully monitored good breeding would weed out the Wheatons' notorious inclination toward destructive behavior, but if the recent arrest of her brother, Oliver, was anything to go by, the longer their lineage grew, the grimmer the consequences of their behavioral missteps.

Comparatively, she'd gotten off easy with an old house and a broken heart.

Josh wrinkled his forehead. "Um, if you say so. Oh, hey, wait here a minute."

As if she had anywhere else to go.

"I think I've got something that might help." He strode into the kitchen and returned a moment later to press a cold can of beer into her hands. "Sorry I don't have anything stronger."

Clara wasn't much of a beer drinker. But at this point, it couldn't hurt. She popped the top and took a deep slug. "Blech." Why did men insist on pretending IPAs tasted good? She dropped her head between her knees and employed a deep-breathing technique she'd observed once when accompanying her cousin to Lamaze class.

"Hey . . . uh . . . you're not gonna toss your cookies, right?"

Bile rose in the back of her throat at the suggestion. This guy was about as helpful as every other man she knew. "Perhaps you could say something reassuring?"

After a few seconds, he blew out a breath. "Your body destroys and replaces all of its cells every seven years."

Clara sat up slowly. "Okay, well"—she pursed her lips—"you tried. Thanks," she said with dismissal.

"I read that in a magazine at the dentist's office." He shot her a weak smile. "Thought it was kinda nice. I figure it means no matter how bad we mess up, eventually we get a clean slate."

"So you're telling me in seven years, I'll forget the fact that I uprooted my entire life and moved across the country because a guy who's not even my boyfriend encouraged me to, and I quote, 'follow my bliss'?"

"Right. Scientifically speaking, yes."

He had nice eyes. Big and brown, but not dull. They looked warm, like they'd spent time simmering over an open flame. *Cute but not handsome*, she reminded herself.

"Well, okay. I was expecting a banal detail about your job, to be honest. But not bad for off the top of your head." She wiped her hand across her mouth and handed him back the beer.

"Somehow I don't think hearing about my job would reassure you." He took a long sip from her discarded can.

Guess that answered the question of whether Josh was the kind of roommate who would eat her leftovers. "You're not a mortician, are you?"

He shook his head. "I work in the entertainment industry."

Figures. Clara immediately lost interest. The last thing she needed was some wannabe filmmaker asking her to read his screenplay.

Josh gave her a blatant once-over. "You're not what I expected."

Well, that makes two of us, buddy.

She'd expected to live with Everett. She'd pictured the two of them cooking dinners together, their shoulders touching as they worked side by side. She'd imagined watching action movies deep into the night like they did back when they were thirteen, only this time instead of separate sofas they'd curl up together under a shared blanket with glasses of wine.

This house should have set the scene for their love story. Everett should have written a song in that window seat inspired by their first kiss.

Instead, she got to share a toilet with a stranger.

Clara stood up and shook off her unfulfilled wishes. "What do you mean?"

"I'm surprised a girl like you"—he gestured to her Louis Vuitton luggage—"would slum it with a roommate in a place like this."

Clara gathered her dark hair over one shoulder and smoothed the tresses. "I received the luggage as a gift from my grandmother." She lowered her eyes to the carpet. "I took the room because I'm between jobs at the moment." The lie sat sour on her tongue and she quickly swerved back into truth territory. "I've known Everett forever. When I graduated a few weeks ago he offered me his spare room."

"Oh. A graduate, huh? What were you studying?"

"I recently completed my doctorate in art history," she said with as much bravado as she could muster. As a kid, she'd dreamed about making work of her own, but eventually, she'd realized art required exposing parts of herself she'd rather keep hidden—her hopes and fears, her passions and yearning. Analysis and curation let her keep art at arm's length while using school as a way to extend the exit ramp to adulthood.

Josh smirked. "Is that like a special degree they only give out to rich people?"

Clara ground her teeth so hard she thought she heard a pop. "Let's keep the interpersonal chitchat to a minimum, shall we?"

She grabbed her purse and hunted for her move-in checklist, finding it buried underneath her airplane pillow and first-aid kit. Clara had compiled the six-page document to include all manner of questions and instructions on what to look for to know whether a new home was up to code in Los Angeles. Holding the document made breathing a little easier.

When she looked up, Josh hadn't left. "Please don't take this the wrong way, but frankly, Everett didn't tell me he had to go out of town until right now, and no offense, I'm sure you're probably nice, but this"—she gestured to the space between them—"falls a little outside my comfort zone."

"Hey, me too." He put his hand to his heart. "I've seen a lot of made-for-TV movies, you know. You're exactly the kind of pint-sized, tightly wound socialite who goes crazy and paints the walls with chicken blood. How do I know I'm safe from *you*?"

Clara cocked her hip and stared at the over-six-foot man across from her. His threadbare T-shirt, featuring a vintage picture of Debbie Harry, barely obscured his muscular chest and broad shoulders. "You're honestly worried about me?"

His eyes sank to the move-in checklist in her hand. "Oh my God. Is that laminated?" He looked positively delighted.

"My mother got me a machine last Christmas," she told him defensively as he took it from her for further inspection. "It prevents smudging."

He pitched his head back and laughed. A loud rumble without a trace of mocking in it. "'Check the water pressure on all taps for inconsistency,'" he read from the sheet. "This is too good. Did you write this yourself?"

"California is known for its propensity toward forest fires. You have to document pre-move-in conditions to arm yourself for possible insurance claims. The smoke damage alone—"

He laughed some more in what she deemed a rather overblown display of mirth.

Clara snatched back the sheet. "Should we discuss some house rules?"

Josh's eyes twinkled. "Like no parties on school nights?"

"You're right. *Rules* sounds a bit aggressive. I'm thinking more along the lines of guidelines for harmonious cohabitation. We might as well make the best of a bad situation."

Josh straightened up. "Of course. I'm afraid you'll need to make the first rule, though. I'm out of practice."

"Well, for instance, Everett mentioned a while back that the lock on the bathroom door doesn't work. So until we can have that fixed, I suggest we employ a three-knock strategy."

"Why three?"

"It would be easy to miss one or two knocks . . ." She spoke to the beat-up coffee table. "If you were in the shower, for example."

"Well, we wouldn't want that, certainly."

She looked up to find his whole body changed with the tilt of his lips. Goose bumps broke out across Clara's arms despite the balmy June afternoon. Josh had some kind of magnetism she hadn't noticed before. Even when she went and stood behind the couch, putting a physical barrier between them, her body hummed *closer, closer, closer.*

"Hey, listen. You don't need to guard your virtue from me, okay?" Josh dropped the charm like someone shrugging out of a jacket. He must have noticed that the energy between them had shifted from playful to something meatier.

"I'm taken, so you've got nothing to worry about. I'm only living here until I can convince my ex-girlfriend to let me move back in. She's a tough nut, but I'm sure I'll be able to wear her down in a week or two, and then I'll be out of your hair for good." He broke the news in the practiced gentle tone of someone used to getting people's hopes up and having to let them down easy.

"Oh," Clara said, and then as she caught his meaning, "No." She crossed her hands in an X. He had the wrong idea. Obviously. She wanted Everett. Had loved him almost as long as she could remember. She didn't even know this guy with his ripped jeans and his bedhead. "Of course not. I didn't think that you'd want to . . ." She waved a hand down her body and stuck out her tongue in disgust.

His eyes followed the path she'd tracked. "Wait a second. I didn't mean I wouldn't want to under different circumstances. You're very . . ." He held his hands out in front of his chest like he was assessing the weight of a pair of overripe melons.

Clara's eyes went wide.

"Oh God. I can't believe I did that. I'm sorry. I just meant that you . . . um . . . what's a respectful way to say . . ." He put his hands back up.

Blood rushed to her face. "I got it."

"Right. Sorry. Again." He shook his whole body like a wet dog. "Besides, I thought for sure you and Everett were a thing. The way he talked about you, it definitely sounded like you two had history."

At the mention of her beloved, the faded bruises on her heart bloomed anew and throbbed. She didn't know how much to share without seeming pathetic. She and Everett certainly had history, even if the romantic part was one-sided.

Something in the earnest set of Josh's brows gave Clara the impression he could handle more than the sugarcoated version of her past with Everett—more than the BS stories she'd given her friends and family back east, so they wouldn't judge her or worry about her rash decision to up and move.

For some reason, she found herself spilling her guts to this unkempt stranger. "Everett and I grew up together. Despite living on different coasts for almost ten years, we've kept in touch with phone calls and visits. I don't know if you got to know him at all, but he's this amazing mix of sweet and smart and funny—"

"And he encouraged you to drop everything and move out here only to abandon you the first chance he got?" Josh arched an eyebrow.

Clara took a step back. The truth stung. "That's not exactly what happened. I know how this looks." She lowered her voice, embarrassed at how she'd let it climb in volume. "But when Everett called a couple of weeks ago and painted this picture of life in L.A., all sunsets and ocean air and people who don't have to wear mouth guards at night because they can't stop stress-grinding their teeth . . ."

A dimple appeared in Josh's left cheek.

"I know it sounds stupid, but it seemed like a sign or something. This felt like my chance. At love, adventure, happily ever after, the whole Hallmark thing."

"Let me get this straight. You, a woman who created a laminated move-in checklist, made a huge life-altering decision based on a hazy sign from the universe?"

Clara shrugged. "Haven't you ever done something stupid to impress someone you liked?"

Josh plopped down on the sofa, propped his feet on the coffee table, and crossed them at the ankles. "No. Never."

"I think you mean 'Not yet.'" Clara grabbed the handles of her rolling suitcases. "So which one of these bedrooms is mine?"

chapter two

BY THE NEXT morning, Clara had managed to maroon herself among a sea of her possessions. Having covered the majority of the floor space in her new bedroom, she now stood on the wooden desk chair trying to decide where to begin.

Unpacking was supposed to make her feel better. More settled. She'd read that in a study on how humans adjust to new environments.

But she'd checked half a suitcase with mementos to share with Everett, and now, laid out in all their faded, adolescent glory, the memories took turns punching her in the stomach.

Curling photo booth strips, the sagging cardboard box from their sad attempt at making their own board game in the seventh grade, even a Ziploc of their favorite hometown bagels—formerly frozen—currently dripping all over her bathrobe.

Everything hurt. Clara dropped her chin to her chest.

A single knock sounded on the door behind her.

"Come in." The chaos on the carpet mirrored the mess she'd made of her life. How poetic.

"How's the unpacking going?" Josh offered her a chipped mug full of steaming coffee.

Clara created a visor with her hand and turned away, but not before she got an eyeful confirming that Josh's happy trail matched his dark brown eyebrows rather than the blond curls on his head. "What the hell are you doing?"

"I kept hearing these sad little sighs from the hallway. I thought coffee might cheer you up." He surveyed her perch. "Did you climb on that chair to avoid a spider?"

Clara stepped carefully down. "You're not wearing enough clothes." She closed her eyes, but the lean muscles of his bare chest had imprinted on her retinas.

"What do you mean?"

"Didn't you see the list of rules I slipped under your door last night?" She'd spent an hour and a half after dinner writing out provisions on college-ruled paper. She'd even included designated spaces for both of their signatures.

"I thought you said they were guidelines?"

"They *are* guidelines." She tried to weave patience into her tone. "And the guidelines say all parties must wear at least three pieces of clothing when entering public areas of the house and/or during direct interaction with another roommate and/or guests."

Josh stared down at his bare feet. "What about socks?"

"What do you mean, 'What about socks'?"

"Do they count as one item of clothing or two?"

Clara placed her hands on her hips. "Socks don't count."

He sucked in air between his teeth. "Unfortunately, that's unclear in the literature."

"A sock is a nonessential clothing item."

Mischief entered his gaze. "Only until you're playing strip poker."

"Thank you for bringing me coffee." Clara accepted the mug mostly so he'd stop talking.

"No problem. I didn't know how you take it . . . but we also don't have any cream. Or sugar." He grimaced. "But listen, I'll take you to the grocery store as soon as you're done . . ." His eyes tracked the mess she'd made of the bedroom. ". . . redecorating."

Tired of making eye contact with his dusting of golden chest hair, Clara grabbed the first piece of clothing she could find—a huge old sweatshirt strewn across the back of the desk chair—and threw it with her free hand toward his rippling pectorals.

While he pulled it on, she went to grab his copy of the guidelines.

As soon as she entered the master bedroom, Clara had to force herself not to look at the bed. Everett's bed. The pillow probably still smelled like him. She took a surreptitious sniff from the doorway. Yep, this whole room smelled like Everett. Irish Spring and the vinyl of hundreds of records.

She shook her head and scanned for notebook paper, finally spotting her draft on the nightstand. Josh had already managed to spill coffee on the corner of the document. If only she'd thought to pack her laminating equipment.

By the time she returned to her room, Josh had managed to cover himself. The sleeves of her Columbia hoodie ended at his elbows. She refused to find him charming.

"I figured you made those as a jumping-off point." He pointed at her sheet. "We should collaborate on the final copy, no?" The struggle with the sweatshirt had aggravated his already disheveled hair.

An unwelcome image of him, tangled in sheets warm from his body heat, floated across her mind. She took a big gulp of coffee, using the bitter taste to rid herself of the unsettling vision. "Oh, sure." She handed over the paper. Frankly, she'd assumed he wouldn't care enough to fight her on any of the line items.

Josh sank onto her bed and reached into his wild nest of hair. From somewhere within the depths of his mane, he uncovered a pair of horn-rimmed glasses and put them on.

"Some of the stuff you've got here works."

Clara bit the inside of her cheek. Josh packed a powerful punch of allure to begin with, but her inner nerd started panting at the sight of him with readers.

"Splitting utilities. Fine. A chart outlining weekly cleaning responsibilities. Very organized. We'll need to pick up some of these supplies you listed. I don't think we've got organic furniture polish." His tongue peeked out between his teeth as he scanned the rest of the page, giving the occasional nod. "I see you've entrusted me with changing lightbulbs."

Josh glanced over to where she stood, awkwardly lingering by the doorway, and gave her short frame a once-over. "Makes sense."

He flipped the sheet. "Quiet hours from midnight to five a.m. Okay. That's reasonable . . . but you're missing a bunch of stuff."

Clara folded her arms. "Like what?"

"Like sex."

Her pulse broke into a gallop. "What do you mean?"

"Well, what's the plan if we're . . . you know." He made a pumping motion with his fist.

Clara swallowed the lump in her throat. "You mean like a scrunchie on the doorknob?"

His eyebrows shot to his hairline. "What the fuck is a scrunchie?"

In answer, she retrieved one from her makeup bag and flung it at him like a slingshot.

He caught the soft material in front of his chest and tested the hair tie's durability between his fingers.

Clara averted her eyes again. *So he has nice hands. Big whoop.* "Haven't you ever seen an eighties sex comedy?"

"Oh, I see," Josh said. "I thought they used tube socks."

"Maybe guys use tube socks. Let's assume any item decorating the doorknob means *do not disturb*." Normally she would have fought against a tacky dorm room signal, but she figured her lack of a sex life would keep her from having to employ this particular rule.

"Okay. That's cool. Although I've gotta warn you, these walls are thin. When I moved in on Sunday, I could hear Everett and the manic pixie dream girl he brought home going at it like I had a front-row ticket."

Clara inhaled sharply. Of course, she knew Everett hadn't been celibate for the last ten years, but she hadn't had cause to picture him with other women . . . and in the bed she had slept in last night. Could she get away with burning the sheets if she replaced them?

"Oh. Shit, I'm sorry," Josh said.

She must have made a face. Clara quickly schooled her features back to calm.

"If it makes you feel better, she made this super annoying screeching sound when she came."

Clara fought the urge to gag. "Let's move on."

Josh squinted at the ceiling. "Hmm." He snapped his fingers. "What are you afraid of?"

"Excuse me?"

"Like if you're afraid of snakes or big dogs or cotton balls, I should know so I can protect you."

She squinted. "You realize one of those things is not like the others?"

"What about mice, cockroaches, opossums?"

"Exactly how many kinds of vermin do you think live here?"

Josh rolled his shoulders. "I'm trying to prepare myself, as your roommate."

Clara saw his point. She stared at the carpet. "I'm afraid of driving."

"But . . . you moved to L.A.?"

Her cheeks grew hot. "Yes. It's all very stupid. I've ruined my life.

What are *you* afraid of?" Her glare, warding off further questioning, must have worked.

Josh grimaced. "Ketchup."

"You don't like ketchup?"

"No," he extended the vowel in emphasis. "I don't like radishes. I'm afraid of ketchup."

"That's not funny. I told you a real thing."

"I'm not joking! The sight of ketchup skeeves me out the way other people can't look at bugs. It's the viscosity or something." He covered his mouth with the back of his hand. "Ugh, seriously I can't even talk about it. It's making my blood run cold." He held out his forearm, where the hairs stood on end, as evidence.

"All right, but if someone dared you to eat ketchup, you could do it?"

"Why would someone dare me to eat ketchup?" He balked.

Clara shrugged. "You're playing one of those games. Truth or dare."

"Have you ever played truth or dare?"

"Of course I have." She flipped her hair over her shoulder.

"Yeah . . . but I bet you only ever picked truth."

"I'll have you know I've completed many dares."

Josh's mouth pulled to one side. "Oh yeah? Name one."

Despite a prolonged sip of coffee that she used to barter for time, nothing came to mind. "Well, I can't think of any off the top of my head. It's been a while."

"That's a shame." Something bright sparked behind his eyes. "Dares are fun."

"Fun for whom, exactly?" Why did her voice sound so breathy?

"Everyone?" A blast of charm accompanied his words.

Spoken like someone who's never been mocked. "No, they're fun for the person issuing the dare and various spectators. The person performing the dare feels mortified at worse and inconvenienced at best."

"So dares are against the rules, huh?"

"Guidelines," she said automatically before clearing her throat. "I think it's safe to say they are now."

A high-pitched jingle sounded from her nightstand.

Clara grabbed her cell. *Crap.* She forced false cheerfulness into her tone. "Hi, Mom. . . ."

Yes, everything's fine. . . ."

Mm-hm. Just unpacking." She glanced over her shoulder to find Josh watching her with obvious interest.

"Everett?" Clara shifted her weight from one leg to the other. "Um, no. He's not here right now. He ran to get coffee."

She lowered her voice. "Sure, I'll tell him you said hello." Clara was so not ready to confess her humiliation to her perfect mother.

"Listen, Mom, I have to go. I've got a pot on the stove. . . ."

Yes, I'm cooking. . . ."

Uh . . . soup. And it's burning. . . ."

Okay. I love you too. Bye."

Josh narrowed his eyes. "You didn't tell your mom about Everett bailing."

He could have at least pretended he wasn't eavesdropping. "She'll worry."

"Right."

The silence between them brimmed with awkwardness.

"So, grocery store?" Josh gestured to her abandoned mug. "I can't drink black coffee to save my life."

"Wait. Did you make coffee, realize you didn't have milk, and pawn off your leftovers on me?"

A guilty grin cut across his face. "Can't a man make a nice gesture *and* responsibly repurpose resources? Come on. I'll drive."

"All right." She followed him into the hallway. "But I'm buying like three bottles of ketchup."

21

. . .

CLARA'S EYES TRAVELED from Josh's well-formed backside to the items currently occupying the grocery cart he'd insisted they share.

Cereal with a higher sugar content than most candy, enough frozen burritos to feed a family of five for a week, and a jumbo-sized bag of Flaming Hot Cheetos. How could a person eat all of this and still look like that? The math didn't add up.

She glared at the lone container of nonfat yogurt in the cart, her only contribution thus far. Clara felt better when she avoided eating things with too much sugar or salt, but all the leafy green vegetables in the world wouldn't make her look like the svelte fitness moms in this L.A. grocery store. No matter what she ate, her prodigious boobs refused to shrink. At least her posterior had caught up over the last five years to create an illusion of balance.

By the time she looked up, Josh had managed to add an outrageous flavor of toaster pastry to his haul. He seemed to navigate the store based on spontaneous whims, completely disregarding the carefully constructed layout.

Clara parked the cart beside him. "Can I ask you an impertinent question?"

He lowered the frozen waffles in his hand. "Only if I get to ask you one back."

"I suppose that's fair." Why had she let her life slip so far out of control? "How do you eat so much junk food and stay so . . ." *Mouthwatering*, her brain supplied unhelpfully. "Trim."

He raised a single shoulder. "I fuck a lot?"

Clara succumbed to an alarming coughing fit and had to wave off the worried glances of several concerned shoppers. It served her right for asking.

Seemingly unperturbed, Josh led the way to the produce aisle and helped himself to an unsanctioned sample of grapes. "Okay. My turn. What's your plan here?"

Clara held up the watermelon she'd just picked out. "I thought I could make a summer salad."

"No. Not what's your plan for the produce. What's your plan for L.A.?"

She adjusted her sundress to avoid meeting his eyes. "My plan pretty much blew up in my face."

It was only a matter of time before her mother found out Everett had split and politely suggested that Clara return to the coastline of her birth. "I suppose I'll try to lie low for a few weeks. Lick my wounds. If I'm lucky, the gossip hounds won't sniff out my humiliation before I can slink back to New York and make my excuses."

She shivered. If anyone from back home realized Everett Bloom hadn't bothered to stick around long enough to give her a proper brush-off, she'd have to move to Guam to escape the satisfied snickers.

"Wait a minute." Josh stopped walking and she had to yank the cart to a halt to avoid running into his heels. "You can't just go back. Maybe Everett got you out here, but if your old life was so good, you wouldn't have jumped at the first chance to leave it."

He plopped a massive bottle of root beer into the cart sideways. That was definitely going to explode and spray everywhere when he opened it.

"I don't buy for a second that you didn't make contingencies."

Clara didn't appreciate his attempts to diagnose her within a day of making her acquaintance, but she couldn't fully deny his argument. "I don't think my backup plan wants to hear from me."

Did it count as a backup plan if the plan was a person? A person who would have every right to slam her door if any Wheaton came calling. After all, some hurts don't heal, and Clara had a suspicion this one hadn't faded, even after a decade.

She tried to let the conversation die off, but Josh waved a pack of pretzels at her. Her grip tightened around the handle of the cart. This guy already knew enough to be incriminating.

"My aunt Jill moved out here ten years ago. She started a PR firm in Malibu, from what I could find on the Internet. I haven't seen or spoken to her since I was in high school." Clara diligently double-bagged her skinless chicken breast.

"You don't have to keep in touch with blood relatives. The shared DNA works like a get-out-of-jail-free card. No way did you do something bad enough to keep her from wanting to see you."

"I don't know about that." Worried for Josh's health despite herself, Clara kept trying to sneak junk food back on the shelf when he looked away. His metabolism might defy science, but judging by some of the ingredient lists, he consumed well over the FDA's recommendation for corn syrup. As they passed an endcap, she covertly positioned his bag of Cheetos behind a jumbo pack of paper towels.

"Jill moved out here because my family disowned her."

Josh took a paper ticket from the dispenser in front of the butcher's counter. "People still disown each other in this day and age? I thought that practice only applied to ancient dynasties."

Clara studied the array of deli turkey. "Wheatons don't like a scandal they can't cover up with money or influence, and Aunt Jill released the Greenwich version of the shot heard around the world."

After they'd ordered lunch meat, they stopped in the cleaning aisle to find items to accommodate the chores laid out in the guidelines. "So what did this lady do that was so bad? Sell a family heirloom? Oh, I know." His eyes danced. "She wore white after Labor Day."

Clara inspected the various brands of furniture polish. He had no idea about the scope of the scandal she'd witnessed. "You joke, but it's not uncommon for Wheatons to donate libraries and hospital wings in order to undo the damage wrought by their poor impulse control."

"So she . . . killed a guy?"

"What? No. She did something stupid, not illegal. Jill slept with the deputy mayor of Greenwich when she was nineteen."

Josh grabbed both of the bottles she couldn't decide between and tossed them into the cart. "Let me guess. The deputy mayor was married?"

"How'd you know?" Clara resumed her position behind the cart. "It probably would have blown over after a while, but when he denied the affair, she chained herself to a statue in the town center and read a bunch of love letters he'd written her over a megaphone." She selected some detergent, an all-purpose cleaner, and several room deodorizers. "By all accounts, they were very, very raunchy."

Josh jogged alongside the cart. "I like her already."

The details popped in sharp contrast across her memory. The first Wheaton scandal that directly affected her. "The mayor's office had to call the fire department to get her loose, and by that point, it was all over the local news." Her entire class had heard about it by the next day.

Another headline that had singed her family tree. And now, like Jill, Clara had climbed out on a limb for love and met the ground face-first.

"Your aunt sounds like a badass." Josh got in the long line to check out.

"Unfortunately, my grandfather did not agree with you." Clara swallowed the sour taste in her mouth. "The spectacle cost him his job. I probably should have mentioned that my grandfather was the mayor at the time?"

It amazed her that a man who'd always doted upon her had turned on his own daughter. "Jill moved out to Los Angeles not long after that. My parents didn't burn all her pictures or anything, but we don't talk about her. It's like she never even existed."

Clara's heart twisted to think of her grandmother and her parents standing by and letting a colossal void open in the middle of the family, isolating Jill enough that she'd fled. The idea of loneliness compounded by embarrassment made Clara shiver. She'd worked her whole life to avoid Jill's fate.

From perfect report cards to her strict adherence to curfew, on paper, Clara was untouchable. She'd stayed close to home for college and then grad school, always on call to put out a fire or smooth over ruffled feathers.

But no matter how hard she tried to live up to her family's expectations, failure seemed inevitable under the weight of her responsibility to defend and uphold the Wheaton name.

"You should reach out to her," Josh said as they reached the conveyor belt.

Clara bit her tongue as Josh unloaded the cart willy-nilly with no regard for essential principles like grouping perishable items together to enable efficient unpacking. "I'm sure she's busy."

"Come on," he said. "What harm could come from one phone call?"

chapter three

♡ ♡ ♡

T HE NEXT DAY, Clara fully expected her phone call to Jill's office to
end in disaster. Josh didn't, couldn't, know how deep the wounds
in her family ran. Wheaton scandals ruined lives, ended marriages, dissolved businesses. What if Clara reached Jill only to find out her aunt
had faded to a shell of her former self?

But for once all her worrying turned out to be for naught. After a
brief albeit awkward exchange, Jill recommended they meet for lunch at
a restaurant near her office. Dressed in a skirt set usually reserved for job
interviews, Clara ordered a car and set out for Malibu.

She arrived to find a cheerful restaurant with a sunny patio and two
full menu pages dedicated to various types of avocado toast.

After an embarrassed hug, where they each bobbed while the other
weaved, Jill leaned back in her chair. "I'm so glad you called, Clara.
What a nice surprise. I can't believe how grown-up you look."

"Thank you." Before she'd moved away, Clara had always admired
Jill for the way she conveyed a kind of effortless cool that stood out
among the country club crowd in Greenwich. "I'm sorry I didn't call
sooner. Or . . . ever really."

The word *aunt* stuck on her tongue. For ten years, Clara had heard the woman across from her referred to as "a blemish on the family legacy." Jill certainly understood the consequences of thwarting familial expectations firsthand.

"Relax." Jill waved away her apology. "I don't blame you." Her voice reminded Clara of honey mixed into whiskey. As if someone had warmed her vocal cords, softening the edges.

When the older woman shook out her long dark hair, Clara caught the resemblance between them. She'd always known she didn't take after her mother. Everything about Lily Wheaton stayed neat and compact, from her manicured bob to her perfectly tailored pastel capris. If Lily was a ruler, Jill and Clara were French curves.

"You're not mad?" Clara chewed her bottom lip.

The laughter died in Jill's eyes and she stared at the menu for a long moment. "I may have some choice words saved up for my father, but time and space provide a lot of perspective. I'm very happy to see you in any case. Your hair's shorter than in the pictures your mom sent me from your graduation."

Iced tea splashed onto the tablecloth as Clara halted her glass's progression toward her mouth. "My mother sent you pictures?" As far as she knew, her mother never put a toe out of line. Contacting Jill, a persona non grata, counted as positively reckless.

"Yeah, every couple of months for years now. Lily sends them by email after most major occasions." Light returned to Jill's eyes. "She's very proud of you."

Guilt climbed up Clara's throat. "I was supposed to be her consolation prize, but I've abandoned the mantle."

Leaving a gaping hole in her wake.

"I know what that's like." Jill smiled ruefully. "Somehow the men in our family tend to get away with a lot more than the women. Your mom's weathered a lot of storms from my father and brother, and now Oliver. It can't be easy."

Lily didn't know the definition of easy. At six years old, Clara had padded downstairs in her nightgown to find her mother sitting at the kitchen table, sobbing into her palm as the news of another Wheaton family scandal broke. She'd crawled into her mother's lap and promised to be different. Vowed to never give her mother cause for concern—never cause her a moment's heartache—and up until a few days ago, she'd faithfully fulfilled her vow.

Jill placed her hand on top of Clara's. "You okay?"

Clara nodded, washing down the lump in her throat with her remaining iced tea. "Do you miss it? Greenwich, I mean?"

Snowflakes of carbs rained down from between Jill's fingers as she tore her breadstick to pieces. "Sure, sometimes. I'll never get used to warm weather on Christmas. But I'm grateful for the blank page I got out here. I've made a lot of mistakes, but at least they belong to me. There's a strange pride in taking full responsibility for the consequences of your actions, however they fall." Wiping the lenses of her sunglasses with her cloth napkin, Jill continued. "But enough about me. What brings you to Los Angeles?"

Where should she start? Most of Clara's rationale for moving was mortifying. She struggled to select the one that made her look the least idiotic. *I moved out here because I'm pushing thirty and I've spent my entire life in the cocoon of academia, avoiding the real world. Because I was chasing a fourteen-year-long unrequited crush. Because I could no longer bear the burden of maintaining our family's expectations.*

She decided on an abridged version of the Everett story. Thinking of his abrupt abandonment still gave her a stomachache, but at least that version of the narrative spoke of only one weakness instead of a whole tangle of them.

Sharing the embarrassing episode, even in part, further eased the burn of the rejection.

When she was done, Jill propped her elbow on the table and rested her chin in her palm. "Okay, after all that, I have to ask, what's so special about Everett Bloom?"

That question had followed Clara from adolescence to adulthood. "Everett makes me feel safe. Growing up with him was like getting cooked in a lobster pot. We became friends when the water was still cold, and by the time it started boiling, by the time he'd turned into this knockout, I was already too comfortable with him to freak out the way I normally do around extremely attractive men."

"Slow boil or fast, still sounds painful," Jill said.

No counterargument sprang to mind. "We know everything about each other. Our families are friends. It's always been simple. And I know, if I could get him to see it, to see me as someone other than his nerdy, bucktoothed neighbor, we'd be perfect. Besides, I've never done anything selfish or impulsive in my life. All I wanted was a taste of adventure, but instead I ended up with a false start."

A chirp sounded from her pocket, earning their table the stink eye from a few other diners. "Excuse me." She unlocked the screen of her cell. "Oh, for crying out loud."

"What's up?"

"Nothing. Sorry. It's my new roommate. I gave him my number in case of emergency and now he won't stop sending me selfies." The message read, *SOS we desperately need toilet paper!!!* and included a photo of Josh with his mouth open in a silent scream of anguish.

Jill lowered her menu. "Ooh, I want to see this mystery man."

Clara handed the device across the table, thankful that Josh at least had all his clothes on in the shot.

"Wait a second." Her aunt brought the phone closer to her face. "Clara"—her eyes went dangerously wide—"this is Josh Darling."

After taking the phone back, she racked her brain for any recognition of that moniker. She couldn't remember Josh mentioning his surname. But Darling? Come on. "That can't be his real name."

The expression on Jill's face would make the blooper reel of Clara's life. "It's not his real name . . ." She paused meaningfully as the waiter arrived to take their order. Only after they'd decided to split a margherita pizza and he'd trotted back to the kitchen did Jill resume her revelation. "It's his porn name."

Slumping down in her seat, Clara darted her gaze to the surrounding tables. Thankfully, no one appeared interested enough in their conversation to eavesdrop. "Please tell me that means anything other than what I think it means."

Jill leaned forward. "You've never heard of Josh Darling? I'm surprised. I would think you fell squarely into his demographic. *Cosmo* described him as 'catnip for millennial women.'" Her words bumped into one another as she rushed to get them out. "He looks like a nineties heartthrob. Like Zack Morris from *Saved by the Bell*, minus the asshole personality."

Closing her eyes, Clara took a long breath and let it out very slowly through her mouth. Her entire life she'd chosen safety over excitement. She hadn't done drugs. She rarely drank because she knew she couldn't hold her liquor. She had exactly one pair of sexy panties, and she never wore them because they rode up her butt.

How in the world had she accidentally moved in with a porn star? And not any run-of-the-mill porn star, but one mainstream enough to receive a profile in a magazine she regularly browsed in the lobby of her dermatologist's office.

"I don't watch porn," Clara said, barely opening her mouth. She didn't have a problem with people taking care of *business* by themselves, but any time Clara saw porn, usually at the request of a soon-to-be-ex-boyfriend, it featured women getting degraded. She couldn't help it if she didn't find women on their knees with semen dripping down their faces sexy.

The idea that goofy, messy, bedheaded Josh made those kinds of videos didn't make sense to her. How could the same guy who'd brought her coffee tell some girl to "take it all, bitch"? Her stomach turned over and she pushed away the basket of breadsticks.

"It doesn't surprise me that you're not into porn, but word around town is Josh Darling is quite the talent," Jill said.

Clara curled her hands around her middle and wished for an antacid. "If this is a joke, it's not funny."

No one could find out about this. The guys from high school would love the idea that Clara "The Prude" Wheaton was sharing a shower with a man who had a penis more famous than his face. Not to mention the reaction from her mother. She strangled her linen napkin.

Jill smiled helplessly. "Looks like you might get that taste of adventure after all."

chapter four

♡ ♡ ♡

MOST PEOPLE WOULD have a problem with their ex-girlfriend going through their phone, but when Josh stepped off set to find Naomi holding his cell between her thumb and forefinger, he simply grabbed the device without bothering to call out the blatant violation of his privacy. They'd always shared a blurry definition of boundaries.

"Clara says she can pick up toilet paper on the way home." Naomi's eyes ran down his naked body with thinly veiled possession.

Josh let her look. For the sake of his career, he needed to get back together with her eventually, so who cared if she never truly butted out of his business? Their relationship was as inevitable as aging.

"What are you doing here? You're not shooting today." He'd checked the schedule. Ever since word got out about their breakup, producers had tiptoed around casting them together.

"I was in the neighborhood. Thought I'd drop off your fan mail." She shook a hefty garbage bag in front of him.

"Oh. Right. Thanks. I'll go online and start getting it forwarded."

Cool air chilled the sweat drying on his skin, reminding him of his nakedness. Grabbing two towels from a production assistant, he wrapped one around his waist and the other across his shoulders and headed for the showers.

Naomi kept pace with him. The slinky dress she wore accentuated her natural strut. "I didn't realize you'd be shacking up again so soon."

Ignoring her, Josh turned the shower on extra hot and waited for the water to heat. These old warehouses always came with shitty plumbing.

"Your little text message chain sounded positively domestic." Naomi perched on the room's tiny vanity, swinging her long legs.

If their on-screen chemistry didn't sell so well, he would have seriously considered telling his agent, Bennie, to put a Naomi Grant exclusion clause in his next contract. Her tenacity made her an excellent businesswoman, but it also made her a colossal pain in the ass.

"Don't tell me you're jealous." He didn't buy that for a second. Their relationship, both romantic and professional, rested on two key pillars: always wear a condom, and stay in your own lane. They weren't the type of people who fell for love's long con.

He and Naomi understood each other. Had extended a successful business relationship into a partnership for almost two years based on mutual respect and the exchange of countless orgasms. Usually, that evened out to enough. On the rare occasion when loneliness lapped at his heels, well, he could always turn on the TV and watch Meg Ryan, falling in love by proxy.

"I'm pretty sure I could get you back if the mood ever struck." She fussed with her dyed red hair.

Josh rolled his eyes. "Thanks, Stu." He used the nickname she claimed to hate, a riff on her real name, Hannah Sturm. She forbade the use of anything but her stage name on set, but he often forgot when they found themselves alone. Like so much else about her, she'd never told him the reason she hated her given name. Even though they had first met as co-stars almost two years ago, he could count on one hand the number of things he knew about her childhood.

"I can assure you, sharing household goods with Clara is platonic. I had to find somewhere to live when you kicked me to the curb." Josh stuck his hand under the stream of water in the shower to check the temperature again and jerked it back when the icy stream pelted his palm.

"Oh please. You practically ran out of my house." She tapped a finger against her lips. "Platonic Clara." Naomi lingered over the syllables, tasting the name on her tongue. "What's wrong with her?"

"She's some loaded East Coast princess."

Naomi grinned like a cat ready to devour a hapless mouse.

He tried and failed to make his frown disapproving. They shared the same sense of humor, after all.

"Don't even think about it." Josh pointed a finger in warning as he told Naomi the same thing he'd told himself ever since Clara had shown up in his living room two days before. His ex was bisexual and loved novelty in the bedroom almost as much as he did. "I've never met someone wound this tight. You should see this girl. I doubt she's ever kissed a guy without knowing his full name." He didn't mention that the challenge Clara presented raced straight to his dick.

"Sounds like the opening of a porno." Naomi plucked an imaginary pen out of thin air and mimed writing. "Sweet, unsullied small-town girl moves to the big bad city and discovers big bad cock."

Josh shook his head and grinned despite her bluntness. The idea of defiling his new roommate was definitely tempting, but even he knew how that story ended.

The room at Everett's place already felt more like his than Naomi's ever had. All of the seventies wallpaper reminded him of his grandparents' condo. Besides, something about Clara reminded him of a baby deer stumbling around on new legs.

"She's a good person. I can tell." He'd already made a pact with himself to keep his distance.

"So are you," Naomi said, her voice sharp enough that he knew he'd managed to raise her hackles. "And you just met her. She could wind up more wicked than both of us."

"Impossible." Josh pulled his comic book out from under her butt and gently swatted her with it. "Besides, I don't have to mount every beautiful woman I meet."

Naomi scoffed.

"Well, there's an exception to every rule."

"So, she's beautiful, huh?" Naomi uncrossed her legs and recrossed them in the opposite direction.

"Would you stop pretending to be concerned? I'm telling you, she blushed, actually blushed, at the mention of sharing a bathroom with me. Can you imagine the color she'd turn if she knew all the places my dick's been?"

Naomi looked down at her crotch and gasped in mock horror. "What's she gonna do when she finds out?"

"She's not gonna find out. Trust me. There's no way that girl watches porn."

"Haven't you heard? We're mainstream now. *Elle*, *Cosmopolitan*, *BuzzFeed*. Everyone and their mother is talking about our last video. Even nice girls know how to use the Internet, Josh."

"Speaking of that video," he said. "I've got a meeting with Bennie tonight. He wants to discuss my contract. I'm hoping he's got an extension for me to sign."

Naomi wrinkled her nose at the mention of his agent. He could admit that Bennie fit the profile of a smarmy bastard, but he'd picked up Josh like a stray cat back when he was an aimless college dropout living on dollar tacos and breath mints.

"Don't give me that look. I've spent two years shackled to a shitty stock agreement. I'm sick of wearing a leash. I want to work with other studios. Hell, I'd like to cut a profit on my own films. Mainstream cover-

age means big money, right? We gotta double down on our fifteen minutes. It's now or never."

No matter what happened in their personal lives, their professional
success tangled together until sometimes he didn't know where Naomi
Grant's career stopped and Josh Darling's began. If she wouldn't capital-
ize on their chance at real stardom, he'd have to grab her hand and drag
her along.

That woman had ten times more brains than anyone in this business
gave her credit for, which was exactly the way she liked it. She dealt in
secrets like currency, and they bought her half the industry wrapped
around her little finger. The whole business would turn upside down if
she ever got inspired to make a fuss.

When Naomi hopped off the countertop and headed for the door,
she had her professional mask back on. "Good luck," she told him, strid-
ing past in a wave of spicy perfume. "Bennie is almost as cheap as he is
repugnant. Trusting him is gonna get you screwed one of these days, and
not in the way you like."

chapter five

♡ ♡ ♡

THE FIRST TIME Josh met Bennie, his future agent declared him the biggest *knucklehead* he'd encountered in almost three decades in the porn business.

Since that day, over two years before, they'd met for burgers countless times.

Bennie's favorite burger came from a landmark diner in Glendale founded sometime in the 1950s. To this day, the interior of the establishment evoked images of sock hops and waitresses on roller skates. They probably filmed sitcoms here during off-peak hours.

Josh spotted his agent's shiny bald head at a table in the back. Bennie didn't look up from his phone when Josh scooted into the sticky vinyl booth across from him, but he did grunt in his general direction. Josh accepted this ritual greeting. He'd spent enough time with Bennie to know that the man issued few words and most of them were expletives anyway.

Bennie smoked unfiltered cigarettes and spat on the sidewalk, but he knew everyone who mattered and never took a vacation, which made Josh's life significantly easier.

"How's it going, Ben?"

The portly man raised his eyes to take in Josh sitting across from him and grinned. "How do you fucking do, Darling?"

Josh pointed to a discarded plate of soggy fries and a sad sliver of bun. "I see you've started without me."

"Ah, I'm sorry. You know me, always starving." Bennie swiveled the plate in offering so the remaining fries faced Josh.

Ugh. He squirmed and shoved the plate away blindly.

"Oh fuck." Bennie threw a napkin over the plate. "I forgot about your ketchup thing again. Forgive me."

"It's fine," Josh said, willing his stomach to settle.

"Is it because it looks like blood?" Bennie waved his hand to bring over their server.

People always asked that. Josh shook his head, not trusting himself to open his mouth at the moment.

A sunshiny waitress approached the table in no particular hurry. She looked down her nose at Bennie but brightened considerably when her eyes found Josh. "What can I do for you two?"

Josh's ears perked up at the attention. He couldn't help it. He specialized in waitresses. They worked similar hours to him and always brought home free food. Naomi gave him flak for his indiscrimination when it came to women, but he didn't mind. He could always find something to like. Hell, even Clara, who had *Don't even think about it* stamped across her forehead, got his motor running.

"Do ya wanna hear the specials?" Fried onions sizzled on the grill behind her.

"He'll have the burger. Medium. Fries. Extra crispy," Bennie said, eyes back on his phone.

She scribbled the order on her pad and pouted at the stolen opportunity to linger.

"Extra pickles," Josh added, giving her his smile at eighty watts. The way she chewed on her pen as she walked away gave him the sneaking suspicion that unleashing the full force of his grin would be writing checks he wasn't prepared to cash.

Putting his palm over Bennie's phone, he tipped his head toward the waitress stand. "Hey, you don't remember by any chance if . . ."

"Yeah, you fucked her the last time we were here."

Josh frowned. He didn't remember the sex, the hallmark of a lackluster performance. He tried to recall the last time he'd had sex with only one girl without cameras. Sometime last year, when he and Naomi could hardly stand each other, they'd opened their relationship to external partners beyond work. At first, he'd enjoyed feasting at L.A.'s buffet of babes, but like anything else too readily available, even pussy got boring.

Bennie shuffled the stack of papers in front of him, reminding Josh of the purpose of their meeting.

"So?" Josh leaned in and tapped the table with both palms. "What have you got for me?"

Bennie handed over the documents.

Two years ago, a few days into shooting his first adult film, Josh had "taken a meeting" with a man from Black Hat Studios. The smooth-as-glass executive had plied him with Johnnie Walker Blue and extended an exclusive contract within thirty minutes of meeting him. Josh, still flush from the fact that someone, anyone, wanted to pay him to fuck, had quickly signed on the dotted line.

The contract meant three years of steady paychecks. It also meant he couldn't work independently or for any other studios, sell his own merchandise, or make any public appearances without Black Hat Studios' explicit approval.

That one night had cost Josh thousands in missed royalties alone. He'd asked Bennie last week to meet with the studio on his behalf, try to grease the wheels a little, and see if maybe the higher-ups would renegotiate a year early.

Josh raked a hand through his hair. "A five-thousand-dollar bonus?" He knew the kind of numbers he brought in through merch and appearances alone. "Is this a joke?"

"I know we wanted more, but I had to fight dirty for that much." Bennie reached across the table to pick up the papers in a white-knuckled grip.

"But why? I'm the closest thing they've got to a household name . . . and they come back with this?"

Before the older man could answer, the waitress returned with Josh's burger, bending from the waist to put down the plate. When Josh didn't spare her an extra glance beyond a cursory "Thank you," she huffed and stomped away.

Bennie folded his arms across his ample stomach. "Look, you're hot right now, but the bigwigs at Black Hat say these new ladies you brought in with the last video won't stick around. They say your self-proclaimed 'Darlings' don't pay for porn, and definitely don't fork over for subscriptions. They'll watch that one video until they get bored and then go back to their cold beds and their colder husbands.

"Besides, you've got all kinds of rules about who you'll work with and what kind of stuff you'll make. You're like some monk with your self-imposed code of conduct. Black Hat likes people they can bully." His agent took a long drink of his soda. "As long as they've still got you hooked on the stock agreement, they don't have a lot of incentive to crack open the old checkbook."

"I know I'm not a genius, but I've seen the numbers I bring in, and they've grown steadily for the past year. I've got bags of rabid fan mail spilling out of my closet and the back of my car. I'm worth at least three times this much. Even Black Hat negotiates. What aren't you telling me?"

Bennie mopped his brow with a paper napkin. "Ever since you and Naomi broke up, your stock's taken a major hit. The domestic fantasy of the two of you together made you more palatable to mainstream audiences, but the powers that be aren't convinced that a man alone, even a good-looking kid like you, can pull numbers like that as a headliner."

He grimaced. "I never knew people cared about my personal life."

"You kidding? You two were like the Brad and Jen of adult entertainment. I thought I'd give a speech at your wedding."

"What?"

"Forget it. Hey, where are you living now that the old lady kicked you out?"

Josh took a halfhearted bite of his burger. "Found some sublet on Craigslist. Came fully loaded. The only downside is now I've got a socialite for a roommate."

"Yikes. That's the last thing we need. Look, they said if you want the big dollars, you gotta start doing more of the hardcore stuff. That's where Black Hat sees the best margins. They want you working in their new extreme division. They're businessmen who don't give a damn about your morals. You want more money, you're gonna have to compromise."

Josh's appetite deserted him. He liked sex as much as the next guy. Hell, maybe more, all things considered. But he'd set boundaries when he entered this business and he wasn't going to abandon them. "It's never gonna happen."

Bennie threw up his hands. "I get it. It's no skin off my nose if you wanna stick to the basics. Take the five thousand and invest it." He eyed Josh's burger with more than a hint of interest.

"Come on. Some of the stuff they get up to in that division makes my skin crawl. You should have seen the waivers they tried to make Naomi sign." Under the table, Josh's hands balled into fists. "Let them loop in some other sap to do scenes with the misguided Midwestern chicks they con into contracts. It's not gonna be me. They can keep me from working for anyone else, but that contract doesn't stop me from spending the next year sitting on my ass eating bonbons. I've hit my performance quota."

"I hate to break it to you, but you don't have to approve." Bennie rolled up his sleeves. "You know how it is nowadays. No one wants to pay for porn anymore. Not the kind of stuff that's easy to get for free from amateurs on the Internet. Black Hat wants to invest in a specialized audience. One that's willing to pay for exclusive content. This is the way of the future. You can't coast on those dimples forever. Sooner or later, you're gonna have to ask yourself, do you wanna make real money or not?"

As realization washed over him, Josh's face turned to granite. "How much did they offer you to convince me?"

Bennie shook his head. "You don't wanna know."

Josh extracted himself from the booth.

"Stop it. Don't be like that," Bennie said, groaning as if Josh were a child throwing a tantrum. He pointed a French fry at the stack of papers with the offer. "Five K is not nothing."

Josh pulled enough bills out of his wallet to cover the burger he hadn't eaten, and an extra twenty to make it up to the waitress for his abrupt dismissal. "Don't take that," he said, pointing at the money and practically growling.

Bennie shouted at Josh's back as he walked out the door, all trace of composure gone. "You wanna walk away? Let me give you a clue, Darling, fucking is the only thing you're good at, and you're not as good at fucking as you think. Give me a call when you wake the hell up!"

chapter six

D**O NOT GOOGLE** *your porn star roommate. No good can come of it.*
Clara repeated the mantra every time the quiet of the empty house gave her dangerous ideas.

The knowledge that Josh starred in explicit videos had infected her brain. A contagion with only one cure.

No matter how hard she tried to distract herself, or how many "concentrate" playlists she made, her mind kept floating back to Josh and his great big . . . occupation.

Josh in a skimpy pizza delivery uniform. Josh as a sexy mailman with an extra-large package. The endless possibilities tormented her. She knew porn came in all shapes and sizes. Which kind of videos did Josh make? She could hardly have peppered Jill for details. Porn wasn't exactly the type of topic one could comfortably discuss with a family member, even an up until recently estranged one, at length.

But despite her overactive imagination, she couldn't imagine a man that playful as sexy enough to sell.

She supposed Josh did have his moments.

Having dedicated most of her adult life to a field of academia favored by introverts, Clara knew a lot of men who shied away from eye contact. The guys in her doctoral program at Columbia could stare at a painting of a wild orgy for hours but only managed to talk to her left ear at the bar afterward.

Josh didn't suffer from any such aversion. Holding his stare for too long made her dizzy. Did nature or nurture make him electric?

Even with all the windows open to tempt any trace of cross breeze, and the lights off, she couldn't get cool. Her bedroom was worse. A blistering inferno without the benefit of a ceiling fan. Everett had neglected to mention the house's lack of air-conditioning when he offered her free rent. She'd changed into an old cotton nightgown that evoked comforting memories of wistfully journaling in her girlhood bedroom, even if it didn't quite fit her the same way it had when she was twelve.

She stared at the ceiling and tried to blow a long strand of damp hair off her forehead. Clara mentally recited the reasons that finding out any more information about Josh's professional prowess would ruin her life.

One, seeing him naked would make it impossible for her to ever speak to him again without spasming into a tornado of awkwardness. Which meant, by extension, she could no longer ask him to reach things off the top shelf of the kitchen cabinets. She'd already stored several bottles of expensive shampoo up there.

Two, she might see something completely reprehensible, forcing her to confront him on the basis of her feminist morals. Those types of interventions had high price tags in terms of both time and energy.

Three, what if he had a weird penis? She supposed he probably didn't, otherwise they likely wouldn't have cast him. Did they have some kind of checklist for porn-ready genitalia?

Her mind crept back to unbidden curiosity, shunning all ideas of alternate entertainment, food, or sleep.

Fine. A quick, cursory search. In and out.

Like his dick.

Oh lord.

Josh had left a note on the fridge. *Dinner meeting after work. Home late.*

It was only seven. Plenty of time for a quick information-gathering session. By the time her roommate returned, she'd have slaked her curiosity and put on some sleep shorts.

Clara swung her legs off the sofa and padded across the carpet on bare feet, unconsciously tiptoeing. She grabbed her trusty laptop from its resting place on her desk and carried it back to the living room.

Imagining herself as a secret agent, hunting for information in enemy territory with bated breath, she flopped back down stomach-first on the sofa and tucked one ankle behind the other. Opening a private browsing window, she typed in *Josh Darling.*

Pretending her mission served a higher purpose, like perhaps defending national security, made it easier to click on the first link she found, an article about how Josh stood out among the fabric of the porn industry.

> *Is Josh Darling evolving porn? In an industry that famously caters to the male gaze, Darling has quietly stolen scenes for almost two years with his signature smolder and his reputation for prioritizing his female co-star's pleasure. Unlike mainstream media portrayals of female desire, Josh Darling is not afraid to get up close and personal with the clitoris. Industry insiders clamor to work with him, and audiences will do the (increasingly) unthinkable to watch him: pay.*
>
> *His boy-next-door looks may appear unassuming, but his magnetism defies definition, especially when he plays opposite his fiery on-again-off-again girlfriend, Naomi Grant. Executives for Black Hat Studios, who hold Darling's exclusive contract, widely credit the smokestack duo with bringing in female*

audiences across age groups. While Miss Grant's long-limbed grace rivets, to watch Josh Darling perform is to witness a master perfecting his craft. In the age of lukewarm hookups and rampant dick pics, Darling gives women a reason to believe sex is still worth getting out of bed.

Clara couldn't help noticing that the article linked to a video.

Her fingers tingled against the keyboard, and her heartbeat kicked up like a sprinter's before a race. How sad was it that just thinking about watching this content was more exciting than the past six months of her sex life?

For God's sake, woman, it's just a little porn.

With a quick glance behind her at the closed front door, she hit play.

The video opened with a pretty redhead swimming in what looked like a small community pool. Her statuesque body sported a perfect golden tan that glistened as she completed expert butterfly strokes.

Clara hadn't expected the woman in the video to look so lovely. The camera traveled appreciatively over her body underwater, panning across her tight red suit—Clara rolled her eyes—before pulling back to reveal none other than Josh, roommate and apparent porn heartthrob, in a lifeguard's uniform, complete with a sunscreen-covered nose and aviators, perched atop a guard's chair high above the water.

Even though she knew what to expect, the sight of him caused a hitch in her breath. As she watched, he arranged his long limbs casually across the chair as he intently watched the swimmer's strokes.

Clara saw immediately why women liked watching him. Unlike stereotypical male porn stars, he didn't sport unnatural muscles. He carried his slim but toned frame with an ease that she supposed must come with having the kind of penis that qualified you as a porn star.

Her eyes snagged on his face. Even hidden behind sunglasses, she could feel the pull of his eyes, currently directed at his co-star. They dared you to jump and promised to catch you. Apparently, he could turn the smolder on and off at will.

The gorgeous girl's swimming faltered, her pretend "drowning" a transparent play for the lifeguard's attention.

Without missing a beat, Josh whipped off his T-shirt and glasses and dove in for a quick rescue. Once he pulled the damsel to safety and had her laid out on a nearby lounge chair, he began resuscitation efforts that looked quite different from what Clara had learned as a camp counselor.

As Josh set to work divesting the revived athlete of her swimsuit, Clara paid special attention to the way he performed—although the word *performed* didn't quite fit.

Josh and his co-star didn't look like two actors getting paid. Now that the pretense of the "plot" had ended, they seemed merely like two people who really had the hots for each other.

Clara fanned herself with her hand, having grasped why this video in particular had caught the eye of the article's reporter.

Lifeguard Josh somehow conveyed with alarming dexterity that he found his co-star simultaneously the sexiest woman he had ever seen and also his best friend. The undercurrent of trust and intimacy made Clara want to look away almost as much as it made her want to press her thighs together.

The enthusiasm with which he explored that woman's body seemed impossibly sexy. Like he couldn't get enough of her. And if her wails of pleasure acted as any indication, the feeling was mutual. Clara couldn't help but compare the on-screen enactment to her own decidedly less enthusiastic experiences.

She had a problem. Josh repositioned on screen. A huge problem.

Either Josh Darling had transcended her current definition of intercourse or someone needed to alert the Academy that he was the best actor in the world.

chapter seven

♡ ♡ ♡

J OSH OPENED HIS front door to find a spectacular ass pointed right at him.

The ass in question, he noted with surprise, belonged to his uptight roommate. Unsuspecting of his admiring review, Clara lounged on the sofa watching something on her computer. The thin nightgown she wore rode up her thighs, treating him to a barely obstructed view of her legs and sweet ass peeking out of pale pink cotton panties.

He bit down hard on his fist to avoid groaning.

Closing his eyes, he said a silent prayer to a God he didn't believe in. *Lord, give me the strength to not fuck my roommate.*

His rough grunt filled the room.

Except he hadn't made a sound.

Josh's eyes snapped open. Because he'd honed that grunt into his calling card. Used it countless times to indicate to co-stars and audiences alike that he'd hit his stride. That noise meant his body wavered dangerously close to nirvana, that a few more deep strokes would make him see stars.

That grunt meant Clara was watching porn. *His porn.*

Josh's chest expanded with pride. *Well well well, Miss Wheaton.*

Obviously, he knew people watched the videos he made. He made them for that purpose. But he'd never walked in on someone viewing his work before. And the fact that his stuff might fuel the naughty dreams of a girl like Clara? Maybe he hadn't wasted the last two years of his life after all.

Josh watched his own ass clench as he got closer and closer to his on-screen crescendo. Clara's head tilted to follow the trajectory of his body as he maneuvered his partner into a particularly impressive final position.

Crossing his arms, he leaned back against the door frame, basking in this moment of unexpected glory. After locking this image away for a rainy day, he finally announced his presence by dropping his duffel bag on the floor.

Clara responded to the soft thud as if someone had fired a gun in the living room. She slammed her computer shut and bolted off the couch, pulling her nightgown toward her knees to no avail in the process.

"I thought you weren't going to be home until later," she blurted out, squirming like a fish caught on a line.

Words caught in his throat. From the front, her pajamas turned positively sinful. Clara's impressive tits strained against the well-worn fabric, and he made direct eye contact with her hard nipples. Everything about her read as wanton. *Fuck.* Did that little wiggle signal guilt or was she simply that horny?

Pink swatches stained her cheeks, and her bee-stung lips parted as she tried to catch her breath.

"My meeting ended abruptly. What were you watching?" He feigned ignorance. He knew he should walk away from this terrible temptation— knew no good could come from lingering in this room and imagining what he might have found had he walked in ten minutes later. But as her face transitioned from pink to crimson, and her gaze bore holes into the carpet, he couldn't resist the urge to push her buttons.

"Oh, it was a video about . . . um . . . meditation." She bobbed her head as reinforcement to her statement.

Josh let his gaze travel over her body in a way that he knew she'd notice. "Yeah?" he asked, testing the truth of her words. "Must have been pretty exciting."

She crossed her arms.

"You're flushed."

Clara finally managed to stop her head from bobbing and instead bit into her bottom lip, drawing his attention back to her lush mouth. "Well, it is exercise for the mind." Her pitch climbed with each word.

Josh cradled his chin in his hand, stroking his jaw. "Awful loud for meditation."

"You're right. I'm a terrible liar." Clara straightened her shoulders as if steeling herself for battle. "I can't believe I couldn't come up with anything better than meditation. People assume I can think on my feet because I was All-State in debate, but it really is a very different skill set." She hung her head. "Anyways, that's not the point. The point is," she continued with incredible gravity in her voice, "I was watching pornography." She brought a hand up to cover her eyes as she completed her confession. "I was watching *your* pornography. But I swear I wasn't doing anything untoward."

Thank God. His dick wouldn't have survived walking in on that visual.

"I was curious! I've never met anyone who . . ." She gestured at her closed computer.

His chuckle reverberated low in his throat. "Why am I not surprised that you've never met an adult performer?"

"Oh. Is that the, um, preferred vernacular?"

"I guess it depends who I'm talking to." He stopped to consider, sinking onto the sofa. People didn't usually ask for his opinion on the matter. "I can't speak for everyone, but if I'm with someone from the industry,

I'm more likely to say *performer*. *Porn star* is the term I hear most often in a cultural context, and I'm fine with it as a more universal shorthand, even if it does feel a little goofy to apply it to myself."

Clara eyed the couch wearily for a moment before joining him.

He'd meant to make this more comfortable for both of them by taking a seat. Not scare her further with his proximity. Josh reached out a hand to reassure her with a gentle pat on the arm, but pulled back at the last moment and tossed her the blanket hanging off the back of the sofa instead.

His life revolved around touching strangers. It was no wonder he had all these instincts to offer Clara physical comfort. He had to keep reminding himself that they hardly knew each other. Josh never worried that his job affected his mental state, but maybe he should.

He didn't bat an eyelash at licking a strange woman's pussy ten minutes after meeting her, so why did the idea of patting Clara's forearm give him a thrill?

"Any other questions?" No one ever had only one when it came to his job. Better to get the inevitable inquisition over with now.

Clara wrapped the throw around her shoulders and Josh mourned the loss of the view.

"Yes. Sorry. What's your name? Your real name, I mean."

At least that one was easy. "It's Josh. Joshua Conners."

"Don't tell me 'Darling' is your middle name?"

He shook his head ruefully. "Plenty of people spend a lot of time and energy coming up with a fake name when they go into porn, but I fell into mine. My first day on set, we had this crazy British director. The guy wore a beret unironically. Anyway, I walked up and introduced myself. He asked me my name, and I told him. I didn't know any better."

"You didn't think to use the name of your first pet and the street you grew up on?"

"I'm not sure Dingus Winslow would have gone over well." Josh warmed at the memory of his beloved hamster.

"Probably not."

"It was dumb luck that every time the director wanted me to lift my leg or whatever he would yell out 'Josh, darling.' The PA on set that day must have thought it was my stage name. They took it down, and the next thing I know the video comes out and there it is in the credits."

"How did you . . . ?" She cleared her throat. "Why do you . . . ? That is to say . . . How did you find yourself in this particular line of work?"

Ah yes. The careful Clara version of *How did you end up fucking on camera?*

"I used to valet for big Hollywood parties in the Valley. One night, some guy caught me going down on his wife in his Maserati. I thought for sure he'd hit me, but instead, he offered me a job if I could keep going and keep my hard-on while he watched. I was twenty-four and a college dropout. The idea that someone wanted to pay me to have sex sounded a hell of a lot better than trying to get a real job."

Josh tried to gauge her reaction. She hadn't fled from the room or curled her lip in disgust, so he kept talking.

"It turned out I had a knack for it. Not everyone can handle the stress of all the cameras and having to perform on command, you see." He refused to admit any shame in that moment. He'd never let anyone make him feel bad about his work and he didn't intend to start now. So what if Clara didn't approve of his choices? She could get in line behind the long list of other people. A line that started with his mother.

A tiny crease formed between her brows. "But you must have considered other occupations?"

"Oh, I see. You're fishing for my secret pain."

She tugged on the hem of her shirt again. "Secret pain?"

"Yeah, you know. What terrible tragedy occurred to force me to take up a seedy career in adult entertainment? Why would anyone undamaged fuck for money, right?" He clenched his jaw.

He'd participated in this conversation countless times, especially with women who wanted to redeem him. If Clara found his job distasteful, she could walk out at any time. He would even lend a hand as she packed her bags.

"That's not what I meant." Clara rubbed her throat with an unsteady hand.

"Well, I hate to break it to you, but I don't have a sob story. I like what I do and a lot of other people like what I do. In fact . . ." Even when they were sitting down, she had to tilt her head back to look him in the eye.

Her sooty lashes lowered. It wasn't fair that she could make bashful look sexy.

"I think *you* like what I do." He returned his gaze to her nipples with obvious innuendo.

"Excuse me." She put a hand on his shoulder and gave a little shove. "I'll have you know that I was watching that video through a very professional, even artistic, lens."

He had to hand it to her, a lesser woman would never have managed to convey righteous indignation in that nightgown.

But all the gumption in the world hadn't saved her from falling into his trap. "Great, so what did you think?"

"Of what?" The sounds she emitted amounted to more squeaks than words.

He dropped his hands to his lap, intentionally drawing her eyes below his waistline. "You know what."

Her throat worked as she gulped. Stray locks of her dark hair clung to the damp skin of her neck.

"Well, I thought the performance seemed very . . . well executed. I can see how your methods would prove effective." Her face filled with alarm. "Not that I was affected. Because, you know, that would be inappropriate." Clara's eyes shot nervously to his forearms and then back to the carpet, her clear refuge.

What was it with women and forearms?

He couldn't resist flexing them by making a fist. "Ahh, yes. Well, I'm looking for strictly professional feedback."

"Like constructive criticism?"

"I'm always looking to improve my craft," he said, his voice just serious enough that she would have difficulty discerning whether he meant the request. He draped his arm across the back of the sofa. "And you seem like the kind of girl who would take notes."

chapter eight

♡ ♡ ♡

CLARA CONSIDERED HOW much of the truth to withhold from the infuriatingly confident man sitting next to her. He'd already imprisoned her in this conversation. She ached to withhold any further satisfaction. Part of her wanted to tell Josh she found what he did degrading, if only to wipe the smirk from his mouth. She envisioned lifting up her nose to show him how far beneath her she found pornography as both an industry and an art form.

But she couldn't do it.

Whether she wanted to admit it or not, that video had achieved its desired ends.

She'd watched him have objectively great sex with a beautiful woman, and it had made her so hot her skin should have burst into flames.

Not because she wanted to sleep with him. No. It was because the words that best described her love life were *tepid* and *careful*.

In contrast, Josh had given the woman in that video pleasure that seemed shockingly wild and vivid. Now he wanted her to provide notes on his craft or, heaven forbid, his form? Lust still swarmed her brain like raging bees. She could barely think over the buzzing in her ears.

Sure, this was probably a mistake. Nothing more than a way for Josh to call her out on paying too much attention to a video of him having sex. But the lifelong student in her couldn't pass up an opportunity for first-hand research.

The silence in the living room swelled, waiting for her reply. Finally, she let fly the words she'd held hidden under her tongue since he walked into the room. "You do that mouth thing a lot."

His lips formed a perfect O—clearly, he had anticipated a different piece of feedback. "You're going to have to be more specific."

Clara desperately drew air past the vise around her throat. *You're a grown woman. You can do this.* "Oral sex," she said, taking great pains not to whisper it.

"On her or on me?"

"On her." If the floor could open up and swallow her right about now, she would really appreciate it.

"And?" The blank look on his face said he was trying to follow the situation but not grasping her point.

"I found all your . . ." She prepped the next word on her tongue. ". . . *mouth attention* surprising."

Josh looked around the room as if the lamp or coffee table might offer a translation of her feedback. "I'm not following you."

Clara believed that he wasn't being purposely obtuse. "It's not really my cup of tea, I guess. Although the woman in the video certainly seemed to enjoy it, so I think we can mark it down as a matter of personal preference." She folded her hands neatly in front of her.

Josh's eyes narrowed. "How do your partners usually get you off?" His tone lacked all traces of lechery. She expected him to pull his glasses from his pocket at any moment.

Their conversation had taken an unexpected and dangerous turn toward her less than stellar track record of sexual experiences. Clara trailed her foot across the carpet in front of her and watched the fibers fold back.

"Wait a minute." Realization must have dawned. "You've gotta be kidding me." Josh placed an urgent hand on her arm. "Clara Wheaton, please tell me that a man has brought you to orgasm."

Clara wished for a white flag to wave. "It's not that some of them didn't try," she said, wanting to stand up for a couple of the sweet, well-meaning men she'd dated. "It just never happened, and I could tell that, after a while, they felt bad about it. It seemed more efficient and less awkward for all parties involved if I took care of things myself."

He shook his head so vehemently, she wondered how it didn't snap his neck. This time, when his eyes swept over her body with blatant heat, she knew he didn't do it to embarrass her.

"What a waste."

She didn't know what to make of his reaction. He seemed almost angry, more bothered than she'd seen him since she moved in. Perhaps he felt sorry for her. Well, she didn't need his pity. She gave him the withering stare she usually reserved for people who made snide remarks about her family.

"Excuse me." She sat up as straight as possible. "I happen to bring myself to very satisfying orgasms."

His eyes blazed at whatever image her confession conjured. "I'm sure you do. But it's not the same. Doesn't the thought of losing control excite you at all?"

When he continued, his voice ran like honey over her body, slow and sweet and sticky. "Don't you ever ache for someone who doesn't care how bad you want it? Someone who doesn't grant you release until you're begging for it?"

Clara clenched everything below her waist. She had to remind herself that his voice was full of promise, not because he liked her, but to prove a point. Unfortunately, that knowledge didn't keep her from wishing he'd press his tongue against her racing pulse point.

"Haven't you ever let someone learn your body? Let them taste every inch of you until the line between pleasure and pain blurs because it feels too good? Too much?"

Clara couldn't stop her mind from playing back lurid images from the video she'd just seen with herself in the place of Josh's co-star.

"Don't you want someone who gets so. Fucking. Hard. Watching you squirm and pant and arch your back as you get close?"

Clara's eyes fell shut. Josh had transported her to a place both splendid and wicked.

Nothing mattered except that he kept talking, kept using that voice that was more potent than any kiss she'd ever been offered.

But he didn't. Instead, Josh snapped the invisible thread of tension hanging between them. When she opened her eyes, he'd sat back against the sofa.

"Jesus, Clara." He ran a careless hand through his hair. "You've dated a bunch of lazy assholes if they let you get away with that shit. Sex isn't about efficiency."

"Maybe not for you," she said under her breath.

Josh's gaze bore through her for a moment, so deep she wondered for a ridiculous instant if he could see through not only her clothes but her skin as well, to the yawning chasm of insecurity underneath.

He got to his feet. "You know what? No."

She followed the movement of his arms as they crossed in a show of defiance.

"No?" Clara licked her bone-dry lips.

"No," he said again as if even more convinced of what needed to be done. "This is unacceptable."

"It is?"

Josh shook out his neck and shoulders, like a swimmer preparing to dive before a race.

"Take off your underwear," he said, his voice calm and deadly serious.

Clara's eyes went heavy-lidded at the conviction in his words, but then her mind caught up with her body. "I'm sorry. What did you say?"

"I'm going to rectify this situation," Josh stated simply. "Right now."

"You can't be serious." She tried to laugh but couldn't in the face of his stoic determination. "This is insane."

"Look. I don't have delusions of grandeur, but at this point in my life, I've made it my singular mission to help women get off more and better. Your existence as an outlier throws off the entire curve."

"Well, when you put it that way it sounds so sexy," she deadpanned.

"You want sexy?"

"No!" His appeal was already potent enough to stun. She threw her arms up in front of her. "It's just that . . . I don't know if you've noticed, but I'm not exactly the kind of girl that has casual sex."

"You don't say." He waited expectantly. When she didn't move to act as instructed, he had the audacity to wave two fingers to the side in a *let's hurry this along* gesture.

Clara fidgeted with her hem. "I appreciate the sentiment. I think. But I can't take off my underwear out here. I barely know you, and while I get that you've got a lot of experience in this area, it seems really unlikely that I could, well . . . you know what I mean."

She rubbed her arms, overwhelmed by the unexpected turn the night had taken. She never should have Googled her roommate.

"What's the big deal? There's no non-asshole way to say this, but I get about fifty women a week asking me to do this. It'll be totally clinical. Scout's honor." He saluted her with three fingers.

"Yeah. I'm going to go out on a limb and say this conversation is not sanctioned by the Boy Scouts of America." She couldn't help imagining the havoc he could wreak with that hand.

"If it makes you feel better, we can do it over your underwear."

"We can?" He was volunteering to take a lot of handicaps here.

He nodded, easy smile back on. "Don't think so much. We'll get this pesky problem taken care of and then the next time you have sex with some Melvin you meet at the library, you'll be prepared to demand what you deserve."

Clara almost slipped off the couch. Something must be seriously wrong with her because she found herself considering his crazy offer. Women like her didn't get many indecent propositions. Apparently, Clara liked them. She'd traveled across the country for a taste of love and adventure, and while this encounter might not strictly qualify as either, the idea did make her heart pound in a way her old life never had.

Think of it as a scientific experiment.

"What if it doesn't work?" Her words trembled with the force of her fear. "What if *I'm* the problem?" She'd heard it before. Too controlling, too in her own head, too prudish to enjoy sex like everyone else.

Josh didn't waver in his conviction. "If I can't get you off with my hands," he said, his voice soft and incredibly kind, "that's my problem. Not yours. And if that's the case, we'll figure something else out. Every body is different, but none of them are wrong."

Clara wiped her hands on her traitorous nightgown and gathered her strength.

She could do this. She could be the kind of girl who did things like this.

"Okay." Her voice sounded far away to her own ears.

Josh's eyes gleamed with a new kind of triumph. "You're saying yes?"

"I'm saying yes." Her stomach churned with mutinous nerves. "So, what should I . . . I mean, where do you want me to . . ."

For once Josh didn't heighten her discomfort by teasing her. His eyes locked on her mouth as he crowded her on the sofa.

She could map his freckles at this range, but the constellation of dots barely registered. God, kissing him must be heaven. But when his mouth came within inches of hers, she chickened out, instinctively leaning back until her head hit the wall behind the sofa with a *thunk*.

His soft chuckle was almost a purr. "Don't worry, Wheaton. I won't forget the rules."

With deft movements, Josh guided her into a reclined position. He approached her more like a skittish animal than a lover. His every touch careful. Controlled. A reminder that he saw this engagement as professional. Not pleasure, but his job.

He guided her knees apart, creating enough space for him to kneel between them. "You can close your eyes if you want."

Clara gratefully accepted the opportunity to detach. Tonight might turn her into a cautionary tale, but she'd wasted enough chances to recognize a once-in-a-lifetime offer.

She slid an inch lower on the couch, letting her body open further, the tiny movement the closest she'd ever come to a deviant act.

Josh brushed his thumb across the tender skin of her upper thigh, making her shiver. "Good?"

Clara opened her mouth to respond but the words died, nervous, on her tongue.

"It's all right," he said in a rough voice, as if someone had taken sandpaper to his vocal cords. "You don't have to answer." The heat of his breath across her already hot skin was decadent torture. "I'll learn what you like."

As Clara tried desperately not to think, Josh kissed along the line where her panties met her leg. The contact shot through the lower half of her body like a current. It had been an embarrassingly long time since anyone had touched her with sexual intent.

Josh employed his mouth and hands like a maestro as he made his way down one leg and then the other with devious patience, but he didn't follow any discernible routine. He tempered his touch across various pressures and patterns, never lingering on one spot for long and avoiding the most pertinent areas of her anatomy entirely. Each maddening stroke made Clara more indignant, more desperate.

Finally, his knuckles brushed against the front of her underwear, the barely-there friction against the cotton leaving her breathless. But just when she thought he'd finally give her some relief, Josh did the opposite, moving away and starting another round of openmouthed kisses down her leg.

"Oh, come on."

"Excuse me." Josh nipped her lightly behind her knee and Clara let out a tiny, wholly involuntary squeak. "Was there something you wanted?" He had the nerve to sound innocent.

Clara clenched the arm of the sofa and bit back a groan, not knowing how much more of this slow-burn stuff she could stand. Was it rude to politely ask him to cut to the chase?

It wasn't that she couldn't appreciate his technique. The slow, tender touches loosened her limbs, making everything languid and hazy. But she'd been promised an orgasm and no matter how talented he was, Josh wasn't going to deliver one by kissing her thighs. Clara raised her hips, offering him a helpful hint.

Instead of following directions, Josh removed his hands altogether, giving her nothing but the wet heat of his mouth as he kissed the cotton covering her core. "I'm not gonna let you rush me."

When he brushed his hand over her knee, she swore she'd go mad. Sometime in the last five minutes, all of her nerve endings had multiplied.

It felt like a punishment, though not like any one she'd ever earned, when he circled her ankle with his fingers and brought it to his mouth to suck on the thin, tender flesh he found there.

Familiar doubts and fears began to play across her mind: this was taking too long. He was going to get tired. Or bored.

Josh seemed to notice her mind drifting because he applied a particularly sharp bite to her calf. The acute press of his teeth, mingling pleasure and pain, made her gasp. Her entire lower body tingled, begging her to remove her own hand from its death grip on the sofa and provide the relief he continued to deny her.

Clara swallowed a choked breath.

"Wheaton," Josh said, lightly. "This only works if you relax. Erase the finish line, okay? I don't have any expectations for you to meet."

He moved to lick a fiery stripe across her hip.

"I don't care if this takes hours."

Hours?

"I've got nowhere to be."

The timbre of his voice alone was making her sweat at this point.

"I'm going to make you feel good until you tell me you're ready to stop."

Clara could feel his words between her legs. Each syllable pulsed, filling her with eager emotions that she couldn't separate, couldn't name. They blended together into a single insistent *need*.

Josh pushed the heel of his hand against her sex and sparks exploded behind her eyelids. Clara made a very unladylike sound. To think, a minute ago she'd thought his teeth on her ankle felt good.

Josh ran both thumbs up and down the damp seam of her sex before bracing one hand on her leg and using the other to slowly circle her clit.

With each caress, he inspired a sharper, deeper hunger until she found herself keening, as he worked her over without mercy. It was a cruel twist of fate that for twenty-seven years she'd settled for a pale imitation of the pleasure Josh wrought as he laid siege to her senses.

To act this way with a veritable stranger, right out here in the living room, without a carefully curated playlist of R&B slow jams, the casual carnality had her drunk on rebellion. At this point, she'd take anything Josh gave her and beg for more.

He played her body like a golden fiddle, ruthless in his quest to prove that he could make her come, fully clothed, barely skimming the surface of his amorous arsenal. That edge, the spike of superiority in him, as he bent her to his will made everything a little bit hotter. She couldn't pull enough oxygen into her lungs. Clara didn't understand—couldn't even follow—his movements as they blurred together into a single heavy throb in her pussy.

For as varied as his touches had been earlier, they were constant, unflinching now. Clara knew she had soaked through her panties at this point. She didn't care. Somewhere along the line, Josh had stripped her of every ounce of shame and replaced it with raw desire.

She hovered on the precipice of orgasm, her body so sensitized that every moment, every movement, almost but not quite sent her over the edge. The louder she got, the firmer Josh made his strokes, but it was never enough.

Still, even as the minutes continued to tick by, Josh never rushed her along to "get to the good part." He never tried to take advantage of her compromised state to barter for services-in-kind. Everything he did, he did for her to enjoy, to savor, until she couldn't survive another second on the edge.

"Please," Clara choked out.

Josh slowed the motions of his hand. "What do you need?"

They both knew the answer, but saying it out loud? She shook her head.

The bastard took his hand away entirely. All that pleasure—just paused.

Clara opened her eyes to find Josh leaning back on his heels. He would have looked ready to discuss the evening news, if not for his dilated pupils and the strain beneath his belt.

"I want to come, you ass," she said slowly through her teeth.

Josh smiled. "Oh. Do you? Why didn't you say something sooner?"

Clara groaned in frustration and closed her eyes again, blocking out his stupid, smug face. She tried to picture Everett. Hoping that a familiar fantasy carved into the grooves of her brain would do the job. She imagined running her hands through dark hair, Everett's eyes tracing her mouth. But for some reason, the images barely elicited a flutter in her belly.

Tears of frustration formed at the corners of her eyes as Josh's voice racked over her frenzied flesh. "Open your eyes again and I'll give you what you want."

Against her better judgment, she complied.

His easy swagger had faded. There was nothing but conviction and a hint of possession on his face now. She'd never realized that eye contact could cause hyperventilation.

This interaction might be all about her body, her pleasure, but here was Josh's consolation. Clara could never deny the identity of the man who made her whimper. She would know exactly who brought her over the edge.

"Wild looks good on you," Josh said, and this time when he put his hands on her he didn't hold back. The difference in tempo and technique was staggering. He'd been playing with her before. Pulling his punches. And it was obvious why. No one, especially a novice like her, could last against an onslaught of pleasure like this. Clara had no power in that moment, not even an ounce of the control that she considered her constant companion. Nothing mattered anymore, nothing but the way he let her fall apart. All the tension evaporated from her limbs as she shook in his arms.

After a few moments, as the sensations slowly began to fade, Josh cleared his throat and eased her thighs closed. But the passion in his touch was gone. His face had turned impassive, more like a man shutting the trunk of his car than a lover drawing out aftershocks.

"Well, that's done then."

Clara tried to gather her bearings. Right. Josh. Orgasm. Her and Josh. Orgasm. She'd . . . Oh dear.

"I'm sorry," she said automatically as she wiped her hand across her forehead, brushing hair that probably resembled a tumbleweed.

Josh stood up.

Clara's eyes found the bulge in his pants like a heat-guided missile.

Wow. Okay. So he'd suffered an involuntary response. To phero- mones. That was fine. Casual. Nothing to get worked up over . . . again.

"Don't worry about it, Wheaton. There's no need to be embarrassed. Think of it this way, this will make a great story when you go back to Connecticut. You can dine out on your 'The Time a Porn Star Made Me Come' story for at least a year. Hell, considering the circles you run in, maybe for the rest of your life."

Clara flinched. How sad did he think she was? Had she really gone through that earth-shattering situation alone? She admittedly didn't share his wealth of experience, but Clara had thought maybe that had been something extraordinary.

He picked up his bag and held it in front of his body.

Idiot. How could she think that a little rubbing over her underwear would even register on Josh's sexual radar? His mind and body were understandably at war.

Hadn't she watched him with the redhead? He routinely went all the way with incredible-looking women.

Josh could probably have chemistry with a ficus.

"Right." Clara pulled at a loose thread on the sofa. "I suppose for you that was just like work?"

Part of her wanted him to argue. To tell her she was special.

"Don't be ridiculous." Josh backed toward his room. "At work, I get paid."

Her shame turned into a living, breathing thing panting against her neck.

Clara had assumed she'd reached peak embarrassment the day

Everett left her on his doorstep with a one-armed hug. She saw now that she'd made a mistake.

She could withstand an inelegant dismissal. Could weather a few weeks of unemployment. She could clean a year's worth of dirty dishes in forty-eight hours. But she knew, from the roots of her hair to the depths of her soul, she couldn't stay in this house with the knowledge that she'd gotten a pity fumble from her roommate.

chapter nine

♡ ♡ ♡

NOTHING SAYS APOLOGY like caffeine and carbohydrates. At least, that was what Josh had learned over the course of his lifetime.

So when he couldn't sleep he'd gotten out of bed and driven across town to the best bakery he knew. At the ungodly hour of eight in the morning, the roads were filled with commuters, but he couldn't risk bringing Clara overcooked croissants or a burnt muffin from some run-of-the-mill gas station or national chain coffee shop. Based on her reaction last night, he'd be lucky if, presented with the best babka in L.A., she ever spoke to him again.

Josh knew, almost the second the words left his mouth the night before, that he'd taken the wrong approach in the moments after he'd made Clara come. But in all fairness, the experience had thrown him for a total loop. He'd expected a small thrill at the novelty of a new woman. Maybe a surge of competitive spirit at the chance to pull a passionate response from a pearl-clutcher like Clara. Not a spike of lust so powerful it made him dizzy.

He got paid on the regular to do stuff way sexier than a little over-the-clothes fumbling on his own sofa. Cotton panties shouldn't do it for him. He shouldn't savor the smoothness of Clara's skin or the way she hummed slightly when she liked a particular move.

Josh had gotten women off with his hands thousands of times, but he hadn't relied on heavy petting alone since high school, when he'd downgraded it from the main course to an appetizer.

He should have been safe, but something about Clara, about the noises she made, or the way she moved, or the wicked combination, threatened to pull him under her spell. Because when he'd watched her, squirming against his hand, panting, his skin had grown too tight for his body. Especially the moment when she said *please*. She hadn't looked like a buttoned-up blue blood then. She'd looked greedy. He couldn't think of another, more delicate, word to describe it. Her hair mussed. Full lips parted and wet from where she kept running her tongue across them. His dick liked it all. The whole naughty picture. Apparently, he had a good-girl fetish he'd never discovered before.

He'd gazed at her like some green teenager, his eyes so ravenous for her pleasure he must have scared her. Because as awareness returned to her body, she'd gone totally silent. Josh felt that quiet like a bucket of cold water over his head. He'd almost ruined everything. He'd promised Clara a professional and acted like an amateur.

He'd failed. At the one thing he was supposed to be good at.

Josh entered the bakery, opening the door to a cloud of air that hung heavy with the scent of sugar and butter and fruit pretending to add nutrients to devilish confections. He recognized the guy behind the counter from previous trips.

"Hey, Frankie. What's the special today?"

"Banana cream pie and fig tartlets." He pulled out a couple of trays from the display.

Josh shook his head. Neither of those treats sounded like his new roommate. He didn't know her yet, but he found to his surprise that he wanted to. There was something about her that intrigued him. That challenged his preconceptions about a rich girl from Connecticut.

The way she'd fidgeted last night when she admitted that her previous partners had left her to her own devices made his blood boil. He'd become determined to give her everything those other guys couldn't, or worse, *wouldn't*. Offering to help her out had felt more like a religious calling than a job. So despite the sirens ringing in his ears, he'd stepped up to the plate, telling himself the gesture was basically a public service.

Enter his massive erection.

Josh had gritted his teeth through the unexpected pleasure, and it had almost worked. But as she got closer and closer to falling apart, as the walls she built against the world turned to rubble, he'd forgotten his pledge to let her escape into a boilerplate fantasy.

Afterward, Josh had watched, transfixed, as she came back to earth. As her eyes cleared and her breath slowly evened out. He'd drunk his fill of her rosy cheeks and pink lips until he remembered that this moment didn't belong to him. Clara's postorgasm glow, bright as any star, wasn't his to savor.

Neither of them could afford to forget that he wasn't some average joe, free to fall for her. No. Josh Darling was a second-rate adult performer who would probably fade into obscurity by this time next year.

He couldn't give Clara any of the things that she probably expected after sharing an intimate moment with someone: comfort, security, romance. Out of the question. Off the table. Better to head off the discussion.

His contract left him with a huge mess on his hands. He couldn't even begin to untangle his relationships with Bennie and Naomi. The last thing he needed was Clara Wheaton asking him to go steady.

So he'd cut to the chase. Let her know that their experience had expired as quickly as it had begun.

"What would you recommend for a woman scorned?"

Frankie didn't miss a beat. "Lemon scones."

"Are you saying that because *scone* sounds kind of like *scorn*?"

"Absolutely."

While he couldn't fault Frankie's logic, Josh needed more. Despite his best efforts to shake off Clara's final wounded look, he'd tossed and turned for hours last night while one thought chewed on the corner of his brain. What if he woke up to find her gone?

He'd finally bit the bullet and checked the bathroom. Only seeing her toothbrush next to his by the sink had eased his fears.

There was the kicker. Josh didn't want Clara to leave. Even if it meant he could have the house to himself. That he could walk around naked eating peanut butter out of the jar and blasting the Ramones until the cows came home.

"What about those chocolate croissants? Women like chocolate, right?"

"Excellent choice." Frankie packaged a few pastries for him in a pink box. "And if you're really concerned about the lady's reaction, might I suggest adding an éclair or two?"

Josh didn't like Clara's rules. They'd turned his life into one big game of Operation. If he forgot to use a coaster or left the milk on the counter instead of putting it away immediately after use, he'd kill his imaginary patient.

She already hated him. At this rate, he'd be lucky to keep her on Danvers Street for the rest of the week. "You know what, you better give me the whole tray."

chapter ten

♡ ♡ ♡

EVERETT BLOOM BE damned. The sooner Clara got out of this town the better.

The unrelenting crush of traffic mocked her through the window of the car she'd called to take her to Jill's office. She never thought she would miss the subway. She pulled up a map on her phone. *Just a few more miles.* After barging back into her aunt's life after so long, Clara couldn't stomach leaving without saying good-bye.

Josh had been gone before she woke up that morning, saving her the torture of having to face him in the harsh light of day. He wouldn't understand why what had happened between them last night made her so embarrassed.

For the second time this week, following her gut instead of her head had landed her in a scandalous situation. Josh would never imagine that she couldn't sleep because her body didn't know how to come down from the most intense sexual experience of her life.

It was almost ten in the morning. He had probably done things ten times dirtier to women ten times hotter than her by now.

Fresh-cut flowers, bright topaz curtains, and an ancient floral rug softened the harsh industrial lines of the offices of Wheaton + Partners Public Relations. When Clara knocked on the door of Jill's office, she looked up from her laptop with a harried scowl.

"Hey there." Her aunt shook stiffness off her face. "What brings you here? Everything okay?"

"Yes. I mean, it will be. I'm sorry to bother you at work. I wanted to say good-bye before I headed back to New York." Her five o'clock flight couldn't come fast enough.

Concern arranged Jill's features. "But you just moved here."

"Yeah, well, it turns out things aren't going quite as well as I might have hoped with my new roommate." Talk about an understatement. She had completely blown whatever fragile friendship might have blossomed between her and Josh. "I think it's best if I get out of here before I cause any permanent damage."

Clara had gotten so far out of control last night, she didn't even recognize that woman panting on the couch. She'd made a spectacle of herself and now she had no choice but to pack her bags.

Jill opened her mouth to reply, but a young man holding a clipboard against his chest rushed into the room before she could get any words out.

"The DA finished her call. She's ready to resume your meeting in conference room B." His eyes resembled those of a frightened hare. Apparently, district attorneys didn't appreciate waiting.

"Shit." Jill's fingers sifted through the massive pile of documents on her desk. "Sorry, Toni's a new client. She's asked me to run her reelection campaign. It's a big deal for us. Normally someone in her shoes would go to one of the big corporate firms." Jill beamed and Clara could see why the men of Greenwich had once fallen at her aunt's feet. "She said she likes that we're famous for championing underdogs."

"Of course. I can see that this is a bad time. I should go," Clara said, already edging toward the door. She could call later on her way to the airport.

"No, wait. Don't leave. What time is your flight? I'm a bit underwater at the moment. One of my associates quit last week without notice." Jill continued riffling through the mess on the desk. A folder careened off the edge, splashing papers in a waterfall at her feet.

Clara bent to retrieve the fallen items. "Is there anything I can do?"

"Actually"—Jill cocked her head—"what do you think about sitting in on the rest of this meeting with me and taking some notes? You'd be doing me a huge favor, and it shouldn't take more than fifteen minutes. Once it's over, we can sit down properly and talk."

"Oh, well. I'm not really . . ." Clara stopped herself. She could hardly argue that she couldn't take notes. She owed Jill whatever favors she required after interrupting her work twice in as many days. "You know what, sure. I can do that. Do you have a notepad?"

And that was how Clara found herself sitting across a conference room table from the district attorney of Los Angeles County.

Clara had never seen anyone wear a suit half as well as Toni Granger. She didn't know if the woman had them custom made to fit her tall frame, or if she commanded the material through sheer force of will. The oatmeal Clara had had for breakfast began swimming laps in her stomach.

"Please accept my apologies for keeping you waiting. This is Clara. She'll be sitting in to capture some takeaways from our conversation." Despite the calamity in her office a few moments ago, Jill's voice now radiated calm professionalism.

The DA gave Clara a nod.

Pushing her nerves aside, Clara happily sank into a familiar position for the first time in almost a week.

Josh might excel in orgasms, but with the number of hours she'd logged in classrooms over the course of her lifetime, Clara knew her way around lined paper like nobody's business.

Toni sat back in her chair. "As you know, I've had a contentious relationship with my constituency over the last few years. When I decided to run for DA, I knew there would be people in this town who wouldn't like the idea of a Black woman in such a prominent office, but lately, it seems like the press is going out of their way to tear me down."

Jill folded her hands together on top of the table. "Yes, I've noticed that as your term comes to a close, your critics have grown more persistent."

"That's one word for it." Toni shook her head. "I've always been so stringent about keeping my nose clean. A sniff of scandal and my opposition would make sure I never work in this town again. But playing it safe has left me polling fifteen points behind my challenger."

With a judge for a father, Clara had grown up around more than her fair share of political and legal officials. With polling numbers that bad, Jill certainly had her work cut out for her.

"You'll need a big marquee case, something that will stir up public attention and bring in free airtime for the campaign." Clara scribbled a few notes. *Headlines. Big-name endorsements.*

Toni looked at Clara for the first time since Jill had introduced her. "Excuse me?"

She hadn't meant to say that out loud. "Oh. I'm sorry. I'm sure Jill would know better. I watch a lot of political dramas on TV."

Toni's face evened out. "Well, it sounds like Hollywood got it right for once. No one in this town gives a damn about run-of-the-mill cases. I need something big." She turned back to Jill. "That's where your firm comes in. I need to galvanize people."

Twenty minutes later, Clara and Jill waved at Toni's car as the DA pulled away.

"I like her," Clara said. "She's got that magnetism that makes people fall in line. Do you think she stands a chance?"

Jill cocked her hip to the side and gave Clara a once-over. "Do you wanna come work for me?"

Clara laughed until she realized her aunt wasn't joking.

"Me? No, I can't. I bought a plane ticket." Clara had a plan to save her reputation. It mandated that she get out of this city and away from Josh Darling's pheromones ASAP.

"Right, but what if you didn't leave? What if I hired you as a junior associate?"

Clara wrung her hands. "I don't have any experience."

"Please. You've got a PhD from Columbia."

"In art history." *A made-up degree for rich people.* "Sure, if you need someone to discuss the privatization of culture in fifteenth-century Florence, I'm your gal, but I don't know the first thing about public relations."

"You've got good instincts and, since you're a Wheaton, years of practical education in crisis management and reputation rehabilitation. The associates mainly do grunt work. Collecting research, drafting press releases. Nothing you couldn't handle."

"I prefer to stay under the radar." Thanks to her infamous family, she knew how the limelight could burn.

Jill leveled her gaze. "You need a reason to stay in Los Angeles. No matter what happened with your roommate, I know you don't want to go back after four days and face your mother. Do me a favor for a couple of weeks until I can fill the position. The pay isn't great, but I do supplement it with needlessly fancy green tea."

Clara shook her head. She wanted to help. She liked Jill, obviously, and Toni Granger inspired a surprisingly strong sense of civic engagement, but working across town from Everett's place wasn't a long-term option. The logistics alone made her brain bleed.

"I can't. Thank you, but I'm not cut out for this whole take-'em-as-they-come, fly-by-the-seat-of-your-pants lifestyle. I did one stupid, huge, impulsive thing." *Two.* "But from here on out I think I'd like to return to my comfort zone and set up camp."

"No. See, I don't buy that. You claim to have come out here for a guy, but what if Everett Bloom was an excuse to abandon a life built around pleasing other people?"

Why did people keep saying things like that to her? Sometimes a cross-country move didn't represent a quest for adventure so much as a failed booty call. Everyone had the entirely wrong idea about the capacity of Clara's courage.

"I'm not asking you to do anything crazy. Go home after you've had a few weeks to relax and recover. Let everyone back home wonder how you spent your time on the other side of the country. They'll never guess that I had you behind a desk from nine to five."

Clara chewed on her thumbnail. "It's not that I'm scared." Not *only* that.

"Well, then, what is it?"

Why did L.A. insist on ripping off all of her emotional Band-Aids at once? "I can't drive." The expense of taking a car forty miles each way, Monday through Friday, was doable, but certainly extravagant.

"Since when? Didn't your dad buy you a Beemer in high school?"

Clara couldn't help but crack a faint smile. "He did. Technically I have a license, but I prefer not to get behind the wheel. In New York, it wasn't an issue. I took public transit or walked most places. But here . . . I think I could catch a bus, but I have to imagine it'd take a while?"

Jill raised her eyebrows. "You're omitting an obvious third option."

"That's by design." Clara grimaced. It smarted to show another weak spot to this family member she barely knew. To arrive with so many broken parts and missing pieces and still expect acceptance.

Her aunt leaned in and hugged her. Somehow, the squeeze released all the shame and fear of the last few days.

"I get it. I do," Jill said. "But maybe it's worth giving driving another shot? Like it or not, you moved to L.A., kiddo. You're smart and capable. I know because I hired you."

Clara shook her head but couldn't stop the surge of pride that warmed her chest.

When Jill spoke next, her words took on gravity. "Some fears kill us. They drain us our whole lives, and we die filled with regret. But this isn't one of those fears. Make a plan. It doesn't have to be now, but you know the only way to get better at driving."

Clara tried to dust off whatever sense of conviction she'd tapped into a few weeks ago when, drunk on a combination of red wine and nostalgia, she'd decided to move to L.A., changing the course of her future.

Her answer resounded like a dumbbell tossed into her gut. "Drive."

Jill tapped her chin with a single finger. "I don't suppose your new roommate has a car?"

chapter eleven

♡ ♡ ♡

CLARA'S PLAN HINGED on her ability to make pancakes.

Batch four had the right color, golden brown, versus anemic batch two. But batch three had a better texture, less cakey and airier. She tightened her ponytail. After spending the entire ride back from Malibu plotting, she had to get this right.

The smell of roasted meat filled the small kitchen. At least popping bacon in the oven was foolproof.

She attempted to see down the hallway to Josh's door while keeping an eye on the half-cooked pancake in front of her. Having passed his car on the way in, she knew he was home. As Clara considered banging a few pots and pans in summons, Josh emerged from his bedroom, rumpled as usual.

Her heart hammered in her chest as her gaze dropped immediately to his hands. Hands that he'd had all over her last night. The plane that should have carried her far, far from their last, mortifying interaction had taken off over an hour ago. She lowered her shoulders away from her ears and gathered her resolve.

As she hastily hid the evidence of her failed batches under the sink,

Josh sank onto a well-worn bar stool at the island. Clara attempted to hum casually.

He swiveled to survey the scene of her culinary implosion. "What happened in here?"

Clara gestured to her army of pans and filled her voice with false cheer. "I thought I'd make dinner. Last night was rather awkward, as I'm sure you know." She winced. "I figured we could start over. Wipe the slate clean, as it were."

"You decided to wipe the slate clean by making the kitchen incredibly messy?"

She might have called the playful quirk of his lips shy if she didn't know better.

"I don't actually have a ton of gastronomic experience. I thought breakfast for dinner would be easy." She dabbed at the raw egg dribbling down the front of her apron with a wet paper towel. "I may have miscalculated."

"That's funny. I . . . ah . . . actually bought you some apology pastries this morning." He reached up to rub the back of his neck. "But then you weren't here when I got back. Anyway, they're in the fridge." He coughed into his fist. "Most of them are still in the fridge."

"You have nothing to apologize for." Clara tapped her batter-smeared fingers on the countertop. "You're an extremely talented performer and I appreciate what you did for me. I'm the one who . . . well, let's just say I got a bit skittish." Raising her eyes, she took in his guarded expression. "I'm better now, at any rate."

"Oh. Well, good." Josh tapered his gaze. "Are you wearing overalls?"

She turned over her shoulder, spatula in hand. "I am." Overalls represented no-nonsense hard work. "The food will be ready in a minute."

"I can't believe you cooked for me." Josh squinted at her. Hopefully he didn't find her motives suspect.

"I think technically this counts as baking." Clara piled a plate high with the best of the batch of pancakes, bacon, and fresh fruit, and placed it in front of Josh. She'd arranged the berries in concentric circles.

Dipping her chin, she nudged the plate closer to him encouragingly. "I guess we both came to the conclusion that we should break bread together."

"You know you've got flour . . ." He pointed to his nose, then his cheek, then his neck, until eventually he waved his hand around his entire face.

Clara tried wiping herself down with a dishcloth.

"You're making it worse." Josh dismounted from his stool and came to stand in front of her. Taking the soft material from her sweaty hand, he bent his knees and gently scrubbed her face. His warm fingers held her chin delicately, guiding the direction of her neck so he could address the worst of the culinary carnage. Clara's heart rate climbed as he brushed off her nose. The strange intimacy of the act hung in the air between them, until she had difficulty catching her breath. Proximity packed a powerful punch.

He stepped back and Clara turned away, tamping down the confusing appetite he'd unleashed that had nothing to do with food. She grabbed a second plate for herself. Somehow his tender assistance shook her almost as much as his choreographed pleasure-wringing last night.

When Josh returned to his stool on the other side of the island, Clara sat next to him, skootching to ensure their elbows wouldn't accidentally brush as they ate. "Oh shoot. I forgot the syrup!"

"I'll get it," Josh said, keeping one eye trained on her as Clara munched on a piece of bacon.

He placed the maple syrup in front of her. "Is this a trap?"

Clara cut her pancake into tiny squares and concentrated on keeping her voice even. "Is what a trap?"

Josh pointed at his brimming plate. "This is a lot of effort for someone you just met."

"You think I have an ominous agenda for making pancakes?" Clara tried not to blink.

"You're literally buttering me up." He thrust his chin at the pat of butter she had carved off on her knife and moved to drop on his plate.

Clara imbued her voice with false innocence. "I'm sorry. Did you not want butter?"

"I definitely want butter." Josh took the knife from her, brushing her index finger with his thumb. "But I've lived in this town long enough to know there's no such thing as a free meal. You sure you're not up to something?"

"You said yourself that you bought me pastries. If there's no such thing as a free meal, consider this dinner payment in kind."

Josh poured a healthy dose of syrup onto his stack and then scooped up a big bite, complete with berries. As he swallowed, his eyes closed, and a groan rumbled deep in his throat. He brought his palm down on the counter with a resounding smack.

"This. Is. A. Trap." He punctuated each word with a slap of his hand.

Her chair groaned as she tipped it back on two legs, caught in a fit of nervous giggles. "Do you really like them? Are you sure they're not too chewy?"

"Jesus." Josh stared at her like she'd hit him over the head with one of the frying pans. "You look like trouble when you laugh."

"I'm not. I swear." Clara's voice stalled on a squeak.

Her eyes fell to where his faded T-shirt hugged impressive biceps. She dug her fingernails into her palm.

Stick to the plan. "It is, however, possible I have a favor to ask."

"I knew it," Josh said around a massive bite. He flew back from the stool and shook his head. "You look innocent but really, you're a wily minx."

No one had ever accused Clara of nefarious motives before. She discreetly dabbed her forehead with a napkin. "Will you at least listen to my proposal?"

"All right, but I'm commandeering payment in kind." He reached over and claimed her last slice of bacon.

"Okay," she said, bracing herself for the big speech. "Try to keep an open mind here. What are the chances you'd let me borrow your car?"

"Slim to none," he said vehemently. "That car is the only thing I own that means anything at all to me. I've had her since high school. Do you know how much work it takes to keep a 'Vette that old running?"

"I wouldn't ask if it wasn't important," Clara said, lacing her tone with practiced calm. "I got a job and I need to work my way up to commuting." Her mother had taught her that any negotiation could be solved with reason and controlled voices.

"Wow. You work fast." Josh brightened. "It's great that you got a job, and listen, I know you're not from around here, but asking to borrow someone's car in L.A. is a massive deal."

"It would only be for a few hours," she assured him. "I'll work around your schedule, and of course I'll pay for gas. I could even get it washed. Maybe get the tires rotated?" She elbowed him like an old-timey salesman. "What do you think?"

"You don't understand how much I love that car. Can't you think of another favor I could do for you? Are you sure you don't want to fuck?"

Clara's fork clattered to the ground and they bumped heads when they both reached for it.

"Sorry," he said weakly. "That was a bad joke. I forgot you were . . . you." He moved and fetched her new silverware. "Why don't you have your own car? I know you moved from New York." He waved away her interjection. "But why wasn't 'get a car' on your little laminated checklist?"

She fiddled with one of the hooks on her overalls. "I knew I would need to drive eventually. L.A. traffic is famous, but Everett said I could borrow his Jeep and I thought I'd have more time to practice." The confession cost Clara her appetite.

"Well, hey, you could get a lease. I'll even drive you to the dealership." He gave her a brief once-over. "We'll get you set up in a nice VW Bug with one of those stickers for the window that says *Student Driver* or *Baby on Board* or something."

"I don't think I can get a lease yet. I've got that . . . emotional impediment to driving, remember? That's why I wanted to borrow your car, to see if I could handle getting behind the wheel at all. I would take it around the neighborhood. Nothing crazy. I'd hire an instructor, but I'm worried I might—"

"Crash?" He nodded sympathetically.

"—lose my nerve," Clara finished. "It's embarrassing enough admitting my weakness to you. I don't need to throw another stranger into the mix if the point is moot." She chased a blueberry around the plate with her fork. "I figured that since you've already seen me in flagrante delicto, the embarrassment veil is lifted."

Josh frowned. "Is that a fancy way of saying I gave you an orgasm? Because like I told you, that was no big deal."

Clara ignored his piercing comment. She didn't need a reminder of how little last night meant to him. "I got a job helping some people I really care about. I know it's a lot to ask, but I'm desperate. It'll probably take all of five minutes. I'll sit in the car, freak out, and then we can throw driving on top of the list of failures I am rapidly accumulating."

Josh resumed eating. "I don't get it. Why are you so sure you can't drive? I know you have a license. I saw it the other day when you bought wine at the grocery store."

"I caused an accident," Clara finally admitted, the words ripped out of her. "It was a couple of nights before cotillion. That's like a fancy society event," she said in answer to his blank look. "I was late to rehearsal and I was so worried that if I didn't show up, Everett would end up escorting someone else."

He raised an eyebrow. "Everett Bloom?"

"The one and only."

Josh sighed. "You know, I'm starting to think that guy sucks."

"The exit was coming up fast, and I needed to change lanes. I hate changing lanes. I can never time it correctly. In the end, I turned on my blinker and hoped for the best. I don't recommend that strategy."

"Hey, accidents happen."

She struggled to control her breathing. "My younger brother, Oliver, was in the passenger seat. He ended up with fourteen stitches, a bruised collarbone, and a broken arm."

"Clara," Josh said gently, "even good drivers make mistakes."

"Mistakes?" She let out a tight, painful laugh. "I've got terrible instincts. Whatever inner voice other people have telling them what to do, mine's broken. Every time I try to follow my intuition, someone gets hurt. For a long time, I couldn't get behind the wheel without hearing Oliver scream."

She tried to shake away the memories but only managed to set flour raining from her hair.

"You're being too hard on yourself. You were a kid."

"I had a series of expensive instructors over the years, but it was always the same story. My father wrote me off as a lost cause. Told me to move to New York where I could take the subway and hail a cab."

Clara's shoulders slumped forward. "Look, I'm being pragmatic. I've never been able to do it before. It stands to reason I won't be able to do it now. But I told Jill I would try, and I don't want to be another family member who lets her down." She stared at her plate. "I realize you have no reason to help me, that I'm already more trouble than you'd prefer, but since you haven't actually said no yet, I'm gonna ask one more time. Please, Josh?"

He squinted at the ceiling. "You want it bad, huh?"

Visions of lurid double entendres chose that very inappropriate moment to invade her senses. Josh was sexy even when he wasn't trying. Nothing in his body language suggested innuendo. If anything, she saw concern woven across his features. Still, his words affected her.

Please try to focus. "I feel like if I can do this, the move won't have been for nothing. I'll have something to show for it, even without Everett. If I can get over this fear, I can stop avoiding my mother's calls and tell her I accomplished something."

"Okay, fine." Josh tipped his head back and closed his eyes. "But you owe me."

"Really?"

He nodded. "Man, you look like I just won you a giant teddy bear at the county fair."

"Thank you, thank you, thank you!" She launched herself at him without thinking, gratitude outweighing her anxieties about touching him. Josh endured the hug, patting her head awkwardly. He smelled like an orchard, crisp and sweet.

"Okay. Well." He detangled himself from her arms and moved to transfer some of her used pans to the sink. "I'll do the dishes, try to minimize the damage from the flour bomb that went off in here, and then we'll go."

Her grin faltered. "Wait. You're coming with me?" She really didn't need Josh to stand witness to another humiliation.

"You didn't think after that whole speech I was gonna let you go alone? I'll be your vehicle supervisor." He pulled on the yellow rubber gloves she'd bought as the sink filled with soapy water. "That's my offer. Take it or leave it."

She wished she could leave it, but she knew that come Monday morning, she'd have both Jill and Toni waiting for her, depending on her. Looking stupid or weak was nothing next to the idea of not meeting the expectations of people she admired. Josh already thought of her as an anomaly, an alien from Planet Stick-up-the-Butt.

Why not throw one more log on the trash can fire of her reputation?

chapter twelve

♡ ♡ ♡

C LARA HAD STUMBLED on the one area of Josh's life in which he had trouble relinquishing control.

"Repeat rules seven through nine one more time," Josh said from the passenger seat of the Corvette thirty minutes later.

They'd sat in the car, in the driveway, for the past fifteen minutes while he tried to get fully on board with the plan.

Clara inhaled slowly through her nose and then repeated Josh's "rules of the road" in the monotone of someone for whom words have lost all meaning. "No slamming on the brakes. No riding the brakes. Proper footwear must be worn at all times." She tilted her head at him in exaggerated question, her hands firmly at positions ten and two on the steering wheel. "Can we please go? I promise I will follow all traffic laws and in no way intentionally endanger this vehicle. Under no circumstances will I engage the high beams without permission."

At least some of the nerves threatening to eat her insides had given way to aggravation and tedium. Whether he'd suggested the rules to intentionally lure her into a false sense of security or not, they'd had that effect.

Josh buckled his seat belt and then double-checked it. "I've noted your lack of enthusiasm for the rules, but you may proceed."

Not exactly a vote of confidence, but better than the alternative.

Clara gave him a look out of the corner of her eye. "You're weird in the car."

"Excuse me? Are you choosing this moment to mouth off to the owner of the extremely valuable vehicle you're preparing to pilot?"

"Really weird," Clara muttered as she made final adjustments to the mirrors. She'd already set them in different positions four separate times. She started the car and the purr of the engine made her jump.

Stalling seemed like a good idea. "You know, Josh, it's nice to see you so passionate about something. You really love this old Camaro, huh?"

"This is a Corvette," he said, white-knuckling the armrest. "And she doesn't appreciate being called old. Let's get this over with."

So much for diversion tactics. Clara braced herself and then slowly backed the car out of the driveway.

Josh's eyes kept flickering between her face and the road.

She chewed on the inside of her cheek. "You're making me more nervous."

"Sorry." Josh slumped back in his seat. "No one's ever asked me to be the good guy before."

"What do you mean?" The street they lived on didn't attract much attention, but she needed to navigate all the cars parked along the curb. Each time she passed a new obstacle, she held her breath.

"I mean this whole situation, being the hero, the one who comes through in a damsel's moment of need. It's new for me. I'm finding it a bit unsettling."

"I'm not a damsel." Clara's sweaty palms threatened her grip on the steering wheel. She wiped them one by one on the shorts of her overalls.

"Sure, you are. A young, unmarried woman of noble birth."

Clara shook her head as they approached a stoplight. "Did you just quote Merriam-Webster?"

"My mom used to read us fairy tales when I was little. I looked up the words I didn't know."

A smile threatened the corners of Clara's mouth until they reached a four-way intersection.

"Clara? Hey. Are you okay?

Her eyes began to water. She tried to tip her chin up without losing sight of the road.

Josh dug in the glove box until he'd removed a handful of tissues. "Are you sure you wanna do this?"

"I'm sure," she said, with only a hint of a tremble in her voice.

When she didn't reach for the Kleenex, Josh dabbed carefully at her eyes, stemming the leak.

"Thanks." Clara's cheeks heated. "I know it doesn't look like it, but I feel like I'm close to overcoming this." She straightened her shoulder blades. "Like if I can just reach out far enough, I can brush victory with my fingertips. That probably sounds dumb, right?"

"No. I'm pretty sure you're the smartest person I've ever met. Objectively." His eyes warmed in the same way they had during dinner when he'd said she looked like trouble. She didn't have time to worry about the meaning behind that look.

"My aunt's going out on a limb for me and I want to show up for her, you know?"

"I know," he said. "Hey, would it help if I sang? Ya know, something soothing." He started in on the first few bars of "Walking on Sunshine."

Josh had terrible pitch and he smacked his hand on the armrest in his attempt to emphasize a high note, but the gesture cut through some of Clara's numbness.

I used to think maybe you loved me . . . now, baby, I'm sure. Her heart fluttered. "You're a terrible singer."

"I'm sorry, what was that?" He cupped a hand over his ear. "Sing louder?"

Clara tapped the brakes too hard and winced.

Josh fell silent.

They'd reached the entrance to the freeway. Clara slowed the car at the metered on-ramp, even though she knew the green light meant *go*.

She brought the Corvette to a halt and the car behind her honked in protest.

Clara tried to focus on breathing. *In and out. In and out.* Each time a new horn blasted she took it like a kick to the temple. *In and out. In and out.*

Her hands shook on the steering wheel, vibrating so intensely the kickback reverberated in her shoulders.

"Jesus, Clara. This isn't nerves. This is terror." His voice wavered. "Let's forget it," he said gently. He coaxed her to pull onto the shoulder. "I'll drive you wherever you need to go. Driving isn't worth *this*."

Clara's teeth chattered despite the early summer heat as she set the Corvette to a crawl while other cars whistled past them. She caught Josh's gaze from the corner of her eye. "I can do it."

He nodded his head once, making his long curls bounce. "All right. Then talk to me."

"What?" She shouldn't be on the shoulder. Someone had probably already called the cops on her. Any minute now the guy in that truck would get out and get in her face.

"Focus on my voice," Josh said. "It works on set when people get nervous. When they can't get past the cameras and the lights."

"This was a mistake." Oliver's screams started, playing on a loop along with the sounds of metal crumpling and tires screeching. She fought the impulse to plug her ears with her fingers.

"Just keep talking."

"I'm a judgmental person," she blurted out.

His chuckle came out in a rumble. "Now why doesn't that surprise me?"

Her eyes flicked to her rearview mirror. "I'm serious. I readily admit it. I meet a person, and I make a decision about their character within half an hour. I have an outstanding track record. My hypothesis is right roughly ninety percent of the time. But on the rare occasion I'm wrong, it's a thrill. Some people are like an iceberg, with the dangerous and beautiful parts hidden below the surface."

"Are you trying to say I'm a dangerous and beautiful iceberg?"

Clara huffed. "More like an ice cap." Her gaze shot from the freeway to her hands on the steering wheel, and then back at the road. "I'm trying to say thanks."

"Thank me after," Josh said.

"There may not be an after. I think I've reached my limit."

"Okay, here are our options. You can merge, or we can sit here and talk about yesterday when I had my hands on your—"

Clara pressed her foot to the gas pedal almost without thinking. Josh had managed to find the one thing that made her more nervous than driving.

JOSH HOWLED TRIUMPHANTLY, pumping his fist in the air to knock the roof of the car. "Do you see what's happening right now? Because you, Clara Wheaton, are keeping pace on the freeway. I feel like you need to let out some kind of primal yell."

Aside from a tiny arch in her eyebrow, Clara didn't acknowledge him, but he noticed that her hands relaxed slightly on the steering wheel. Color returned to her cheeks. She even suggested he put on the radio, as long as he kept the volume in the vicinity of a whisper. A win if he ever saw one.

The concern that sat heavy and unfamiliar in his stomach slowly faded. He'd never dealt with anything like this with Naomi. A woman who was self-sufficient to a fault. The last time he remembered worrying about her was when she'd insisted on getting her tongue pierced on the Venice Beach Boardwalk.

After about fifteen minutes of uneventful cruising by the ocean, a familiar cluster of palm trees gave Josh an idea. "Hey, how would you feel about a little detour?"

"You mean a chance to get out of the car?" Clara laughed tightly. "Yes, please."

"I know just the place." Josh directed her toward the next exit and then down a few streets until they found themselves pulling into the empty parking lot of a high school.

He raced to help Clara out of the driver's seat, mostly because he didn't want to risk her getting a case of jelly legs and face-planting on the pavement. While her color had returned, she still had a sheen of sweat across her forehead.

When she put her tiny, clammy hand in his, he tightened his hold on impulse. She sighed as her feet met solid ground. "Please tell me it gets easier?"

His body, betraying all instruction from his brain, buzzed from the contact with her skin. "I'm pretty sure it has to." He wasn't positive whether he was talking to Clara or himself. As soon as she stood up, Josh backed away, out of the pull of her orbit, as she took in their surroundings.

"How did you even know this place was here?" Clara shook out her hair.

"This was my high school." Josh greedily inhaled the scent of fresh-cut grass. "My family moved here from Seattle right before ninth grade. You wanna look around?"

When she nodded, he guided her around the building. "So, what was Josh Darling like at eighteen?"

He watched, momentarily mesmerized as her long dark hair whipped in the wind. "Well, Josh Darling didn't exist yet, but Josh Conners was your classic fuckup. I cut class so much they almost held me back."

"Ah." She took two steps to keep pace with every one of his. "A rebel."

"That's one word for it. I think the law prefers *truant*. You see, over there"—he pointed to a set of corner windows—"is where I served a month's worth of detention. It took a lot of sweet-talking to get the principal to agree to let me graduate on time."

"That doesn't sound so bad." Clara tilted her head back and offered her porcelain skin to the dying sun.

"You've never met Principal Carlson. I tried to spin my life into a sob story, but there wasn't much to work with. Only child, on the light side of latchkey. My parents worked all the time to pay the bills, but they've always been good people who loved me and I guess I never figured out how to hide that."

Josh swallowed the lump of guilt in his throat. He hadn't seen his parents since Thanksgiving two years back. Ever since, turkey made him nauseous.

Clara stopped walking and looked up at him. "The principal didn't buy it?"

His chest burned as he remembered the assessment sent to his parents, left carelessly on the kitchen table waiting for him when he got home from school. *Underachieving, pleasure-seeking, lazy, reckless to the point of endangerment.*

That had been almost ten years ago, but he knew not much had changed. If he saw Principal Carlson again, she'd probably add to the list. *Defensive, closed off, hopeless.*

With a hand on her back, Josh guided Clara around a pothole. "She didn't buy it."

What was he thinking, spilling his high school woes to someone with a doctorate? Josh could picture her at eighteen. One of those golden girls with all of the privilege and support he'd resented his whole life.

When Clara walked into a room, people respected her.

When Josh walked into a room, people wondered why he was wearing so many clothes.

"Don't feel sorry for me." The words came out rougher than he'd meant them.

"I wasn't." Clara actually crossed her heart.

The sun slipped below the skyline and the stadium lights around the baseball field came on.

Clara wandered in that direction. "What about extracurricular activities? Did you play any sports?"

"No, but I did stay active." He pointed to a patch of trees and a well-worn bench. "Had sex over there." He gave a fond wave to the dugout. "Went down on Olivia Delvecchio there. Found out about squirting—"

"Okay, okay, I get it. You're a stud."

"Even back then I knew where my talents lay." He pictured his last meeting with Bennie. "Although I guess that might have been wishful thinking."

"What do you mean?"

He lowered his chin to watch the grass grow. "Black Hat, the studio I work for, gave me a real lowball offer recently when my agent asked to renegotiate my contract."

She'd shown him her weakness, and now he'd revealed his own. For all his big talk and his "viral" video, no one who mattered considered him worth opening up the old checkbook.

"Really? I'd think they'd jump all over the chance to keep you on the books." She sat on the bleachers. God, everything she did looked so polished and proper.

Josh sat down next to her. "It's my fault. I signed this terrible contract a few years ago. Didn't even read it. I got drunk off the idea that someone thought I could do something, anything, well. The loss of revenue from merchandise alone . . ." He buried his hands in his hair.

"Merchandise?" Clara's voice had gone up an entire octave.

Her discomfort broke through some of his self-pity, lightening his mood. She was a good sport, his new roommate. "Don't worry, Wheaton. Any time you ask, you've got the real thing."

Clara gasped as she took his meaning and pulled the edges of her cardigan closer together. "What will you do about this contract situation? Get a lawyer?"

He admired her determination to change the subject, but the mention of lawyers went down like a bitter pill. "Nah. I can't afford a lawyer, at least not one good enough to go up against Black Hat. I assume you know that parts of the porn industry deserve the bad rap. That there are some not-so-nice people with skin in the game?"

"Until I met you I didn't think there was anything worthwhile about porn."

He'd figured as much. "As a performer, you've got very little say in what gets made. The producers and studio heads pull the strings. I've got a solid fan base but not much sway. Believe it or not, women aren't the primary audience of most pornos."

"Is that why so much of it is gross? Why don't the major studios invest in female audiences?" She wrinkled her nose. "Sounds like bad business to me."

"Are you saying that if the studios invested in the right kind of porn, you would watch it?" Josh conjured up the embers of his signature smolder.

"That question is negligible at present," she said, crossing her legs at the ankles.

"Damn. You can make anything sound fancy, can't you?"

She squinted into the darkening sky. "Surely not something completely pedestrian."

"Are you kidding? You just did it."

She had the nerve to wink at him. *Get this girl out of the driver's seat for five minutes and suddenly she's a scoundrel.* He couldn't remember the last time a woman, or anyone for that matter, had surprised him so much.

Clara reached down to pick a weed. "So if you can't get a new contract, would you quit?"

Josh covered his face with his hands and sighed into them. "I have no idea." That question had haunted him for days. If Bennie put him off pickles for life, Josh would never forgive him.

"Lots of people transition between careers in their late twenties," Clara said. Always striving for diplomacy. "You need to make a list. Maybe two. I wish I'd brought my notebook. What's your primary skill set?"

Josh put his hand on her bare knee. Half challenge, half invitation. He didn't apply much pressure, just enough to raise goose bumps. The vision of her spread out across the sofa last night made adrenaline pump in his veins. Clara didn't look down, but he felt the tightness in her body, the rapid awareness. She immediately brought her hand to cover his, and he waited for her to push him away. Instead, she . . . held. For an incredible moment, he let himself believe she might guide him higher until his fingers brushed under the shorts of her overalls to caress the top of her thigh, light as the lazy breeze. She sucked in a sharp breath but didn't move.

Clara would probably sock him in the mouth at any moment. Was probably gathering her strength for the windup. Her eyes stayed on the field as she sank her teeth into the pillow of her bottom lip. Was it possible that Clara Wheaton liked her sex with a side of exhibition? That knowledge raced straight to his cock. But before he could invest in his revelation, she cleared her throat and put his hand back in his lap. "What else?"

While his heartbeat slowed he racked his brain. "Driving. I could become a truck driver or a pizza delivery guy." He was only half joking. He loved pizza.

"That's a start. Keep going." She jumped at the chance to move the conversation back into safe territory. Her family had probably hired a career counselor for her while she was still in preschool.

"Taxes. I could do the shit out of your taxes," he said, getting into the game despite himself. He stood and started to climb between the bleacher seats. "You should see the refund I got last year."

Clara turned to watch him and quirked her mouth to the side. "You'd have to go back to school to become an accountant."

He'd probably have to wear a tie to work too. "Forget that."

Just because Clara had started to see past what he did—what he was—didn't mean the rest of the world would follow suit. Relative success in porn equaled relative failure in the real world.

His head hurt trying to process all these *what if*s and *maybe*s. He'd stayed in a shitty contract, not to mention a dying relationship, for years because he preferred the path of least resistance. All he knew was he liked working in porn. Not just the getting-paid-to-have-sex part—though he admitted that didn't hurt—but the people and the process of making something that others enjoyed. He wasn't ready for long-term planning, didn't have that kind of endurance, but Clara kept staring at him expectantly. Like together they could solve all of his problems.

"I know a decent amount about production," he said finally, making his way back toward where she sat. "Just from being around it all the time, ya know." He ran his hand over his jaw. "You wouldn't believe how much editing affects the tone of a piece. Or music selection. I know it's a porno, so how emotional can ya really get, but I've seen some stuff that's closer to art than most commercial blockbusters. And it's production that controls casting, sets, even making sure that we adhere to health and safety regulations."

"That sounds promising." She jumped on his first sign of interest. "You should produce something."

"No one would hire me. I've got a high school diploma, thirty college credits, and expertise in anal beads. Not exactly a stellar résumé."

Clara tipped her head back to look up at him where he stood in the row above hers. "Don't sell yourself short. I Googled you, remember?"

He swallowed hard. As if he could forget.

"One of the headlines that popped up—which I definitely didn't click on, mind you—said you have over a million fans on your website. If you made something, I bet those people would pay to watch it."

Josh sank back down beside her. "I don't know. The porn industry doesn't exactly cater to women's pleasure. My skill set . . . if you can even call it that . . . it's like being the da Vinci of macaroni sculptures. No one gives a shit."

"You're an artist, and you've found a way to make a living from your art." Clara turned pink. "That's pretty enterprising. Most people quit before they ever get a chance to fail."

Josh couldn't recall the last time someone had given him a pep talk, especially when the subject matter made them so obviously uncomfortable. "You're impressive."

Clara waved the compliment away.

"No, really." He pulled up a handful of grass and counted the blades. "You're a study in contradictions. A week ago you'd never heard of me, and now you're sitting here adamantly defending my 'art.'"

She lifted a delicate shoulder. "What can I say? I'm a desperate optimist."

"Is this the part where birds and other woodland creatures come out and sing backup on your ballad about why I shouldn't abandon the dream of fucking my way to fame?"

Clara let out a bitter sigh and straightened her shoelaces. "Unfortunately, animals hate me."

"What?" Josh snorted and stood, reaching out to help her up.

"They can smell my fear." There wasn't a hint of a joke in her voice as she took his hand.

"It's kind of cute that you're such a little nutjob," he said, more to himself than to her.

"*Cute*'s one word for it." She started back toward the car.

"Wait up." He moved to stand in front of her. "Hey. Look at what you've done in less than a week." Josh spread his hands out in front of him. "Moved across the country, started a new job, got behind the wheel. Not to mention fooling around with an acclaimed adult performer." His dimples bloomed. "As far as I can see, Wheaton, you're pretty damn extraordinary."

Clara's shy smile made him want to grab the straps of those ridiculous overalls, yank her mouth to his, and *finally* taste those strawberry lips he'd been dreaming about since she first walked into his life.

"We should probably head back." He needed doors between them, ones he could lock.

"Oh. Sure." Clara brushed off her butt and Josh tried not to notice the way her hands glided down the generous swell.

Fuck. If he wasn't careful, he was going to end up with a crush on his roommate.

chapter thirteen

♡ ♡ ♡

T WO WEEKS INTO his self-imposed underemployment, Josh had grown dangerously bored. It was disastrous, having so much free time in the vicinity of Clara Wheaton.

He first noticed the symptoms when he found himself timing his showers to follow hers. Something inside him perked up when he walked in and their tiny bathroom still held the scent of her soap. It was like stepping into a meadow. And if that meadow also made him think about Clara, naked, wet, and covered in bubbles? Well, he shot those daydreams on sight.

It was easy to blame this new, strange behavior on his first physical dry spell in recent memory. Even though his romantic relationship with Naomi had fizzled more than a few months back, up until last Thursday, work had kept his libido in check. His right hand hadn't seen this much action since he'd hit puberty.

Josh displayed mental symptoms of decline as well as physical. He had grown so desperate for conversation he resorted to waking up early to catch Clara before she went to work.

Unlike Josh, she loved mornings. As soon as he stumbled into the kitchen, she put on cheesy pop music to accompany her as she made coffee and packed her lunch.

He'd never seen so much Tupperware in his life. She even had little containers for the dressing, so small he could fit three of them in his palm. They were almost cute. Baby Tupperware.

Everything seemed to deflate when she left promptly at seven thirty. He felt so useless sitting around that by day three he offered to drive Clara out to her office in Malibu. Josh had nothing better to do. In the evenings, he picked her up and let her drive home for practice. It was pathetic that basically acting as his roommate's chauffeur gave him a small, twisted sense of purpose, but these days he had to take the wins wherever he could find them.

He still spent most of the day alone with nothing but the possessions Clara left like footprints across the house. Each afternoon a new box of tchotchkes got delivered to their door. While her changes were subtle, they touched every single room. He'd open a drawer to find coasters or oven mitts. Hand towels appeared in the bathroom, along with some kind of basket of dried flowers and twigs.

She might have a doctorate, but where he came from, that shit would not pass as art.

Clara even bought curtains for his bedroom. He opened the door one day to find them hanging jauntily above his window, both charming and useful. Somehow, while working, she still found time to turn Everett's man cave into something resembling a home. As if he needed further evidence of her competence to press on the bruise of his stalled career.

He'd started running in the afternoons to have something to do. Trying to burn off the itch he felt in his limbs. On those long jogs to the ocean, he tried to think about his future. Tried to brainstorm production partners, and people within the industry who owed him a favor, but even if he could find someone to let him produce, Josh didn't have a clue what he'd make.

When he returned home from his latest jog he knew, even before he bumped into Clara's five separate hampers, that she must have run out of clean underwear. The whole house had filled with sweet-smelling humidity radiating from the small laundry room next to the porch.

He balled his hands into fists and immediately moved to open a window.

Tonight, like every night this week, Clara had deposited herself on the couch surrounded by piles of documents. He didn't know what kind of workload she'd agreed to when she took that job, but it seemed to involve a lot of take-home reading.

Josh rearranged her laundry baskets so he wasn't barricaded out of his own kitchen.

"You don't need to separate your clothes into that many separate cycles," he told her as he deposited one of the full hampers at her feet.

"I know you probably don't care since you seem to live in jeans and T-shirts," she said prissily, "but different types of clothes require different water temperatures and speeds."

"Yeah, that's the wrong way to think about it."

"Excuse me?" Clara lowered the document in her hand.

Bending to examine her system of organization, Josh began to sort through her clothes, rearranging items into new piles on the carpet. "Fabric content determines ideal washing conditions, not color. For example"—he held up a soft T-shirt—"cotton is prone to shrinking. You should only use cold water and air-dry cotton of any color." He tossed a set of shorts over his shoulder. "Linen wrinkles like a bitch, so you should be pressing those shorts immediately after they come out of that washer." Two pairs of pantyhose tangled together around his wrist. Josh separated them and placed them over the arm of the couch. "Hanging nylon will avoid that aggressive static situation you've got going on."

Lesson over, Josh followed his nose into the kitchen. He opened the oven to investigate the source of a pleasant peppery smell. "Oh, you can do whatever you want with polyester," he yelled so she could hear him through the doorway. "It's hard to mess up polyester." Josh eyed a lasagna bubbling under the broiler. "Can I have some of your pasta?"

"Of—of course. It's vegetarian . . . and I made the sauce from scratch."

Josh's stomach growled. Another symptom. In such a short time, Clara had already gotten him addicted to vegetables. Probably tricked him into some kind of iron dependency with her magical menu that disguised an ungodly amount of leafy greens. Sometimes he woke up in the middle of the night craving spinach.

Clara shook her head slowly as Josh joined her on the couch with a steaming plate. "How do you . . . how do you know so much about laundry?"

"I've got more than your average experience. My mom works for a dry cleaner. Has ever since I was little. She browbeat that stuff into me as a kid. Last I heard she's still there. At this rate, her hands will never stop smelling like bleach."

"Last you heard?"

"I haven't seen anyone in my family in a few years. Not since I told them about my job." Josh blew on his loaded fork. "They didn't get it."

The guilt from that moment had eaten at him until he'd stopped returning their calls. He'd even gone so far as to change his number and his email address. He didn't need lectures or quiet concern.

He cleared his throat. "I guess they feel responsible. I think my mom's convinced that if she had taken me to church more as a kid maybe I'd work in a bank or something now."

"I know what you mean."

He lowered his fork and frowned. Clara was a parent's dream. Polite, respectful, studious. What more could her family want?

Pain washed across her face. "I resent my own mother for taking my family's decisions so personally. She wears other people's mistakes like scars. Like she's keeping score of all our crimes against her. I had a clean ledger until I moved out here and veered off the chosen course. But now . . . it would be easier to face her if she lowered the bar."

Josh never considered the cost Clara might have paid for her freedom. That they were both running from something. That they might have something in common after all.

"I'm not mad at my mom," he said. "Not exactly. I get where she's coming from. No parent dreams of their kid growing up and making porn. But it's hard, carrying around the weight of her disappointment. I think if she and my dad supported me, even if they didn't understand, hell, even if they didn't like it, it would be easier to bear the rest of society looking at me like I'm dirt under their shoe."

"Do people really look at you like that?"

"I mean, not everyone knows what I do. It's not like I'm walking down the street handing out dick-shaped business cards."

Clara covered her mouth with her hand. "Do you have those?" Her eyes had gone almost completely round.

"No. Although it's not a bad marketing idea. People find out anyway. It almost always comes up at parties. My buddies from high school think it's funny." He gave a small, bitter laugh. "I don't mind the scorn so much. At least those people usually keep their distance. The handsy ones are worse. The ones who think my job turns my body into public property."

"You mean people grab you?"

"Oh sure. You ever had a guy brush against you on the subway when you know he could have avoided it? Or maybe you're standing at the bar and some bro puts his hand on your lower back to 'scoot by'?"

"Ugh, yes." She glared.

"It's like that. I get a lot of unwelcome hands in places I'm too polite to mention. When people find out I perform, they stop seeing me as a man. It's like in their eyes suddenly I'm a big fat Christmas ham. Everyone wants to carve off a slice."

"I'm so sorry," Clara said.

Josh stared at his food. "Lots of people have it worse. Almost every woman I know working in the industry has stories about experiencing harassment, even abuse." How many times had Naomi come home spitting because someone tried to take advantage of her? Tried to make her do things she didn't want to and often had explicitly refused? Josh tried to use what little power he had to protect her, but the power imbalance remained overwhelming, and besides, he couldn't protect everyone.

"It's not a zero-sum game. Acknowledging your pain doesn't take away from anyone else's."

"Thanks, but enough about my pain." He smiled to let her know he wasn't fatally wounded. "That's my cap on feelings for one night." He balanced his plate on his thigh and reached for his comic book on the coffee table. "I'm going to spend the rest of the night with the X-Men."

Clara scooted closer. "What's going on there?" She pointed at a panel.

"Mystique is about to steal Forge's interference transmitter."

A moment later, she stopped his progress with a hand on his arm. "Wait, I'm not done with that page!"

Tingles raced toward his shoulder. "More exciting than work, huh?"

"I feel like I'm going cross-eyed trying to find something interesting in all those files. Ever since Jill hired me to work on Toni Granger's re-election campaign, I've been trying to combat the fact that I'm completely unqualified with a rigorous dedication to research. Granger's office delivered like thirty boxes of these documents for us to go through to help craft our PR angle. Lawyers love paperwork."

"I've heard that," Josh said. "If I help you look through these boring files for let's say, thirty minutes, would you be allowed to take a break and watch a movie? I'm worried about your big brain combusting."

"Oh my gosh. That would be amazing." She handed him a huge pile. "But who gets to pick the movie?"

"Obviously me."

"Why obviously you?"

"Because I'm the one saving you from early-onset cataracts."

"Fine." She resumed reading. "But can we please watch *Speed*?"

His eyebrows sank together. "You like *Speed*?"

"No." She highlighted something on the paper. "I love *Speed*."

"You mean you love Keanu Reeves?"

"Are you trying to minimize my excellent taste in movies to a mere celebrity crush?"

"Oh no. I wouldn't dream of it."

"Good. Because I'll have you know I am a dedicated and lifelong fan of the action movie genre." Clara reached for a set of documents at her feet. "I actually wanted to ask you about one of these." She handed him a file. "Does the name Black Hat mean anything to you? I thought I came across the name in one of those articles that popped up when I Googled you."

He wanted to tease her about reading his press coverage, but the quip died as he paused on the third line. "Wait a minute . . ."

"What is it?" Clara leaned to read over his shoulder. Her tits brushed against his shoulder and he almost yelped. He definitely needed to lift his embargo on masturbating to the thought of her. He couldn't risk even platonic touching until he got his rocks off again. Josh would have called one of his regular hookups—hell, he'd even considered driving by Naomi's place—but he knew his strike would last longer if he avoided people in the business who would tell him to suck it up and get back to work. A little intercourse hiatus wouldn't cause any permanent damage. Probably.

Josh could feel her breath against his neck. He turned his head only to find their faces closer together than he'd anticipated. Clara had something shiny on her lips, making them pinker than normal. He found himself staring at them, imagining them wrapped around his . . .

"Do I have a booger?" She rubbed her nose. "If I do, you have to tell me."

"Relax. Your nose is as clean as a whistle." Josh directed his eyes back to the page in front of him.

"Did you find something in there? From what I read at the office, Toni's a good lawyer with a solid case record, but so far nothing has jumped out as headline fodder."

"I need my glasses." Josh returned from his room a moment later, bespectacled. "Okay. Yeah. Look at this." He ran his finger below where he wanted her to follow. "Toni Granger didn't just mention Black Hat, she wrote a whole paper about them."

As Clara reached to take the doc from his hands, the sweatshirt she wore fell off her shoulder. "Where did you get that sweatshirt?" He knew she hadn't gone to Berkeley.

"Oh, um." Clara tugged at her fallen collar. "It's Everett's. All of mine are in the wash."

Josh ground his teeth together. *Everett. Again.* He kept letting himself conveniently forget her lifelong crush. "It looks like she wrote this when she was applying for the assistant district attorney's office." She flipped a couple of pages. "Hey, what's Big Porn?"

"It's like Big Tobacco. Black Hat is the largest distributor of pornography in the world. They own three of the five major streaming sites, more than a handful of big studios, probably a bunch of other stuff I don't even know about. Their reach is long."

Clara's eyes widened as she took in more of the position paper. "It looks like they completely decimated the structure of the porn industry in a handful of years. Toni argues that their end-to-end distribution model creates a dangerous power imbalance, with their workers paying the cost. You know these people?"

"Sure. I mean, everyone knows Black Hat. They're hard to avoid. I don't deal with corporate directly, they usually go through Bennie, but their holding company controls the studio that holds my exclusive contract. They've invited me in for meetings a few times over the last couple of months, but I'd rather gnaw off my own arm than listen to business-men talk about synergy."

"This is serious." Clara skimmed her finger underneath a new para-graph. "She's implying wrongful termination, unsafe working conditions, sexual harassment. This place sounds like a disaster. She could have de-manded they improve their policies during her first term. Why isn't Granger's office prosecuting on any of these violations?"

"My guess? Not enough witnesses to testify." Josh needed a beer. "My contract might be a raw deal, but when it comes to porn, the performers are the lucky ones. I've got an agent, arguably some market value to trade on. But the directors, the crew, the people emptying the trash cans? They can't afford to risk their jobs to take down a corporation with this much power and influence."

"Well, someone should do something. I can't believe the press isn't talking about this."

"Really? You're shocked that Hollywood isn't in an uproar because someone might be getting mistreated in the porn industry? Nobody out-side our bubble gives a shit."

"Well, somebody does. Toni obviously—"

Josh scoffed. "Toni wrote that five years ago so she could follow in the footsteps of countless politicians before her who have made a career out of demonizing sex workers. What has she done since then?"

Her silence sat heavy between them. Clara put down the papers and straightened her stacks.

He adjusted his tone. "I hate to break it to you, but the government and the porn industry don't exactly see eye to eye."

"Toni's not like that. I grew up in a family of local politicians and other influential people and I've never seen one of them speak with the same unwavering dedication to civil reform as she does. She cares."

Josh's face curled with exasperation. "You don't think she's like that because you don't have a clue what it's like to live in the real world.

You've spent your entire life in fancy schools. I bet you never learned how to do laundry because you could always pay someone to do it for you. Out here not everyone gets taken care of. You think all of us have rich family members handing out jobs like peppermints?"

Clara winced and hauled a pillow to her chest, refusing to look at him.

"I'm sorry." Josh softened his voice. Their discussion tonight had stirred up so many painful memories. But that was no excuse. His stomach sank. "Clara, I shouldn't have said that—"

"No, you're right." She met his gaze with her big doe eyes. "I was born with a silver spoon in my mouth. I've always known that. This is my first foray into the real world and I'm stumbling. I don't know what it's like to do what you do." She frowned. "Or apparently how to wash different types of fabric. I'll be the first one to admit I'm a bit of a mess."

Josh ignored the way his stomach flipped over at her raw admission of vulnerability. "We're both on uneven ground here. Will you please forgive me?"

Her eyes dropped to his lips and he found himself breathing more heavily.

"If I say yes, can we watch *Speed*?"

He needed to find a way to get his attraction to her under control. She wasn't fuel for his fantasies and she definitely wasn't a whipping post for all his personal failures.

"We can watch *Speed*," he conceded.

IN TIMES OF turmoil, some people turned to a pint of ice cream, and others ran a hot bath. When Clara needed comfort, she put on an action movie.

Despite Josh's apology, awkwardness hung heavy in the air. Clara knew the palpable weight of words left unspoken. She'd spent a lifetime tiptoeing around a household teeming with words people wanted to say but never dared.

"Shouldn't someone with a fancy degree in critiquing old paintings prefer grainy documentaries and foreign films with subtitles?" Josh eyed her from his end of the couch as the opening credits of *Speed* rolled across Everett's flatscreen.

"You think I'm way more highbrow than I actually am," Clara said, cutting the slice of lasagna she'd retrieved into neat bite-sized squares. The recent strain about their socioeconomic status and upbringing reinforced the fact that Josh would never look at her as anything other than his pampered roommate. She didn't need to guard her emotions against him because the world provided ready-made barriers to any future between them.

Still, whether it was because he wasn't working and didn't have anything else better to do, or because he found her odd, Josh paid her a surprising amount of attention. If he were any other man, she might have squirmed under the scrutiny.

He was the most charming person she'd ever met. She had no idea how to navigate the minefield of their day-to-day interactions. With Everett, at least she'd had home field advantage when it came to trying to win his favor: hard-earned years' worth of studying his likes and dislikes to ensure that their interactions always went down easy.

Josh studied her like a slide under a microscope. "What about period pieces? You know, lots of ruffled collars and weepy-eyed longing. I bet you go for those."

Clara gracelessly bit off a long string of cheese from her fork. Thank goodness she didn't have to bother trying to impress Josh with her table manners.

It was kind of nice, actually. The lack of romantic expectation let her relax. Someday she'd look back on this summer with fondness and laugh.

"I do like a good Regency drama, but I also like Keanu Reeves running hard toward danger in a tight T-shirt to save the city of Los Angeles with nothing but his bare hands and his mettle." The sauce needed more basil. She added the herb to her mental grocery list. "My personality contains multitudes."

Keanu Reeves's character, Jack, came on screen and Clara emitted a happy little hum. That man sure knew how to wear a pair of cargo pants.

"Ohhh, I get it." Josh slumped back against the couch. "This stuff makes you hot."

"I beg your pardon?"

"You get off on the heroics." He gestured to the TV, where the characters attempted their daring rescue mission. "Look at you. Pink cheeks, wide eyes, breath coming out in little puffs. Those are classic signals."

Her heart pounded unnaturally. She supposed having sex on the brain was an occupational hazard for Josh. What was her excuse?

"First of all, stop watching me and watch the movie. Second of all, you're confusing lust with wholesome excitement." She moved so one of the throw pillows blocked his view of her face, just in case. "They're climbing into an elevator shaft. This is a suspenseful situation. I'm worried about the well-being of the hostages."

Josh lowered the pillow and shot her a filthy smile. One that worked so well that for the first time in her life, Clara had to temper down the impulse to purr. "Oh please. Wait until Keanu slides under the bus to dismantle the bomb, I bet you go nuts."

That moment did make her swoon. "My devotion to *Speed* is not motivated by anything remotely carnal." At least, not entirely. "This film is a triumphant celebration of the human spirit."

"You're reaching," he said, stretching his arms above his head until his shirt lifted high enough to reveal his lower stomach.

"I'm not." She folded her arms to cover her duplicitous nipples.

"*Speed* is about rising to the occasion. About average people like Jeff Daniels and Keanu and Sandra Bullock who are good and noble, and yes, hot, but in a soft, restrained way."

"Restrained, my ass. You don't get biceps like that without extensive personal training."

Clara ignored that impertinent comment. "*Speed* is an action movie for the female gaze. Do you know how you can tell? The heroine has got on sensible shoes."

Josh squinted at the screen. "So you identify with Sandra Bullock's character?"

"I wish. Keanu falls for her as soon as she takes the wheel. I, on the other hand, would never recover from the embarrassment of Keanu calling me *ma'am*."

Clara dabbed a napkin at a drop of sauce that had landed on the sofa. She never should have eaten dinner in front of the TV. She'd started picking up bad habits from her new roommate.

Josh fetched her a wet paper towel to better attack the burgeoning stain. "What's wrong with *ma'am*?"

"*Ma'am* is so sexless." She pouted. "The word tastes like sawdust in my mouth."

"Aha! Sexless. Implying that you'd like for him to call you something *sexy*. You totally wanna do the horizontal mambo with Keanu."

"The horizontal mambo? Seriously?" She threw the balled-up towel against his chest. "No one says that."

He jump-shot the towel into the trash can. "Don't like that one, huh? How about 'buying a ticket to pound town'?"

Clara wrinkled her nose. "No, thank you."

"Crashing the custard truck? Engaging in a little gland-to-gland combat? I can keep going."

"Please don't." She sank down in her seat, trying to hide how even those ridiculous names somehow made her want to drape herself across Josh's lap.

"Suit yourself."

"I'm not denying the hunk factor here," she conceded, "but there's so much more to love about *Speed*."

Josh pretended to cough into his hand. "*Speed* is a poor man's *Die Hard*."

Clara clutched her heart. "How dare you."

He chuckled and reached for her empty plate.

Clinging to the edge of it, she tilted her head. "What are you doing?"

"Tidying up?" He tugged on his end until she let go.

"Oh. Thank you." He'd taken to mirroring her behavior as if they were a team. A team unfit to accomplish anything, surely, but still, she appreciated the effort.

"*Die Hard* is a masterpiece. I'll give you that," she said when he returned from the kitchen. "But *Speed* has a uniquely endearing ensemble. There's that nerdy tourist in the blazer, you know? I relate to him. I, too, came to L.A. with big dreams only to wind up circling the airport on a bus with a bomb."

Josh raised his eyebrows as he returned to his seat.

"A metaphorical bus, obviously."

"Wait." He frowned and paused the movie. "Am I the bomb?"

"Don't be silly." She grabbed the remote and hit resume. Josh was absolutely the bomb. He was a big tangle of hormones trying to lure her to an untimely end. A bomb masked by cheesy jokes and kind eyes. One that could blow up her whole life if triggered at the wrong moment.

She tucked her legs underneath her with her knees pointing away from him. Best not to dwell. "Which character do you identify with?"

Josh chewed on his bottom lip. "I guess the bad guy."

Clara made a dismissive huff through her nose.

"Well, I'm not Keanu, that's for sure. I'm not saving anyone. I see that first bus blow up and I'm running in the other direction. There's no movie with me as the lead."

"Stop it. You're nicer than you give yourself credit for. You're helping me learn to drive out of the goodness of your heart."

"Only because you remind me of a wounded woodland animal."

"Thanks," Clara said, the word dripping sarcasm.

"See? I'm totally the villain. Disillusioned and angry. Drunk on self-importance."

"You are not Howard Payne." Yesterday, she'd caught him trimming their elderly neighbor's hydrangeas.

"Is that his name? Talk about on the nose. You know, if you flip the script this is a story about a broken system of law enforcement that abandons an officer disabled in the line of duty. Maybe he wanted to draw attention to the crumbling infrastructure of the LAPD."

"Josh. Howard murders a bunch of people."

"Yeah. That's not cool."

She tossed a pillow at him. "Pay attention."

The rest of the movie passed in companionable silence. At the climax, Clara tried to wipe her leaking eyes without drawing attention to herself.

"Are you *crying* at *Speed*?" Josh sounded both amazed and appalled.

"Keanu is so sweet here." Clara hiccuped. "He knows they might die and he sits on the floor with Sandra Bullock and holds her. He doesn't try to grab her boob or kiss her. He wraps her in his arms, providing a shallow sense of safety. Isn't that what all of us want deep down? Someone to hold us at the end of the line?"

"Are we watching the same movie here? I feel like you're getting a much deeper read from Keanu's potato face than I am."

"Potato . . . face?"

Josh shrugged. "My mom used to say Keanu's face looks as blank as a peeled potato."

Clara grinned into her palm.

"Besides," Josh said. "This isn't even the end. What about happily ever after?"

"What about it?" Clara turned off the TV as the end credits began.

"Well, they don't last. Jack and Annie."

"Sure, they do." She straightened the pillows on the couch.

"They don't. There's a sequel and Keanu's not even in it. Sandra Bullock gets with some other cop."

Walking into the bathroom to brush her teeth, Clara left the door open so she could respond. "I don't acknowledge that."

Josh followed her, accepting when she offered him the toothpaste and preparing his own brush. "What do you mean? The sequel exists. It's not open to debate."

Clara moved her toothbrush to rest inside her cheek. "If I never watch it, then it never happened."

"Is that right?"

She nodded around her busy bristles.

"You invent an alternate reality. Figures," Josh mumbled around his own minty mouthful.

After a full two minutes, Clara rinsed her brush. "Art belongs to the audience, not the artist. I would think you'd know that by now."

Josh shook his head. "The more I learn about you the less I understand."

"I've always wanted to be an enigma." Clara smiled over her shoulder as she exited the bathroom.

chapter fourteen

♡ ♡ ♡

JOSH HAD TO decide whether he wanted to spend the rest of his life resenting people like Clara for their money and their brains and their success, or if he wanted to remove his career from cruise control. A call from Bennie a few days later dialed up the deadline on his decision. Black Hat wasn't taking no for an answer.

The big dogs had invited him to visit their headquarters to discuss his contract demands in person. They didn't want to wait almost another year for more Josh Darling content. He decided to gamble. What did he have to lose?

"Now that's a lot of chrome." Josh whistled under his breath as he entered the reception area of a nondescript office building in Burbank. He'd heard there was a lot of money in porn. Turned out, it had all ended up here.

He checked in with a receptionist who made him spell his last name twice and checked his ID before ushering him to an uncomfortable metallic chair to wait.

Despite Clara's idealistic outcry to reform an industry she knew next to nothing about, Josh had no plans to ride in, Indiana Jones style, and call out this corporate fortress. Even if he wanted to, and maybe part of him did, he wasn't that guy. He didn't have the same luxury of opportunity that Clara enjoyed. If anything, their heated discussion a few nights ago about the power structure of porn had made him realize that he'd never get anywhere if he didn't play nice with the people in charge. He had to decide between swimming with the sharks or becoming their chum.

The man he'd come to see today, H. D. Pruitt, could change Josh's life with a snap of his fingers.

He figured he might as well get a look at the guy.

"Josh Darling?" A short, tan man in a very well-tailored suit carried himself with an air of defiance as he stepped into reception.

Josh recognized H. D. Pruitt from his headshot on the company website. Last night he'd taken a leaf out of Clara's book, staying up late to do his homework. He'd learned that Pruitt had started building an empire a handful of years before Josh signed his contract. A venture capitalist turned entrepreneur, Pruitt had made a lot of money selling search data before he'd decided to bring his talents to the adult entertainment industry.

His company had gobbled up a bunch of mom-and-pop studios out of the gate, and nowadays you couldn't swing a dick in porn without hitting something owned or operated by Black Hat. According to his bio, Pruitt "lived for pushing boundaries" and "going beyond what's polite."

In Josh's social circles, the man had a reputation for chasing every depraved fantasy the Internet could think up. Until today, Josh had avoided Pruitt like the plague. He'd never had any interest in playing corporate games. But he couldn't get that position paper from Toni Granger out of his head. Couldn't stop hearing Clara's indignant voice as she recounted the injustice of a system he lived in every day.

Josh tugged down the sleeves of his own navy sports coat. "That's me." He followed Pruitt into his corner office.

"You're a tough man to get hold of." Pruitt's chair sat a few extra inches above the one relegated for visitors, so its petite owner could stare down at his guests.

Josh pulled out the cushy leather armchair across from the imposing dark wood desk.

"Believe me, it's only because I'm wildly irresponsible." Josh pulled his cell phone out of his pocket. "You wouldn't believe how many of these things I burn through."

Pruitt steepled his fingers and gave Josh a once-over. "You're even taller than you look on film."

Josh hunched down in an effort to take up less space. In his experience, short men tended to resent his height. As if Josh were trying to one-up them simply by existing. "That's probably because in the movies I'm usually lying down."

Pruitt didn't smile.

Tough crowd.

"So, what's your deal? You're talented, clearly. Audiences seem to respond to you, but your portfolio of work is decidedly bland. Don't get me wrong." Pruitt held up a hand. "You and Naomi Grant kept it spicy for a while, but how many times can you really watch the same couple fuck?"

The question hung in the air, while Josh tried to decide if it was rhetorical.

"I'm hoping you finally decided to grace us with your presence because you're ready to take your work to the next level? I'm sure I don't have to tell you, but amateurs are all the rage now. Big-name performers don't bring in the same numbers they used to. Variety over quality. It's not good for business. Our shares are down over the last two quarters. The only way we can protect our margins is by going further. Getting creative. Do you consider yourself a man of great ambition?"

"No, sir. I can't say that I do."

"Well, you should. Porn is power. Never forget that. We may not get the respect of other industries, but we shape culture and technology in ways they can only dream about. You've made a name for yourself. Got a nice, young following. Fresh. That's what I like to see. How many subscribers do you have on your videos?"

"Uh, I'm not sure." Josh didn't keep tabs. Clara had mentioned a number the other day. "About a million?"

Pruitt smiled. "Potential lifetime customers, even if most of them are women. Many of my colleagues don't agree with me about investing in male talent. Not unless you're willing to do male-male?" He raised an inquisitive eyebrow.

Josh politely shook his head. He had tried it exactly once, because you didn't have as much sex as he did and not get a little curious, but he found he strongly preferred women.

"Pity. I've gotten a lot of requests for that from both fans and performers. Still. You're what, almost thirty? You've got at least three, maybe even five good years in you if you take care of yourself. Lay off the red meat. Invest in some under-eye cream."

Josh brought his hand up to feel for bags beneath his eyes. The skin felt relatively tight. Maybe he should ask to borrow some of the fancy lotions his roommate left in the bathroom.

Pruitt chuckled. "Oh, don't worry. Only the girls can't age. One of those harsh truths of the business. Older men want to see themselves on screen, but we don't want to see our wives."

The CEO turned around a photograph on his desk so that Josh could see a snapshot of a middle-aged brunette with her arms wrapped around two teenage boys. The woman in the photo looked sweet, pretty if a little tired.

"People are quick to demonize porn, but how many marriages have we saved? Porn keeps men from cheating when their wives no longer do the trick. It's our duty to provide ever-evolving fodder for the sexual imagination. To take audiences places they'll never go in real life."

Josh dug his fingernails into his palms. He couldn't believe this man could talk about his wife and the mother of his children this way, let alone to a complete stranger. When he answered he couldn't quite keep the edge out of his tone. "I'm not so sure I'm ready to let the most extreme audiences dictate the direction of my career."

The older man straightened his tie and sat even higher in his throne-like chair. "I'm going to level with you, Josh. Man to man. You got lucky. You rode the wave of your girlfriend's hot ass to a modicum of notoriety, but there is no such thing as happily ever after in this industry. Without Naomi Grant, you're gonna fade fast."

Josh slammed his back molars together with enough force to make his jaw ache.

Pruitt picked up a glass paperweight from his desk and juggled it. "I'll tell you what. I'll start you slow if you want. Real gentle. I'll even let you work with other studios as long as you give my hardcore division fifty titles a year and exclusive appearance rights."

It was a better offer than Bennie had ever brought him, almost generous. Josh's throat clenched. He hated himself a little for the next words out of his mouth. "How much?"

Pruitt brought his hand up to cover his mouth for a moment before lowering it. "What did you make last year?"

Through the haze of his simmering rage, Josh took last year's income and doubled it before writing it on a piece of paper from a pad in front of him. He slid it across the desk to Pruitt.

The executive picked it up and read it, giving a little laugh. "I'll start you at twice that amount."

Josh tried to wrap his head around that kind of money. A paycheck like that would validate his career.

"Welcome to the big leagues." The most powerful man in porn sat back and folded his hands across his chest. Pruitt was convinced he'd gotten his way, and maybe he would have if Josh hadn't thought of Clara's face at that exact moment.

If he hadn't pulled up her profile in the driver's seat of his car at sunset after a whole day of facing her fears. The shadows of a dying sun across her face made her look like a 1940s movie star. Biting her lip. Determined to do what she thought she must. No matter how much it scared her. He wished his brain hadn't replayed the catch in her voice when she'd protested the mistreatment of people she'd never met by the man sitting across from him. He could no longer claim ignorance. If he took this money, Clara would always know he'd done it because he was weak.

"I'm sorry." He placed the paper back on the desk. "I can't accept." Once his contract expired he could find work with other, smaller studios. Maybe he'd never be rich, but at least he could go to sleep at night without worrying about his work putting money in the pockets of men like this guy. He could look Clara in the eye over breakfast tomorrow. He'd never be good enough for a woman like her, but at least he wouldn't fail this basic moral test.

"Are you sure about that? I feel I've been very generous, Josh." Pruitt's eyes had gone hard and cold.

Josh ran his hands down his itchy dress pants. He wanted desperately to get out of this room, this building. "I appreciate your time, but I think I'll try my hand at some other ventures when my contract ends."

Pruitt sat up straighter in his chair. "I'm not sure that would be a wise choice, son."

"What are you implying?" Josh had a sneaking suspicion he knew.

"If you choose to walk away from this company and our *very generous* offer, you might find it difficult to find other people in this business who are prepared to work with you. Do I make myself clear?"

"Yes, thanks. Think I've managed to crack your code." Josh stood up, letting his height send a final message.

Pruitt rose to his feet quickly. "Why don't you take a few days to think about it?" He straightened his lapels. "Decisions like this shouldn't be made in the heat of the moment. Weigh your options. Check your bank balance." Pulling a business card out of his wallet, he flipped it to Josh, who caught the tiny rectangle against his chest.

There goes my career, Josh thought as he tossed the paper into the first trash can he found in the parking lot.

chapter fifteen

♡ ♡ ♡

When she came home to find Josh in a terrible mood, Clara immediately suggested they open a bottle of wine and watch *Die Hard*. She'd never seen her new roommate frown so much. His face seemed to resent the expression. She wanted to ask what had happened while she spent the day at her aunt's firm, but at the same time, she didn't want to pry.

Clara had a funny feeling action movies were becoming a bridge between her and Josh. A mutual appreciation that gave them something to talk about, or at the very least allowed them to both occupy the living room with minimal awkwardness.

"Hey. Would you want to go to a *Rocky* marathon in Silver Lake with me at the beginning of August?" She took a casual sip of her Cab. "I saw a poster at this coffee shop near work and I love *Rocky* and obviously I can just go alone unless you think you might—"

"You can stop rambling." Josh patted her foot where it rested near his thigh on the couch. "I'd like to go with you. I've never seen *Rocky*."

"Oh. Good. Well, I'll get the tickets then. To pay you back for all the driving lessons."

Clara exhaled. *It's not a date. Of course it's not a date. I don't need to clarify because there's no way he'd ever consider it a date.* They might not have much in common, but at the very minimum, they both appreciated a movie where the lead actor sweated profusely.

Unfortunately, her brilliant plan to turn around Josh's surliness met an almost immediate obstacle. John McClane had barely arrived at Nakatomi Plaza when the power in the house cut out like a blink held too long. For a few seconds, neither Josh nor Clara said anything. Nobody moved.

"Do you have a flashlight?" She spoke toward the end of the sofa where Josh had been sitting before the world plunged into darkness.

"If one of us had a flashlight, it would be you."

"Right." Clara fumbled for her phone on the side table. "I suppose we can make do with these."

Josh followed suit. "I'll go check the breaker."

Clara opened the drapes and peered down the street. "Don't bother. The whole block is out." A summer storm raged across the sky in a rare bout of L.A. weather, making Clara jump.

She navigated her way to the bookshelf where she kept a few scented candles. "I'll light these, I guess."

"Great. Now the entire house is gonna smell like the inside of a pumpkin pie," he teased before helping her arrange the candles around the living room so that the space took on a cozy glow. The claps of lightning and booms of thunder mingled to form a malevolent orchestra.

"Wow. This is kind of ro—"

"Spooky." Clara finished Josh's sentence on the off chance he'd been about to voice the same forbidden word she'd thought watching the candlelight dance across his features.

"Right, yes." He shoved his hands in his pockets. "That's exactly what I was going to say. Hey, the stove still works during a blackout, right?"

"Yeah. It's gas so you should be able to light it with a match. Here." She grabbed the box where she'd abandoned it on the coffee table and offered it to him.

His fingers brushed the tender skin on the inside of her wrist and she gulped. No matter how hard she tried, she didn't seem to be able to avoid touching him, and every time they touched, a feverish wanting threatened to consume her.

"Cool. Thanks." Josh's voice came out lower than normal. "I'm gonna make popcorn." He hurried into the kitchen.

Clara took a moment to collect herself. *He's not being sexy on purpose. Stop fetishizing him.*

She took advantage of the fact that Josh had left the room and tugged at the underwire of her bra where it dug into her rib cage. Clara wasn't one of those women with a manageable bust size where you could hardly tell if they went au naturel. You could definitely tell. So she kept everything locked down instead of flinging off her unwieldy undergarments the moment she got home from work the way she longed to and certainly would have if she lived alone. She didn't need Josh's pupils growing dark and urgent again the way they had when he'd walked in on her in nothing but her stupid, reckless nightgown.

"Ta-da." He returned from the kitchen a while later with a giant bowl of popcorn, held out for her inspection.

She only had to inhale to know he'd loaded up the stove-top-popped kernels with a pound of Parmesan, red pepper flakes, and olive oil. He considered this a "healthy snack" and she didn't have the heart to correct him.

They settled back into their designated seats on the sofa, Clara on the left, Josh on the right, with the middle cushion as a buffer. Rigid respect for the buffer usually lasted for about half an hour. They each tended to unfurl their bodies as they got comfortable.

When Josh tried to inconspicuously wipe his hands on the back of the throw pillow, she unthinkingly grabbed his forearm. Normally she wouldn't touch anyone without an explicit invitation, but Josh didn't seem to live by normal rules of personal space, and so sometimes she forgot too. For a moment, she imagined leaning forward and running her tongue across his palm. Imagined slipping his index finger into her mouth and savoring the way butter and salt seasoned his skin. Her face overheated. *Stop acting like a pervert.* She marched into the kitchen for paper towels.

"Do you wanna play a game?" Josh held up a deck of cards when she returned. He'd repositioned himself on the very edge of his side of the couch. Either he wanted to escape her lustful gaze or—she clenched her thighs—the dark was getting to him too.

"What kind of game?" Clara choked on her tongue. Surely he wouldn't, couldn't, suggest strip poker.

"I thought I could teach you Slap Jack," he said, the picture of innocence.

A few hands in, Clara knew Josh was cheating, but she didn't know how.

She pouted into her glass of wine. She had not expected Josh to roundly trounce her. "Are you hiding cards under your butt?"

"That statement is incredibly offensive. First of all, a Conners never cheats. We're incredibly honest and upstanding. Second of all, and more importantly, there's no way my ass is big enough to hide cards. I've put in hundreds of hours of rigorous thrusting to get these tight buns."

Clara licked a drop of wine off her lips. She had a hard enough time sitting on this couch, in the candlelight, facing Josh, their knees almost touching, without him mentioning sex. Or his tight ass for that matter.

She reminded herself that Josh wasn't Everett. Like at all. Somewhere around sophomore year, Everett had decided that big emotions weren't cool. He committed himself to a "mellow way of life." He never cried at movies or laughed so hard that beer came out of his nose. Josh, on the other hand, seemed to naturally suck all the juice out of every moment. When Josh ate something that tasted good, he threw his head back, closed his eyes, and groaned. Clara bit her lip thinking about it. "Just deal the cards."

He did as she bade him, shuffling with an impressive flick of his wrist. Clara hadn't anticipated how much this game would make her focus on his hands. Perhaps she was losing so badly because she couldn't stop thinking about all the ways he'd used those long fingers to make her moan? Knowing she'd barely scratched the surface of his sexual talents made her a little crazy. According to that article, he was the Michael Jordan of cunnilingus.

Clara lost another round.

"Good thing we're not playing for money, huh?" He gave her an impish smile.

She squirmed. *Get a hold of yourself.* She was doing the same thing as all of those other people who treated Josh like a piece of meat. If he were an investment banker or a plumber, she wouldn't be imagining ripping off all her clothes and begging him to take her. His illicit profession had warped her brain into some kind of frenzy.

"How many glasses of wine have you had?"

"Two?" Oh no. Was she drooling?

"You're all rosy." Josh brushed his knuckles against her cheek. "Do you want me to grab you some water?"

Clara's hands flew to her cheeks. "No. I'm fine. Must be feverish with competitive spirit."

"I've gotta admit." Josh leaned forward. "I like watching you lose."

Heat spread across her chest at his gravelly tone. "That's a horrible thing to say!"

"No, I mean it's cute."

Clara brightened.

"You get all pouty like a little kid."

Oh. Like a kid. Of course. "I am not pouting. I'm concentrating. This is how my face looks when I concentrate."

Josh shot a glance at the ledger. "Maybe you should concentrate less."

Clara handed him her discarded cards with more force than necessary. "This game is rigged."

"I offered to give you a handicap." Josh tossed a handful of popcorn at her.

The soft kernels bounced off her nose and she gasped. "You've got an evolutionary advantage. Your arms are longer, making it easier for you to reach the cards, and your hands are bigger, meaning you can flip through your stack faster."

Josh laughed. "Your ability to rationalize knows no bounds."

"Maybe we should switch to gin rummy?"

Josh pulled a face. "Are you kidding? How about Texas hold 'em?"

Clara rose up to her knees on the couch in indignation. "What's wrong with gin rummy? I used to play all the time with my grandfather."

"Exactly. It's a game for old people. I rest my case."

From somewhere deep in the cushions, a phone beeped. Josh and Clara both stuck their hands down the seam of the sofa and their arms brushed. Goose bumps broke out across her skin and she prayed he didn't notice.

"It's mine." Josh's mouth twisted like he'd sucked on a lemon as he looked at the message on the screen.

"What's it say?"

Josh tossed the phone behind him. "Nothing." Then he shoved a bunch of popcorn in his mouth.

"It's obviously not nothing. Come on. Who's texting you?"

"H. D. Pruitt."

"Why does that name sound familiar?"

Josh bent to pick up the dispersed kernels. "Because he's the CEO of Black Hat."

Clara gasped. "The one Toni wrote about?"

"Yeah. I took a meeting with him this morning and he offered me this insane deal. Six figures to headline his hardcore division."

What the hell did they do in the hardcore division?

"Before you freak out, I turned him down. He, uh, may have threatened to blacklist me."

"He what? Josh, that's terrible. Not to mention illegal."

"Pretty standard for Black Hat as far as I can tell. I figured he might try something similar when I agreed to the meeting. It's not a big deal. I've got a year left on my contract with them, but I've fulfilled my film quota. I'll take a hiatus. They can't sue me or anything."

"But what are you going to do for a year? What about your talent?"

Josh raised his eyebrows. "I guess I'll have to go back to using my talent recreationally."

Clara's heartbeat skidded to a halt.

"The only rights not locked down in my stock agreement are for voice-over."

Putting a pin in why she cared so much about Josh's "recreational activities," Clara narrowed her eyes. "Wait, so you're saying you could narrate something?"

Josh cocked his head to the side. "Yeah, I guess, in theory. People aren't usually looking for a narrator in their pornos. That kinda thing probably goes from zero to wildlife special real quick."

Clara sat up straighter. "But what if you didn't make porn?"

"Then I wouldn't have a job?"

An idea ran like a charge down her spine. "Okay, remember that thing you helped me with?"

He raised a shoulder and frowned.

"That thing." She looked down at her lap.

"Sorry, no."

"Ugh. Remember that time you gave me an orgasm?"

"Ha. Yeah. I knew what you meant. I wanted to hear you say it."

Clara rolled her eyes. *Jerk.* "Well, a lot of women have problems like that. I looked it up."

"Of course you did."

"Their partners don't know how to get them off. Or they know like one way to do it and they ride that horse into the ground." She'd once dated an engineer who insisted that any position besides missionary gave him a migraine. "But you could help them. You said you wanted to produce something. What if you made something somewhere between porn and sex ed?"

Josh rubbed the back of his neck. "Like an orgasm how-to guide?"

"Yes! Exactly. You could narrate tips and tricks and . . . I don't know . . . scenarios focused on women's sexual pleasure. Your fan base would eat that up."

Josh bit his thumbnail. "It's not a bad idea, but the start-up costs associated with something like that would add up fast. You're talking hiring performers, renting a sound stage. You need a ton of expensive equipment. Lighting, editing, web hosting, marketing. I've got some savings, but I'd burn through it way before I ever saw money back. Even if we set up a subscription model."

"Well, I could help pay for it." She'd always imagined that eventually, she'd sponsor the creation of meaningful art with her wealth. While this particular type of venture had never entered her mind, she found she wasn't opposed. In fact, she could barely catch her breath for how excited the idea made her.

"What? No. I'm not taking your money."

"Why not? Lots of projects get investors. I've got a trust fund just sitting there. I wouldn't suggest it if I didn't believe in the concept."

"No. Seriously. Borrowing money ruins friendships."

Clara's cheeks heated. "You consider me your friend?"

"Of course you're my friend, and I'd prefer to keep it that way."

"Then don't let the money thing make it weird. Women need this. No." She corrected herself. "Women *deserve* this." She stood up. This felt like the kind of moment when a person should stand up. "Women need to know that their pleasure matters. If we build the right resource, the world would no longer have an excuse not to know how the clitoris works."

Josh stared up at her. "I can't believe you said *clitoris* at full volume. I can't tell if I'm afraid of you right now or turned on. Possibly both. Are you sure you only had two glasses of wine?"

If only his attraction didn't extend to the entire female half of the population. "Does that mean you'll do it?"

He looked at his hands folded in his lap and sat uncharacteristically still. "Why me?"

Couldn't he see it? "You're the perfect inspiration. God knows I don't want to inflate your ego further, but I can imagine you're a gateway to porn for a lot of women. Must be your massive . . . personality."

A smile broke across his face. "I'm pretty sure that somewhere in that little soapbox speech was the nicest compliment I've ever been paid." Josh stood up from the couch and bumped her shoulder with his own. "But don't I need, you know, women for an idea like this? I'm not exactly an authority on the female body."

Clara snorted. "Obviously. But you wouldn't have to do it alone."

"Are you volunteering?"

"Me? Oh no. Absolutely not." Her vision swam at the very thought of tying her name to a project like that. "Just think of me as an anonymous bag of money. You must know someone, a woman someone, who wouldn't mind being on camera." She stared at the ceiling. "Naked."

"I know a lot of someones like that. But someone who wouldn't be deterred by Pruitt's threat? That narrows the list considerably. There is one person who comes to mind, but that might make things a little complicated."

"Well, call her." Clara knew he meant Naomi Grant. That this business idea she'd had would likely provide the setting for their inevitable reconciliation. Attempting to ignore the panic climbing up her body, Clara realized that she'd just handed Josh a one-way ticket out of her life.

chapter sixteen

♡ ♡ ♡

JOSH LEARNED THE definition of the word *awkward* underneath the disco lighting of a West Hollywood bowling alley.

"Clara, I'd like you to meet Stu . . . or uh . . . I mean, Naomi Grant," he said a week and a half later, raising his voice over the clashing of pins as he introduced the last woman he'd touched sexually to his ex-girlfriend.

He'd attempted to be strategic with the location for extending his business proposal. Nothing corporate or fussy. Bowling seemed smart because it gave everyone something to do with their hands, but he hadn't anticipated that the only available lane at two p.m. on a Sunday would be smack-dab between a middle school birthday party and league practice for seniors.

Clara shifted the pair of bowling shoes she held to free up her right hand and extend it for Stu to shake. "It's nice to meet you. Do you prefer Naomi or . . . Stu, was it?"

"If you call me Naomi there's a better chance I'll answer." His ex looked around the bowling alley with a deep glower.

They all stood in a little circle staring at one another and holding shoes that didn't belong to them. "Shall we?" He gestured for the two women to precede him in selecting their bowling balls.

While Clara wore a pair of jeans and a simple white short-sleeve shirt, Naomi had on some kind of ridiculously tiny leather shorts and one of his old Metallica T-shirts chopped up until it hung off her shoulders and showed her stomach. Outwardly at least, the two women didn't have a thing in common, besides the obvious fact that they were both beautiful. Josh fought the impulse to run.

"Next time don't let him pick the activity," Naomi said to Clara.

Clara dipped her head. "Noted."

"I'm standing right behind you."

Both women stared at him with their hands planted on their hips. Why had he ever thought this was a good idea?

Oh right, because beggars couldn't be choosers. And, after verifying with Clara several times over the last few days that she still wanted to fund this endeavor while sober, he'd agreed to take her money. Now he owed it to her to secure the best possible "leading lady." No one else in the industry had the lethal combination of talent, intellect, and business savvy that Naomi did. Unfortunately, she also alternately hated his guts and wanted to fuck his brains out, making negotiation rather treacherous.

After a couple of awkward rounds of both bowling and beers, Clara discreetly elbowed Josh. "Quit stalling," she said under her breath while Naomi waited for her ball to come back out of the machine. "We've been over the pitch a hundred times over the last few days. Ask her now before we lose our audience."

"Now? You think so? We've only bowled twenty-four frames."

Clara furrowed her brow. "Now. I get frumpier every second I spend standing next to that woman." She pulled the contract they'd had a lawyer draw up out of her purse and shoved the papers hard against Josh's chest. "I'm saying this not as your friend, not as your roommate, but as your business partner: if you don't ask her to look at those documents in the next five minutes"—her gray eyes flashed dangerously—"I'm going to make you eat them."

Josh swallowed. "Got it."

Naomi returned from her turn.

"Hey, Stu, will you sit down for a second? There's something I . . . I mean, we, want to discuss with you." He laid out the situation, hitting most of the key points from Clara's project proposal. She only winced once when he accidentally said "resource to pleasure women" instead of "resource for women's pleasure."

When he finished he sagged back in his hard plastic chair. Mission complete. Maybe now they could order nachos. "So, what do you think?"

Naomi stared at Clara and Josh over the rim of her beer. "I've heard my fair share of wild propositions over the years, but I've got to hand it to you, this one takes the cake. You wanna give Black Hat the middle finger and you want to use my hand, not to mention other body parts, to do it?"

Josh leaned forward and rested his elbows on his knees. He lowered his voice so that the birthday boy in the paper hat wouldn't overhear them. "The concept only works if it's got a woman at its helm. No one needs a site focused on how to get *men* to orgasm. Clara says we've gotta play to the needs of the market."

Clara took a healthy gulp of her beer and lowered it with a shaky hand. He shouldn't have begged her to come, but he didn't think he'd get through this without her.

"Come on, Stu. I'm not arrogant enough to think I know everything about women's pleasure. But lending my dulcet tones as your pretty-boy front man? It could work."

Naomi's fiery-eyed glare would have stripped paint off a Buick.

Clara came to his rescue. "You can hire whomever you want. Female writers, directors, editors, as many positions as you need. We'll let them know about the risk up front from Pruitt, but the beauty of the plan is that we don't need Black Hat distribution. Josh can harness his Darlings, and you'll bring your own fans to the table. That's enough of a viewing population to get things rolling. But if our goal is to bring in male audiences too, we need a carrot."

"I'm the carrot?" Naomi gave a little wave to the shoe attendant, who hadn't taken his eyes off of her since she walked in.

"You're more than a carrot," Clara said. "Separately, you're two of the hottest names in the industry, and the idea that you're coming back together to build something for women, focused on their experience and satisfaction, will make people curious. I can help you get press coverage. I'm learning a lot at my aunt's PR firm. The hook is built in. A site focused on women's sexual pleasure shouldn't feel revolutionary, but it does a little, don't you think?"

Naomi raised a finely crafted eyebrow. "Exactly how much do you know about pleasuring women?" Her tone was civil but her subtext was pointed: *Who are you and what gives you the right to walk in our world?*

Clara straightened her shoulders. "Not as much as I'd like, but I'm a quick study."

Naomi's eyes shot to Josh. "Is that where you come in, Romeo?"

Josh knew she thought he'd seduced Clara into some kind of sex fog, but that wasn't the case. She was just that good a person—one who wanted to use her money to help people. And he'd brought her here and fed her to a lioness because he only had conviction in his potential when she stood within ten feet of him. Sweat beaded at his temples and he tried to drown himself in his beer.

Naomi tapped her foot and the bottom of her bowling shoe slapped the linoleum. "So it's what, porn with more kissing? Better lighting? Rose petals?"

"It's not porn," Josh said. "It's sex ed with a makeover. Less clinical, more entertaining. Built for grown-ups."

Clara picked up on his momentum. "You two could make it fun, exciting. You're experts in pleasure. The primary focus would be instruction rather than titillation. The people on screen would perform different positions and techniques, you and Josh could explain what they're doing and why it works. What works for everybody is different, so we'd never run out of material."

"We could give advice and tips for partners to act out together and for women to try solo," Josh added, feeling like the Robin to Clara's Batman.

"Sounds quaint," Naomi said. "But it won't matter what you call it. Society sees naked women and immediately registers spank bank material."

"But it's got a completely different goal. We want to rewrite the narrative with a focus on establishing healthy intimacy and equal-opportunity orgasms," Clara said as the lane next to them celebrated a particularly good spare with a loud round of hollering.

Naomi picked up her ball and, after a practiced windup, sent it flying down the lane, knocking over a neat nine pins before saying over her shoulder, "That's a sweet vision. Delusional, and self-important, but sweet for certain."

"I should have stayed home," Clara whispered to Josh.

But he wasn't ready to throw in the towel. "That's why we need you, Stu. I know you look at the direction the industry is going and wish you could change it, dismantle the machine from within. How many times have you had to work with a man who made you feel gross?"

"Josh mentioned you've had some trouble with the producers and directors trying to get you to do things you don't want to," his roommate added, wringing her hands. "This is your chance to call the shots. To make what you want with whomever you want to hire. Complete creative freedom."

"Come on, Stu. How many of us get an opportunity like this?"

Naomi narrowed her eyes. "Who's funding this benevolent endeavor? I don't suppose you recently came into an inheritance?"

"That would be me." Clara raised her hand and then immediately tucked it under her thigh.

Naomi laughed. "Now that's an unexpected twist. You'd be my creative partner? You're full of surprises."

"My involvement would be exclusively financial. If that's what you're worried about."

"That's exactly what I'm worried about." Naomi turned to Josh. "I'll do it, but only if Connecticut here is involved in the development, casting, cutting, the whole process."

Clara's face drained of all color. "Why would you want me involved?"

"This is a huge risk. No matter what the two of you wanna tell yourselves. I'm treating this like a business decision. A serious one. If we only reach the people who are already watching porn, it's too niche. You're the target audience. The kind of woman who will watch this stuff, benefit from it, if we're successful, right? I need you as a stand-in for what the average American woman wants to know and what's a step too far. Plus, if you've got more skin in the game, you're less likely to get cold feet and pull the funding."

"I'm only comfortable with nudity in Renaissance artwork, and even then sometimes I get overheated."

Naomi smiled a genuine smile, the one that changed almost her whole face. From ice to inferno. "That's my final offer, Connecticut."

Josh grabbed Clara's elbow. "You don't have to do this. It's too much. You've already got a full-time job. We'll find someone else."

"There is no one else," Clara said between her teeth. "Not like her." She wiped her palms on her jeans and extended her hand for Naomi to shake. "You've got yourself a deal, but I'm warning you now I might need a fainting couch."

chapter seventeen

♡ ♡ ♡

CLARA HAD NEVER seen this many topless people outside the south of France. It had taken two weeks to register their new business, obtain a federal employer identification number, open a company bank account, and obtain all the necessary licenses and permits mandated by California law, but they were finally ready to start recruiting performers for their as yet untitled project.

Two more weeks of lying to her mother about spending "all her free time" visiting art museums and brushing up on her ancient Greek. Every time Lily wanted to Skype, Clara told her the Wi-Fi was spotty and Everett was working on getting it fixed. She would probably get a stomach ulcer from all the lying, but she couldn't bring herself to stop.

Josh, Clara, and Naomi had rented out a small studio space in Burbank to hold auditions. Of course, Naomi showed up looking way more chic than anyone had a right to. *That's the type of woman Josh goes for.* All legs and hair and collarbones sharp enough to take out an eye.

Any and all thoughts of him ever touching Clara again needed to cease. She'd never carry herself like Naomi. Never ooze sex appeal or skewer a man with only a few words. Josh bedded bombshells, not bookworms.

He and Naomi had arranged the logistics of recruitment while Clara worked her day job for Jill. True to her word, she still reviewed everything. The unlikely trio had daily status calls at night.

Today they'd be seeing a mix of seasoned adult performers and a handful of students recruited from Naomi's psychology program at Cal State. In addition to being insanely hot, Naomi was also a genius studying for her master's in social psychology and family dynamics. Clara made sure everyone signed an ironclad nondisclosure agreement at the door.

They wanted to cast an array of backgrounds and body types, and they needed people who were comfortable in front of the camera as well as with the risk and who believed in the mission of the project.

Clara stood at the water fountain in the hallway, filling her reusable bottle, when Naomi sashayed out of the casting room. "So far so good, Connecticut, but today the real fun starts. You nervous?"

Clara thought about lying but decided that, like animals, Naomi could probably smell fear. "Yes."

"That's all right." Naomi adjusted the straps of her tank top. "As long as your nerves don't keep you from doing your job."

"Remind me of my job again?"

"Barometer for average."

"Right." Clara's eyes shot down the hall. "There are a lot more people here than I expected."

"Hey." Naomi's voice relaxed from granite to shale. "You can do this."

The vote of confidence was surprising but nice. Clara smiled. "Thanks."

"But if you can't, I'd rather figure it out now."

Her smile died. "That was less reassuring."

Naomi shrugged and walked away.

"Um . . . I think your bottle might be full," a man's voice said from behind Clara.

She turned to find a handsome stranger gesturing at her overflowing water bottle. He had a similar jawline to Josh's, actually, though this man's wasn't quite as strong and lacked the golden stubble that Clara had come to appreciate on her roommate.

"Sorry." She stepped out of his way.

"No trouble." The man flashed a set of very white and very straight teeth at her. "You here for the auditions?"

"No. I mean, yes." Clara pulled down the sleeves of her favorite blazer. "I'm part of the casting team. I'm not, like, a performer."

"That makes sense. I'd remember a girl like you." He extended his tan hand. "I'm Matt. Masterson. I know Josh and Naomi from filming *Infinity Orgasm*."

"Oh." She laughed nervously. "Gotcha."

"Have you seen it?"

"No." She took a careful step backward. "No, I'm afraid I'm a bit of a pornography novice."

"Well, if you ever want any recommendations or . . ." He leaned toward her until she could smell the spearmint of his breath. ". . . a practical demonstration, I'd be happy to help you out." He flashed his giant, shiny teeth at her again. *This guy must floss like ten times a day.*

Clara tried not to stutter. "That's a very generous offer, Matt."

"Put it away, Masterson."

She hadn't heard Josh come up behind her. "Oh. Hi."

"Just being friendly, Darling." Matt wasn't as tall as Josh. He had to tilt his head slightly to look him in the eye.

"Direct your friendliness elsewhere. We're running behind schedule." Josh let his hand rest lightly on Clara's back, a few inches below where her shoulder blades ended, and gently steered her toward the conference room. "We need to get going." He used a much lighter tone with her than he had with Matt.

Clara leaned in to whisper to him as they walked. "What do you think of that guy? Should we cast him? He certainly seemed . . . hygienic." The spicy scent of Josh's soap washed over her and she inhaled superfluously.

Josh pulled out her chair and then his own. "I guess women like him," he said in clipped syllables.

Clara stared down at her notebook. At the checklist she'd made last night in an effort to come up with an objective ranking system for potential performers. "You don't think he was flirting with me, do you?"

"Of course he was flirting with you." Josh had the tip of his pen in his mouth, leaving a faint impression of his teeth on the plastic.

Clara found herself smiling at her notebook. "Really? I think I might have liked it." It was hard to tell. She didn't have much practice receiving male attention.

"Matt's not the guy for you, trust me."

"Why not?"

"Because you should be with a doctor or a firefighter . . ." Josh sighed. ". . . or at the very least a kindergarten teacher."

"Oh, I get it." Her shoulders slumped.

Josh's mouth turned down. "Get what?"

"I'm not . . . *sexy* enough." Her stomach clenched. Matt had probably only turned on the charm because he thought she could help him get a part.

Josh dropped his pen. "What the hell are you talking about?"

"I know I wear too many cardigans. And I can't, for the life of me, figure out how to use a curling iron." She lowered her voice. "Even my nice bras are neutral colors."

Josh closed his eyes and lowered his forehead into his hand. "That's not what I'm saying."

"It's all right." She swallowed down her discomfort. "You don't have to sugarcoat it. It's been this way my whole life." *Everett never would have walked away from Naomi.*

"Clara—" Josh placed his hand over where she'd started to anxiously twiddle her thumbs in her lap.

"Are you two ready?" Naomi took the final seat behind the card table and Josh bent to pick up his pen, taking his hand with him. "We've got a line down the hall."

"Yeah. We're good." Clara folded herself in as small as possible. Legs, shoulders, neck. Josh's opinion of her ability to heat a man's blood didn't surprise her as much as it confirmed her bleak self-assessment. She didn't belong here among all the beautiful, sexually advanced people.

"Number one, please." Naomi's voice resounded with authority.

A full-figured brunette with a sleeve of tattoos and a nose ring came in. "Marissa Martinez," she said.

"Hi, Marissa. Before we get started, you've signed the release forms, performer questionnaire, and nondisclosure?"

Clara was grateful that Naomi had taken the lead on this part of the process. She would talk to a thousand lawyers, notaries, and bankers if she didn't have to figure out how you determined whether someone had what it took to perform in a sex ed resource.

"Yep." Marissa handed over a stack of papers. "Here you go."

Naomi scanned the forms. "I see here you've stated you're comfortable with full nudity, sex acts solo or with one to three partners. Both male and female. Excellent."

"And you read the documents about the risk from Black Hat?" Josh, especially, insisted they make sure that every person who might get involved went in with full knowledge of the gamble.

"I did. I'm not surprised, honestly. I've got friends who got on the wrong side of the studio before. They got blacklist threats and worse."

Worse? Clara mouthed at Josh, her panic rising.

He winced before turning his attention back to the audition.

"I'm glad someone is standing up to those assholes." Marissa unfolded a new piece of paper from the pocket of her shorts. "I really like the company manifesto you provided."

Clara's ears perked up. She'd written that part, her only contribution to this piece of the process. To help with recruiting like-minded individuals. It was a couple of paragraphs about the impetus for the idea, a vision for how the resource would help both women and their partners, and a company commitment to respecting everyone involved.

Naomi pushed a file across the table. "Clara, why don't you read the audition requirements?"

Clara shifted in her seat. "Me?"

Josh gave her an encouraging nod.

"Uh . . . All right." She picked up the sheet. "First, please remove your clothes." Her stomach flipped over, but Marissa smiled, shoving off her shorts before Clara had finished the sentence. *A blazer was the wrong choice for this occasion.*

Once she was fully nude, Naomi and Josh both jotted some notes down. Clara wrote the word *naked* in cursive on her own pad so she wouldn't look completely unprofessional.

"Ready to move on?" Naomi used a kinder voice with Marissa than she'd ever used with Clara or Josh. "We know this process can get awkward. As a reminder, you can stop at any time."

Marissa chuckled. "I appreciate that, but I've done this a million times. Plus, my body rocks."

"Is the room warm enough?" Josh had insisted they set the room to a balmy seventy-five degrees.

"Oh yeah. This is way better than the usual icebox casting calls."

"We've been in your shoes. We're trying to make the process as comfortable as possible. Clara, I think we can move on to the next part."

"Of course, sure." Her grip made the paper curl. "Please make yourself comfortable and . . ." *Good lord.*

Josh touched her forearm. "You okay?"

Clara forced the words out over the ringing in her ears. ". . . and bring yourself to orgasm. Lube has been provided. You're welcome to use any kind of reading or viewing materials to help you get in the mood."

"No problem." Marissa reclined on the comfy chaise Naomi had brought in and covered with a clean sheet and proceeded to stimulate her breasts.

"Oh dear." Clara automatically raised her eyes to the ceiling.

Naomi cleared her throat. "If you wouldn't mind amplifying your reactions? We want to make sure everyone's really comfortable with vocalizing their pleasure."

Clara forced herself to make eye contact with the performer as Marissa gave a thumbs-up with the hand that hadn't made its way between her thighs.

She'd never seen anything this explicit before in real life. Even though Marissa seemed like she was having fun, Clara couldn't stop sweating.

"What do you think, Clara?" Naomi's face didn't look menacing, but Clara knew a test when she saw one. "Would you like Marissa to try any techniques in particular?"

"No, I think this is fine. Good, I mean."

Naomi nodded. "Marissa, feel free to improvise with dirty talk if you'd like."

The performer let out a string of sentences that made Clara's face go from hot to scalding.

"Please excuse me a moment." Clara pushed back from the table and rushed into the hallway, following the frantic direction of her feet until she could pull fresh air into her lungs.

She closed her eyes. Tried to picture Zen gardens or any of the meditation mantras from the forty-five-dollar yoga classes she'd taken in Manhattan. She couldn't do this. The proof lay in her shaking hands. She'd been kidding herself. Kidding all of them.

"Clara?" Josh came barreling out the doors. "Are you all right?"

She urged her wobbly legs to a bench to the side of the building entrance. "I'm sorry. I thought I could handle this. I thought I could be calm and cool and collected but I obviously can't."

Josh sat down next to her and brushed the hair off her sweaty neck as she worked to regulate her breathing. "No. I'm sorry." His eyes traced her face and he ran his thumb up and down the side of her neck soothingly. "This is all my fault."

His touch worked like a balm, calming Clara both physically and mentally. "What are you talking about? I asked you to make a website featuring naked people and then I got weak in the knees on day one."

"There's a big difference between theoretical nudity and the real thing. I knew that. You didn't. I saw you blush the moment you realized we'd have to share a bathroom."

She managed a weak smile at the memory.

"Now we're trying to build this site and it's a huge leap for you." He tucked her hair behind her ear, fussing over her in a way that made her want to preen despite her humiliation. "No wonder the process is turning your face into a burnt tomato."

Well, that's an unflattering picture. "I should have prepared myself more. Should have, I don't know, read a lot of *National Geographic* magazine."

Josh's eyes crinkled. He was trying not to laugh at her.

"Marissa wasn't doing anything wrong or shameful in there." Clara thrust her chin at the building. "I'm just still a prude."

Josh steepled his hands. "That's not such a bad thing, you know."

Clara laughed, the bitter kind that hurt. "Sure."

"I'm serious. It's sweet and maybe even . . . sexy, actually."

Clara scoffed. "Don't pander to me. My lack of chill is not sexy. Marissa and Naomi, women who are confident in their bodies, are sexy. I'm a PG movie about a cartoon bunny."

Josh stood up and took her hand in his, threading their fingers together and helping her to her feet. He used their combined grip to tilt her head until she was looking at him. "No. You're really not. Do you know how many dirty thoughts I've had about your overalls?"

She wrinkled her nose. "You're kidding." Something warm inside her blossomed until she realized he'd said *your overalls*, not *you*. He probably pictured them on Naomi's lithe frame.

Josh ran his free hand through his hair, making the strands stand on end. "I'm not. Unfortunately. You're like an untapped gold mine. Waiting for some guy . . . or girl . . . to come and discover you. To work out all your hidden layers, reveal the depths of depravity I know are in there somewhere." He used their joined hands to chuck her on the chin. "You're a challenge."

Clara stared down at where their feet pointed at one another. The ridiculous idea to tilt her hips toward Josh's, to close the scant inches between their bodies, rose to the forefront of her brain, but she swatted it away. He could joke about wanting her because he joked about wanting everyone. The sooner she stopped gobbling the crumbs of his attention, the better. Still, her throat grew dry and she wished she hadn't left her water bottle inside. Clara licked her lips. "You think someday someone might accept that challenge?"

Josh pulled his full bottom lip between his teeth and closed his eyes. "Hell yeah." His eyes snapped open. "I mean, theoretically. Most likely someone with a vast collection of loafers and money clips."

Right. Someone the opposite of him. At this rate, Josh would try to set her up with his optometrist sometime next week.

"But listen, if you don't wanna do this." His voice had turned serious.

"I'll go in there right now and call the whole thing off." Despite his lighthearted comments from a few moments ago, Josh's eyes now held a tremendous amount of gravity. He brushed his thumb across her knuckles. He was a good man. *A good friend*, she reminded herself.

"No. I'm okay. Mind over matter, right?" Clara was an adult. She could handle some nudity. A handful of orgasms. That was the whole point of this crazy scheme, right? That if you pushed through the discomfort of social stigma you learned something that made your life exponentially better. Hell, maybe when Everett got back from his tour she'd have a whole roster of new moves in her repertoire. She'd blow his mind.

Josh's shoulders visibly relaxed, though the heat hadn't fully retreated from his eyes. "Exactly. Look, it gets easier. You get used to it. All the discomfort kinda fades after a few days. You realize we're all human. We've all got bodies and nerve endings. Attraction and orgasms—" His gaze slipped to her throat and he swallowed. "—it's just a biological response."

"Right." She brushed off a thread from his shoulder and let her hand linger. "It's science."

Josh's muscles flexed under her fingers. "If it would help, I could start walking around the apartment naked as a desensitization tactic?"

"Yeah, no, I think that might kill me."

"Well, if you change your mind you know where to find me."

Clara rolled her eyes. "I'll be fine."

"Good." Josh narrowed his eyes like he wanted to say more, like he was looking for a clue somewhere on her face.

Clara opened the door back to the studio. "I'll go home and watch a ton of porn."

The way Josh's mouth dropped to the ground made the whole embarrassing ordeal worthwhile. She tapped her foot. "You coming?"

"I mean, I'm gonna try not to," Josh muttered.

chapter eighteen

♥ ♥ ♥

IT DIDN'T SURPRISE Josh that Clara had never visited a sex shop before. She entered the store with gigantic eyes, like she'd wandered into some kind of erotic snow globe in the middle of the Valley.

"It's so quiet," she whispered before wandering down the first aisle.

Josh grabbed a cart from the front of the store and followed her. "What were you expecting? A soundtrack of high-pitched moaning?" They had a lot of errands to run for the project and a limited amount of time to accomplish them.

"It looks very clean."

Any minute now she'd pull out a magnifying glass.

The store had white walls and hardwood floors with neat hand-lettered signs marking each section. Like most boutiques opened in the last five years in Los Angeles, it resembled an artisanal coffee shop. Except instead of lattes, the chalkboard behind the counter listed flavors of organic lube.

"Did you base all your assumptions for this experience on a movie from the 1970s?"

Josh had tried desperately to avoid having Clara accompany him on this leg of the trip. He would have gone while she was tucked safely away at her day job, but the store manager who'd promised to cut him a deal on sex toys only worked on weekends.

Despite his best attempt to subtly grab his keys this morning while Clara lounged on the sofa, the jangle of metal worked like a cowbell and she'd come running, desperate for more driving practice. She'd already bamboozled him into granting her four trips behind the wheel of his car this week. After he picked her up from work, they'd spent the evenings traversing L.A.'s many neighborhoods, stopping for dinner in restaurants from Koreatown to Pasadena. Admittedly, the practice seemed to make a difference. Her driving had really improved since their first fateful trip. She could now merge with minimal hyperventilation.

Josh hadn't figured out a way to say no to her doe eyes in nearly two months of living with her. So now, he'd have to spend the next hour suppressing a hard-on while Clara carefully examined objects and implements meant to inspire debauchery. He didn't need the explicit stimuli to get him hard. These days, even watching Clara brush her teeth made all the blood rush to his groin.

"Do we need this?" She handed him a pair of handcuffs.

Josh ignored the way his dick jumped at the blatant excitement in her tone. "Fifty bucks? For plastic? No way. I could snap those flimsy things in my sleep."

Clara's breath hitched. "You could?"

Josh nodded, imagining breaking free from the ridiculous contraption to crawl across her naked body.

"Good to know." She carefully placed the merchandise back on the shelf. "I told you not to worry so much about the budget. We've got plenty of money in the account."

"It's not about the money." Though he had spent almost an hour last night searching for deals on bulk condoms online. "I want everything to be perfect."

He tossed a few satin blindfolds into the cart and bit the inside of his cheek. He'd give anything to know what Clara fantasized about. If any of these accessories featured in her dreams. If *he* did.

He'd lain in bed last night with his hand wrapped around his cock, imagining her touching herself under those ridiculous cotton panties, pretending she wanted him the way he wanted her. Desperate, all-consuming, so hungry for him she had to stifle her whimpers with the back of her hand. If his brain worked half as hard as his dick he might have something to show for it. Josh didn't want to tell Clara that, in addition to blue balls, he had a major case of writer's block.

The whole project depended on his ability to craft the next Kama Sutra, and he couldn't shake the nerves threatening to eat his intestines. Once they finished this errand, he'd have nothing left to do but actually put pen to paper. A truly terrifying prospect.

"I'm scared." The words fell out of him like a leaky faucet.

Clara lowered the box of butt plugs she'd been studying with a furrowed brow and looked around. "Of what?"

Josh took a deep breath. "Of blowing this chance. I've always just shown up and pointed my dick wherever someone told me to. Now, if I fail, there's so much more on the line. When no one expected anything from me, I couldn't let anyone down." He pinched the bridge of his nose. *Except for my family, but that is a different story.*

"Hey." Clara handed him a novelty mug that read *Fuck the Pain Away.* "I've got complete faith in you."

He relaxed as he watched her attempting not to giggle. At least one person found this whole process entertaining.

She picked up a twelve-inch vibrator. "Can you imagine using something like this?"

Josh covered his teeth with his lips and raised an eyebrow.

"Right." Color splashed across her cheeks and she carefully replaced the box on the shelf. "Of course you can."

She pointed at the next item that caught her eye, a set of stainless-steel Ben Wa balls. "Are those like whiskey rocks?"

Josh felt like her sexual Sherpa. The trouble was, he'd much rather have given a practical demonstration. *Don't think about readying her sweet pussy with your hand. Don't think about her breathy gasp as you slip the cool metal inside her hot, tight body. Don't . . .* He threw up mental walls.

Trying to break through to his hormone-hijacked brain, he picked up a set to the left of her selection and placed them carefully in the cart. "They go inside you, actually. To strengthen your pelvic floor. But you can also use them to practice edging."

"What's edging?" Her words dripped with curiosity.

He swallowed hard, trying to keep himself in line. "It's when your body is kept primed to arousal but release is postponed . . . or withheld."

When she spoke, her words came out huskier than normal. "Why did you pick that set?"

Josh leaned toward her until he could breathe in the scent of her perfume. He closed his eyes for a moment, trying to collect himself. "They . . . uh . . . come with a remote."

Somehow they'd moved until their noses were almost touching. With barely a tilt of his head, he could capture her lips. Each exaggerated rise and fall of her chest snapped another thread of his feeble control. He tore his eyes away from hers and scanned the shopping list clamped in his fist. "We're done in this aisle."

When Clara disappeared around the corner, he carefully adjusted his jeans.

A few minutes later, she paused in front of a row of packaging so long that Josh abandoned his search for cock rings to see what had captivated her attention. The items in question turned out to be a set of whips with Naomi posing on the packaging in a leather bustier and poisonous-looking red lipstick. He'd forgotten she had her own line.

"I didn't realize Naomi had so much merchandise," Clara said, tensing her shoulders. "Have you made any progress in your plans to reconcile with her?"

"I hadn't thought about it in a while." A bucket of ice water doused his arousal. "We've both been so busy." He supposed at this point that was still his most likely future living situation. He kept forgetting that his current home came with an expiration date. That sooner or later Everett would return and kick him out.

"Have you heard from Everett lately?" She hadn't mentioned anything, but that didn't mean they weren't calling and texting each other out of his earshot.

"I got a few postcards and a promotional beer koozie with the band's name on it in the mail." She shook her head. "I don't know how much longer I can keep making up excuses for him when my mother calls." Clara turned an aggressive-looking set of nipple clamps so the box faced away from her.

"What's the deal with your mom? I didn't realize avoiding someone who lives across the country could be so difficult."

Clara paused in front of a rack of magazines and frowned. "She wants me to be like her. I'm supposed to find a respectable man from a good family and settle down. Pop out some babies and then run the charity of my choice."

"Sounds boring." Josh winced. "I mean unless that's what you want?"

"I think part of my problem is, I spent so long trying to please her and my dad, I never gave much thought to what *I* wanted. And now . . ."

Josh found a sliver of hope in those last two words. "Now?"

"It doesn't matter." Clara flattened her skirt. "If my parents found out the truth, about my job with Jill or . . . you know, you. Oh my God. They'd die."

Lava swam in his stomach. "So that's a no-go on fraternizing with porn stars, then?" He shouldn't be surprised. Had known from the second she arrived that she'd never consider him anything other than a pit stop on the way to the things she really wanted.

"Big time. Wheatons are very sensitive to optics. My mother didn't want me to date a law clerk during undergrad because he rode a skateboard. I'm supposed to be her saving grace—the one she doesn't have to worry about embarrassing her."

Josh clenched his jaw. Occasionally he let himself forget where Clara came from. Right now, that willful ignorance felt fatal. "And she likes the idea of you and Everett?"

Clara leaned over and rearranged the items in the cart from the haphazard positions he'd given them. "She likes his family. Likes that she knows where he came from and how he grew up. I'm pretty sure she and Mrs. Bloom picked out our wedding china when we were in eighth grade." Her voice took on an edge. "Nobody seems to care that Everett and I have never even kissed."

A wicked satisfaction spread across his chest. Even if Everett Bloom got to marry her someday, Josh would always be the first man who made her come. But if Clara had the Greenwich version of an arranged marriage, what the fuck was Everett waiting for? Josh could hardly spend more than fifteen minutes with her without wanting to eat her out until he sprained his jaw. "I'm sorry, how is it possible that you've carried a torch for that guy since you were a teenager, but somehow you've never kissed?"

"Sometimes the anticipation of a kiss is better than the actual experience anyway." Josh tracked the way she ran the hem of her dress through her fingers, exposing half an inch more of her pale thigh.

If she believed that, clearly she needed more practice. "I'm pretty sure physically kissing is better."

"That's because you're accustomed to instant gratification." Clara gave him a Cheshire cat smile as she strolled ahead of him, leaving Josh panting at her heels. "Half the pleasure in kissing is the buildup. The obsessing over the other person's mouth. Thinking about the shape of his lips and the taste of his tongue. Imagining his hands in your hair. Or the way that he'll hold you." She stopped and turned toward him. "You can spend a whole night wondering if he's ever going to pull you in unexpectedly and capture your breath in the middle of a sentence. Or lean in so slowly one morning that the wanting curls your toes and singes your fingertips."

Josh dug his nails into his palm, hard enough to leave marks. His body didn't care that she was describing pining for another man. He had no trouble pretending that all the *he*s in her sentences could be replaced with his name.

"Does he taste like cinnamon or whiskey?" Clara absently traced her bottom lip with the tip of her index finger while holding his gaze. "You imagine, over and over, in a thousand renditions, how he'll push you up against the wall and press his entire body against yours until you're trembling with how much you want him to take you."

His eyes shot to the exposed brick behind her. He'd have no trouble walking her back until the rough stone pressed against her soft body before dropping his mouth to her neck as his hands shoved that flimsy cotton hem to her waist.

Clara's eyes turned liquid as they found his lips. "Or maybe he won't. Maybe he'll barely brush his mouth across yours. Make you lower your chin and beg."

Josh let out a sound, caught between a groan and a whimper.

The noise seemed to draw Clara out of her stupor. "Are you okay?"

"Yes." The word came out in the wrong register. He tried again. "Yes. I was thinking, maybe you should write for the website."

"Me? Really?"

He focused on keeping his eyes above her nostrils. "You're good at channeling your emotions. All this thinking about sex but not actually having any is boiling my brain." His cock pressed angrily against his zipper. She was right. Josh's body didn't understand the concept of wanting and not having. Of constant exposure to the object of his desire with zero hope of ever crossing the finish line.

"I know what you mean. All this thinking about sexy people doing sexy things with sexy toys." She fanned herself with her hand. "I've never said the word *sexy* so much in my life. I feel strung out."

"I don't know what to do." He couldn't do any of the things he wanted. They all involved different parts of Clara's body. Sweat beaded on his brow as he watched her eyes grow heavy-lidded. It took everything he had to keep from dropping to his knees and pleading with her to put him out of his misery.

"It's like having an itch you can't quite scratch." Her pink tongue traced her pinker bottom lip.

His jaw went slack. "Yes." God, even her voice was starting to do it for him. Was it possible she was as turned on as he was?

"Well, I suppose you should channel all of that energy into a productive direction." Clara hauled in hectic breaths.

He hoped "a productive direction" was code for between her thighs.

She shook her head as if to clear it. "Have you tried journaling?"

Josh's head snapped back and he blinked stupidly. "I'm sorry. It sounded like you said *journaling*."

"I did. You should use all of your erotic energy as fuel for next week's scenes."

"Oh. Yeah. That's the plan." Just because he'd never attempted to produce something academic with his sex drive before didn't mean he would fail. The fact that he'd never written anything longer than an email wasn't a bad sign. He'd take all of his pent-up lust, all these inexhaustible urges and he'd . . . package them. Make them neat and useful instead of messy and maddening.

When they finally made it to the checkout counter, Clara placed their purchases into designated rows for the manager.

The tall woman with a pink Mohawk totaled them up, including the promised thirty percent discount, and handed over an impressive number of bags. "If you don't mind me asking, is all this stuff for business or pleasure?"

Clara blushed. "I guess you could say our business *is* pleasure."

As soon as they got home, Josh was going to lock himself in his bedroom and journal until his hand fell off.

chapter nineteen

♡ ♡ ♡

CLARA HAD INTENTIONALLY put on the least sexy sleepwear she owned in an effort to smother the inferno of her libido. Even though she normally wore cozy, rather than alluring, sleep sets, this evening she'd gone so far as to wear a pair of extra-large men's pajamas she'd ordered by accident last Christmas. She looked ridiculous, like the ghost of her great-grandfather had spit plaid all over her, but she didn't care. At least these pj's didn't antagonize her carnal thoughts.

For the umpteenth time in the last hour, her eyes jumped from her computer screen on the coffee table to Josh's closed bedroom door. Behind that thin strip of wood, she knew he was writing X-rated fantasies. All the moisture in her mouth relocated below her waist.

Going to that sex shop was a mistake. Watching Josh select items for their project with authority and expertise fired off a thousand pleasure sensors in her brain. She tugged her top away from her heated skin. Cotton wasn't as breathable as the manufacturers claimed.

In order to complete her to-do list for the evening, she needed to secure a domain name. Unfortunately, she, Josh, and Naomi still hadn't agreed on what to call the project. LadyBoners.com and Orgasms4All .org, Josh's latest suggestions, didn't exactly roll off the tongue.

The man of the hour opened his door. "Hey." He had a worn black notebook in his hands.

"Hi." Clara crossed her legs. "How's it going in there?"

"It's going all right." He pointed the open notebook in her direction and fanned through several pages full of his dark, spiky handwriting. "Once I got started it turned out I had a lot to say."

Clara swallowed hard. "I can imagine." *So many things.* A million Josh fantasies played on loop in her mind. She needed some kind of anti-libido medication. Or a therapist. Probably both.

Josh descended onto the sofa beside her. Close enough for her to feel the heat rolling off his body. She gritted her teeth to keep from inhaling his scent.

"The trouble is, I can't tell if any of it is good or if I'm dribbling garbage across the page."

"Do you want me to take a look?"

"Actually, I was thinking maybe I could read it to you?" His voice held a hint of insecurity. "Since it's supposed to be delivered as narration." Josh ruffled the fluff of curls in front of his eyes. "Unless that's weird? Since it's sexy. I could always call Naomi."

"No." She shoved her computer under the coffee table and faced Josh with her legs tucked together in front of her. "I can listen."

"Oh, okay. Great. So it's a part of the introductory series. For partners who are getting to know each other sexually and figuring out what works. I thought that rather than diving right in, the woman, the performer in our case, could show her partner how she pleasures herself. Help them get a sense of where she likes to be touched and with how much pressure."

"That sounds smart." Clara forced herself to look away from his mouth. *Damn it.* She wanted him bad.

"Okay. I'll start then?"

"No time like the present." She steeled herself. *No one ever died from an overdose of desire.*

"Begin by helping your partner get in the mood." Josh altered his pronunciation slightly so that his syllables came out with more authority than his average speaking voice. He poured the magic of his charisma across the innocent words, making them smoky and tempting. "Ask her to describe one of her favorite fantasies. As she gets comfortable, encourage her to touch the parts of her body that become stimulated by the story."

Josh lowered the notebook as Clara ran her hand up and down her thigh. "What do you think of that exercise? Heather, one of Naomi's friends from Cal State who's a certified sex therapist, suggested it."

Her tongue felt big in her mouth. "I think it's good. And the tone you're using, deep and slow. That's good too. It's sexy but not over the top."

The corner of Josh's mouth kicked up. "Thanks." One of his reckless curls fell in front of his eye and Clara fisted her hands in her pajama pants to keep from reaching out and running the glossy strands between her fingers.

He flipped a few pages in his notebook. "So then I mapped out some blocking for the performer, though I think we can give her a lot of creative freedom to explore her own desires. The idea would be that we explore several erogenous zones starting with the mouth, ears, and throat, and then make our way down her body, lingering at her breasts."

"Wow." Her body burned for his touch in each of the places he'd mentioned.

"Oh, good call." He scribbled the word *collarbone* in his notebook and Clara realized she'd begun tracing her clavicle with two fingers, imagining his mouth. She hastily shoved her hand under her butt.

"I think a lot of men write nipple stimulation off because they don't know the right way to do it. Women often spend more time exploring that area on their own bodies than their partners do."

Clara's breasts grew tighter as each word slipped from his perfect lips. She raised her eyes to see Josh running a hand over his mouth as he stared at her chest.

"We could try it," he said. "The exercise. If you wanted to. It's normal to be overstimulated when you first take up pleasure as a profession. When I got into the business my dick practically fell off from all the solo sessions I needed to take the edge off."

"I have noticed an increase in my sexual . . . appetite." A drop of sweat slipped between her breasts. "I suppose, in a sense, we have an obligation as the creative leads to make sure what we're suggesting works." Her heartbeat kicked into an alarming staccato. "We wouldn't want to show up on set, with the performers we're paying, and waste their time on something that hasn't gone through careful vetting."

His eyes burned, an expression of hunger unlike anything she'd ever seen. "Right. It's not like we'd be having sex."

"No," Clara agreed around a heaving breath. "Definitely not sex."

"It's masturbation." He shifted in his seat. "Perfectly normal. And you said earlier you've been worked up lately."

Clara bobbed her head. The massive bulge in his pants made her lips part. A thousand alarms rang in her ears, warning her of their crumbling boundaries, as her hands strayed to the hem of her top. "I really have."

"I bet if you touched yourself—relieved that distraction—you'd be a lot more focused on your work. Both for Jill and on the project."

An excellent point. "And a relaxed mind is more creative."

Josh positioned the notebook in front of his lap. "I'm always reading about the long-term health benefits of regular orgasms."

Her fingers stilled. "You are?"

"Sure."

"So I would, what . . . take off my shirt and touch my breasts?" That sounded like the kind of thing a self-possessed, sexually liberated, hot person might do.

Josh cleared his throat. "That sounds like a good start."

A combination of nerves and blistering arousal brought goose bumps to her arms. "I can do that?" The words came out as a question.

His molten eyes devoured her mouth. "I think you should."

Clara willed her body into action. "I can't seem to make my arms move." How dare her limbs betray her? "Sorry. I don't even like being naked by myself," she said. "Let alone with an audience."

"What's wrong with being naked?"

A sad sigh climbed out of her mouth. "Well, nothing if you look like you. But when I'm naked, it's all soft and everything wobbles." She leaned forward to hide her curves.

Josh shook his head. "Those are the best parts." He rolled up the sleeves of his henley. "Would it change anything if I told you how attractive I find you?"

"What?" Clara's attempts at playing it cool went up in smoke.

"Would it help if I outlined how I find you sexy? Objectively speaking, obviously." He showed her another page in his notebook. "It's one of the partner tips. If the woman you're with is feeling nervous or having trouble conjuring up a fantasy, stating your desire for her can help set the tone for the session."

Clara's mind went blank. "Okay. Yeah, let's try that."

Josh took his time looking at her, starting at the top of her head and making his way down to her sock-covered feet.

She held still as he drew his gaze across her body.

"Well, there's a lot of good stuff going on," he said so quietly she almost didn't catch it. "There's the obvious stuff that I notice when you enter a room." He started counting things off on his fingers. "Your hair is nice. All shiny and inky. And you're always tossing it around. So I get big whiffs of your shampoo when we're sitting on the couch whether I want to or not. And then there are your breasts, of course. God, your tits are torture. The way you insist on hiding them in those ridiculous high-necked shirts. Why are you doing that? They deserve to experience fresh air. It's summer in Los Angeles, for crying out loud." He rubbed his jawline as if it pained him. "I think I've imagined twenty different ways to rip your top off. Just so I can get a look at them."

They'd barely begun and already Clara's breath was coming too fast. She might faint.

"But the stuff that really drives me crazy is subtler," he continued. "The way your skin feels when I help you out of the car and how you kinda glow in the face region. I also like that thing you do where you arch your back when you're stretching in the morning. Oh, and the tiny mole at the top of your lip. Like an X marking treasure."

He brought his thumb up to brush the thin skin.

Clara's eyelids grew heavy. Yearning filled her throat, making it difficult to breathe. Had anyone ever said so many nice things about her in one sitting? Sure, they were superficial, but they were also sweet. Hearing Josh admire her body somehow made up for every guy in middle school who had called her chubby or made fun of her big teeth.

She couldn't fight the sudden, overwhelming desire to open her mouth. When she indulged the instinct, Josh let his finger slip between her lips. Clara couldn't help herself. She dragged her tongue across the rough pad of his thumb, tasting salt, as he closed his eyes and groaned.

"Show me what you like," he said, eyes still closed. It was a request and a command and a plea all at the same time.

And suddenly she needed to. It didn't matter if she liked every part of her body. What mattered were Josh's words and the way they elevated her to a position both wanton and powerful. He'd handed her the opportunity to blow on the spark of desire behind his eyes until it blazed. She'd be a fool not to take it.

Before she could lose her nerve again, she moved her legs behind her so she could sit back on her heels. "This is professional, right? We're doing this for the good of the project?"

Josh breathed slow and even through his nose, holding himself rigid. "Yes. Absolutely. We're working right now." His eyes were practically all pupil.

Clara thanked her lucky stars that Josh was a master performer. Who cared if he was pretending to want her right now? It felt impossibly real.

She relaxed her shoulders as his confirmation washed over her. They'd explicitly agreed that whatever happened next didn't mean she had feelings for Josh. Wanting him, she could handle. But anything deeper . . . anything more with Josh was impossible. Unacceptable. A recipe for a broken heart.

But she could still indulge one of her fantasies. Just a single, harmless confession. For the greater good.

She peeled off her top in one fluid motion. Thankfully the material didn't get caught around her elbows.

The overhead fan blew cool air against newly exposed skin. Of course, the bra she'd chosen today was too small. Her breasts spilled over the top of the unadorned cream fabric.

Josh moaned like someone had stabbed him with a dull knife. "I'm burning every single one of those fucking sleeveless turtlenecks. How the fuck are they better than I imagined?"

Clara ducked her head and laughed a little at that. A throaty purr that sounded like someone else but felt good in her throat. "Bra next?" She needed guidance, but she also liked the idea that announcing her progress would drive Josh wild.

Sure enough, when she met his eyes he shuddered like a man enjoying the electric chair.

"Do you want me to stop?" She feigned a tone of concern.

He gave her his most charming smile in reassurance, dimples in full effect. "Don't you dare."

Clara got up and turned around so that her back faced him, hoping that not having to make direct eye contact would make removing her bra, a significantly larger hurdle to her insecurity, a little easier. She bent slightly forward and reached back to unclip it, fumbling with the clasp.

"Let me help you." As Josh deftly undid the hook, more of her reservations melted away.

He let the back of his fingers brush along her spine as he removed his hand. "If you refuse to turn around, there's a good chance I'll spontaneously combust." His breathing was no longer slow and even. It sounded like he was trying to climb a flight of stairs while carrying a wheelbarrow.

Clara swiveled, forcing her body not to obey the impulse to cover herself as Josh licked his lips, staring unabashedly at her chest.

He hissed in a breath. "What I'm about to say is gonna sound like a line. But please believe me when I tell you that I've seen thousands of tits in my lifetime and I've never wanted to get my hands and my mouth and, if I'm being totally honest, my cock, on a pair as much as yours."

Clara's face warmed at the ridiculous praise. "No one in their right mind would ever think *that* was a viable line." Still, she lowered her shoulder blades, pushing her breasts further out, and cupped one in each hand until the heavy flesh spilled over her fingers. *See. This barely counts as second base.* Equating adolescent baseball metaphors to levels of intimacy was oddly soothing. Josh's talent was almost enough to make her brazen. She let her thumbs graze her nipples, feeling the rush of pleasure even that small gesture sent down through her belly to her clit. She hadn't touched herself like this in a while, and half the time she was so embarrassed about the size of her breasts that she pretended they didn't exist.

"Okay. So, umm . . . In my fantasy, I'm on a beach somewhere." She glanced at him. *With you.* "And the sun is warming my skin." Her eyes consumed the wide slabs of his shoulders. *And you're naked.* "I'm sunbathing topless." Josh drew his hands into fists. *Because I wanted to tease you.*

The attention she gave her breasts, starting slow and varying the pressure, made her want to writhe. She'd forgotten the way the pleasure could build, more complete than when she started below the belt. Clara closed her eyes and threw back her head until the long strands of her hair brushed the middle of her back.

"The knowledge that you love having your tits played with has taken at least five years off my life." The raw lust in his voice made her melt.

Clara hadn't accounted for Josh's dirty talk when she agreed to this plan. How his words made everything more exciting and urgent and deliciously undignified.

She opened her eyes to find him wrestling with control. He moved until he was facing her on the couch, every inch of his long, lean form bent forward in anticipation. She let her eyes wander between his legs and pinched her nipples hard between her thumb and forefinger. The bulge in his pants was truly obscene. He seemed unaware that he'd begun to subtly rock his hips.

"You should take that out," she said, and then immediately covered her mouth with her hand.

Josh froze. "Huh?"

Clara removed her fingers from her lips slowly. "Your . . . cock." She wrapped her mouth around the word he'd used earlier. "You should take it out and touch yourself. If you'd like." She ducked her head. "I'm sorry. I shouldn't have said that. I got carried away."

"Are you fucking kidding me?" Josh tore off his T-shirt, treating her to a view of his abs rippling as he raised his arms. He pulled his pants and briefs down his legs so fast she'd barely blinked before he had his hand wrapped around himself.

"Oh my God." Her voice shook as the temperature in the room

blazed. "It's like someone gave a Caravaggio painting a gym membership."

Josh stilled his hand around the base of his thick shaft. "Is that . . . good?"

"Yes." It was so much more than *good*. The screen of her computer really hadn't done him justice. No wonder he was mad about losing all those merchandise dollars. Women across America had probably emptied their 401(k)s for a silicone simulation of the heat Josh was packing.

"Are you going to . . ." He nodded toward her still pajama-clad thighs. "You have no idea how much I want to see you right now."

Clara would have traded anything to get Josh to keep looking at her exactly like that, so she pushed the rest of her clothes down and off.

"Fuck. Me," Josh said when she was bare before him. He stopped moving. In fact, she wasn't sure he hadn't stopped breathing. "Please touch your pussy. Please. I know I'm begging. I know it's not macho or suave or cool. But please, Clara. I'm losing my mind." Josh ground out the words in an aching voice.

Blind lust gave her the confidence to bring her trembling hand to her stomach, to let her fingers slowly slide between her thighs. The moment her hand made contact with her sex, she and Josh both swore.

He moved closer until each of his harsh breaths fell against her neck.

She whimpered as her hips bucked, seeking penetration. Begging for the man beside her.

Josh's eyes grew darker, wilder, until he looked like the victim of a pheromone shipwreck.

Suddenly everything, the pressure of her hand and the pleasure she wrought, doubled. Josh worked himself in smooth strokes, swallowing every time his thumb grazed the head of his cock. He let his mouth fall open as he watched her work herself closer toward release.

Without thought or intention, Clara moaned the one word she'd forbidden herself to utter. "Josh."

The sound of his name on her lips seemed to break him. His whole body started shaking. "Say it again," he ground out through clenched teeth. His working forearm had pulled so tight she could count the veins. He lowered his voice to a litany. "Keep saying my name."

She held his gaze as she inserted two fingers into her tight body, unable to find any room in her mind for shame.

Not when his breathing was as ragged as hers.

Not when she chased an orgasm that promised to ruin her.

It made perfect sense to turn Josh's name into a mantra. Even though he wasn't touching her, she could feel him everywhere. The heat and tightly coiled energy rolled off his body in waves.

Everything she'd ever believed about sex and her body became ancient history as she moved like a woman who had never apologized for chasing her own pleasure. *Let him look.* Let him see the frantic motion of her hand as she brought herself exactly what she wanted.

His presence acted like sensory deprivation, everything heightened, focused on a single point.

"Please tell me you understand how amazing you look right now." His eyes rolled back in his head as she added another finger. He grew rougher with his strokes. "I'd do terrible things, Clara, to suffer the perfect torture of watching you fuck yourself again and again." He didn't touch her, but his words sank into her skin.

Clara was caught up in him. Drowning in sensation. So distracted that when she fell over the edge, she cried out in not only pleasure but surprise. Her eyes fell closed as she let the orgasm break across her body without shying away. When she blinked to find Josh watching her face, the naked longing in his eyes drew out the shudders of her body.

It wasn't until a moment later when her body finally relaxed, when she fell back against the sofa like a limp noodle, that Josh allowed his own release, painting his stomach with the evidence of his desire. Sweat began to cool on her trembling body. Nothing had ever felt as good as the illusion Josh wove of wanting her.

The living room was quiet except for the mingling of their desperate breaths.

"That was . . ." Josh finally said. "I mean, you did . . . Your body is . . ."

"I hope the ends of those sentences are complimentary." Clara smiled as she handed him a handful of tissues from the box on the end table, spent and happy and different from the woman she'd been an hour before.

"Yes, very," he said as they locked eyes. The room filled with something more than attraction and unbridled lust. Josh clenched his jaw and Clara was the first to look away.

He gestured with a thumb over his shoulder. "I should probably go type up my notes. My findings, if you will."

Clara hunted on the floor for her pajamas. "Right. Yes. You do that." She admired his bare ass as he got up to walk away, weaving slightly.

"Oh, and Josh?"

He turned, holding his balled-up clothes in front of his waist.

"I'd say your strategy definitely worked."

He huffed out a sound that was almost a laugh.

After Josh had locked himself back in his room, Clara cleaned up and changed into a fresh pair of pajamas. Then she picked up her discarded laptop and typed a single word into the domain search engine.

She grinned as she added her selection to her cart. Finally. Their fledgling project had a name. A word waiting to be reclaimed. One that beat in time with the thump-thump of her heart.

Shameless.

chapter twenty

♡ ♡ ♡

CLARA WHEATON HAD experienced her fair share of embarrassment. She'd tripped down staircases in front of her peers, used the wrong French pronoun when addressing a native speaker, and once accidentally screamed "abort" when she ran into an ex-boyfriend at a Manhattan bodega.

Having endured so much worse, she decided not to let her little "living room rehearsal" with Josh ruin their strange, unnameable bond.

She needed him. Professionally now as well as personally. She would simply redraw some boundaries between them. *No harm. No foul.* It would probably be a good idea to stop getting off to the memories of him stroking himself. Just a thought.

In a desperate attempt to return to her comfort zone and get to know the performers and crew they'd hired over the course of the week, Clara convinced Josh they should host a barbecue in Everett's backyard.

Entertaining was a skill set ingrained in Wheaton women, practically from birth. Clara could fold napkins in fourteen distinct shapes. That skill did not come in handy in this situation.

In an effort to appear laid back and unfussy, she'd purchased red Solo cups and rented card tables and folding chairs. She'd even gone so far as to allow Josh to write *potluck* on the invitations.

"No one our age can show up to a party empty-handed without feeling like an asshole," he'd said. "At least let them bring beer."

Clara had consoled herself by making a plethora of dips to accommodate any and all dietary preferences. She *was* still the hostess, and after the spectacle she'd made of herself at casting, this was her chance to make friends. To show them all she wasn't a boss or a banker, but one of them. With delicious appetizers and stimulating conversation.

As the start time of their party neared, Josh came out of his room in a cheesy Hawaiian shirt.

"Are you seriously wearing that?" She didn't know why she bothered to ask. She stirred fresh raspberries into a bowl of punch.

"Sure am." Josh stole a piece of fruit before she could swat him away and popped it into his mouth. "Is that what you're wearing?"

Clara straightened the full skirt of her vintage dress. It had a halter neck. She'd thought it was charming. "You don't like it?"

"No, I like it." He let his gaze trail down her form. "But it's white. At a backyard barbecue. With red punch."

Clara frowned. She hadn't considered that. "Perhaps I could wear my apron during the meal?" She pulled a pile of gingham and flounces out of the closet and held the material up for his inspection.

"That seems on brand." He turned toward the fridge and Clara noticed a Band-Aid across his temple.

She stood on her tiptoes to inspect the bruised area. "What happened here?" He probably hadn't thought to apply an antiseptic.

"Nothing." Josh pulled away. "Just clumsy."

The doorbell rang.

"They're here early." She wrung her hands. "I haven't put the place cards out on the table yet."

Josh steered her toward the door by her shoulders. "You go and greet our guests. I'll set the place cards."

Clara dumped the paper triangles with each person's name written in calligraphy into his cupped hands and hurried to the door.

Naomi stood on the doorstep, along with a handful of other cast and crew members that Clara recognized but didn't know by name. Naomi pressed a large plastic veggie tray into Clara's arms. "I don't cook and I don't chop."

"I don't blame you." Frankly, the idea of Naomi wielding a knife was terrifying. "Thanks for coming. This is perfect." Clara pointed to the door that led out back. "Party's through there."

Clara collected a few other food items as guests in flip-flops and tank tops snaked by, introducing themselves and thanking her for the invitation. The crowd grew larger than she'd originally accounted for. Good thing she had plenty of food.

After some last-minute prep, Clara joined the rest of the group in the yard. Despite the music playing, the scene had not achieved the air of jovial camaraderie she'd hoped to inspire. She noticed with bemusement that a few of the guys had turned her place cards into paper footballs. Oh well. At least they'd put them to use. She made her way over to where Josh and Naomi stood in a corner talking. With more than her typical nonchalance, Josh's ex handed him something small and black, smoothly, the way Clara's dad passed a tip to the valet.

Clara caught only the tail end of the sentence that accompanied the covert gesture. ". . . that's got my stuff and everything from Ginger."

Josh shoved the item into his pocket when he noticed her approach. "All done in the kitchen?" He turned his dimples to high beam.

"Uh, yeah. Everything okay out here?" Clara's brain flipped through a dozen explanations for that handoff. Not the least ridiculous of which was that Naomi had passed Josh some kind of electronic key to a hidden sex dungeon. But what kind of "stuff" did one keep on a key? More likely it was a flash drive of some kind which was . . . only slightly less disconcerting. *It's none of your business anyway*, a prim voice in her head reminded her.

"I think we're off to a bit of a slow start." Josh frowned at the tepid gathering.

Now that he mentioned it, the party wasn't exactly lively. Most of their guests looked as uncomfortable as Clara felt.

"You need to encourage interaction," Naomi said. "Half these people don't know one another. You've got a bunch of strangers together and is that *Shania Twain* playing from your phone?" She stared at Clara accusingly. "No wonder it's awkward."

Who doesn't like 'Man! I Feel Like A Woman!'? "Ooh. I have an idea. I've got a list of questions, originally developed by Marcel Proust to rouse meaningful conversation, in my room. I could grab those—"

"No," Josh and Naomi said in unison.

Josh turned down the music and called the guests to attention. "How about a round of old-school Never Have I Ever?"

A couple people exchanged sly smiles. Others laughed and moved to top off their drinks.

"You're on, Darling," a woman who'd introduced herself as Stacy said. Her date, one of the place card abusers, whooped and drained his beer before punting it on the ground.

"Adult performers love Never Have I Ever because it gives them a chance to brag about all the sex they've had," Naomi explained as she led Clara over to the table to play.

Interesting. Clara had played the game a few times at camp. She knew that more often than not the questions centered on illicit activities. Though she had to imagine this crowd defined *illicit* differently than the counselors of Camp Sparrow.

Still, drinking games were a good idea. A social lubricant would set everyone at ease. She poured herself a glass of punch and joined the fray.

"All right, everyone. Let's play with both hands up, and the final person standing can shotgun a beer at the end of the round. Last time we played with the rule that you had to drink for everything you'd done, the whole party ended up trashed." Josh smirked. "I'll start. Never have I ever fucked both members of a married couple."

His ex dropped a finger along with a few others. Clara lowered her eyebrows before anyone noticed her surprise.

"Never have I ever come so hard I passed out," Stacy said. Many more fingers fell.

Clara shifted her weight from side to side. She had never considered that possibility. *How . . . ?*

"Never have I ever fucked ten times in one day."

Even Josh had lowered a finger on that one. But . . . that defied science. She wanted to call a doctor.

"Never have I ever been offered a million dollars for a one-night stand."

Only Naomi lowered a finger on that one.

Clara turned to her. "Are you serious?"

"I didn't take it," Naomi assured her.

"Never have I ever turned down a million dollars," the next player said.

Naomi flashed him the middle finger, conveniently the only one remaining up on her right hand.

All heads turned to Clara for her turn. "Umm. Never have I ever broken a bone?"

"You mean like a boner?" Stacy bent a finger halfway down. "Like breaking someone's dick during sex? 'Cause I've totally done that."

Clara forced herself not to recoil at that mental image. "No, I meant like a regular bone." She held up her arm and mimed wearing a sling.

Stacy deflated. "Oh."

Naomi took her turn. "Never have I ever fucked a celebrity."

"How are we defining *celebrity*?"

"B list and above," Naomi clarified.

"Damn. Close but no cigar," said Stacy's date. "Never have I ever fucked a world leader."

Most people had one hand left up or less. Clara's ten fingers stood out like a neon sign announcing her as an outcast. A couple people looked at her with arched eyebrows.

"You're supposed to lower a finger when you've done something," Stacy whispered to her unhelpfully.

"Oh no." She craned her neck, trying to see the drinks table. "I think we're running low on ice. I'll check." Clara walked into the kitchen and opened the freezer, letting the blast of air cool her heated cheeks.

"You need any help?"

She shut the door and faced Josh. "No. I'm sorry. I know I'm making a habit of running out of rooms."

"That game wasn't fun for you, huh?"

"Not so much. My sex life is very vanilla." She sucked in a breath and looked away. *Present company excluded.*

"We can play something else."

"It's not the game, Josh. Look at me. I don't fit in. You go back out and have fun. I'm sure no one wants to be on their best behavior because of me."

"Come on. No one thinks of you like that. Everyone wants to get to know you. You're a mystery to them."

"*Mystery* is a nice word for *weirdo*. The cool kids in high school used to use *buzzkill*." Clara had tried blending in with Everett's new friends after he'd started getting attention for his burgeoning looks, but casual had never come easily to her.

Josh reached over and wrapped her in a hug. "You're not in high school anymore." He bent his knees so her chin could rest on his shoulder without strain and applied the perfect pressure, firm but loose. The scent of fresh laundry filled her nose. "Clara, those people out there are showing off. Half that stuff is exaggerated, guaranteed. Besides, our sex lives are hardly average. You've done tons of stuff none of those people have ever even attempted."

She stepped back from the hug, grateful he'd let her break away first. A part of her could have stayed there forever. "Yeah, right."

"Throw up some fingers."

Clara waved him off.

"Come on. I'm serious. Put 'em up."

She rolled her eyes and held up her right hand.

"Never have I ever earned a doctorate."

Clara folded down a finger. "A lot of good it's done me."

"Never have I ever made brussels sprouts taste good."

"Anything tastes good if you fry it in bacon fat," Clara said, but she smiled a little despite herself. She'd vowed to get Josh to eat vegetables by any means necessary.

"Never have I ever come up with an idea for my own business."

He had her there. Shameless made her proud.

"Never have I ever been generous enough to fund a ragtag band of sex workers that no bank would ever give the time of day." Josh's voice conveyed his respect and she found herself blushing.

Clara lowered her ring finger and shrugged. "I believe in you guys."

Josh touched the Band-Aid on his forehead. "Never have I ever made someone walk into a door frame because I exited the bathroom in a very tiny towel."

Clara tilted her head. He'd lost her with that one.

Josh reached over and lowered her last finger.

Comprehension dawned. "What? This morning?"

Josh gave her a self-deprecating smile. "You might think you don't fit in, but those people out there are as intimidated by you as you are by them. If you relax, they will too. I promise." He punched her lightly on the arm. "Now let's go back out there before Felix finishes all the crab dip."

She'd entered this business endeavor with one foot out the door, but with Josh by her side, maybe she should stop telling herself that the "cool kids" would never accept her. "Thanks."

The noise of the party barreled on outside. "Anytime, Wheaton."

JOSH NEEDED TO get his feelings for his roommate under control. His physical symptoms had started to cause him bodily harm. And his mental ones? Well, those had gotten so powerful, he could hardly go ten minutes without thinking of Clara.

All he knew was that he always wanted her to be happy. When she smiled or laughed, he felt powerful and good. If something hurt her, he wanted to Hulk smash.

He'd been grateful when she suggested the party, a chance to blow off steam that didn't involve blowing his load. His dick was officially on lockdown after he'd almost blurted out, "I think you're the girl of my dreams," while whipped into a sexual frenzy by the sight of Clara's naked body. His capacity for longing terrified him.

"Come on, Darling. We're picking teams for flip cup. You and Naomi are captains. Battle of the Exes."

Naomi caught his eye. He knew she'd seen him follow Clara inside after the earlier debacle.

Josh gave her a subtle nod and watched as her shoulders relaxed. Her cool demeanor didn't fool him. Naomi was starting to like Clara, whether she wanted to or not.

"You pick first," she told him, gesturing to the gathered guests who wanted to play.

Josh found Clara where she stood rearranging the plastic cups near the keg. Despite the talk they'd had in the kitchen, he knew she would love to spend the rest of the party doing hostess chores instead of inter-acting with other people.

"Wheaton," he called across the yard. "You're with me."

She turned toward him with wide eyes. "Me?" She looked around at all the guests. "No. That's okay. I'll sit this next one out. You all go ahead."

Josh shook his head and curled his finger. "Get over here." He'd made it his personal mission to ensure that she spent the remainder of the barbecue having fun.

Clara obeyed with visible reluctance as Felix and Max lined up the long rows of cups on either side of the table, pouring light beer across them.

Josh pulled Clara to his side of the table and bumped his hip against hers. "This one's easy," he said, showing her the motion with an empty cup. "It's all in the wrist."

"I know how to play flip cup." She raised her chin defiantly. "I spent the last nine years on various college campuses."

"Fair enough," Josh said. "Naomi and I are the anchors. So stand next to me and I can make up for any lag time."

Clara crossed her arms. "Why are you assuming I'm going to lag?"

He didn't get the chance to respond before Felix climbed on a chair and bellowed. "Okay, folks. You'll go on my command. The first player on each team must answer my question before they start drinking. Play-ers ready? Would you rather fuck Santa Claus or the Easter Bunny?"

The shouted replies of the first player on each team mingled in an alarming calamity and then they were off. The other team members cheered and the spectators heckled through the megaphones of their cupped hands. A bolt of competitive spirit ran up Josh's spine.

He held his breath as the line sped toward Clara. *Please don't let her get flustered.* Josh could barely watch as the player in front of her, Stacy, scrambled. The other team gained on them as she attempted over and over again to land her cup. Josh gritted his teeth.

Shit. Now the round would end on Clara's turn and she'd feel awful again. He could hardly stand to see her upset. It was like watching a puppy with a broken leg. Josh chose not to examine why he cared so much that Clara fit in with his friends.

Finally, Stacy landed her cup. The other team would end it all at any moment. *God damn it.*

Except . . .

Josh's mouth fell open as Clara downed her entire beer in a single gulp and then flipped her cup on the first try, using only her index finger.

"What the hell are you waiting for?" Clara's cheeks were flushed and beer glistened on her lips as she yelled at him.

Josh shook off his stupor and flipped his own cup as Naomi floundered across from him. The cup landed after a few tries, winning the game at the last possible second in a blur of stale lager and admiring shouts from their team members.

Without thinking, Josh grabbed Clara around the waist and swung her in a circle, setting her skirt swinging.

She laughed in his arms, her grin gleaming against her cheeks. "Put me down, or I'll throw up all over you and then we'll both be in trouble."

"Josh loves trouble," Naomi said, crossing her arms and narrowing her eyes as she observed their embrace. He wanted to chalk up her sour expression to her reputation as a sore loser, but that didn't explain why he felt so guilty.

Immediately, he stopped spinning. With reluctance, he lowered Clara. A terrifying thought lit a fire in his brain. *Fuck.* If he wasn't careful, trouble might not be the only thing he loved for long.

The way he felt about Clara, heart pounding every time she entered a room, greedy for her approval, laughing at everything she said. He hadn't recognized the signals. Had always assumed he'd been born immune.

Clearing his throat, he popped open a new beer, letting the cold, bitter liquid linger on his taste buds like a wake-up call. *No. Not possible.*

"Where did that performance come from?"

She raised her shoulder toward her ear. "I've always been good at flip cup. Not that you asked." She stuck her tongue out at him and reached to help Felix arrange the next round.

Josh tried not to panic.

He didn't mind admitting he wanted to sleep with Clara. Or even that he liked her a lot as a person. Josh could talk to her more easily than most people, even about stuff he'd never shared with anyone else. But that didn't mean he wanted to be with her. He'd never wanted to be someone's boyfriend. All the responsibility and expectations. *No thanks.*

He couldn't be falling for her. He wouldn't. The laws of evolution shouldn't allow it.

Josh watched as Clara laughed at something Felix said. He furrowed his brow. What was so funny?

Naomi offered him a plate of spinach dip and crackers. "Don't do it."

"I'm not doing anything." He wiped his palms on his shorts before helping himself to the food.

"Good. Because it wouldn't work anyway." Even though Naomi used the same argument he'd made for himself a few minutes ago, he found himself balling his hands into fists.

His mother used to say, *If you want something to happen, tell Josh it can't be done.*

chapter twenty-one

♡ ♡ ♡

CLARA TRIED TO focus on her press release for Toni's latest fund-raising event, but she'd had to read the same paragraph four times because Josh kept emitting distracting sighs from across the studio. She rubbed the back of her wrist across her eye and ignored him.

Josh had sworn he'd only need twenty minutes to conduct a final equipment check before shooting began tomorrow, but they'd already spent over an hour here while he obsessively inspected their modest workspace.

The setup certainly looked professional. Their skeleton crew, two film students from UCLA, had rented all the necessary lights, cameras, microphones—everything. Naomi had come by earlier and given the green light, but Josh refused to take anyone's word for it.

Clara should have told him to go without her when he brought up driving out to Burbank after dinner. But he'd offered her a set of his spare keys that morning, and she didn't want him to think she was rejecting his gesture.

At least she'd brought her work with her. Between the PR firm and all the extra hours she'd put in over the last few weeks on Shameless, she'd been burning the candle at both ends. If she didn't finish this round of re-leases for tomorrow, even her extremely laid-back aunt would have her hide.

Another pitiful sigh made her look up, only this time she found Josh flat on his back, thrusting his hips in the air.

She gaped at him as her eyes inhaled the sensual image. "What on earth are you doing?" He should realize she didn't have time to sift through any less-than-friendly feelings she might have developed for him. To figure out where the boundaries of living together, working together, and now canoodling fell. She'd made the executive decision to blame everything on repressed hormones and move along. She desper-ately hoped he'd done the same.

Josh paused midthrust and covered his face with both hands. "They framed the shot all wrong. The angle's too wide. They'll cut off Lance's feet."

"Are you sure?" Clara vaguely remembered Lance from auditions. He had some *very* unique piercings.

"I'm almost positive. Do me a favor, look through the lens and tell me if you can see my whole body in the shot." Josh held the bridge posi-tion with annoying ease. As far as she could tell he didn't submit to a traditional exercise regime outside of running. All those muscles just from sex? *Despicable.*

She cautiously approached the tripod and stood on her tiptoes to peer through the viewfinder. "You're right. It cuts off at your knees."

Josh got to his feet and turned his gaze to the ground. "Shit. We're going to have to redo all of this gaffer's tape. Somehow they blocked everything a foot to the right."

"Can't we just move the camera?"

"Not unless you want to move all the lights and the boom. We'd need a ladder." He pointed at the vaguely feather-duster-looking thing mounted above his head.

Clara took in the fluorescent tape scattered across the ground. "Those little marks are where the performers go?"

"Yeah. Ginger and Lance came in this morning and Naomi blocked all the positions for the intro scene."

"So we need to move the tape? That sounds simple enough."

"Sort of. In order to know where the new tape goes, we'd need to reblock all of the performers' positions. We're probably close enough to their heights, but . . ."

Clara's palms grew slick. "What kind of positions are we talking about?"

Josh's eyes flashed. "Ones that make it easier for women to orgasm during intercourse."

Her pulse picked up as she wandered closer to where he stood. She'd been afraid of that. "All right." The words wavered as she wrestled to control her excitement. Despite her best efforts, she couldn't seem to call forth her defenses against touching him. Her chest filled with anticipation. "Let's run through the positions quickly. I'm exhausted, and I still have to find an accessible synonym for *magnanimous*." She frowned so he wouldn't see that she'd agreed to this salacious exercise to take advantage of his incredible body.

Josh blinked a few times. "I'm sorry, are you offering to simulate all of the sex positions required for the scene?"

His incredulous tone made her question herself. "I thought you were suggesting that's what we needed to do?"

"Oh." Josh rocked back on his heels. "Yep. That is what's needed. No way around that." He immediately went into a crouch and started ripping tape off the floor.

Once they had a clean slate, he got behind the camera and motioned for Clara to stand at a specific position. "Stay right there."

He ran around and lay down so his shoulders lined up with the current position of her feet. "Okay. So now you straddle my thigh and place the tape at our feet."

Why did both *straddle* and *thigh*, two seemingly innocuous words, sound filthy coming out of Josh's mouth? "But . . . I'm wearing a skirt."

His breath caught. "I could straddle your thigh?"

She massaged her temples. His long body was laid out before her like a horny feast. "Just tell me which direction to face."

"On your knees with your back to me, put one of your legs on either side of my left leg."

Clara held on to her hem as she carefully lowered herself into position, until her butt was almost but not quite aligned with Josh's groin and her calf rested against his inner thigh. How anyone had the confidence to attempt a maneuver this complicated while naked was beyond her.

She couldn't for the life of her figure out how their necessary body parts would align. "Where does my foot go?" She shifted backward until her sneaker slipped, slamming into something that forced an agonized wail out of Josh.

"Oh God. I'm so sorry." She scrambled to her feet and stood helplessly as Josh rolled into the fetal position, clutching his unmentionables. "Should I go get an ice pack?"

"I'm fine." The vein throbbing in his neck said otherwise.

"What if there's permanent damage? The women of America will need a day off to mourn the loss of Josh Darling's prized asset."

"Please stop talking." His eyes welled with tears.

Clara watched helplessly while he took slow, deep breaths for several minutes, until he eventually unfurled his body. "You can get back into position now," Josh said with decidedly less enthusiasm than the first time he'd instructed her to kneel. "Gently."

Once she'd done as bidden, Josh ripped off a few pieces of tape from the roll with his teeth and handed them over. "Mark little *X*s by each of our feet."

She leaned toward his toes in acquiescence and felt her skirt travel with her. "Are you sure ladies like this?"

"Yes." Josh's voice had gone rough. "It's a similar concept to reverse cowgirl. You're in control of the depth, the speed, the angle." He shifted his hips. "Let's, uh, get into the next position."

She hesitated. "I don't want to hurt you again."

He waved dismissively. "Don't worry about it. My dick's insured."

Clara flung her hand to her heart. "Are you serious?"

"No. Of course not." Josh brought the weight of his upper body onto his elbows. "But I really like that face you just made. The next position is girl on top. So if you can—"

"I know what girl on top is." Clara tried to retain a ladylike demeanor as she adjusted her straddle. She purposefully perched on Josh's lower stomach, rather than risk entering the danger zone below his belt, and fluffed out her skirt so she wasn't flashing an exorbitant amount of thigh.

She pushed her hair behind her ears. "Is this right?"

"Almost." Josh pressed his hand gently against the middle of her back.

"What are you doing?" Her voice came out sounding more like a squawk. She'd managed to get this far without encountering his erection. Not that he necessarily had one. He probably didn't. Considering she'd almost unmanned him. Also, he did this stuff for a living, minus the layers of fabric. She schooled herself into a professional expression.

The heat of Josh's fingertips through the silk of her blouse sent pleasant tingles up and down her spine. He guided her until their chests came into contact. "We're going for this angle."

"I see," she said, trying not to notice the way her nipples rubbed against his chest each time she breathed. "I always thought I should sit up straight. You know, for leverage. This is much more intimate." She inhaled through her nose as she studied the hard line of his jaw. "But I don't have as much room to . . . bounce." Surely steam poured from her ears.

Josh dimpled at her. "You don't actually need to bounce. I mean you can, the view would be nice." He dropped his gaze for only a moment. "But in the tutorial, we're suggesting more of a rocking motion to get your clit in contact with my pubic bone." To his professional credit, Josh delivered the titillating description with a straight face.

"How would that work?" She could barely get the words out. His scent, a heady mixture of skin and soap, had caused a fog of lust to roll in and cover half her brain.

"I could show you, but I'd . . . uh . . . have to put my hands on your ass."

"That would be all right," Clara said with as much dignity as she could muster. What had happened to her willpower?

Josh cupped her behind, bunching the delicate fabric of her skirt until the tips of his fingers seared her bare skin. His eyes fluttered closed as, from that point of leverage, he ground her against his pelvis in a fluid figure eight.

Holy shit. She bit her lip to keep from moaning. Riding the rough denim of his jeans through only the thin cloth of her underwear created an exquisite friction. "Oh my God."

"Are you okay?" Josh froze, clenching his jaw so hard a muscle twitched in his cheek.

Clara murmured confirmation and squeezed her eyes shut. If she opened her mouth she'd say something desperate. Something filthy. She knew she could come like this if he repeated that motion.

Josh shifted his grip to her hips. "We still have to place the tape." His breathing had gone ragged.

Clara couldn't believe she'd ever wasted a second of her sex life on any position but this one. She pressed her palms to the floor on either side of his face, rocking over him as her breasts dragged across his chest.

When she opened her eyes he was gazing back at her.

She bit her bottom lip hard enough to taste blood. Dry-humping was tragically underrated.

"Damn it, Clara. You're driving me crazy."

He brought his hands back to her ass and opened the span of his fingers so he could knead her overheated skin.

Clara wantonly rubbed herself against him as her pleasure built. "Oh God. I'm close."

His grip grew rough enough that she imagined she'd wake up tomorrow to imprints of his fingertips. The idea made her shiver against him. "Don't stop."

"Whatever you say." Josh grunted as he dragged her lower this time, across his unmistakable erection.

"You know, it works even better if you take off your clothes," Naomi said in a dry voice from inside the room.

Josh and Clara both scrambled to their feet, or at least they tried to. Her feet slipped on the shiny laminate flooring and she waved her arms wildly, trying to regain her balance.

"Fuck," Josh said as Clara's elbow slammed into his solar plexus.

"Not quite." Naomi examined her manicure. "But I'm sure if I'd shown up ten minutes later . . ."

Clara opened her mouth to apologize or explain. Whichever came out first.

"I'm a patient woman, but if you utter the words *this isn't what it looks like*, I am going to lose my shit."

Josh's low voice contained traces of both weariness and warning as he said, "Stu—"

"Clara, would you please give us a moment?" Naomi bared her teeth like a rabid panther.

Indecision locked Clara's feet to the floor. On the one hand, she probably shouldn't abandon Josh. After all, it took two to drop down and gyrate. On the other hand, Naomi was his ex. An ex that he still hoped to reconcile with, last she'd heard. Perhaps he wanted the opportunity to explain the problem with the tape directly? Clara hardly wanted to stand around and listen to Josh write off her amateur response to what the two professionals probably considered an everyday ask.

She gathered her things slowly, giving Josh plenty of time to signal if he needed moral support. She even bent to retie her shoelaces.

"Clara, it's okay." He kept his eyes locked on Naomi. "I'll meet you in the car."

As she fled, a thousand scenarios for what was going on back in the studio ran in Technicolor through her mind. Each one more incendiary than the last. She started the engine and turned on the radio. Because the two most likely outcomes of a disagreement between Josh and Naomi were yelling and screwing, and in either case, she didn't want to hear it.

NAOMI POINTED A menacing finger directly at Josh's heart. "You can't turn it off, can you?"

Josh sighed. He was already drowning in the quicksand of his feelings for Clara. The last thing he needed right now was a lecture from his ex-girlfriend.

"I can't believe you would gamble all of our futures to get your dick wet."

He reached out and batted Naomi's hand away. "Don't talk about her like that. Clara and I are not having sex." At least, not the kind Naomi was accusing him of. Jesus, when had his life gotten so complicated?

"Wow." Naomi took a step backward that set her dress swinging around her knees. "I never thought I'd see the day when you'd lie to my face." She spread her arms out away from her body. "I knew this was gonna happen. I knew as soon as she moved in. You can't resist a woman that will never commit to you."

Josh rejected the burn of embarrassment in his throat. "You don't know what you're talking about. We were fixing a blocking mistake. One that you didn't notice, by the way." Had they both needed to get on the ground? Probably not. But Clara had on that flirty little skirt with pleats and he couldn't help himself.

"I did not make a blocking mistake." She stomped over to the camera mount and peered through the lens. "Are you talking about the framing of the shot? Josh, I had the wide angle professionally cleaned." She pulled the expensive lens out of her purse. "That's the standard on the rig. I came back to switch it out. Now, thanks to your amorous shenanigans, I have to move Lance and Ginger's call time tomorrow up an hour to fix this mess."

He rubbed the back of his neck. "Oh."

That made sense. *Shit.* He'd been nervous about having everything ready. Add in the increasingly dizzy feeling he got whenever Clara came within ten feet of him, and he'd clearly jumped to conclusions.

Naomi tapped her foot. "Besides, even if I *had* made a mistake, what you two were doing was not blocking."

"Jesus. You're right. Okay? Look, if it makes you feel any better I got kicked in the balls for my efforts." He still had a vague stomachache. "You think I don't know that Clara Wheaton is an impossible pull? She's a rich, cultured genius and I'm a degenerate college dropout with more dick than brains."

Everyone thought it was the jealousy thing you had to worry about when trying to date in his line of work, but that was only the tip of the iceberg. Jealousy assumed that nonindustry people accepted the moral and social implications of his profession. That they wouldn't mind introducing someone who made porn to coworkers and parents. That the object of your affection could imagine standing up next to you in front of friends and family and declaring love and allegiance to someone who large swaths of the rest of the world considered unclean. Clara had been clear that her family would never accept him.

Naomi's eyebrows shot together. "When was the last time you had sex?"

He looked at the ceiling, trying to remember. A vision of Clara, her eyes closed and her mouth open as she arched her back in pleasure, entered his head. Clara didn't count. Now that he came to think about it, maybe there hadn't been anyone for a while.

"Too. Long," Naomi snapped. "If you have to think about it, it's been too long."

"I've been busy." Starting a business was significantly more labor intensive than he'd assumed when he signed up.

"Yeah," Naomi scoffed. "Busy falling for someone completely inappropriate. Did you ever stop to think about all the people who could get caught in the crossfire if you break Clara's heart? What's gonna happen to Shameless when the two of you can't stand to be in the same room together?" She ran her hands through her hair. "If she pulls our funding, we're done."

"Who says I'd break her heart?" He didn't want to hurt Clara. Yes, he wanted to fuck her. But he'd fucked lots of people and they all seemed to like it. For the first time in a long time, he had a lot more than sex on his brain. That impossible word sprang to mind again, but he tucked it away. Later, when he was alone, he could let it out of its box and examine it.

"Don't insult me by pretending you don't know what I'm talking about," Naomi said.

It was Josh's turn to throw his hands in the air. "What you're talking about is none of your business."

"None of my business? Josh, you're the one who made this my business. And not just me. What about all the performers we convinced to follow us on this suicide mission against Pruitt? What happens to them when the paychecks dry up?"

"All right." He held up his hands. "You've made your point. I'll back off Clara."

"Swear to me." Naomi held out her hand expectantly.

Josh stared at her bloodred fingertips and tried not to let his fear read on his face. "Don't be dramatic."

"Do I look like I'm acting right now? Swear to me that you won't have sex with Clara or enter into any other kind of screwy romantic entanglement, or I'm walking off this project tonight." She shoved her hand at him until he clasped it briefly with his own.

"Don't you think you're being a little hypocritical right now? You and I did it." He wanted Stu to tell him it was okay. That of course he and Clara could find a way to make it work. He wasn't entirely sure he'd survive the alternative.

"I can't believe we're still having this conversation. You and I never exchanged money. But more importantly, you know as well as I do the only reason our relationship worked was because, for the most part, we left each other alone."

She had him there.

"I never pushed you and you never tried to rein me in. We always owned up to the fact that we were two people who liked to fuck each other, desperately trying to keep the cameras rolling." She gave him her signature smile. The one where she barely moved her mouth, but her eyes sparkled. "I liked you 'cause I never had to worry about you falling in love with me, Josh."

He hated when she was right. "For the record, you are lovable. If you'd give anyone half a chance."

Naomi shrugged. "In that case, I guess we'll never know."

Josh swallowed hard. He had to ask. "What if Clara's different?" He knew it wasn't right. That he'd let his infatuation with his roommate go too far. But his feelings for her were too messy, too powerful, to reel back now. In the grand scheme of things, was loving Clara Wheaton really so bad?

Naomi shook her head. "Nobody's different. They all want the fantasy, but nobody wants the reality."

"I'm serious, Stu. You should have seen her when I wanted to quit. This whole thing, this insane idea, she did this because she believes in me." He scrubbed his hand across his face. He couldn't reconcile Naomi's words with Clara's actions. "It sounds ridiculous, I know, but for the first time in my life someone wants me to live up to my potential. Whatever the fuck that means."

"I know." Her mouth sat in a thin, straight line.

"She thinks she's soft, but sometimes she gets this look in her eyes. I don't even know how to describe it."

Naomi sighed. "Like she could eat nails for breakfast."

Josh smiled at his shoes. "Yeah."

When Naomi spoke, her voice came out deadly serious. "That's why I made you swear."

chapter twenty-two

♡ ♡ ♡

EVERYTHING THAT COULD go wrong did on the morning of Clara's first big presentation to Toni Granger's campaign team.

She overslept, having forgotten to set an alarm the night before. She ran out of toothpaste, stubbed her toe in the living room on one of Everett's wayward amps, and now, worst of all, the bus to Malibu, her archnemesis, had gone MIA.

Not for the first time that morning, she wished Josh were home. He'd driven her in to work before, but she'd barely seen him since shooting for Shameless had started a few days earlier. After dropping her off last night, he'd gone back out in a cab to meet some of the crew for drinks and hadn't returned.

She tried not to let herself linger on the way Ginger's eyes had gobbled him up every time he gave her a scene direction last night or how Naomi could still call him to heel with a whisper. Had he spent the night with one of them? Or, she gulped, *both* of them? Her heart swam up between her ears and she closed her eyes against the ache. How Josh spent his free time wasn't her concern, but that didn't mean she didn't care.

Besides, likely she was overreacting and he was merely busy with business matters. She couldn't deny that Shameless created a black hole of work. But she also couldn't shake the feeling that his sudden absence from the house coincided more specifically with Naomi walking in on them at the studio the other night. When he'd finally returned to the car afterward, Josh had been unusually quiet, opening his mouth only long enough to ask her, "You wanna drive?"

She'd stolen glances at him at every stoplight on the way back to West Hollywood, trying to suss out his thoughts, but the night sky had painted his face in shadow, reducing him to jawline and cheekbones and the hollows beneath his eyes.

The car filled up with the words she wanted to say but couldn't bring herself to utter. Men like Josh didn't entertain questions like *What's going on between us?* from girls they hadn't even slept with.

Clara tried to school herself into a calm and detached demeanor, but instead, she'd grown absent-minded and clumsy. Almost as if Josh's presence in her life had been the rope tying her boat to shore and he'd suddenly cut her adrift.

She swiped the back of her hand across her damp brow and, keeping one foot on the sidewalk, looked down the street. Nothing.

She checked her watch. 8:07. If the bus arrived within the next three minutes, she would only be five minutes late for her meeting with Toni. Five minutes late to a nine-thirty meeting was plausible with L.A. traffic. Not good, but excusable. The kind of thing you could play off with a charming apology.

8:08. Each minute she waited took away her options for alternative transportation. They'd entered prime time for L.A. commuters. If she called a car at this point it would take them twenty minutes to get out here.

She had no choice but to call Jill.

Her boss picked up after only one ring, so Clara knew she too had been obsessively counting down to the meeting. "Hey, what's up?"

Clara heard the faint cracks in her aunt's practiced calm.

Juggling the phone, she shifted the stack of printouts she carried to her other arm. "I'm so sorry. I overslept and now the bus is late." The truth tasted sour.

She'd overslept after staying up half the night waiting for Josh to come home. Somehow she'd let her feelings for him enter into treacherous territory. Every day the way she cared about him became less friendly, but a romantic relationship between them was impossible. Pathetically preposterous. Her family would flip if they knew she shared a roof with someone who made such excellent tabloid fodder. Besides, as far as she could tell, Josh didn't date. At least, not women like Clara. They'd let off steam together a few times. But like he'd told her that first week, he had no trouble separating sex from feelings. Clara wanted to believe that she'd learned her lesson when Everett left. So why did she feel so sick when she thought about Josh touching someone who wasn't her?

"I don't know what to do," Clara said, half to Jill and half to herself. "I've been here for twenty-five minutes already. You might have to start without me."

There was a long pause on the other line, and she could tell that her aunt, her boss, wanted to choose her words carefully.

"I can't start without you. You have the copies of the presentation. If you're not here when Toni arrives, I'm not confident she won't turn around and walk out the door."

Crap.

The stack of printouts in Clara's arms included weeks' worth of research, meticulous impression projections, and advanced ROI models. They'd been working tirelessly on this first-round campaign proposal for weeks. Not the kind of thing someone, even Jill, could re-create in thirty minutes.

"I could send you the file and you could print it at the office?" Anxiety clawed at her throat.

Jill sighed over the line. "With our ancient printer, it'll come out looking like garbage. That's why we went with professional-grade prints. I'll have to reschedule." Her clipped, resigned tone made Clara close her eyes.

So this was how it felt to let down people you loved. Her mother's face frowned from behind her eyelids. She'd seen that look directed at her father and Oliver countless times, but before moving to L.A., she'd never found herself in its direct trajectory.

Clara found herself hedging. "No, don't. I'll figure something out. I'll be there." What was that saying about making promises you weren't sure you could keep? She hung up before her brain could catch up with her mouth. *8:13.*

The heavy rays of the sun slammed against her back, threatening to liquefy her where she stood. Clara dug in her purse for a tissue, and her hand grazed cool, sharp metal. Josh's spare key. His vote of confidence.

She began walking the short block back to the house. Until the shiny black paint of the Corvette winked at her from the driveway. She imagined where Josh was at that moment, probably lying naked in bed, kissing the shoulder of last night's conquest. Clara's stomach threatened mutiny.

He would lose his mind if she drove his car without him. The idea of taking advantage of her key without permission made her shake her head at her own train of thought. She couldn't violate the only rule Josh had ever given her. Not to mention that the idea of driving alone made her legs shake.

But Jill needed her. Her aunt had taken a huge chance, hiring her to work on this high-profile project. Clara couldn't let the firm suffer the consequences for its most junior member's selfishness. She had to take responsibility for stretching herself too thin.

Josh did let her drive the Corvette almost every night to the studio *and* she'd bring it right home after the meeting. After pulling his number up on her phone, she stared at the digits. *8:15.* Who was she kidding? If she asked he'd definitely say no and then she'd be out of options.

Clara curled her fingers around the key until the edges bit into her palm.

Please don't let him hate me for this. With one last glance down the street for the bus, she ran to the car.

The thirty seconds when she had to move the driver's seat to accommodate her short legs almost stopped her in her tracks. The seat seemed to resist sliding forward, like the 'Vette wanted to save her from herself. Silence smothered the empty interior as she turned the key in the ignition until the sudden roar of the engine made her jump.

Josh would understand. He had to.

"This isn't so bad," Clara said to the empty passenger seat a few minutes later. If she kept up a steady stream of conversation, she could almost pretend Josh rode with her.

But then the adrenaline started to wear off and panic threatened to claim her.

She gulped as she sped up to keep with the flow of traffic. So far she'd only had to merge twice.

As she tried to relax her grip on the steering wheel, she realized her fingers had gone slightly numb. The second the meeting ended, she and Jill would take the car back, and Josh would never be any the wiser. She practiced her lines for the presentation over and over in her head.

At last, she exited the interstate and slowed at the four-way stop sign a few blocks from the firm.

Almost there.

The Corvette made it about halfway across the intersection before Clara heard the familiar squeal of rubber against pavement followed by a metallic crunch.

chapter twenty-three

♡ ♡ ♡

EXCUSE ME, MISS? I'm looking for suspected felon Clara Wheaton."
Josh entered the hospital room in last night's rumpled clothes. Despite the teasing tone, he had dark circles under his eyes, obvious traces of strain.

His familiar presence washed over Clara, soothing her in a way nothing else had.

"Josh," she said the way someone might utter *Wow* as they watched a shooting star pelt across the sky.

But then she remembered. Remembered that she didn't deserve to have him rush to her bedside like some fairy-tale knight in shining armor. She sucked in a shaky breath and fought off the threat of tears, unwilling to risk Josh offering her sympathy instead of the scolding she'd earned.

It felt like weeks since she'd seen him, rather than hours. She'd grown too accustomed to having him around. To the breadth of his shoulders and the steep slope of his nose. To the way he made her laugh even when her brain insisted on working overtime. Clara had taken the gift of his kindness and crushed it under her heel. Why did he always look so handsome? She tore her eyes away from his face long enough to notice the slightly limp bouquet clutched in his fist. The inevitable avalanche of her sobs burst forth.

"Whoa there," Josh said. "Hey, now. Are you in pain? Do you want me to get a nurse?" He moved closer to her bed, his face drawn, and brought the back of his hand to her forehead.

"What are you doing?" She hiccuped, looking up at him from under his palm.

The tops of Josh's ears went pink. "It always made me feel better when my mom did it. Like whatever hurt was being taken seriously." He swiped at the tracks of her tears with his warm thumb.

She had stolen his car and ruined their friendship. Why was he so calm? So sweet? Her shoulders tensed, waiting for him to yell or, worse, quietly express his disappointment.

Josh must have mistaken her guilt for pain because he said, "Easy, tiger. You've had a big day," and then, seemingly remembering the flowers in his other hand, he placed them gingerly on her lap.

Her heart rate monitor picked up. It was stupid and vain, but Clara hated that he was seeing her in her hideous hospital gown. She considered this whole scene overdramatic for what amounted to a glorified fender bender. The damage to her pride would take longer to heal than her body.

Despite her protests that she was fine, just shaken, the EMTs at the scene had insisted she go to the hospital to get checked out when her blood pressure wouldn't come down. She'd tried to explain that the physiological response stemmed from concern about her roommate's and boss's reactions, but her reasoning had not mollified the medical professionals.

At least they'd let her sign a release form and ride with Jill, who had left Toni Granger in the waiting room to rush to her side, instead of making her ride in the ambulance. Once at the hospital, she found no effective argument against the hours-long series of tests and waiting. She had only just managed to convince Jill to go back to the office and run damage control when Josh arrived.

Clara pointed her chin at the ceiling in an effort to slow her water-works. If she looked at Josh she'd lose it again. Why was he acting like she hadn't done this awful, selfish thing? If her family had taught her anything, it was that when you let people down you suffered the consequences. Hurt feelings at best, news articles and jail time at worst. You didn't get flowers and you certainly didn't get affectionate nicknames.

"Sorry, they're a little smushed." Josh turned the flowers so the less crushed side faced her and held them under her nose. "I, ah, may have accidentally sat on them on the ride over."

Her heart throbbed, two sizes too big for her chest. His sweetness tortured her guilty conscience. "I'm so sorry, Josh. I know you must be livid, but whatever happens, I'll make sure your car comes out of this whole thing as good as new."

A tiny wrinkle appeared between his brows. "Wheaton, I could give two shits about the car right now. Someone tried to mangle you." He was still holding her face in his hand, stroking back and forth over her jawline like she was made of glass.

"That's not exactly true. The guy got confused. He's from out of town, like me, and isn't used to driving in L.A. and he felt so terrible, Josh. He really did. He was a wreck." She pictured the older man with salt-and-pepper hair and a big mustache sitting on the curb next to her with his face in his hands.

"Mm-hm," he said, noncommittal. His eyes traced over her face and neck, her arms, and he even peeled back the blankets to inspect her legs. "Where are you hurt?"

"I have whiplash in my neck and shoulders. The seat belt did more damage than anything." *I'm mostly worried you'll never forgive me when you see what I let happen to your car.*

"Jesus." He traced a finger very lightly over the angry red line cutting across her clavicle. "They keeping you here?"

Clara shivered, but not from pain. Somehow his gentle handling wrought more havoc on her heart than any of their previous flagrant gyrating.

"No. They've run all the tests and everything came back clear." These touches probably meant nothing to him, but Clara had once spent thirty minutes convinced that letting her thigh touch a boy's at the movie theater equated to a steamy moment of intimacy. "Last thing I heard they were processing discharge papers. How did you even know where to find me?"

Josh stepped back and took his hands with him. "The police called me. My name is on the car's registration. Don't worry, I told them I'd given you the all clear to borrow the car, so you're not in trouble." He looked at his shoes. "I wish you had called me. Lance had too much to drink at the bar last night so I crashed on his couch to make sure he was all right. If I'd known you needed help, I would've come home sooner."

Clara sank back into her pillows. "I panicked. I wanted to call you, but I thought you'd be mad."

"Why don't they put any chairs in here? Scoot over, would ya?" His tall frame filled the space she'd made for him and then some. "I *am* mad, you little jerk. You scared the crap out of me. I got home and the car was gone. No note. Nothing." He shook his head. "I went wild. I thought someone stole it and I didn't know if you'd been home at the time. If they'd tried to hurt you."

Josh reached up and pushed her hair off her forehead. His eyes searched hers.

"You shouldn't have borrowed the car without asking me. But if you thought for one second something like that would have stopped me from coming for you when you needed me . . ." He gave her a smile sexy

203

enough to take out a whole legion of nurses. "Well, then you're not as smart as you think you are."

She brought her hand to her heart, hoping in vain to prevent it from escaping the cage of her body. "I'm still sorry. You have no idea how sorry. I took the car because I didn't want to let Jill and Toni down."

She folded her hands in her lap. "I'm not trying to excuse myself. There's no excuse for what I did, but I thought you deserved to know why. I make myself really sick over not meeting other people's expectations." Clara released a hollow laugh. "But even when I try, I still end up hurting people. I'm really sorry that this time you were one of them."

"Clara." Josh tilted her chin until she met his eyes. "What you're talking about? That kind of perfection? It's impossible. You're never gonna please everybody. Don't get me wrong. You're good, but nobody's *that* good."

Clara pressed her face into his chest, so he wouldn't see the return of her embarrassing tears. He smelled sweet, like powdered sugar. "Did you buy donuts again?"

He rested his chin on top of her head. "What, are you a bloodhound? Yes, okay, I got you a 'get well' donut when I picked up the flowers, but the traffic on the way over was terrible and I had to eat it. For sustenance. It was an emergency."

"I deserve that," Clara said, trying to hide the amusement in her voice.

"You did crash my Corvette."

"Very true."

"You wanna know how I got that car?" He took her hand in his, drawing little circles over her knuckles with his thumb.

"Is this story going to make me feel better or worse?"

"Well, it belonged to my grandfather."

"I wrecked a family heirloom? Seriously?"

"No. No, listen. I'm not done. Here. Drink this water." Josh thrust the plastic cup from her nightstand into her hand.

"So my granddad bought the 'Vette back in 1976. Called it his midlife crisis car. Anyway, he loved it. All through my childhood, I have these memories of him waxing and buffing the thing. My grandmother said he wanted an excuse to stand next to it."

Josh tucked the blanket carefully back around her legs from where it had slipped.

"Anyways, when I was old enough to drive there was no way in hell my parents could afford to buy me a car. Not a single fucking chance." He accentuated the story with wild hand gestures. "But I got home one day after school and there was my grandfather with the Corvette parked in the driveway, holding out the keys."

Clara warmed at the animation in Josh's face.

"I couldn't believe it. I told him I couldn't accept it. Even though it was a total babe magnet, I knew how much he loved that car. But he looked me in the eye and said, 'Take it. Please. Giving her to you, making you happy, feels better than the day I got her.'"

Josh took her empty water cup and returned it to the table. "For me, that car has always represented the idea that people are more important than things. Even things you love. Watching you driving this summer, conquering your fear, hell, even imagining you gathering your courage to start that engine by yourself this morning . . ." He looked up, catching her eye. "Somehow, it feels better than the day I got her."

"That's a really good story."

Josh shifted so he could lean back against her pillows and gingerly put his arm around her shoulders. "Thanks, I thought so."

"Josh, how am I ever going to make this up to you?"

"I wouldn't worry about it, Wheaton," he whispered, pressing his lips against her temple. "You look extremely goofy in that hospital gown and it's going a long way."

chapter twenty-four

♡ ♡ ♡

"OW...OWWW...OW...OW!"

Josh could hear Clara alternately yelping and whimpering through the bathroom door where she'd locked herself after insisting she could manage to shower alone despite her whiplash. The doctor had agreed to discharge her with the recommendation that she rest and take ibuprofen twice a day until the pain subsided.

Clara refused to acknowledge that maintaining her stringent daily routine now included unexpected challenges.

He leaned his face against the cheap plywood separating them. He'd been standing outside the bathroom for fifteen minutes since she'd gone in, in case she fell or something and he needed to break down the door. "For Christ's sake, Clara, let me help you."

So far she had spent the morning waddling around like a lost duckling. From his perch at the kitchen counter, he watched her putter into the living room, sigh dramatically, and turn around. A few minutes later she wandered into the kitchen and opened the fridge before seeming to decide it was all too much effort and settling for handfuls of dry cereal out of the box. *His* dry cereal.

He offered to make her scrambled eggs or grilled cheese, his two specialties, but she told him she didn't deserve warm food after the mechanic said the 'Vette would be out of commission for at least a week.

She was acting like doing one bad thing could never be absolved, and it was getting on his nerves. Only someone who had never done anything wrong before would think borrowing a car deserved this level of self-flagellation.

He broke down and used the stupid three-knock system to request entry, browbeaten enough to employ her ridiculous household rule.

"Absolutely not," she shouted over the noise of the shower.

"Clara, this is next-level crazy, even for you. The doctor said you shouldn't raise your arms above your waist until the whiplash subsides. That's half your body. I'm the one who has to be around you all the time. If you stink, it's my nose that suffers."

The sound of the water abruptly cut out. "But you'll see me naked. Again. It breaks the guidelines for harmonious cohabitation."

"I saw at least twenty naked bodies this week alone shooting for the website and nothing happened." It was an occupational hazard. Years of on- and off-camera escapades had dulled his sexual senses. Even though they had worked with gorgeous women every day over the last few weeks it was like he was wearing earmuffs or dirty glasses during filming; nothing penetrated.

"I cannot express enough how your bruised and battered form is not going to send me into a sexual tailspin. This is all very simple. You're hurt. You smell. Let me in there. It'll be so impersonal you'll think you ran through a car wash."

A moment later, Clara opened the door, holding a towel around herself with one hand.

The tiny bathroom was easily ten degrees hotter than the hallway and full of steam. He blinked a few times to clear his vision. The combined effect of the environment and the sight of Clara with damp hair, her skin beaded with water was . . . arresting.

"Holy shit." Her cleavage made him see stars.

Clara pulled the towel tighter around her breasts. He didn't have the heart to tell her that the harder she pulled the material, the more he wanted to drown in the valley between her luscious tits.

Okay. So he might have miscalculated. Turned out he wasn't totally immune. He'd forgotten that being on set meant lots of people, working and talking and eating. It meant cameras and lights and costumes and makeup and other signals of artifice.

The intimacy of seeing Clara in such a small, heated space made him want to peel off that towel and lick every inch of her.

Fuck.

"I'm sorry," he said, turning away from her to pull himself together. He was probably scaring her. *She's wounded, you asshole. She needs help, not you slobbering all over her.*

He closed his eyes and thought about sitting in traffic.

He thought about getting his teeth cleaned. Sitting in traffic while getting his teeth cleaned. *There we go.* That did it.

He turned back around to find her with a drop of water running down the slope of her nose. His heart squeezed.

"Sorry," he said again around his thick tongue. "Overestimated my own endurance."

"What do you mean?" Her fragile voice broke through his lust stupor, at least for a moment.

He finally took in the blue and purple splotches blooming on her neck. He straightened his shoulders with renewed resolve to take care of her. "Just that I should have prepared myself more before I came in so that I could help you without sporting a rampant erection."

Clara's eyes wandered to his groin at his words. When she licked her top lip, the tiny gesture made him almost double over.

"Jesus fucking Christ." *Traffic. Dentist. Grandma Pearl.*

Clara's eyes widened. "I'm sorry. I didn't see anything. Honest." She kept her eyes firmly trained on the sink behind him.

"Let's get you clean." He remembered he was going to have to get in the shower with her. Naked. The guidelines did not cover this shit.

Clara seemed to have come to the same conclusion because she'd directed her gaze to the tile floor.

"We don't have to do this," he said, taking the coward's way out. "I could call Jill." Yes, Jill. Her aunt wouldn't be in danger of coming in her pants over Clara's convalescing body.

Clara's wet hair dripped into a little puddle at their feet. "It's fine. I'm fine. Are you fine?"

"Yep." Josh swallowed twice. "Fine."

She's just a naked woman. Just another naked woman. Seen one, you've seen 'em all. No big deal.

He ripped off his T-shirt like a Band-Aid. If he lingered in the act of undressing, his cock would continue to get the wrong idea. As he reached for the zipper of his jeans he made the colossal mistake of looking at Clara. The spark in her eyes, the hunger that she didn't know how to hide made his hands shake.

This is how I die.

He left his briefs on.

They would be clingy and uncomfortable once they got wet, but even that thin layer of cotton felt like a shield against the siren song emitting from Clara's skin.

He turned the knob to restart the hot water, holding his hand under the spray until it was warm enough to step inside the glass doors. "Ready?"

She held on to the towel for another long moment but then gave him a tiny nod and released it, draping the material over a hook by the sink before reaching for the hand he offered to help her step inside. There was about a foot of space in front of him for her to slide into.

Have mercy. He'd thought he'd be safe back here, out of the direct line of sight of her tits, but the sweet dip of her waist into her perfect peach of an ass was almost worse. Especially considering there was now only about four inches between his cotton-covered cock and her soft, slippery body.

When she turned to look at him over her shoulder, probably because he was breathing like an asthmatic, he ground out, "Turn around."

He hadn't meant for it to come out a gruff command, but he'd never get through this if he had to make eye contact with her.

Josh needed to unlearn his entire persona. Over the years he'd honed God-given charisma into a finely crafted weapon. He'd wielded his charm without thought for so long that Josh Darling became a natural extension of him, as unconscious as breathing. But he couldn't risk flirting with Clara, not now that he knew he might be falling for her.

He picked up her floral shampoo and poured some into his hand. Her head was a safe place to start. Nothing erotic about her hair. Besides how silky it felt.

"Close your eyes." The words felt jagged in his throat. He massaged his fingers across her temples with quick, efficient movements.

But Clara didn't play fair. She tipped her head back ever so slightly into his hands. He found himself slowing down, watching as her mouth fell open a little when he applied the right amount of pressure. She made tiny noises, breathy little moans, and he didn't know if they were signals of pleasure or pain.

"Is this okay?"

Clara bit her lip and nodded.

What was happening to him? He felt insane. Hadn't he done things fifty times filthier than this with five times as many women involved? Why was he falling to pieces over washing the hair of a pocket-sized WASP?

He kept his hands moving, down to the base of her skull, where he pressed in with his thumbs, making her gasp. It was becoming impossible to remember that this wasn't supposed to be foreplay, especially when he could easily see her puckered nipples over her shoulder.

After what felt like a million years strung up on a rack, it was time to rinse the suds from her scalp. He guided her under the spray of the shower, avoiding any unnecessary touching. He received a brief reprieve when the water ran clear . . . before he realized he still had ninety percent of her body to cover.

"Just gonna keep washing." He broadcast his mission for both of their sakes.

"Okay," Clara said, but kept her eyes closed. Probably so she could pretend this wasn't happening.

He picked up her body wash next, his eyes lingering on her lime green loofah. But as much as he knew he should, Josh couldn't bring himself to give up direct contact with her skin. The cool liquid heated quickly in his palm. Clara was so much smaller than him. He'd have to kneel to reach the bottom half of her.

Luckily the shower was long enough for him to come to his knees. Contact with the hard, cold floor momentarily brought his body out of overdrive.

"Hold on," he said, not knowing whether he spoke to her or himself.

Her eyes fluttered open like a princess waking from a dream, and he helped her put her hand on his shoulder for balance as he picked up her left foot and placed it on his bent thigh.

Any pretense of humility seemed to have burned up between them, replaced by another hot, pulsing emotion, as she bent forward to comply. Surely she was aware that this position presented him with an unobstructed view of her pussy?

He ran his soap-slick hands across her foot and around her ankle, massaging his way up her calf. Her thigh was taut as he glossed over it, and by the time his fingers reached her ass, she was thrusting her hips forward, issuing an invitation he didn't have the strength to refuse.

"Please don't do that," he choked out. "Clara, I can't stand it."

Her eyes shot open. "I didn't mean to. I wasn't trying to imply—I'm sorry." She went to turn off the shower, half her body covered in soap.

"No." The word came out too loud, ringing in the small space. He corrected his volume. "It's fine, remember?" Josh gritted his teeth. "Try to hold still."

He sped through washing the rest of her body, feeling like Keanu trying to defuse a bomb. Clara didn't close her eyes again.

Finally, he finished rinsing the thin skin behind her ears. He stepped back until his back pressed against the cold glass wall. "There. Done."

He deserved a fucking medal.

"Great," Clara said, standing under the spray with unsure eyes. "Thank you. For helping me." She curled her shoulders in.

Josh should probably make an excuse for his hard-on. There weren't enough dentists in the state to temper how much he wanted to fuck her right now. Of course, he wouldn't. He couldn't. Even if she wanted to. Even if she begged him. *Oh sweet Jesus, please don't let her beg.*

Why again? *Oh right.* Because he'd promised Naomi. He couldn't break his word. His vow. Shameless had come so far in the last few weeks. People were counting on him. He was finally making something important.

Clara took a step toward him, and then another, until he could have stuck out his tongue and licked her lips.

"What are you doing?" His voice came out gruffer than a cement mixer. Naomi screamed in his head. *No. Stop. Don't.*

Clara closed her eyes and tilted her head slightly, carefully.

Josh brought a shaking hand up to cradle her face. He wanted to kiss her so much it hurt. Had dreamed about tasting her so many times he lost count. Kissing Clara had become imperative. As if her full bottom lip held the antidote to a poison that had been pumping through his veins for months. All of the arguments against this moment flickered from his brain like blown bulbs.

Fuck it. He closed the last inch between them. Until their wet bodies pressed together from knees to chest.

Clara slipped and almost fell, squeaking as her chin landed against his shoulder.

Josh caught her under her arms. "Are you all right?"

She brought a hand to her head. "Yeah, I think so. I feel a little dizzy."

Shit. What if she had a concussion and they'd missed it? He grabbed a towel and wrapped it carefully around her before guiding her to sit on the closed toilet seat. "Stay here and put your head between your legs." That was what they said on TV, right? "I'll go get you a glass of water."

"Josh, I'm fine. It passed." She held out her hand and looked up at him, beads of water caught on her eyelashes.

"Don't worry," he said, backing out of the bathroom in his sopping briefs. "I'm not going to let anything else hurt you." *Especially me.*

chapter twenty-five

♡ ♡ ♡

JOSH TREATED CLARA like a pneumonia patient for the rest of the week. He went out and bought her chicken noodle soup and orange juice, both with and without pulp, despite her protests that there was nothing wrong with her immune system.

He flat-out refused to let her come to the studio after work, instead dictating that she needed time off to rest.

So tonight, while Josh instructed hot people how to get each other off, Clara found herself relegated to the more commonly accepted Clara Wheaton Friday night activity of cleaning out the inside of the fridge. She might even go crazy and descale the coffee maker.

Josh's message came through loud and clear. He didn't want her. Despite whatever "signs" her desperate heart presumed to detect, he'd gone so far as to run from the room when she offered him her naked body on a silver platter.

Apparently, sometimes a raging hard-on was nothing more than a biological consequence.

When the doorbell rang, she didn't bother removing her yellow rubber gloves before answering it.

"Are you Ms. Wheaton?" The delivery guy held a stunning bouquet.

"I am." She signed her name and carefully accepted the colorful flowers, waiting until she had her back to the closed door to stick her face in the middle of them and inhale. The manicured stems contrasted vividly with the plastic-wrapped wildflowers Josh had brought to the hospital.

She knew without looking at the card that they were from her father. Or rather that her mother had sent them using her father's credit card. Some women regularly received flowers from suitors, but Clara wasn't one of them.

No. With the recent exception of infirmity, she garnered bouquets not for her allure, but for graduations and birthdays. Even the occasional bittersweet Valentine's arrangement that smelled equally of freesias and pity.

She no longer indulged the girlhood fantasy of poetry accompanying her roses. So when she did glance at the folded greeting tucked behind petals, the signature made her hand fly to her racing heart.

C—Your mom left me a voice mail saying you were in an accident. She seemed to think I was taking care of you, so figured I could at least send flowers. Hope you're back on your feet soon. See you at the end of August. Love, E.

The word *love* struck her right between the eyes. She knew Everett didn't mean it romantically. He'd surely signed the card without thinking. The way she often scribbled out a missive to her great-aunt Barbara. But still.

She'd waited fourteen years for those four letters.

"*Love.*" The word got even better when she said it out loud.

Her mother had ignored her express wishes and called Everett directly to check up on her. The physical distance between L.A. and Greenwich did nothing to dim Lily Wheaton's tenacity.

Her stomach flip-flopped as she hunted for a vase. Everett would return in just over two weeks; there was a chance he'd see their last breath. An unfamiliar knot formed in her belly. She'd almost forgotten about Everett.

And she had one person to thank.

Clara didn't owe Everett any loyalty, obviously, but at the same time, surely when he returned things would change. Josh would move out, for starters. Why did that idea hurt?

She frowned. Surely, Everett coming home was good? Clara would finally have the chance she'd come to California for . . . but at what cost? Her days of plotting perfect lighting, nostalgic activities, and figure-flattering outfits felt so far away. Like plans that belonged to another person entirely.

With no vase in sight, she settled for a pot and arranged the bouquet to the best of her ability on the windowsill. Josh's flowers had already claimed the space on her nightstand.

She removed the rubber gloves and wandered into her bedroom. After several minutes of hunting, Clara found her Everett-snaring accessories in the closet, behind the raincoat she hadn't touched since she'd arrived. She carried the small hatbox out to the back porch. A trip down memory lane would remind her why she'd risked so much for the one that got away.

Settling herself in an Adirondack chair with peeling paint, she pulled out a handful of photographs. Her thumb snagged first on a shot of her and Everett from peewee soccer, arms slung around each other's shoulders. He had mud spattered across his cleats and shin guards, while Clara's uniform remained suspiciously pristine.

Everett had always picked her in gym class, even though everyone gave him a hard time. They were a pair. A foregone conclusion. Until they weren't.

She'd been so excited to come out here and renew their bond, but now she realized she was nervous about Everett's return to L.A. For better or for worse, when Everett left her on his doorstep, she'd had to write her own destiny for the first time. No one could have imagined she'd like freedom so much.

There were definite benefits to anonymity. The people here didn't immediately link her surname to the library or the wing at the hospital like people she met back east. No one said, *Oh yes. Of course I know your father* or *Such a shame about Oliver's insider trading snafu* five minutes after bumping into her.

In L.A., Clara had her own identity. The future wasn't carved in granite.

"Mosquitoes are gonna eat you for dinner." Josh came out carrying a citronella candle.

"They do love me," she agreed. He really was unusually thoughtful. The familiar notebook under his arm told her he'd come home straight from the set.

"It's late." He frowned. "You should be in bed."

"You have to stop mothering me. I'm totally fine. I could cartwheel right now." Assuming she'd ever learned to cartwheel.

Josh pulled up a second chair next to hers. "What are we looking at?"

She handed him the box of images. Sure, they contained evidence of several awkward phases, but Josh had already seen her stripped bare both emotionally and physically. She had nothing left to hide. Her heart hammered . . . reminding her of all the things she'd taken "off the table." *Fine. Almost nothing.*

The night had that unique summer energy when the air grows heavy and sparkling. When each breath in feels like freedom and the sky seems so glad to be rid of the sun it sighs in relief. If Clara wasn't careful, an evening like this could get her tipsy on its potential.

"Look at you." Josh lingered over a headshot from second grade. "Man, you look exactly the same. What kind of seven-year-old wears sweater-vests?"

Clara smiled sheepishly. "I picked that one out myself."

"Of course you did." He flipped her a shot from the middle school debate team. "I like those bangs."

"My mom loved that haircut. Even though I clearly don't have enough forehead to sport fringe." Clara wrinkled her nose. "It took me until eighth grade to stand up to her and demand to grow them out. There's a distinct headband phase in there if you keep digging."

"Wait, this one is the best." Josh passed her a faded Polaroid. This one featured Clara posing with a huge oak tree, exposing her terrible teeth pre-orthodontia. "I had a gap too."

"No way." Josh had a perfect grin complete with dimples.

"Oh yeah." He moved to light the candle with a matchbook from the pocket of his faded Levi's. "Huge gap. I thought it had personality with a capital *P*. I cried when I got braces and it closed up." Josh dug for more pictures. "Now wait a minute." He tapped the image with his thumb. "Who's this babe?"

Clara glanced at the image and then stared out into the darkness of the backyard. "That's my mom."

"You have her eyes."

But not her tiny waist or perfect poise. Not her patience or her self-control.

"I've never seen another pair your shade of slate."

Clara shifted in her seat. No one ever mentioned the color of her eyes.

"She didn't know the picture was being taken or she would have said it was undignified. See?" Clara pointed to her mother's bare feet. In the photo, Lily stood in the kitchen drinking a glass of iced tea with the sun setting behind her.

"She always liked to look put together, head to toe. It wasn't until the end of the day when she would come home and kick off her heels that I really recognized her. I used to think that was the signal that she was morphing from director of the board to mother."

"I bet she's a firecracker."

"Usually," Clara said. And then for some reason, "She cried the day I left. To fly out here, I mean. She's used to having me an hourlong train ride away."

Chirping crickets filled their silence.

"She wouldn't even drive me to the airport. Said I was being selfish, leaving her alone." Clara took a deep breath. "I think she was scared. My family's been through a lot, and my mom has always borne the brunt of it. Cleaned up other people's messes. I promised her she'd never have to worry about me, but then I woke up one day and everything in my life was disposable. Nothing was mine."

"So you came out here." Josh handed her a new image. Another shot of her and Everett, though this time from senior year of high school. Clara recognized the yellow dress and the sunburn on her nose from senior week.

Everett's arms and legs had filled out. He looked like a boy on the cusp of becoming a man. They sat on the hood of the Wrangler, waiting for graduation rehearsal to start. "It always ate at me," Clara said. "My mom got to choose her life, but I never once asked for what I wanted."

Josh propped his elbows up on his knees and sank his chin between his hands. "I didn't realize that you'd been gone on Everett that far back."

Clara nodded. "As long as I can remember."

The line between his brows grew deeper. "I don't get it."

"What do you mean?" The idea of wanting someone who didn't want you back? She had no trouble believing that Josh had never encountered that situation.

"You and this guy. Is it the butt-chin? The good family name? The inheritance?"

"No." Clara pushed her heavy hair off her neck. "Or I don't know. I guess none of those things hurt, but I think the real answer is simpler than any of that." She shook her head as the truth sank in. "I think I've wanted Everett for so long because he always held his love just out of arm's reach."

Josh fiddled with the sleeve of his shirt, avoiding her eyes.

"I was always looking for the right light switch. That one moment that would make him see how good we could be together. My life is built around rhythms and routine. Chasing Everett became familiar. Comfortable. No one would worry about me with Everett on my arm."

Beside her, Josh's shoulders tensed.

"God. That sounds so pathetic. I moved across the country, away from my family, my friends, and Everett barely saw me. Even when I was standing right in front of him." Her stomach swam with shame.

Josh shook his head. "You really have no idea, do you?"

Clara lowered the photo and brought her hand to her temple. "What?" She couldn't decide if she wanted a stiff drink or fourteen hours of sleep.

Josh stood up and began to pace across the porch. His shoes struck the wood with each jerky movement until he balled his hands into fists and planted his feet. "Fuck." She worried for his scalp when he ran his hand through his hair with alarming force. His chest rose and fell under his T-shirt.

"Listen, I can't think of a polite way to tell you that if that guy"—Josh pointed at the photo of Everett where it lay on the ground—"doesn't drop down on his knees and beg to fuck you, he's a moron." He threw up his hands. "If he doesn't wake up every morning and pray for the privilege of kissing you and touching you, and God, just looking at you, then something within him is deeply deranged."

Clara's mouth fell open. Every sound except Josh's voice faded away.

"Clara." Some of the darkness in his gaze receded. "If Everett can't see that you are epically, painfully beautiful, and so sexy"—he closed his eyes as if in pain for a moment—"that I practically rub myself raw thinking about the way your mouth moves, then he's the one who's pathetic and he's making the biggest mistake of his miserable life."

chapter twenty-six

♡ ♡ ♡

THE TRUTH HUNG in the air between them, and for a moment Josh knew both glory and triumph. Admitting the depth of his attraction to Clara, challenging her misconceptions about herself, made him feel like the tight band that had been wrapped across his chest for the past few weeks had finally been snipped.

But then that moment ended and he had to live in the aftermath of his words. As he took in Clara's enormous eyes, he realized he might have made a mistake. With a handful of clumsy, impulsive sentences, he'd unleashed a new reality. Had done the exact thing he'd sworn not to do. All of the stolen glances and lingering touches he and Clara had diligently skirted addressing rearranged themselves inside an alternative narrative: one where she knew he wanted her beyond physical desire.

Naomi would have him for breakfast when she found out about this. Impassioned speeches definitely counted as "funny business."

To his credit, he'd tried to avoid Clara, actively worked to create distance while he craved closeness. Hell, he'd even considered trying to sleep with someone else. To take the edge off. Unfortunately, the idea of other women made his balls threaten to curl up inside his body.

Maybe everything wasn't ruined. He'd merely defended her against slander. Friends did that for other friends all the time. Of course, most friends probably could have accomplished the task without multiple references to their genitals.

So he'd gotten a bit carried away. The idea that Clara wasn't desirable, wasn't inherently lovable, made him irrationally furious. Josh didn't claim extraordinary intelligence, but Everett Bloom was a first-degree fool.

Even in the oversized T-shirt and ratty boxer shorts she currently had on, Clara took his breath away. These days, the only part of her body that didn't make him hard was her chin.

Clara moved her mouth a few times, shaping different letters that didn't make it past her lips.

"What are you thinking?" His confession left him cracked open and bleeding at her feet.

"You're saying *you* want *me*?" The words trembled in the night air.

Shit. He'd hoped beyond hope they might avoid direct confirmation. The site was set to launch in less than a week. As much as he didn't want to admit it, Naomi had a point about his track record. But what could he do? Lie? Tell Clara no? That when he said he got off most nights thinking about her he'd meant it metaphorically?

"I definitely want you. But to be clear, I'm not asking for anything here. I know you don't think about me like that." Clara might find him sexy, but she'd never consider actually dating him. At least she hadn't asked him if he was in love with her. He'd never been any good at lying.

Clara gaped at him from her chair. "Uh . . . are you kidding?"

"I'm not kidding." He bent down and blew out the candle so he wouldn't have to meet her eyes. "But I've got zero interest in being your consolation prize. If you wanna wait for Everett to come back, we can forget this conversation happened, okay?" As elation faded, his insides turned black.

"So this is what it feels like," Clara said, so quiet he almost didn't catch it. "It's like someone shook a soda can and opened it inside my chest."

Josh winced. "Any chance that's pleasant?" It sounded painful, but something in her eyes made him hope.

She massaged below her clavicle, giving him a weak smile. "It's amazing."

He knelt down in front of her, slowly bringing his hands up to cradle her face. "How amazing, exactly? If you don't mind me asking."

Clara rubbed her cheek against his palm. "Let's just say when I imagine the most incredible moment of my life, I'm usually wearing a better outfit."

Josh ran his thumb across her jawline, mapping the topography of her face. As he drew their mouths closer together he watched her eyelashes flutter closed. "If you'd like, I'm prepared to help you out of these pajamas."

He captured her startled laugh with his lips, sighing as the first taste of her fell across his tongue. The scent of her floral shampoo, so familiarly tantalizing, surrounded him, bringing back lust-loaded memories of her—wet, naked, and wanting. Impossibly, holding Clara was better than he'd imagined. His whole body came to life under the press of her luscious kiss. At the risk of scaring her with the intensity of his craving for more, he tried to school himself into gentleness. He demanded that his body go slow. Tonight, Josh wanted to show her he was capable of more than she thought.

Clara's fingers threaded through his long curls and he shivered as she ran her nails against his scalp. Kisses were the hardest thing to fake on set. Josh had spent hours practicing how to tilt his head and move his mouth so that it looked like he cared. There was nothing performative about the urgency that powered this moment. The intensity of his desire mingled with joy walloped him over the head. Josh caught her bottom lip between his teeth, nipping the tender skin until she gasped.

Naomi was right. He was insane to gamble so much. Too bad he didn't care anymore. Drugged on Clara's softness, on the sweet sting of her bite as she delivered payback, Josh surrendered. How could anything that felt this good be bad? He pulled Clara to her feet. He wanted access to more of her. All of her.

As their mouths grew more frantic, kissing Clara no longer felt like a choice at all. Touching her, wanting her, felt as crucial as oxygen.

She ran her fingertips below the waistband of his jeans, making his stomach muscles clench. Why was he surprised she wanted the grand finale to this thing that had built up between them?

Josh caught her wrists in his hands. "Slow down. I'm trying to savor you." You only got one chance with a girl like this, and he didn't intend to waste it on instant gratification.

Clara let out a tiny whimper, and the sound shot straight to his dick. Relenting, he slipped one of his legs between hers. She seized the opportunity to rock against his thigh. If his cock had been halfway hard before, it could hammer nails now. When she lowered her mouth to his neck and applied pressure, he rolled his hips helplessly. With her body, Clara urged him toward the back door.

"You know, those cardigans of yours are deceptive. I'm not sure you're a nice girl after all." He ran featherlight kisses down her jaw and across her collarbone as his back smacked into the side of the house. "I can't believe this is actually happening."

Josh trailed his knuckles against the hot stripe of abdomen above Clara's shorts. His legendary control threatened to dissolve. He meant to kiss her so long and so well that her legs buckled, but already he was the one leaning against the wall for support. Clara hooked her leg up and around his waist, pressing herself against him shamelessly until he swore.

If only he knew whether she wanted Josh Darling or Josh Conners. The panic racing from his head to his body, making him shake, didn't come from stage fright. Something worse, something bigger made him lock his knees.

Over the last two years, he'd drained sex of any emotional component. Not only in his performances, but with Naomi as well. She didn't allow feelings to mix with her fellatio.

As he ran his fingers through Clara's hair, Josh wasn't just savoring. He was stalling. Fear had coupled with the desire singing in his veins.

He could fuck with the best of them, but this wasn't about fucking. Taking his clothes off tonight would test his ability to open not just his pants but his heart for Clara.

He brushed his hands gently up her sides to rest on her shoulders, ignoring her breasts so obviously that she let out a frustrated groan and pounded her fists against his chest in protest.

"I'm savored, I promise," she told him tartly, reaching for his zipper.

"Jesus." He hissed as he felt her hot little hands through his jeans. "You're perfect. Did you know that?"

He molded his hands to her breasts, giving them each exactly what they wanted. Josh sucked in a deep, ragged breath. "Fuck."

Clara arched into his touch. "Josh?"

He maintained his position but made eye contact with her. The white noise from the street thundered in his ears.

"We're about to have sex, aren't we?" She chewed her bottom lip.

He laughed, bringing his forehead to rest against hers. "Yes, Wheaton." He pressed a tiny kiss between her brows. "We're about to have sex." The idea of not living up to her expectations terrified him, but as he took in her flushed cheeks and her lush mouth, he knew he had no choice. He'd give Clara everything he had, even if it killed him.

chapter twenty-seven

♡ ♡ ♡

ARE YOU COMFORTABLE leaving the lights on?" Josh lingered by the doorway with his hair mussed from her fingers and his lips swollen from her mouth.

Clara's heart rattled against her rib cage. "Yes." In for a penny, in for a pound. She might have done a lot of crazy things in the last few months, but this one definitely took the cake.

Josh rewarded her answer with eyes that promised to watch as she came apart underneath him.

But still, Clara froze. She knew herself, knew that she'd never managed to separate sex from love before. And with Josh, the stakes were so much higher. She already liked him as a person, respected him as a professional, hell, she even knew they could successfully cohabit. Falling for him would be laughably easy, so sleeping with him should have presented an impossible risk. Except for one truth. Loving Josh went against every expectation she'd ever known. Every dream her family had ever set for her. Every future she'd ever imagined.

Maybe those walls would be enough to protect her. Maybe she could have amazing, mind-blowing, earth-shattering sex and still somehow be safe from a broken heart.

Unlike with Everett, this situation was clear. Josh hadn't promised her anything more than a culmination of the unyielding desire between them. He hadn't asked her on a date or to be his girlfriend. It seemed simple: if she could find a way to play by his rules, she could be happy. She could have Josh, for as long as they had left.

For once, take what's offered without expecting more. One night with Josh was more than most women could hope for in a lifetime.

"You're panicking." Josh crossed the room and reached for her hand.

"I'm not," she lied, keeping her gaze fixed on his shoulder. Was the bed too pedestrian a setting? Should she slink into the bathroom and put on something lacy? How on earth could she ever live up to his plethora of kinky experiences? She didn't have any whips or chains. No blindfolds or toys. Novelty and proximity were the only things she really had going for her. Should she dial up the "good girl" thing? Pretend she felt shy instead of wanton and feral?

"Hey." He tilted her chin. "We don't have to do this tonight if you're not ready." Josh tugged her against him and stroked his free hand against her hair before kissing the crown of her head. "I'll happily sit on the couch and make out."

"No," Clara said desperately, pulling back so she could bring her free hand up to his neck and hold him to her by his curls. She poured desire into her kiss, probably bruising him in her eagerness. "I mean," she said against his lips, "no, thank you."

Her body hummed with demands. His mouth should come with a warning label. Josh kissed her like a man come home from war. Like the thought of her alone had kept him warm across a thousand lonely nights.

They kissed until she clung to his neck to stay on her feet. Until her worries dissolved right out of her brain. Josh walked her backward to the bed, tearing at her clothes as he covered her body with his own. Thank goodness. Clothing had become an unbearable burden. She considered every second not spent with him touching her bare skin a second wasted.

His mouth worked hot and sweet against the pulse point behind her ear as he peeled her top over her breasts. Everything he did sent her into a lascivious tailspin. Until she scraped her blunt fingernails against his back through the thin cotton of his T-shirt.

"I don't have any moves," she warned him between heavy breaths as he divested her of her shirt entirely.

Josh sat back to look at her. Gold hair fell against his forehead, casting a shadow across his heated eyes. He discarded his own T-shirt haphazardly. "I'll worry about the moves." He pulled her into his lap so she sat astride him and took her earlobe between his teeth in a way that shot straight to her sex.

Clara let her hands ride the thick slabs of his shoulders. She wanted to taste him everywhere. Wanted him in ways she'd never wanted anyone—frantic and messy and completely out of control.

Helping her out of her sports bra without sparing the fabric a second glance, Josh stroked her bare breasts. As he teased her, Clara writhed from the acute ache he elicited.

"Please." She didn't have words to ask for all of the things she wanted.

He brought his mouth to replace his fingers, using his teeth to apply decadent pressure. Each flick of his tongue was flawless. She'd never considered her body especially carnal, but now she felt made for sex, engineered for pleasure from head to toe.

"Please what?" Josh sucked a love bite into the top of her breast.

Clara moved away from him to shove her boxers and underwear down and off, before sitting back and letting her thighs fall open. "Shut up."

He groaned and leaned forward, bringing his hand between her legs. "I knew you'd be like this." His gravelly voice made her shiver. "So hot for me. So ready. Have you thought about it?" Josh circled the tips of two fingers against her clit. Clara was wet enough that they could both hear it as he handled her. "About what I'd do to you if you ever let me?"

She bucked her hips and whimpered. "Yes. Oh God." Every night for months that passed like years. "Yes."

Josh closed his eyes for a moment as if he wanted to savor her confession.

Bending down, he lifted her hips toward his mouth, tracing over her slick flesh with his lips, teeth, and tongue. All of the things that Clara knew to be true, including the limits of time and space, ceased to exist. Josh wanted her. Every touch, every rough sound he made, confirmed the unimaginable.

Later, when he made her come on his tongue, she keened, feeling more animal than human as she dug her nails into the meat of his arms. Josh brought her down gently. His soothing touches prolonged her pleasure and prepped her body for more. "It's going to be tight." Josh's warning warred with his wild eyes.

"I don't care," Clara said when she could collect enough air to form words again.

Josh looked at her like she was something precious as he got to his feet. The purr of his zipper descending cut through the loaded silence. She let herself stare, gorged on the way his muscles moved under his golden skin. Clara licked her lips. She couldn't decide what she liked best. The curve of his jaw, the curl of his biceps, the flat planes of his stomach, the sharp dip of his hips. Her mouth went dry. *His thick cock.*

Clara inhaled, and let it out slowly. She'd seen the videos, had watched him touch himself, but now, confronted with the reality of his size and . . . girth . . . when it had a new destination . . . well, it wasn't that she wasn't game. Her thighs were soaked with how much she wanted him. But the math of it all remained hazy.

Had another man ever been so confident? So fluid and lupine as he stalked toward her.

Josh's skin was hot and sweat-slick as Clara leaned forward to run her hands across all the places she'd consumed with her eyes. "Your body is unreal. I know you know"—ab muscles contracted under her fingertips—"but I thought it was worth repeating." She dipped her thumbs into the harsh curve between his leg and his groin. "Really . . . ten out of ten."

Josh withstood her appraisal, let her take her time, until she caught his gaze and traced her tongue across her bottom lip.

"If you keep eye-fucking me like that, this is all going to be over before it starts." His voice had turned into a mixture of smoke and flame.

Bending down, he captured her mouth again, threading his hands in her hair. Between each of his drugging kisses, Clara's breathing grew more ragged.

She didn't want to laugh, knew you shouldn't laugh at a gentleman recently divested of his pants, but she let a small nervous giggle escape against his lips in spite of herself.

He pulled back. "What just happened?"

Clara covered her face with her hands. "Sometimes I have inappropriate reactions to stress."

This time the laugh came from him, and some of the tension left his shoulders. "Is my dick stressing you out?"

Clara curled her lips into her mouth and gave a tiny nod.

Josh winced and ran a hand down his face. "I get it."

"You do?" Had he guessed that she was too inexperienced to accommodate him? Was it somehow physically obvious?

"Yeah, I mean, I'm sure you're turned off thinking about my job. Probably wondering if I'm even capable of having sex without cameras . . ." He waved his hand in a broad sweeping gesture below his waist. His whole body carried signs of defeat, although to his credit that erection didn't budge.

Clara's eyebrows jumped together. *Turned off? Was he crazy?*

She tucked a loose strand of hair behind her ear and leaned forward. The quickest way to show Josh she loved his dick didn't involve words.

"What are y— Oh God." Josh sighed as she took the tip of his erection between her lips. His fingers shook as he slid them through her hair, and she lifted a hand, wrapping it around the base. He groaned as she ran her tongue around the head. Clara lifted her eyes, only to have her heart skip as Josh stared down at her with naked lust. Usually, her insecurities dominated this exercise, but this wasn't about her. It was about showing Josh how he drove her wild.

Judging by the way he swelled against the back of her throat as he held her gaze, Josh didn't care about her lack of finesse.

"Holy shit." Each expression and response rewarded her for her efforts. He pulled her hair away from her face into a messy ponytail, but still, he applied no pressure. Instead, he ran his fingertips soothingly against the base of her scalp, making her sigh around her mouthful.

"You're driving me insane, Clara. Look at what you do to me." His fierce brown eyes held intensity she hadn't expected, and when she balked and dropped her gaze he guided her head gently back up with his thumb across the apple of her cheek.

She took in the strain in his jaw as she moved, the way his eyes had gone heavy-lidded and hazy, how his neck went taut. Josh, usually so calm and collected, looked enraptured.

Clara kept her eyes trained on his face as she brought her hands to his ass. When she sank her nails in lightly, he threw back his head. The pulse in his throat jumped. Emboldened, Clara tried something she'd only read about in *Cosmo*. She hummed.

His grip on her hair tightened and he hissed through his teeth. "Clara." Her name came out more breath than word. Josh took a step back, his eyes tortured, frantic, as he pulled her to her feet so her back rested flush against his front.

"I've wanted you for months," he said against the shell of her ear.

"I'm done waiting." Josh traced his hand along her rib cage and hip before moving between her legs, inserting two and then three fingers while his other hand held her in place at her waist.

She gasped, clenching around him, breathless at the promise of being filled. All the oxygen in the room evaporated. Clara had to work twice as hard for every breath. Blood pounded in her ears so loud she worried it was affecting her vision. Every atom in her body demanded more. "Condom?"

He untangled himself from her long enough to pull out a foil packet from a bedside drawer and roll it on.

She lay back down, feeling languid and wired at the same time.

"Are you sure about this?" He returned to the bed to pour his body over hers.

The adoration in his eyes, both vulnerable and possessive, made her heart clench. In answer, Clara wrapped her legs around his waist.

The muscles working in Josh's throat highlighted his elevated pulse point as he positioned his hips. Clara sucked in air like someone had outlawed it as he entered her. The stretch of him was deep enough that she could almost feel it in her teeth. She had to breathe through her nose for a few seconds. Each time he exhaled the tiny movement felt like pressing her tongue against a live wire.

Josh kissed her temple. "Are you all right?" His voice shook as he held his body still.

"Yes." Clara gasped his name, using the word *please* as punctuation. Josh tortured her with pleasure until she dug her heels into his back.

He brought his hand down to where their bodies joined, applying steady pressure like an art form as he began to thrust. The wet slap as his hips met her ass echoed in her ears.

Her peak was so close, so close, so . . . "Oh God. I'm gonna . . ."

"Yeah?"

Her pussy tightened around him as she whimpered.

Josh pulled her closer with two hands on her ass and buried himself inside her, holding the heavenly position. Every cell in her body burst apart and fused back together.

When she reentered reality, Josh's pupils were dark as pitch and his forearms strained where he supported himself above her.

He was trembling, she realized, watching her face.

"Josh?"

"Give me a second," he said between his teeth.

True to form, she didn't listen. She trailed her fingernails over the damp skin of his bare back, hard enough to leave marks.

Josh flipped them so that she was the one on top with so much grace her jaw dropped. The change in position seemed to release any reservations he'd maintained because he brought his hands to her hips and ground her body down on his with vigorous intent. She recognized that figure eight. The new angle made her see stars. He was touching parts of her she hadn't even known existed.

The intensity with which Josh thrust into her made her wild. "You're so beautiful. I can't fucking stand it."

Clara reached up and cupped her breasts, taking her nipples between her fingers and mimicking his earlier ministrations. Josh's eyes raked a path from her face down to her breasts to where their bodies came together. Until finally, he groaned, jerking his hips for a handful of final snaps.

Clara smiled, catlike, against his shoulder. He brought his hands to her back, tracing soothing circles across her shoulders until she sat up and pushed her hair out of her eyes.

He reached up to brush her cheek, letting his hand linger along the side of her jaw. "I've wanted to do that since the first moment we met."

"You said you thought I was a cat burglar." Neither of them could quite catch their breath.

"Yeah." Josh ran his hand down her spine. "I was gonna let you burgle me." Bringing his palms to her waist, he carefully detangled their slippery limbs.

As she lay on her back next to him, Clara pointed and flexed her toes under the covers, testing to make sure this body still belonged to her.

"Are you hungry?" Josh sat up and playfully sank his teeth into the skin where her neck met her shoulder. "Because I'm starving."

God, he's hot. So hot part of her wanted to pause and take a picture so that someday when she was old and gray she could remind herself that she'd once gone all the way with such a veritable smokestack.

Somehow she'd earned this oasis with a man who made her feel divine. If only she could keep him. "I could eat."

"Great. I know just the place." He grabbed his pants off the carpet.

"But it's almost three. Nothing's open."

He walked to her closet and tossed her a T-shirt and her overalls. "Oh ye of little faith."

Clara caught the clothes and smiled, remembering his affinity for the outfit. "I have to be up for work in a few hours. Toni's got a big fundraising event and it's all hands on deck."

Josh's hands stilled on his waistband. "Right. Sorry." He rubbed the back of his neck sheepishly.

The soda-can feeling returned. Bubbles of joy bloomed from her toes to the tips of her fingers. Tonight didn't have to end. Not if she didn't let it. "Let's go."

Someone else could worry about her future. About repercussions. About pain.

Clara had plans.

She loved this messy, sun-drenched life she'd stumbled upon. Suddenly words like *destiny* and *fate* didn't sound so silly. Other people did things like this every day. Slept with a beautiful man, knew he didn't owe her anything.

Josh wasn't the man of her dreams.

He was something better, something more than she'd ever allowed herself to imagine.

What if L.A. wasn't a mistake?

She had a cozy home. A good job. A rewarding, if surprising, passion project.

Hell, she was even making progress with Naomi.

Josh Conners and Clara Wheaton didn't make sense on paper, but what if somehow, impossibly, two wrongs made a right? At least under the covers.

He dusted a kiss across her temple. "I think you might be the best thing that's ever happened to me."

Clara's heart squeezed like a fist. The moment was too good. Too much. *He doesn't mean it. Not like it sounds.*

Shit. She pulled on her clothes and toed on her sneakers. Had anyone ever managed to fall into bed with a pleasure professional without losing their heart?

chapter twenty-eight
♡ ♡ ♡

J OSH ALWAYS WALKED out of Miss Dee Vine's Corner Café with a full belly and glitter stuck to the soles of his shoes. About an hour postcoital, a celebrated drag queen greeted him and Clara with smacking kisses to both of their cheeks. Miss Dee led them to a table tucked in the back and winked.

"Order whatever your heart desires," she said as she handed them menus and a can of crayons, and then, in a conspiratorial whisper, "but we've got the best waffles in the Gayborhood."

Clara ran her palms across the brown wax paper covering the table. Josh tried not to openly stare at her. In the dim fluorescent lights, she looked like everything he'd ever wanted. Every toy that was too expensive at Christmastime. Every sports car he'd ever salivated over. Every ounce of approval he'd never earned.

He sat on his hands to avoid reaching out and caressing her face. The very impulse made him wonder if he'd gone off the deep end. Words left him. Usually having sex with someone made him feel more comfortable around them. He'd successfully used intercourse as an icebreaker in awkward or unfamiliar social situations on more than one occasion.

Somehow tonight he'd walked through a doorway to an alternate reality. Only in another dimension would Clara have let him hold her and kiss her and touch her without a list of reasons on hand to justify the intimacy. His molecules had rearranged to give him this shot at loving her. His seven years must be up.

After a server took their order, Josh focused on making eye contact with the shiny buttons of Clara's overalls. *Oh shit.* What if she thought he was staring at her tits? And now, of course, his eyes had strayed to her tits and yep, they were still amazing.

Clara reached across the table and patted his forearm. "Everything okay?"

"What? Me? Sure." That sounded too casual. He didn't want her to think tonight didn't matter to him. That he considered all sex the same. Josh covered her hand with his own. "I mean, I'm good. Really good. I'm happy." *Happy* was too generic. *Happy* was commoditized. He needed a better adjective. One that spoke of transformation. The elation of reaching a summit. *Damn, he was in trouble.*

Clara sat back against her chair and narrowed her eyes. "You're totally freaking out."

"No." He wiped his sweaty palms on his shorts.

"Are you freaking out because you think *I'm* going to freak out?"

"*Now* I am."

"Well, don't. I promise I'm really happy too." But he could see something sad in her eyes. Clara rearranged the condiments on the table so that the Heinz bottle stood front and center. "Now, please tell me the ketchup story."

"No. It's embarrassing." Josh dropped his face into his hands.

She straightened the sugar packets so that they all faced the same direction. "That reaction is not making me want to hear it any less."

"It's dumb." But at least it gave him something to think about besides how much he liked the smell of her perfume and how he wanted to spray it across his pillow. Did they have a hotline for this shit?

Dolly Parton crooned through the café's speakers and half the patrons at the counter twanged along. Clara swayed side to side and twirled her hand at him expectantly.

"Fine," he said, resigning himself. "Growing up, all my cousins and I used to rag on one another. Just dumb pranks. As the youngest, I was both very devious and very good at talking my way out of trouble."

Clara propped her elbow on the table and rested her chin in her hand. "No surprise there."

"One night when I was seven, my cousin Fred had taken the blame for something I did, maybe melting a Tonka truck, I can't remember. Anyways, in retaliation he waited until I went to sleep, filled both of my palms with ketchup, and then tickled me with a feather until I had rubbed it all over my face."

"That's it?"

She didn't grasp the severity of the situation. He'd made his dad burn his favorite superhero pajamas. "I woke up in the dark with globs of the stuff dripping into my eyes. The vinegar burns like you wouldn't believe." His throat clenched as the memory of the overwhelming odor threatened to suffocate him. "I was scared shitless. I thought my face was peeling off."

Clara hid the ketchup bottle behind two stacks of jelly and the small pitcher of syrup. "That sounds traumatic."

A sound suspiciously close to a giggle escaped her mouth before she brought her forearm up and smothered it.

Josh smiled self-deprecatingly. "I told you it was dumb."

"You were not kidding." Clara's smile was so bright, he expected all the fuses in the kitchen to blow at any moment. His chest tightened.

Talking to women had always been easy before. He liked them. They liked him. The math was simple.

Until now. There was nothing simple about Clara.

"You better take that story to your grave. No one outside my family knows, and they're all gagged by extensive threats of blackmail."

"You can trust me."

With startling clarity, Josh realized that he could. This woman who never should have given him the time of day had arrived on his doorstep. His heart climbed into his throat.

"I scared you again," Clara said. "I have to admit, if I had to guess which of us would go skittish after sex, I never would have picked you."

"I'm sorry. I'm not usually like this." Josh's shoulder drooped. He had a reputation as a respectful bedfellow, sure. His partners counted on him to deliver a good time and a few laughs, but even with Naomi, no one expected any more of him.

"Tonight feels important." He shook his head. "That sounded weird." Any second she'd go running.

"No. I know what you mean." She smiled shyly. "It felt like we caused some kind of cosmic shift by acting out of character." Clara exhaled and tucked her hair behind her ears. "Let's put these crayons to good use, shall we? Whoever draws the best caricature of the pair of us gets to assign the other the chore of their choice."

"How loosely are we defining *chore*?" Lurid visions of Clara folding laundry in lingerie entered his mind.

Clara picked up the crayon closest to her and began to draw. "Use your imagination."

Josh scooted farther under the table to hide his body's reaction to the promise in her tone. His imagination was wicked.

Ten minutes later he dropped his own drawing implement. "Okay. Moment of truth."

Clara added a final flourish and then came to sit beside him. "Which one is me?"

He quickly added green boobs to Clara's stick figure.

She laughed and her arm brushed against his. Josh's mouth went dry.

"I see you've gone for anatomical accuracy."

He pointed to some key details in the illustration. "We're on an adventure. You've got a telescope and a map. I have a sword because you're the brains of the operation and we can't afford to lose you to bandits."

She bent closer to the table covering and her hair brushed along his forearm. "It looks like you've got two swords."

"No. The one in my left hand is a baguette. In case we need a snack."

"I have never met a man who loves baked goods as much as you do."

Josh tapped his chin with his index finger. "And yet you still gave my body a ten out of ten."

Her cheeks turned the delicate pink of cotton candy.

Kiss her, you idiot. You're allowed now.

But what if she pulled away? What if the reason she was unusually calm was because she'd gotten a taste of him and decided not to go back for seconds?

He stood up abruptly and Clara straightened to follow suit. "Let's see yours."

They both shuffled over to her side of the table.

Her picture made his breath catch. She'd managed to use the broken crayons to create something beautiful.

"Are we swimming?"

"No." She pointed to the blue swirls surrounding their cartoon images. "That's the sky."

"So we're flying?" He took an embarrassingly large gulp as he reached out and traced the way she'd drawn herself tucked under his arm.

"I modeled it after Chagall. Often when he draws . . . lovers . . . they're floating in each other's arms. Caught somewhere between awake and dreaming." She cleared her throat. "Like tonight."

Josh's pulse thundered in his ears and his voice came out reverent. "I've never heard of Chagall."

Clara passed him a crayon. "This shade of blue reminded me of his work. It's the crushed velvet of the night sky."

"I have to tell you something," he said, now holding his beating heart in his hands. Ready to confess that he wanted to be with her more than he'd ever wanted anything. The word *love* hovered on the tip of his tongue. He'd never done this before. Not when it mattered so much.

Her brows drew together and fear flashed across her face.

"Here you go." Their server arrived with two plates brimming with waffles.

Josh awkwardly returned to his seat, his courage snuffed. He would tell her tomorrow. If she still wanted him in the morning light.

They finally left the café as Clara's blue velvet sky broke to reveal the vivid orange of dawn. As the woman of his dreams waited by the door, Josh hastily ripped her drawing from the brown paper covering their table, tucked the folded square into his back pocket, and made a wish.

chapter twenty-nine

♡ ♡ ♡

W HILE CLARA HADN'T become immune to the shock of watching writhing naked bodies, at least she could now do so without hiding behind her fingers. The teaser clips on her screen ranged from studious to steamy, with Josh and Naomi alternating narration. As moans of pleasure poured through her headphones, she crossed her arms over her nipples and hoped no one realized just how well their latest segment for Shameless worked.

Naomi's videos always piqued her interest, but every time Josh's voice came on Clara began to pant. When the man himself walked over to her makeshift desk at the studio, Clara's stomach fluttered at the memory of the last time he'd caught her watching something steamy, the Googling that had started it all. As she hit pause, she resisted the urge to minimize the window on her computer.

"Is that the promo footage Naomi sent through? What do you think?" Josh pulled up a chair next to her. He had rolled up the sleeves of his button-down and the sight of the golden hair peppered across the sinewy skin of his forearms made her salivate. Had a human being ever looked so . . . edible? Sleeping with him last night had sent her body into an endless cycle of craving. She'd run around Toni's event all day replaying memories and fanning herself before finally ducking out early to meet Josh at the studio.

"Clara?" Josh waved a hand in front of her. "Did you hear me?"

"Oh yes. Sorry. You did a great job describing the use of biting in the tutorial about oral nipple stimulation." Her face heated to approximately the same temperature as the surface of the sun. Couldn't she have picked something less explicit to comment on? Like the background music?

Josh tugged at the collar of his shirt. "Thank you. I'm . . . uh . . . glad you approve." The air between them smoldered as her body wavered closer to his. "If you need any additional consultation on the matter, don't hesitate to ask."

It was all Clara could do to keep her tongue inside her mouth. "I think a practical demonstration would be helpful. For my professional understanding of the choreography. As a business leader."

Josh lowered his voice so only Clara could hear. "I jotted down three new scene ideas while you were at work today. For some reason, I woke up particularly inspired this morning."

Clara hid a smile behind her lips. She had some scene ideas of her own, but . . . Who was she kidding? She'd never pull off casual sex with Josh, of all men. Her only option was an honest conversation about what they meant to each other. Clara thought she'd seen hope in his eyes last night that reflected her own. It was agony, holding back from letting herself consider a future with him, and she didn't know how much more she could take. "I actually wanted to talk to you about last night."

"Right." Josh turned to look around the room. "Maybe we could discuss that later?"

Oh. Perhaps he was trying to give her the brush-off after all.

He pulled two printed tickets out of his back pocket. "Don't forget, we've got *Rocky* in two hours."

Of course. She'd purchased the tickets weeks ago and hung them on the fridge. Josh must have snagged them on his way out this morning. Clara had been so sure then that the movie marathon would be a platonic outing. *But now* . . . She gulped.

"Ginger said your note about cheating her body to the camera in that last scene made a big difference."

The compliment sent a pleasant warmth blossoming in Clara's chest. "Everyone has been very kind. I think I've gotten more hugs in the past few weeks than I did in my entire childhood."

Josh frowned.

"Wheatons typically reserve physical contact for special occasions," she said in explanation. "Also, everyone has started calling me Connecticut. I've chosen to believe they mean it as an endearment."

"Naomi shows affection in strange ways."

"Asking her to lead the project was the right call. She's got so many ideas. I didn't realize that sex could involve that many hijinks."

"Stu's certainly not afraid to laugh at herself or her partners in the bedroom," Josh said.

"But she also has these stories that are incredibly heartfelt. A lot of the performers do. It's like they've gotten comfortable enough with sex to uncover another plane of intimacy. I'm used to worrying about how my body looks or if the guy is picturing someone else every time he closes his eyes." Clara shook her head. All that was in the past now. In the land before Josh. "But some of the stuff Naomi's directed, it's amazing. I think our videos could help people see what sex is like when partners really trust each other, and the interest from the press has been tremendous. I've lined up all kinds of interviews for the two of you for launch next week."

Clara had grown to appreciate putting her doctorate skills to use in new ways for Shameless, but at the end of the day, Josh and Naomi still had the most to lose. The former flames remained the only A-list names attached to the project. Their reputations had to carry the site, at least until they built a subscriber base.

"Those press releases you drafted were amazing. I guess you're pretty good at mixing business and pleasure."

Clara leaned toward him. What if he kissed her right now, in front of everyone?

"Excuse me." A blonde in glasses and a tool belt stood in front of them. "Can one of you sign off on this lighting design before I start drilling the mounts?"

Josh jumped up from his chair like someone had poured hot coals in his lap. "Oh hey, Wynn. Stu mentioned you were in town visiting. I didn't realize she'd roped you into manual labor during your vacation."

The blonde smiled wryly in the direction of where Naomi bent over a set of test stills. "She called in a very old favor."

"Have you met Clara? She's the brains and the bucks behind this operation. Clara, Wynn's a carpenter and set designer by trade and the only person alive who knows any of Stu's secrets."

Wynn held up a pair of callused palms. "Only because I met her almost immediately after she exited the womb."

Clara quirked an eyebrow.

"Our mothers took the same Lamaze class and became joined at the hip," Wynn said in response.

"Ah. Well, nice to meet you. It's very generous of you to give up your personal time to help us out." Clara extended her hand and Wynn took it.

"No problem. It's refreshing to do work at a place where the people in charge don't all look like a stock photo for white male privilege." She turned to Josh. "No offense."

"None taken. Clara can sign off on your designs. She's got the better eye. I'll head back to the edit bay and try to be useful." Josh excused himself.

Wynn handed over the sketches for the mounts. Each image detailed the way the light and shadows would play across the set and the performers.

"Wow, these projections of the light trajectory are incredibly helpful." Clara studied the images, looking for anything she'd change and coming up short. This design was more than practical, it was art. "I don't suppose there's a chance we can convince you to move to L.A. and join us as a full-time hire?"

The blonde wrinkled her nose. "Tempting, but no. My family, my job, and my boyfriend are all back in Boston. Hannah makes skipping town look easy, but I'm a hopeless homebody."

Clara nodded. "I had to try. You're very talented. Where did you learn all of this?"

Wynn's face crumbled. "I didn't grow up with brothers."

"Excuse me?"

"Sorry, gut reaction." Wynn winced. "Almost any time someone compliments my work they follow it up by asking if I grew up in a household full of boys. You know how girls in movies who can change a tire or throw a football are always explaining their skills away as if talent transferred through proximity to testosterone?"

"Ah, yes. Well, I've got a brother and I'm certain he wouldn't have any idea what to do with your tool belt."

Naomi placed a cup of coffee next to Clara's elbow. Surely the beverage was a nonverbal gesture of acceptance?

"Thanks." Clara leaned over the steaming liquid in the hopes of giving herself a caffeine facial. She'd barely gotten four hours of sleep last night. Right now her eyelids weighed twenty pounds each.

"You look like you need it." Everything Naomi said came out sounding like a threat, but Clara now knew that she meant well. "You two met?"

"Yep. I was just admiring some of Wynn's work."

"She's obnoxiously talented. Practically perfect." Naomi sighed. "If only she weren't tragically heterosexual."

Wynn peppered a kiss on her friend's cheek. "And on that note, I'm gonna go screw something that's not one of your performers."

Naomi turned to Clara. "Why are you making a mess of my studio?" She gathered a handful of the balls of crumpled scrap paper scattered around Clara's computer.

Oops. Clara hadn't realized how many doodles of logo designs she'd accumulated while watching the preview clips. It had been years since she'd drawn anything for eyes besides her own. But something about channeling Chagall for Josh last night had released dormant artistic impulses. *Among other things.* She'd always associated Chagall with love, and not just any love. He painted the romantic love of myths and fairy tales. True love. The kind between soul mates. Love that she and Josh could never have. Except that falling asleep in his arms felt disconcertingly right.

Naomi lingered over one of the first images Clara had sketched, a pair of typefaces that broke down *Shameless* so that while still written as a single word, it read more like a declarative statement: *Shame. Less.* "You like it? I thought that—"

"You don't have to explain it to me."

"Right." Should she mention the change in her relationship with Josh? She didn't want to hide the information from their business partner. Naomi seemed to value honesty above all else. But what if she freaked? Or decided Clara wasn't good enough for her ex?

"Can I ask you a question?" Clara blurted out the words before she could think better of it.

Naomi looked at her with pursed lips. "One."

Clara planted her feet and stood up extra straight. "Do you think people can change?" What she meant, but couldn't bring herself to say, was *Do you think someone like me could ever be right for someone like Josh?*

Naomi didn't answer right away. She twisted her hair up into a bun and stuck a pen through it in a way that Clara thought only worked in movies. When she did respond, her voice was thoughtful and her eyes were sharp.

"Can? Yeah. If the circumstances are right. But you have to want to, and most people don't." She took a deep breath. "Or something big enough has to happen to you. Something that leaves you with no other options."

Something—*no, someone*—big had happened to Clara. But she couldn't figure out if the effects would last.

Naomi stared at her. "That's how I got into porn."

"It was?" Living with Josh and working alongside so many different kinds of performers had significantly opened the aperture on Clara's definition of a porn performer.

"Believe it or not, I had a pretty perfect high school experience. I wasn't as much of a brownnoser as you." Naomi smirked. "But I got good grades and I was captain of the soccer team, class president, the whole thing. I even had the perfect boyfriend." Naomi's lips twisted as if she'd sucked on a lemon.

"Life pretty much came crashing down around my ears when said perfect boyfriend shared the private pictures he'd begged for as an eighteenth-birthday present with the Internet. You see, I'd told him I wasn't ready to sleep with him." Her voice rang hollow.

Clara wrapped her arms around the other woman's shoulders without thinking. She expected Naomi to toss off the physical contact, but instead, she leaned her chin on top of Clara's head and sighed. "If you tell anyone about this, I'll deny it, and then kill you."

Eventually, they stepped apart sheepishly. When Naomi spoke next, her voice allowed pain to bleed through.

"I knew that no matter what I did, those images would be out there for people to see without my permission. Knew that no matter how many years passed, no matter what I went on to achieve, some people would always define me based on my body alone. So I came out here. I took my own pictures. I figured if I flooded the market I could decrease the value of those original poses. That I could reclaim my body on my own terms."

"That's really—" Clara started to say.

"Impulsive? Juvenile? Stupid?"

"Brave."

Naomi looked Clara in the eye. "I was terrified and so mad I couldn't see straight." She picked up Clara's coffee and pushed it into her hands.

Clara took an obedient sip. "What about your family? Your friends? Did they support your decision?"

"I didn't ask for their permission then and I don't plan on asking forgiveness now. Even Wynn, who understands why I had to leave, can't comprehend why I'll never go back." She held her hands up in front of her chest. "That is not an invitation to hug me again."

"I wouldn't dream of it."

"Most people will do anything to avoid change." Naomi brushed her flame-colored hair over her shoulder. "Even the ones who try often revert back to old habits as soon as life gets hard. Remember that before you go doing something crazy. Sometimes we think we want something until it's time to live with the consequences."

The answer wasn't pessimistic, just grounded in the firm dose of reality Clara had grown to expect from Naomi.

As the bitter coffee played across her tongue, Clara tried not to close her eyes. She wanted to believe in change. To believe she could leave her old life, her old responsibilities and baggage, behind for Josh, if he'd have her. She wanted people to say, *Oh yeah. Clara can always roll with the punches. She takes big honking bites out of life.*

But Naomi was right. It was easy to try. To swallow the insecurity triggered by working with so many beautiful women who knew so much more about sex than she could even imagine. To dodge calls from her mother and blame it on the time difference. To fan the fantasy of her and Josh living happily ever after while his performing hiatus helped stall the thousands of obstacles standing in their way.

This was summer vacation from real life, but sooner or later, summer would end. She'd have to face her family, would have to choose between the life she'd been groomed for and the one that hung at the edge of the horizon, outrageously tempting, but with a price tag of all she held dear.

"Change always comes with a closing cost," Naomi said. "But it's still worth trying. Not because the odds are particularly good, mind you, but considering the alternative. There's value in the struggle. Value in touching the raw and bloody parts of our souls, opening them up to the sunlight, and hoping they heal."

Clara got the message. If she wanted a future with Josh, she'd have to fight for it. "You know, you're the first person I've ever met who I think might actually change the world."

Naomi grinned over her shoulder as she walked away. "Tell me something I don't know."

chapter thirty

♡ ♡ ♡

JOSH WOULD STOP at nothing in his quest to take Clara on a real date.

While he'd loved sharing breakfast food with her during the middle of the night, he wanted something more formal. An arranged outing versus the casual hanging out they'd been doing for weeks. Everything had changed for him last night. Now he needed to figure out if Clara felt the same way.

All day he'd felt like a teenager, green and unsure, pussyfooting around. He'd spent enough time with Clara before they got physical to know that this thing between them was more than run-of-the-mill attraction.

He wanted to plant a flag. To show Clara he was all in.

He didn't mind that this movie marathon had been her idea. Ever since they'd first watched *Speed*, whenever he thought about car chases and standoffs, he thought of Clara. She was surprisingly bloodthirsty for a woman who, a week earlier, wouldn't let him smush a spider that had showed up in the bathtub.

"I probably should have tried to take you somewhere more romantic than the megaplex." He helped her out of the rental car.

"Are you kidding? I love *Rocky*. Sylvester Stallone taught me how to punch."

"You know how to punch?"

Clara planted her feet and made tiny fists.

Her form wasn't half bad. "Okay." Josh held up his open palm. "Gimme your worst."

Clara's smile made him overheat and her punch landed with a resounding smack and not an insignificant amount of force.

He shook out his wrist. "Damn. You weren't kidding. Sometimes you're alarmingly scrappy." Josh let his hand linger on her lower back as he ushered her inside.

Josh had dressed up for date night in a crisp white button-down and his nicest pair of jeans, but he still felt like a putz next to Clara. She'd taken off her cardigan and looped it over her arm, revealing a black dress he'd never seen before, held up by two tiny straps that he could, and hopefully would later, snap with his teeth.

He'd gotten used to her beauty on low volume at the house. No makeup, sweats, hair piled on top of her head like a cinnamon roll. All done up, in natural light, she took his breath away. He hadn't used the right words last night when he'd confessed the way he felt about her. Certainly hadn't used the one word that had been swimming in his brain ever since their barbecue.

But that was okay. He could make it right. Tonight he would issue a proper declaration. One that wasn't based on her physical characteristics but told Clara how she made him want to recite epic poems. If she'd let him, he'd do his best to lay cities at her feet, to sail for fourteen years only to find his way back to her bed.

"Did you know *Rocky* is both an invigorating tale of determination and grit and a romance for the ages? You're in for a real treat." Clara used the know-it-all voice that drove him wild.

"You think everything's romantic. You tried to convince me that *The Mummy* was a love story."

"Of course *The Mummy* is a love story." Clara thrust her hands on her hips. "You're off your gourd."

"Off my gourd? No wonder you like that movie. You're one pair of horn-rimmed glasses away from a librarian yourself." He tried to think of a compliment worthy of her. How could he tell her how much tonight meant to him, without saying something ridiculous like *Your eyes shine like diamonds*?

Clara turned up her nose. "Thank you. Librarians are pillars of society."

Josh wanted to dip her, like an old-timey dance move. He wanted to lower her into a dramatic arc and claim her lips for his own while everyone around them cheered.

He'd had to lie low at the studio so as not to attract unwanted attention from Naomi. The last thing he needed right now was to deal with the consequences of his ex-girlfriend-turned-business-partner's rage.

Somehow, defying the laws of logic and science, Clara seemed genuinely interested in him. He was the luckiest son of a bitch alive.

"Next," the ticket collector called.

Josh realized he and Clara had been standing, smiling at each other, holding up the line.

"Sorry," he told the older couple behind them.

"No trouble," said the woman, patting the arm of her companion. "We remember what the early days were like."

He expected Clara to protest, but she simply gave him a shy smile.

Pride added an inch to his height. A stranger had mistaken them for a couple. No, wait. Not mistaken. A stranger had *recognized* them as a couple.

Josh's stomach tumbled merrily, and he managed a nod.

As they headed to the concession counter, Clara reached for his hand. He tried not to let on the way his whole body tingled in response. Josh had participated in sex moves he couldn't spell, but none of them had made happiness pump through his veins like holding hands with Clara.

She studied the menu. "Should we get M&Ms or Skittles?"

"Obviously we need to get M&Ms and dump them into the popcorn bucket."

"People do that?"

Josh pressed his thigh fully against hers. "Oh, Clara. Stick with me. I'm gonna show you a whole new world."

They found seats toward the back of the theater. Not the row occupied exclusively by teenagers who came to make out, but close enough that Josh figured he could at least get away with putting his arm around her.

"Are you ready?" Clara stared at the trivia on the screen with palpable excitement.

Josh stuck his tongue between his teeth. "To rumble?"

She awarded him a glare for his teasing.

"Oh no! The hot popcorn is melting all of the M&Ms." She held up the evidence. Between her thumb and forefinger, she'd captured the perfect bite: two pieces of popcorn melded together by now-gooey chocolate.

Josh leaned forward and caught her offering between his teeth, letting his canines gently scrape against the pads of her fingertips. The salty sweet concoction and the contact with her skin made him almost dizzy with pleasure.

Clara blushed and grabbed her own handful. After a few moments of chewing the treat, she leaned back. "You're a genius."

"Wow. More compliments?"

She nodded solemnly. "Seriously. You're the full package."

Josh examined the half-empty auditorium with mock horror. "Hey, quit talking about my package. This is a family-friendly theater."

When she laughed against his shoulder he swore the vibrations went all the way to his roaring heart. He found himself bending down and smelling her hair. *I'm such a goner.*

The lights dimmed, signaling the start of the previews. He'd never seen *Rocky* but he knew the story. A man no one dreamed could compete wound up holding his own in the ring with a champion.

Speed. Die Hard. Rocky. Clara always seemed to fall for the underdog. Josh reached for her hand, ran his lips across the back of her knuckles, and wondered why he'd never noticed before. She leaned her head on his shoulder as the opening music played.

Throughout the movie, Clara lit up anytime Josh laughed and squeezed his hand when things looked bleak for the Italian Stallion.

When he got home he'd write a letter to his principal telling her how wrong she was. He'd grown up into the kind of man who went on dates with Clara Wheaton.

"So . . . what did you think?" Clara practically skipped as they exited the theater.

Josh would have sat through anything that made her glow like that movie. "I liked it. Rocky's very lovable. Apollo was cool. Adrian's a babe."

Clara stopped in the middle of the hallway. "Well, what was your favorite part?" The rest of the theatergoers shot them dirty looks as they went around.

"Hmmm." Josh wrapped his arm around her shoulders and gave a scowling gentleman a little wave as the hallway emptied out. "I really enjoyed the way you sat forward in your chair and shadowboxed along with Sylvester Stallone."

Clara ducked her chin. "I may have gotten a little overexcited. Speaking of . . ." She backed him into a corner and kissed him.

"We've only got fifteen minutes before the sequel starts," he said against her lips, figuring she'd murder him if they missed the opening credits.

"Maybe we could watch it at home?"

Josh's dick twitched. "At home? You mean you don't want to see your heroes duke it out on the big screen?"

Clara closed the distance between their hips and reached into his back pocket. "I thought I'd teach you a few sparring moves instead."

"Okay, but league rules say all fighters must be topless."

She yelped when he gave her ass a friendly tap and started walking her toward the door. If he had his way they wouldn't get out of bed for the next forty-eight hours.

"You know how much I love rules." She blinked up at him with a devastating set of bedroom eyes. "Oh shoot. I left my sweater in the theater. Wait a second. I'll grab it." Clara made it about twelve steps before stopping short.

Immediately, her posture changed. She stood up straighter and crossed her arms over her chest before taking another small but decisive step farther away from him. "Toni. Hello. Nice to see you." Her voice changed pitch.

Josh recognized Toni Granger from the newspaper, even though the woman wore a casual outfit. She was taller in person than he'd assumed.

"I thought I'd take the team out for a little last-minute morale boost." Toni gestured to a group of seven or eight people waiting in line to get into theater two. "Their boss kept them working late on a Saturday. We looked for you but Jill said you'd already left for an appointment."

Clara wrung her hands.

The DA looked to where Josh stood waiting. "Is this your young man?" She gave him a polite smile.

"No. Of course not," Clara said, going white.

Josh felt each word like a punch to the solar plexus.

"No," she repeated, mercilessly hammering the point home. "I was asking this nice man if he knew where the bathrooms were located." Clara's eyes found his, desperate and pleading. "Thank you again for your help."

"Don't mention it." Josh hauled his lead feet toward the exit.

He'd made it about halfway through the parking lot when Clara ran up beside him. "Josh. Josh, wait up." She caught his sleeve between her fingers. "I am so sorry about that."

Something inside Josh howled in pain, but he smothered its cries. "It's fine."

He'd known no one would buy a fairy tale about a princess and a porn star. "Where's your sweater?"

She shook her head. "I don't know. I don't care about the sweater. I care about you. I . . . I couldn't risk someone on her campaign team recognizing you." Clara worried her bottom lip between her teeth.

He lengthened his strides until she fell several steps behind him. How many times had people laughed when they heard his profession? Or stammered and refused to meet his eyes? How many people had called him disgusting? He should have outgrown this reaction years ago.

Somehow none of those slights compared to this. If he lived to be a hundred, he'd never forget the way Clara had looked at him when she thought someone she respected might see. Even now, the difference in her body language reflected the void opening between them.

He had been a fool and a half to think that a golden girl like her would ever acknowledge him as her equal.

Bile rose in the back of Josh's throat. "I get it, Clara."

"They're politicians." She stared at her hands. "Everyone's skittish about the reelection campaign. Please understand."

"It doesn't matter. Don't beat yourself up." As sad and pathetic as it was, he couldn't stop himself from trying to save face. He'd die if she knew how close he'd come to believing tonight meant something. "It's not like this was a real date."

Clara reared back for a moment. "Oh. Sure. Right."

Another nail in the coffin. Everything made sense now, her unusual calm; she'd never thought they'd make it past the bedroom. He wanted to ease the guilt off her face. She wasn't to blame for his feral hope. "We're having fun. Messing around." His voice sounded far away in his own ears.

Clara's eyes turned the gray of a thousand thunderstorms. "Of course. I know that."

He wished he could trade places with Rocky Balboa. He'd give anything right now to hit hard slabs of frozen meat and run until he puked. Maybe then he could replace the emotional pain that sat like acid in his stomach with physical pain that meant something. That showed up on the outside.

If the world were fair, Josh would have been able to get into a ring and fight for what he wanted. If the world were fair, he would have stood a chance.

chapter thirty-one

♡ ♡ ♡

JOSH'S PAIN MADE him crave sugar, so he and Clara showed up to the studio the next morning bearing brownies. They weren't supposed to arrive until noon, but he couldn't stay trapped in the house with her any longer.

When he suggested they get going early, his roommate, because that was all she would ever be to him, hadn't argued. But her eyes had darted to where the keys to the rental car hung on a hook by the door and she'd shivered like they'd sprouted big hairy legs.

"It's okay," he said, understanding her hesitation to get behind the wheel again after the accident. "I'll drive."

As he talked shop with Naomi, Josh tried his best to pretend he didn't have a giant stamp on his forehead that read *I had sex with Clara and I'll never get over it.*

As his ex-girlfriend had forewarned, getting involved with his business partner and roommate left him nowhere to lick his wounds. He couldn't escape Clara. Every time he turned around she looked carefree and pretty, the opposite of his rotting soul. The worse part was, she kept trying to apologize to him over and over again. Which only made him feel worse. He'd never felt as alone as he had climbing into his vacant bed the night before, knowing she was lying feet away and miles apart from him. He'd read the situation with her so wrong, it might as well have been written in a foreign language.

He would count it as a tiny victory if he could at least avoid Naomi detecting his massive miscalculation. Luckily, his ex seemed distracted.

Josh remained paranoid all morning, convinced there were signs of their indiscretion everywhere. For a moment he thought he saw a lingering love bite on her wrist, but it turned out to be leftover chocolate.

This must be karma. In the past, he would have loved the idea of a no-strings-attached romp, but this was Clara. *Clara.* He wished he'd never gotten a taste of her.

Just a few more weeks. Then at least he could move out. She wouldn't be the first person he saw when he woke up and the last before he went to sleep. God, he felt sick.

Feeling a hand on his shoulder, he hit pause and took off his headphones, turning to find the object of his unwanted affection.

His breath caught in his throat at the sight of her, at the way the lightweight top she wore left her arms and shoulders bare. He faked a cough to cover his reaction. Even though she kept a healthy distance between them, Josh got a whiff of the sunscreen on her skin. Somehow she'd rewired his brain to find all of these formerly ordinary things arousing. She wasn't even showing any cleavage, for fuck's sake.

"Kiana looks great, doesn't she?" Clara said, looking at the screen over his shoulder, oblivious to the effect she had on him.

Josh forced his gaze back to the video, where a blonde was enjoying some heavy petting from her partner. The shot focused on her reaction. Clara openly admiring another woman in the throes of passion was too much for him at the moment. His hindbrain sat up and growled. "You've seen this?"

"Oh yeah. I was there when they shot it last week," she said, nonchalant.

The sensory knowledge he'd gained the other night had only added fuel to his desire for her. He stood up abruptly, needing to put more distance between them, needing to think of anything but licking her warm, wet skin.

"You wanna order Thai for lunch?" he asked.

"Oh, um . . ." She grew enthralled with a crack in the vinyl of the table.

"Clara's got plans," Naomi said, joining them. "But I'll go in on noodles with you."

"Plans?" He looked at Clara for clarification. Since when did Clara have plans that didn't include him?

"A day date," Naomi answered. Her eyes told him not to argue. "I set it up two weeks ago. My dentist is handsome and single. They're meeting at Griffith Park at two."

"A blind date, huh?" Josh tried to ask like a normal person, a person with less to lose.

Clara nodded. "Naomi insisted on setting it up because I haven't gone out much since I moved here."

Josh had kissed her and held her and been inside her, and she would still rather go on a date with some random guy.

"Your phone is ringing," Naomi said, handing him the offending electronic device. Her raised brows said, *What is wrong with you?*

The caller ID made him grimace. "It's Bennie." He moved his thumb to send the call to voice mail. Everything was wrong and he didn't know how to fix it. He needed to talk to Clara. Now.

"Answer," Naomi told him.

He shot daggers at her. "Hello?"

"Darling." His agent's voice sounded in his ear. "It's been too long. I hope you didn't think you were done with me?"

"What do you want, Bennie?"

"Now, now. Better watch that tone. Someone less charitable might take offense. I'm calling to let you know about some industry developments I thought you might find interesting. I believe you know Paulo Santiago and Lucie Corben?"

Of course Josh knew those names. Paulo was the editor who'd given him the Final Cut software download in exchange for a round of beers, and Lucie was a makeup artist who told him dirty jokes until he laughed so hard he cried off all her handiwork. They were two of his favorite people in the business.

"Get to your point."

"They've both been removed from consideration on any future Black Hat productions."

He covered the mouthpiece of the phone with his palm. "Pruitt's making good on his threats."

Naomi cursed under her breath.

"You're a piece of shit, Bennie. Doing that bastard's dirty work is low, even for you," Josh said into the phone.

"Hey, kid. I'm the messenger. For every day you go without signing a new contract, the list of people who find themselves out of work goes up. And if you're thinking about pushing your luck, let me remind you that Mr. Pruitt's holdings are vast. He's got a lot of expendable resources. He can afford to wait. If you change your mind about signing, you know where to reach me," he said before disconnecting the call.

In contrast to the people caught in the crosshairs was the implicit subtext. Josh knew that Paulo and Lucie lived paycheck to paycheck, like a lot of Pruitt's employees. He thought about Paulo's kids and Lucie's expensive ongoing hormone therapy treatments.

He couldn't let them suffer for his actions. His mistakes. He slammed his fist on the card table so hard the legs wobbled. This week was shaping up to be a real kick in the teeth.

"Damn it. I can't be worth this much effort. Why go to all this trouble to get me to bend to his will? This industry is full of white guys with big dicks."

"I don't think it's just about you," Naomi said. "We've been noisy in our dissent. Word's getting around about our little project. People are calling, ready to defect, no matter the risks. We've got interviews set up through next week. I think this is about Pruitt sending a message. About crushing anyone who stands in opposition to him. If he doesn't nip this in the bud he could find himself with a mass revolt on his hands."

"Good," Clara said from the corner. "Sorry. That's good, isn't it?"

"A couple weeks hanging around a bunch of sex workers and suddenly you've got an appetite for rebellion?" Naomi raised a finely arched eyebrow.

Clara gave a demure shrug.

Josh sank back into the folding chair with his head spinning. There was no way he could justify being this selfish. *Look at the cost.* How could he let people he cared about suffer when he had the power to stop it?

"You can't sign that contract," Clara said. "If you sign, Pruitt and Bennie win. Besides." She folded her hands. "There's still nothing to stop him from firing more people after he gets what he wants. You'd be giving up your leverage."

Josh rubbed his palms against his eyes. "My leverage doesn't matter anymore. We can't hire the whole industry," he said. "Black Hat's pockets are deeper than even yours."

Naomi shook her head. "We need to hold out long enough to get to the press. It's only a few more days."

Clara smiled hopefully. She and Naomi and so many other amazing women had given their time and knowledge and experience so this tiny, probably fruitless rebellion could see the light of day.

Josh looked at the screen left up on his computer, at the banner across the top of the website, the first thing people would see when they visited, designed in Clara's hand, brought to life from a sketch Naomi had rescued from among a hundred destined for the trash. *Shameless*, the letters growing out of the earth like fresh blooms.

He could do this for them.

Even if Clara had broken his heart. Even if she continued to baffle him, continued to infuriate him with how much she made him want her. If she wanted to go to war with a porn monolith, well, the least he could do was ride in beside her.

Josh grabbed his backpack, hunting for a nondescript black flash drive he'd taken to keeping on hand. He'd been adding to it sporadically for months now. Even with the stakes raised, he wasn't sure he'd ever have the guts to do anything with it, but holding it, knowing he had it, made breathing a little easier. No matter what the next few weeks held, Josh had underestimated Black Hat for the last time.

chapter thirty-two

♡ ♡ ♡

CLARA WINCED AS Toni Granger exited the stage of the local L.A. County Baptist Church.

This was the third public campaign appearance she and Jill had attended in the last two weeks, and the trend was clear. Toni would need a miracle to defend her position against her brash super PAC–funded opponent with his big mouth and even bigger promises.

"She got bulldozed." Jill agreed with Clara's assessment of their client's performance at the Candidates' Forum. "He made her look soft on crime." She took a sip from a paper cup of instant coffee, courtesy of the event's meager refreshment table.

Earlier this week, supporters of her opponent had released a nasty attack ad, going for the jugular. The crowd today had obviously seen it. They'd practically eaten out of her opponent's hand while he fired off out-of-context statistics about Toni's conviction record.

"She's a reform candidate," Clara said, shifting her weight to the opposite leg and trying to stick up for Toni. "She's trying to correct the criminal justice system of mass incarceration."

Clara's feet throbbed inside her heels. Josh had been in the living room this morning when she got ready for the event. He'd lain on the sofa, eating frozen waffles, right next to where she'd left her preferred pair of work shoes. She'd been avoiding him for three nights. Ever since she got back from her lackluster date with the dentist. A date she hadn't even wanted in the first place. Clara had spent the whole picnic thinking about Josh. She couldn't stop thinking about him. Last night she'd woken up saying his name into her pillow.

She needed to get over her roommate, and fast. He'd made it crystal clear that anything more than sex between them was off the table after she'd humiliated him at the movies. Too bad her heart couldn't separate lust from love as easily.

Still, she wished she hadn't chickened out and had rescued her shoes. Sometime in the last hour, her toes had gone numb.

"The material we gave her wasn't bold enough." The longer Clara worked for Toni, the more she admired her. The public servant worked a truly thankless job, trying to fight for equality and justice. Clara noticed that not a single event went by without some old white man coming up to Toni and trying to explain her own job to her.

"Bold makes her nervous." Jill chucked the coffee into a nearby trash can. "Come on, she'll want to debrief." Her aunt led the way to the lobby of the church where the current district attorney glad-handed potential voters.

Toni's eyes found Jill over the head of an elderly churchgoer, and their client nodded subtly toward the holding room they'd prepped in before the event, a clear signal that Jill and Clara should wait there for her to join them.

Clara's stomach sank. Toni had the same *I'm not mad, just disappointed* look as Clara's mother.

A few minutes later, their client joined them in the room, closing the door behind her and shutting out the din of the crowd. She held a manila folder under her arm.

"Should I get Tricia if we're going to talk about altering the communications strategy?" Jill asked, referring to the Granger campaign's chief of staff and rising from the folding chair she'd been sitting in.

"No," Toni said. "That won't be necessary, thank you."

Clara had spent countless hours observing, asking questions—some more welcome than others—and learning everything she could about her client. She knew that the beautiful slate gray suit Toni wore today used to belong to her mother. And that Toni only wore her current shade of crimson lipstick when she needed courage. *She dressed for battle today. Maybe this really is the end.*

"Clara, may I speak to you in private for a moment?" The DA's voice held an unfamiliar rasp.

Clara looked up from her notebook, surprised. "Are you sure you don't want to talk to Jill?"

"I'm sure."

Jill gave Clara a nod of encouragement as she gracefully exited the small room.

"Clara," Toni began, taking the seat Jill had vacated. "We've worked together closely over these past few months. I like you. You're smart and you're hardworking and you're not afraid to ask for help when you don't know what to do."

"Thank you," Clara said, flattered, but something about the way Toni's voice died off at the end of her last sentence set off a warning signal.

The DA looked out the small window in the room to where friends and families lingered, talking between their cars, unwilling to say goodbye. When her eyes returned to Clara, her gaze was troubled.

"I know my campaign is on its last gasp. I've seen the polling numbers. I pay your aunt and everyone else on my campaign team to pretend it's not that bad, but you're not so good at hiding it. I can see in your eyes that you know I don't have a lot of choices left if I want to keep my job.

That's why I wanted to ask you—what would you tell me to do if I found out someone working on my campaign was involved in an activity that could prove inflammatory in the wrong hands?"

Clara thought about Toni's newly earned razor-thin lead, about that first day at Jill's office when she'd talked about creating a better, safer city for all. She pictured Josh before she'd met him, before he'd ever made a single adult entertainment video. He'd told her stories about working three jobs so he could afford to pay rent.

She thought about Naomi and Ginger and their stories of harassment on set. The stuff they'd "had to put up with" because it "was part of the biz." Her heart ached for the countless people who contracted for Black Hat who might wake up one day and find themselves blacklisted because they'd done something that pissed off a corrupt company.

Toni had the power to protect them all. Not to mention all her other constituents. The people Clara rode the bus with in the morning. The mothers with crying babies, the old men with canes. All of them deserved a district attorney who would fight to keep them safe.

Clara knew what to do when faced with a scandal. She'd heard the phrase so many times growing up in the Wheaton household, from various lawyers and consultants advising her family: *minimize the damage.*

When she spoke, her voice was clear, confident. "I'd tell you to fire them quietly. Distance yourself. Issue a single statement and then don't rise to the bait when you get calls for comment. It'll pass soon enough if you starve the news cycle. There's always another story, new dirt."

Toni pulled the manila folder out from under her arm and held it out to Clara. When she spoke, she didn't sound angry, but her words were hard, resigned. "My campaign manager put this on my desk this morning."

Clara took the folder and flipped it open. Inside were a handful of articles printed out from the Internet. Various gossip sites and entertainment publications she recognized.

One word stood out across the headlines. *Shameless.* For a moment her chest swelled with pride. *We did it.* But then her eyes found a name in the print and it wasn't one she expected to see.

Next to attributions of the property to Josh Darling and Naomi Grant was a third name. Her vision swam for a moment, but it didn't change the letters printed on the page. They spelled out *Clara Wheaton.*

Her shaking hands turned page after page. The first article wasn't an anomaly. Multiple reporters named her as the project's financial backer and one even heralded her as "Josh Darling and Naomi Grant's inaugural novice." *Oh no. No. No.* She couldn't get vomit on Toni's mother's suit.

"Clara," Toni said, "I support your right to do whatever you want with your money and your time, but you must know I can't have my campaign associated with something explicit when my opponent is running on a platform of family values. You've been on the ground with me at events. We've been photographed together. One of those articles mentions your work at the firm. It's only a matter of time before someone makes the connection."

Toni was right, of course. A scandal this late in the campaign was poison. How could Clara have put the campaign, the firm, people she cared about at risk like this? She used to be careful . . . but everything with Shameless had moved so fast. But how . . . She'd made sure her name didn't appear in any of the site copy or metadata. All the performers had signed the nondisclosure agreement. Her name had been left off the press releases she'd drafted for Josh and Naomi before they'd scheduled any interviews. The only way those reporters could have found out, would even care about a nobody like her, was if one of the site's famous founders had named her directly.

After everything Naomi had experienced in high school, Clara couldn't imagine her outing anyone. *But that only left . . .*

Josh wouldn't do that. He knew how much her reputation meant to her. But the how didn't matter so much because no matter what, word was out. Jill and Toni would suffer alongside her. What a spectacular mess.

She mentally shook herself. There would be plenty of time to wallow in self-pity later. Right now she needed to focus on making this right. "The firm had nothing to do with this. My aunt didn't even know. Please don't take this out on her."

Jill was out there somewhere, probably wondering what was going on, drinking more of that terrible coffee to keep her hands busy. Her aunt had been so proud that her firm, most famous for elevating D-list actors and aging musicians, could serve someone like Toni—could have a bigger impact. Losing the Granger campaign account would break her heart, not to mention that it could deter future clients.

Toni rose. "Clara, you're my PR team. I need you to talk to your aunt and find a way to make this go away. I'm sorry. I can't afford to gamble my career on you."

"I understand." The words tasted like chalk in her mouth. "I'll fix this."

Toni took one last look at Clara, her eyes troubled, and left.

Moments later, Jill came back in with a pen behind one ear and a crumbling mini muffin clutched in her hand. "What the hell happened?"

Clara showed her the folder, unable to speak.

"Wow." Jill's eyebrows rose so high they almost kissed her hairline. "You used your trust fund to back a program dedicated to promoting equal-opportunity orgasms at scale?" Her aunt pursed her lips and nodded, impressed. "That's cool."

"It's got naked women masturbating on the landing page."

Jill choked on a bite of mini muffin, and the room filled with her hacking coughs for a full thirty seconds. Clara had reached an unexpected level of rebellion, even by Jill Wheaton's generous standards.

Clara might have laughed if her whole world hadn't been folding in around her. "You have to fire me." She forced the next words out. "Release a statement denouncing me and the site."

Jill pounded a fist lightly against her chest, still recovering from her coughing fit. When her throat was clear, she said, "I'm not gonna do that. Clara, you're my family."

The last of Clara's defenses shattered.

Jill's definition of family, what they did for one another, the way they forgave, defied everything Clara had ever known. But Clara knew too well the destruction a rumor could cause, and the worst part was, this one was true.

"It's the only way. I put the firm at risk and I probably lost the campaign for Toni. You saw that guy up there. He doesn't pull his punches. This time tomorrow it'll be all over the news: *Granger Campaign Staffer Peddles Porn.* Don't smile," she said, reprimanding her aunt.

Didn't Jill know she should frown and glower, sigh deeply as if Clara's existence were a trial? That was the only way to let someone know they'd let you down.

Jill wasn't having it. "There's gotta be another way to salvage the story here. I need some time to figure it out."

Clara's eyes welled with tears. How had she gotten lucky enough to get this woman for not only a family member but a boss, too, even if the latter was short-lived? The rest of the Wheatons didn't realize what they were missing. A decade ago, Jill had fought for love, and Clara now realized she'd never stopped. "There's no other way. You know there's not."

Jill didn't answer, but Clara saw agreement in her eyes.

chapter thirty-three

♡ ♡ ♡

HER KNEES BEGGED for mercy against the hard linoleum floor, but Clara relished the discomfort as she cleaned the kitchen with a diligence and vigor usually reserved for someone covering up a crime scene.

Over the last few hours, she'd had plenty of time to mull over her current situation and work up a healthy cocktail of anger and fear. Scrubbing was the only antidote she knew.

Patsy Cline crooned from a portable speaker perched on the kitchen counter. The soundtrack to pain. Clara had spent her whole life trying to please everyone and somehow wound up pleasing no one. Not even herself.

The Wheaton curse took no prisoners.

Around five o'clock, Josh came in and almost tripped over her, positioned as she was on all fours in front of the doorway to the kitchen. She got to her feet and dusted off her sweat pants.

He wore the dopey grin that made lesser women swoon, but she girded her loins and cut to the chase.

"Did you tell a bunch of reporters that I provided the funding for Shameless?" Clara laced each word with fury.

Josh's smile fell and his eyebrows drew together. "What?"

Her heart twisted. "Have you seen these?" She handed him the article printouts.

Josh took the documents and began to shake his head, tossing his golden curls. "Naomi totally sidestepped those questions. Wait—what the fuck? Clara. Did you see this quote on page three? 'Darling's agent, Bennie Mancusso, says the pair of sizzling stars owes their success to their investor, noted Manhattan socialite Clara Wheaton.'" He swore under his breath.

Clara balked. "How would your agent know my name?"

He thumbed through the pages. "This has Black Hat written all over it. I bet their lawyers can sniff out a paper trail from a mile away. The bank, the website hosting, the rental equipment. It couldn't be that hard to tie all those expenses back to you if someone was looking hard enough. Bennie and Pruitt probably thought highlighting your background would undermine the website."

She strangled the sponge in her hands. "How do you sound so calm?"

Josh's face hardened. "Look, this is bad, I'm not gonna pretend it's not, but come on. I know you had cold feet before we got started. Before we knew what this project could turn into. But now? Your fingerprints are all over Shameless." His eyes became guarded. "I thought you were proud of what we built together."

That was the kicker. She loved every part of their project. The people, the humor, their tiny studio space. Every camera and microphone and monitor. Clara even liked the wild toys with names she could never remember. Why else would she have toiled and gone without sleep or proper nutrition to bring Shameless into the world?

Even if no one else ever used the site, Clara had learned from their creation already. And not just about how to have better sex. It was the first real piece of art she'd ever created.

But now everything she'd sacrificed was corrupted. None of the joy or pride Shameless brought her changed the fact that her public involvement with the property came at a huge cost. Her name. Her *real* name was compromised.

Clara's head pounded as chemically engineered citrus wafted up from the newly polished floor and stung her nostrils. She would never be able to sever the link between her identity and explicit sex. "Those articles cost me my job." The reality hit her again, as fresh and painful as the first time.

She'd failed. More than failed. One day had sent her fledgling career down a trash chute.

"I work in public relations and reputation management for a political campaign," she said. "This scandal might end Toni's bid for reelection, and it puts a huge blemish on Jill's firm's résumé. I can't undo this. When you search *Clara Wheaton* now, do you know what comes up?" She threw her arms in the air. "It's not my thesis on Renoir. It's tits and ass."

Josh moved past her with tight lips and short, choppy strides to pour himself a glass of water.

"I'm sorry," he finally told her after taking a sip.

Clara saw red. "You don't sound very sorry."

Josh lowered his glass to the counter hard enough that the surface of the water quivered. "I'm sorry you lost your job, okay? I really am." His mouth tightened. "I'm sorry that your dirty little secret got out. I'm sorry that for one day you experienced a tiny piece of the backlash that I've faced for the last two years of my life. But I've got to tell you, as far as political sex scandals go, this one sounds pretty fucking tame."

Clara opened and closed her mouth like a fish. Was he actually . . . *angry? At her?*

He flexed his fingers at his side. "Actually, you know what? No. I'm not sorry. Wasn't the whole point of Shameless that women shouldn't be punished for seeking pleasure, and their partners shouldn't be ashamed about wanting to learn how to give it to them? Wasn't that your whole sermon? When are you going to stop acting like a hypocrite and start practicing what you preach?"

"I believe in the site as much today as I did yesterday, but believing that doesn't change who I am. It doesn't mean I'm ready to leave everything else I love behind. The second my mother hears about this—"

Josh shut his eyes and tipped his head back. "Would you stop hiding behind your family? You're a grown woman, Clara. You're twenty-seven years old, for crying out loud. Who cares if your mom gets mad?"

"*I* care." Did he really not see how much this hurt her? How she could barely stand upright long enough to discuss it? "I like making my mother proud. It might be easy for you to write off what everyone else thinks about you, but I'm not like that."

All the heat went out of him. "I never stood a chance, did I?"

Clara was thrown by the dramatic shift in his tone. "What are you talking about?"

"Why did you sleep with me?" His voice sounded unnaturally thin.

Her gaze sank to his lips and she hesitated. "I don't know."

"Yes, you do. Come on. You did it. At least own up to it." His eyes burned straight through her skin.

She felt like prey being lured into a honey-sweet trap. "I wanted to. I'm attracted to you. Is that what you want to hear?"

"So it was just sex?" He kept his tone light enough to discuss the weather.

Clara buried the truth in her belly. "Yes." Just the best sex she'd ever had. Just sex that had turned her whole belief system upside down.

"But you don't have casual sex," he said. "You told me that the first night I touched you."

Clara shivered. How foolish she'd been to trust that she could separate body and mind. Hadn't she known then that falling for this man would ruin her? "Our situation was different. We both knew that it could never go any further between us." The sentiment was true. The knowledge hadn't protected her.

Josh's mouth curled. "Did we ever discuss that? Because I don't remember having that conversation with you. You know what I think?" He lowered his voice. "You're not really upset over losing your job or about ending Toni Granger's campaign. You're terrified that someone might find out what you're really ashamed of in this situation."

Clara shook her head in anticipation of an accusation she knew part of her deserved.

Josh leaned toward her until she could count his eyelashes. "The Greenwich in you is wondering if I'm lying right now. I know you can't help but ask yourself, what if I told the reporters your name? Or worse, what if I stuck my tongue behind my teeth and described the way you taste on the record."

For the first time, Josh's sex appeal made her feel cheap instead of cherished. He was a master, and his powers could destroy as well as delight.

"You said it yourself, you want to make your mother proud, and the last thing she would want is to hear about her baby girl fucking a porn star."

Clara lifted her chin. She wouldn't give him the satisfaction of shocking her. "I never should have slept with you."

"Oh, now. Don't be like that." Josh's face had turned into a hard mask. "We both know why you did it. So that years from now, when your rich, red-faced husband climbs on top of you under the covers, you can close your eyes and remember writhing on my cock."

Clara gasped as his insult connected. Josh had impeccable aim.

"What is wrong with you?" She didn't know this man. He wasn't the one who'd bought her groceries and let her drive his car. He hadn't climbed into her hospital bed or kissed her like she was the last woman on earth.

"I thought it was obvious." Josh let out a bitter laugh. "I'm in love with you." He made the confession like a man on death row. Like it didn't matter because tomorrow would never come.

Clara froze. She'd imagined this moment in spells of weakness, but never like this. The words that should have meant everything felt meaningless.

"What part of this is love?" Her fragile words rang out in the kitchen. Her pain made the question vibrate in the air. "I bet you've never stopped to consider the realities of a romantic relationship between us. Well, I have. And the first thing I realized is that if we're together, Josh, then someone has to lose. Either my family or your career. Two things we love. Two things we've built our lives on. Two pieces of us that will never fit together."

"I can't believe you're disqualifying me out of hand. Don't I get a chance to plead my case?" He sounded wounded, but more than that he sounded like a man whose past has caught up with him. A man who always knew that he couldn't win and wished now that he'd never tried.

"Josh, I'm not an idiot. I spend hours a day surrounded by your former lovers. I've seen your five-star videos. Even if you didn't go back to performing when your contract expires next year, you'd get bored with me in two weeks, a month tops. I could never compete."

"I can't believe this. Listen to yourself. You've already made up your mind. You're jumping to conclusions about things that may or may not happen a year from now when we haven't even gotten a chance to learn how to live together as more than roommates. You wanna be right more than you wanna be happy," Josh said, like a soothsayer.

Clara's eyes burned. "I need to get out of here." He'd once accused her of not living in the real world, but now he was the one painting a fantasy he couldn't fulfill.

"Wait." Josh's voice sounded far away, like she'd sunk to the bottom of the ocean while he stayed on the surface. "Don't run." He reached for her hand and she saw the fear in his eyes.

She tucked her arms behind her back. "I don't belong here." Clara tilted her head back so the tears would pool in her eyes. "There's nothing left for me in this house."

For the second time that summer, she packed her bags.

chapter thirty-four

♡ ♡ ♡

IT HAD BEEN a while since Josh had driven down the highway, hating his life, but he fell into the old habit with ease. After Clara left, he couldn't stay in the house. Every room pulsed with memories and phantom promises of what might have happened if he hadn't inadvertently harmed the woman he loved.

He'd grabbed his keys and jumped in his car without a plan. Without a destination. Without realizing that driving now reminded him, as strongly as any room he'd left behind, of the person he was trying to escape.

Everything hurt. Never before had he registered that eyelids could ache. He couldn't stop seeing Clara recoil when he'd fed her those lies about her future without him. When he'd spit the same vile stereotypes that Bennie had used on him back in her face. It didn't matter how much her rejection stung. Lashing out like a wounded animal wasn't acceptable.

Josh wished he could get purchase on some anger. At Bennie or Clara or even himself. Anger wouldn't have carved out his insides like anguish until the only thing left of his body was a hollow shell. At least not at first.

Somehow he'd done it again. Josh had always had a rare talent for sinking every ship he ever stepped foot on. Replaying his conversation with Clara over and over, he tried to pinpoint, to the millisecond, the moment he'd fucked up. He lowered his window until the wind off the freeway smacked him in the face.

As soon as he'd found out what had happened, he should have offered Clara comfort, not chosen to indulge his ego. He could have gone after Bennie or at least made her a cup of coffee. Instead, he'd had a childish outburst because she didn't appreciate being thrown into the world he'd chosen. Her fear and anger at her name going public along with Shameless had been another cruel reminder that Clara didn't want to be publicly associated with him.

To add insult to injury, he'd picked the worst possible time to tell her he loved her. Really ruined that whole moment. Of course, she didn't believe him. Mixed in with his remorse was a heaping helping of guilt.

While he hadn't revealed her name, he'd thought about it. It had felt wrong during all of those interviews not to give her credit for her idea and involvement. Shameless wouldn't exist without Clara. Neither he nor Naomi wanted all the credit, attention-loving as they were. But Josh wanted partners who would face the firing squad of society alongside him.

In hindsight, the *silent* in Clara's request to be a silent partner was deafening. Had she ever really believed they could win? Or had she considered her investment, in both him and their venture, a lost cause all along?

Shameless represented everything he'd ever liked about porn. A celebration of sex and pleasure that didn't make any apologies. Without all the stuff he resented about certain studios: overproduced, extreme narratives that confused fantasy with objectification, performers and crew treated like garbage so that the machine could drain them for all they were worth. But Shameless without Clara didn't make sense to him.

Josh started to sweat as he pulled up in front of his parents' house. He hadn't meant to drive here. Not consciously. But it seemed a fitting punishment. Now he could see how far he'd fallen. Could catalog all the people he'd hurt. One by one. He killed the engine and let the silence of the suburbs engulf him.

Whether through the interference of fate or simply because of bad timing, his mother stood at the front door, bringing her hand up to shield her eyes from the sun as she bent to pick up the newspaper. Josh took a deep breath and stepped out of the car.

"You know, you look a lot like my kid." Her words were just loud enough to carry across the lawn. The grass had that fresh-cut appearance, all the blades pushed linear, that only lasted for a few hours after his father dragged the old machine he refused to replace across the yard. Josh wanted to dive into it face-first. To fill his hands with the sharp warm blades until his fingers were painted green and he could pretend he'd never left.

Instead, he screwed up his face against the surge of tangled emotions that arose at the sight of his mother, at once familiar and painfully distant. "Hey, Ma."

Her hair was up in a tight bun, the wheat-colored waves shot through with gray. She had on one of his dad's fishing shirts and white capris, frayed at the edges. When she made her way toward him, she walked carefully across the pavement with the kind of short urgent steps that told him the driveway was like coals under her bare feet.

"'Hey, Ma,' huh? That's all I get after two years?" She stopped in the grass a few feet from him. "You always did have an abundance of nerve."

His chest ached to look at her. At her hands and her strong jaw and the freckles so like his own that splashed across her cheeks. He felt rotten, like the core of him had decayed and was spoiling everything from the inside out. Every reason he'd left home, every reason he'd run, seemed almost as stupid as it had been selfish.

"I missed you." Josh had never found any particular talent for apologies.

His mom crossed her arms and didn't give an inch. "You're in trouble."

"I know," he said, surprised to find relief in the words. At least she was talking to him.

"Big trouble." She raised her chin in the way she thought made up for the fact that he was over a foot taller than her. "I'm not exactly sure I know how to punish a twenty-six-year-old man who doesn't live under my roof anymore but believe me, I'll find a way."

He wanted to smile at her but he knew she wouldn't like it. "I don't doubt it."

"You look terrible," she said, in that soft, gentle way that only mothers can get away with. That tone when it's not judgment so much as reproach. *How dare you not take care of my child?* She ran her thumbs gently across the bags under his eyes. "Is this all for my benefit?"

Josh tried not to think of Clara. It was extraordinary that just holding her name in his mind made him flinch. Winning her back seemed unlikely. The most likely outcome of their fight was that Josh would spend the rest of his life thinking about this summer and trying to exorcise his regret. He was lost. In ways both literal and profound. And just like when he was little, he'd done the only thing that made sense. He'd tried to make his way home to the house with the blue shutters.

"I never should have stayed away so long."

His mother stepped back, adjusting the way his glasses rested on his ears in a gesture that sent him right back to standing in the kitchen before the first day of fifth grade. "That's true."

"I hurt you." It was written in the unblinking way she held his gaze. "Yeah."

The one word was all it took for him to lose it. He bent his arm to cover his face as he started to cry.

"Come here, you." She wrapped her arms around him. "Looks like you got a head start on punishing yourself."

"I'm sorry," he said, the words fragile and shaky and not enough.

"I know you are." She brushed his hair back from his forehead in slow strokes. "Sometimes you're a disaster. But you're mine."

She held him long enough for him to soak through the shoulder of her shirt.

God, he felt like shit. To have parents as good as his and leave them voluntarily, when so many people were robbed of the singular security of having their mother hold them.

Eventually, she pulled away, swiping at her own eyes. "Well, you gonna come in or are we going to stay out here and continue to make a spectacle of ourselves?"

He nodded and followed her inside, his throat too raw for words.

"Didn't even bring flowers," she said under her breath as she shut the door behind him, startling a laugh out of him that came out like a bark.

Once inside, she headed to the sink, letting the water run over her hands for so long he knew she was using the moment to collect herself. "Your father's at the store," she said before he could ask.

The tiny kitchen looked the same as he remembered. Time had neglected to reach the Conners' house. Same jaunty tablecloth. Same overflowing pile of cookbooks. Same fridge covered in countless snapshots of family and friends.

Josh couldn't help himself. He wandered over and traced the faces of his cousins' babies with a shaking hand. They'd gotten so big since he'd seen them last. What in the hell was Beth feeding them?

His mouth watered from the scent of spicy tomatoes wafting from the stovetop. When he turned around, his mother had shoved a bowl of soup on the table. Apparently, her anger didn't cancel out her constant desire to feed him.

"You don't deserve my cooking, but I'm a benevolent woman," she said, looking at the spoon she'd laid out expectantly.

Feeling surreal, he pulled out the chair and sat. The first bite acted like an elixir. The pain he felt over the loss of Clara didn't fade, but his vision got a little clearer, and his body no longer felt like it would turn on him at any moment. The soup somehow cast warmth in corners of his heart long gone numb. The feeling of being home was overwhelming.

Despite all the trappings of normalcy, the tension in the room was palpable. After a few bites, he pushed away the bowl. "If you want to yell at me, just yell at me."

His mother pulled ingredients out of the fridge and carried them to the counter. Josh had a feeling she was trying to avoid looking at him. "I'm not going to yell at you. Though I can tell by that look on your face it would make you feel better." She slathered butter on bread with angry, jerky movements. "What the hell were you thinking?"

Josh raised his hands in surrender. He knew he'd fucked up in multiple ways and it was hard to know which ones she was most mad about. "I thought you wouldn't want to see me."

She slammed the knife down on the counter. "Where in the world would you get a stupid idea like that?"

"Well, for starters, the last time I saw you, I told you I was making porn and you turned white and ran from the room."

"Oh for God's sake, Joshua, it was shocking. Maybe your generation is more open-minded, but in my day pornography still raised eyebrows." She picked up the knife and resumed buttering for only a moment before she stopped again. "Besides, you told me while I was trying to take a twenty-pound turkey out of the oven. I needed a moment to process."

"It was more than a moment," he grumbled, reduced to the child who had received regular chastisement at this kitchen table.

"The point is"—she slapped cheese onto the bread haphazardly—"when I came back to the kitchen you'd gone. And when I tried to call you the next day you'd changed your number."

He'd been scared. Josh hated seeing his mom upset. Avoiding her had seemed a lot easier in comparison. He hadn't expected to like performing as much as he did. To find himself unintentionally building a life with Stu. The longer he stayed away, the harder it became to bridge the distance he'd inflicted.

The uncomfortable moment of silence was broken by his mother pulling a frying pan out of the cabinet and setting it down none too gently on the stove. When she did speak, her voice cracked in the exact way he knew she'd been trying to avoid. "Do you have any idea how that felt? You scared the crap out of me. I was worried sick for weeks. I had to run down Curtis Bronson at the pharmacy and threaten him with fingernail clippers to find out you'd moved in with some new girlfriend."

She tossed butter into the pan and it hissed. "I wasn't mad that you'd chosen porn. I was mad that you chose porn over us."

He'd never considered that out of all his choices, his silence would be the one that broke his parents. At twenty-four, he'd felt like a failure. No one had expected anything from him and nothing was exactly what he'd given them. "I always assumed I had to choose."

Bread hit the hot pan with another sizzle. The scent of toast became another memory ignited on this painful walk down memory lane.

His mother finally turned to face him. "That's the worst part. You gave me and your father zero credit. You cut us off before we even got a chance to respond. I felt like a bad mother, not because you chose to have sex on camera, but because you didn't trust me enough to love you while you did it."

Josh realized he'd internalized a lot of the stigma surrounding his occupation. Had let it craft his vision of that November night and the subsequent fallout. "I told myself I was doing you a favor by staying away."

She sighed, turning to flip the grilled cheese. "In your rush to protect yourself from heartache, you're always the first to jump to conclusions."

The truth of that statement was undeniable. He'd rushed to push Clara away before she could condemn him, the same way he'd fled from his family. "If it makes you feel any better, I've come to accept that that's a crummy strategy."

"You owe the people who love you the benefit of the doubt." She piled the steaming sandwiches on a plate.

Josh rubbed his eyes and groaned at what an absolute idiot he'd allowed himself to be for so long. "I'm really sorry, Ma."

Bringing the plate with her, she sat down across from him, separating two halves until they created the kind of cheese pull usually reserved for Kraft Singles commercials. "Jerk." Her smile was contagious as she passed him his own grilled cheese.

"You really don't care that I've been performing?"

"Look, I've had two years to process this information and for me, it always comes down to this: I care about you being safe and happy. And about the blockers your father put on my computer so I never accidentally see you mounting anyone. As long as those three things hold up, you're an adult and I respect your choices."

The acceptance and love meant more to him than he could ever articulate. "Thank you."

"I've always believed in the infinite power of your goodness, Joshua. I'm sure whatever sex you choose to have, on or off camera, both of which I never want to hear about, is an expression of that. Now I'm going to eat the rest of this grilled cheese sandwich, and when I'm done I'd like to discuss things that in no way involve your genitalia for the rest of the afternoon."

"Yes, ma'am." Josh took his own bite, letting his eyes fall closed.

He knew his mom had let him off easy. Knew he'd have to apologize all over again once his dad got home. Most of all, he knew he owed Clara more than an apology. Josh had watched her face her fears over and over in the last few months. Now it was his turn.

He had all the pieces. All he'd needed was the courage to put them together.

chapter thirty-five

♡ ♡ ♡

RECKLESSNESS PUMPED IN Clara Wheaton's veins, as potent as any other poison. Following in the footsteps of many a scorned woman before her, she'd gone and blown an absurd amount of money on a flight and a dress designed to make men pant. The moment she stepped outside the airport in Las Vegas—the last leg on Everett's band's tour—all moisture drained from her body. Well, at least what remained following an onboard crying jag that had drawn concerned whispers from several passengers. She supposed most people cried on the way home from Sin City, rather than on the way there.

The travel-size pack of tissues in her purse had proven no match for the way her confrontation with Josh had stripped her of whatever remaining armor she possessed against the world. Every inch of her felt flayed open. Raw.

Love. He'd said love. Love, in the same breath he'd used to declare she'd never find anything better. Despite all the worrying she'd done in her lifetime, none of her contingency plans covered this type of emotional implosion. For so long, she'd refused to allow herself to indulge the idea of building a romantic future with Josh. Two people as different as they were couldn't fit into each other's lives without carnage and bloodshed. They'd made an attempt and ended up the first victims.

Reverting to her original plan, otherwise known as Operation Everett, made sense on paper. Clara needed to remind herself of what she used to want so she could stop thinking about a love she could never have.

Attempting to swish her hips, she entered a dive bar on the outskirts of town that stank of fried onions and stale beer. Making her sway fluid with luggage in tow was no easy task, but she'd traded in her reputation as a conservative socialite for one as a champion of the clitoris. She might as well act like it. Some sort of sex appeal through osmosis should have occurred after all her time spent around people who excelled at raising pulses. And . . . appendages. The bottom of her heel stuck to the sticky floor and she stumbled. *Or not.*

At seven p.m., the bar held only a smattering of customers, but the band's website said they went on in half an hour. A small stage with a lone mic stand and a despondent-looking amp flopped facedown took up most of the back wall.

"Excuse me?" Clara caught the eye of the surly bartender. "I'm looking for Everett Bloom and the Shot of Adrenaline."

He pointed a rag at the door down a dark hallway. "Check out back. Think he went for a smoke."

"Thanks." Clara wrapped her arms around herself and stepped carefully over piles of peanut shells littering the floor. Reuniting with Everett was supposed to cut through the miserable haze that had engulfed her ever since she'd left Danvers Street. Instead, she just felt numb.

"Actually." She spun around. "May I have a shot of your finest tequila, please?" Fingers crossed that the burn of alcohol reminded her she was alive.

The bartender passed her the drink with an appreciative smile. "On the house."

At least she knew the dress worked.

She found Everett sitting on the curb of the parking lot with a cigarette resting between two fingers. The sunset painted a starburst halo over his head.

She waited for her heart to flip over like a pancake.

It didn't.

Almost as if she'd left the vital organ back in West Hollywood.

"Hey," she said, trying not to cough. Not her finest opening line.

Everett swiveled and his mouth dropped. "Cee? Oh my God, kid." Stubbing out the cigarette on the pavement, he got up and wrapped her in a bear hug. "What are you doing here?"

Brushing her hair out of her face from where he'd accidentally pushed the heavy locks into her lipstick, she aimed for nonchalant. "Thought I'd catch the show."

"Wow." He nodded his chin at her suitcases. "You planning on moving in?"

"Not exactly. I, ah." *It's only embarrassing if you let it be embarrassing.* "I'm on my way back to New York. This is a layover."

"What?" His face fell. "Trip's over already? How much trouble could you have possibly gotten into over the course of one summer?"

"You'd be surprised." Her laugh turned into a wince.

"I can't believe this. I can't believe you're here." Everett's eyes traced her from head to toe. "You look different."

Clara tried not to fidget. She'd waited a long time for him to look at her with unbridled interest. So why did it make her long to wipe off her makeup and pull on sweats? Everett only ever saw her at her best. Her most polished. Josh had seen her covered in flour and raw egg, in lounge clothes that made her resemble a human potato, and in a terrible hospital nightgown—bruised and battered. Not to mention buck naked. He looked at her the same way when she was stripped to her foundation as he did when she was decked to the nines.

Everett gestured at her general form. "Did you do something different?"

She knew he meant had she dyed her hair or lost weight or bought a new shade of lipstick. But the more honest answer went beyond the way she looked.

This summer, she'd done a lot of things differently.

While on paper, she was ending the summer the same way she'd started it—unemployed, single, and in search of housing—she'd recently learned that sometimes the facts only told half of the story.

If her name had never appeared in those articles, today would have gone a lot differently. She'd seen the bottle of champagne Josh had bought weeks ago and tried to hide behind a grapefruit at the back of the fridge. In another life, they were toasting their success right now, the bubbles stinging her nose each time he made her laugh.

"You know," she said, folding her legs to sit next to Everett on the sidewalk, "I think I might be a coward."

He ran a hand across his head, ruffling the dark hair. "Come on."

"I'm serious." She could still feel the tequila hot in her throat, loosening her tongue. "I spent all those years in art school. Countless hours observing creators, their patterns and motivations, their fears, and their pain. And I never once had the guts to make something with my own name on it." Shameless could have changed everything if she'd had the strength to claim it.

"There are worse things than being afraid," Everett said gently. "I was always really proud of you going for your PhD. Keeping art history alive. I'd picture you in a museum somewhere, showing everyone how much smarter you are than them. The path you chose suits you."

The future he described had always been the plan. The Guggenheim. Perfectly tailored pantsuits. A lifetime preserved in a temperature-controlled room.

"I'm more than my job." The words came out bare. Truth without accusation. The first lesson, though not the last, that she'd learned from Josh.

Inside, she heard the band begin to tune up. The drumbeat was almost visible in the stifling Nevada heat. Why had she come here?

Up close, it was stupidly obvious that Everett was never going to want her. He was never going to look back on their friendship and wish for more. Never going to lie awake in bed wondering where he'd gone wrong. Never going to see her name in the Sunday wedding section and taste regret. Hollywood had promised her that if she loved hard enough, pined long enough, threw herself in his path, again and again, eventually, her childhood best friend would fall for her.

But real life didn't account for free will.

It didn't matter how many reasons she could list why Everett should love her. He didn't. Not in the way she'd always wanted. And until she stopped waiting for a love she felt she was due, she'd never be able to imagine the future with anyone else.

Everett ran his hands down his jeans-covered calves. "I guess you're not the girl with Popsicle-stained lips trying to dunk me in the pool anymore."

A giggle made its way out of her mouth. Oddly painful. God. What an absolute nightmare. She'd been waiting all summer for some kind of closure. For him to say something or do something that would complete the narrative of their one-sided love affair. No wonder she couldn't get closure from Everett. As the architect of her own suffering, Clara was the only person who could bring this emotional pilgrimage to its conclusion.

With a glance over his shoulder, he tapped his foot against the concrete, a nervous, itchy tune. "I should probably head back inside."

As Everett got up, turning his back on her for the second time that summer, she realized she didn't have any of her usual responses from close proximity with him. Her breathing was calm. Her face cool. The only impulse she fought was one to check her watch. At some point over the last few months, Everett's position had shifted in her memory and her esteem, the evolution occurring so gradually she hadn't noticed until now.

She could see why she'd once liked him. He was still handsome. Still said her name like a caress. Fourteen years of fantasy built up a lot of scar tissue. But Everett was no longer her "one that got away." No, that title was desperately in danger of belonging to someone else.

Josh might have acted like a self-righteous idiot, but one bad day didn't change the fact that he'd spent his summer making her feel exceptional in every way.

Everett was . . . she considered a handful of words most commonly attributed to women: *flighty, ditzy, bimbo. Figures there aren't as many readily available terms for men.*

The very idea of loving Everett suddenly struck Clara as ridiculous. A wannabe rock star living off his daddy's money who forgot to return her phone calls. She didn't need Everett Bloom with his cleft chin and his Ray-Bans and his halfhearted apologies. What an embarrassing catalyst for her fall from grace.

It's amazing how wrong you can be about a person. About yourself.

Clara pressed her lips together to avoid smiling. She wondered if it was hindsight or the tequila buzzing in her veins that transformed tragedy into comedy. Discarding old dreams was surprisingly liberating.

"I loved you for a really long time," she said on an exhale, letting the truth out into the night air.

Everett froze. "Clara," he started, but then didn't seem particularly inclined to take the sentence further, as if her confession were an inconvenience more than anything.

Oh, for crying out loud. She'd been the one to carry a torch for fourteen years; the least he could do now was hear her say it.

He ran his thumb along his eyebrow. "You're just saying that because we've known each other forever."

She let her eyes swipe across him then and came away cool and impartial. The sky's last traces of sunset surrendered to dusk, and in those impossible blues, Clara saw Chagall. She saw Josh when his hair fell into his eyes. Her heart, which had been screaming in her chest all day, had finally found a way to speak to her brain.

"I think you're right." Everett had eclipsed her ambition, her drive, her hunger, all of the things that she now loved most about herself. All the things Josh celebrated. "I think I loved my idea of love. Of passion and partnership. Of someone else's hand in mine. My name on the lips of a man who wanted me. I craved certainty. The excitement and reassurance of knowing who I was coming home to at the end of the day."

It was strange to want something for so long, to turn it over so many times in your mind, that the image became as faded and worn as an old Polaroid. To become so consumed by the yearning in your heart that when you got what you'd always longed for, you could hardly recognize it. "But still, I pinned that fantasy on you for longer than I'd like to admit."

"I've been a shitty friend." Everett let out a long sigh. "I'm sorry. I want to say that I didn't know how you felt all those years, but I did. I knew and I pretended not to know because it was easier. I didn't wanna lose you. You've always been there for me."

It was a crummy answer, but honest, and at the end of the day, it didn't matter very much. She took the hit like a pinprick.

"You know what's funny?"

Everett pulled a new cigarette from his pocket and lit it. "God, I hope you've got something good, 'cause I feel like a colossal asshole right now."

Clara grabbed the cigarette from his mouth and tossed it on the ground. Even if she wasn't in love with him, she didn't want him giving himself lung cancer.

"You came through in the end. Not intentionally, of course, but through sheer dumb luck. Because you got me to Danvers Street. You got me to Josh."

Everett's eyebrows shot toward his forehead. "Don't tell me you and Craigslist guy . . . ?"

She sighed. "I think he might be the best mistake I ever made."

"The Clara Wheaton I know doesn't make mistakes."

She whistled under her breath. "I guess you don't know me anymore." Her months in L.A. had been about more than Josh. Somewhere in a falling-down bungalow in West Hollywood, she'd built Shameless and a version of herself that she admired.

Honestly, so what if people knew she'd invested in promoting women's pleasure? For twenty-seven years she'd held a nearly perfect record, and all it had landed her was a life she could walk away from at the drop of a hat. Maybe it was her Wheaton blood, or falling head over heels for the last person she'd expected, but somehow, some way, Clara had finally developed a taste for scandal.

She got to her feet, her mind already miles away. "I gotta get out of here."

"What do you mean? You just showed up. The band's on in ten minutes."

Leaning up onto her tiptoes, she gave him a quick peck on the cheek. "Sorry, kid," she said, tossing his favorite nickname for her back over the fence. A quick look at her watch and a few careful calculations confirmed the fastest way back to Josh. She could wait, take a flight tomorrow, but suddenly the idea of getting behind the wheel, of trusting herself and navigating toward exactly what she wanted, was undeniably appealing. Sure, her heartbeat still kicked into high gear. Her hands would probably still tremble a little when she wrapped them around the steering wheel. But Clara now knew that more often than not, the scary things, the ones you spend the most time and energy talking yourself out of, are the ones that make life worth living. "Hey, I actually need a favor."

"Anything you want." Everett shrugged. "I owe you big-time."

Clara held out her hand, palm up. "I'm gonna need your keys."

chapter thirty-six

♡ ♡ ♡

THE LAST THING Josh wanted to do two days after losing Clara was talk to more press. But if he couldn't do right by the woman he loved, at least he could show up for the project they both believed in.

So Josh sat in the recording studio of KXZR radio station in Torrance. Following the mini press schedule Clara had made for them weeks ago, he and Naomi were appearing on Dana Novak's popular syndicated talk show. He'd tried calling and texting Clara, but she must have turned her phone off. The word *gone* flashed across his brain in neon letters.

The well-known host's signature close-cropped silver hair shone under the lights as she fired off a series of questions. Josh tried to smile. The big headphones he'd received from her assistant made his ears sweat. So far, they hadn't gone near Clara, but he knew it was only a matter of time.

"How did you decide to start Shameless?" Dana had the perfect radio voice, clear and direct. "I'll be the first to acknowledge the sad state of sex ed in America. But it's a bit of a stretch to go from porn—and exes, I might add—to creators in the business of promoting female pleasure."

Josh nodded for Naomi to take this one. He didn't feel like talking.

Didn't want to waste another second not looking for Clara, but Naomi had threatened to skin him alive if he missed the interview, and his ex was nothing if not a woman of her word.

"We came into the project with different perspectives but a common goal," Naomi said. "We both believe sex is better, for everyone, when partners understand each other's bodies. When they give each other permission to communicate and experiment and grow. Pleasure isn't one size fits all. Great sex is constantly evolving, and so should the discourse around it."

Naomi gave him a half smile. "Josh and I happen to have more sex than average, so we've learned a few tricks that we share on the site, but we certainly don't know everything. We could never have brought Shameless to life alone."

Dana propped her chin in her palm. "Ah, yes. You've got a handful of creative collaborators. But I'll tell you, the one I'm most interested in, and I'm sure you can guess, is socialite Clara Wheaton. Before Shameless, she'd never dealt in adult entertainment, but her family's got a list of scandals as long as my arm. What made her decide to take a walk on the wild side?" She looked back and forth between them. "Or should I say which one of you?"

Josh had known this moment was coming. Still, his pulse jumped at her name. "We're not going to discuss Ms. Wheaton in any capacity," he said into the mic with a flat tone that brooked no argument.

"Ooh, do I detect a bit of protectiveness? Did I stumble on America's raunchiest love triangle?"

Josh took off his headphones and got to his feet. "I'm done." The vision that greeted him when he turned around stole his breath. "Clara."

A fresh wave of pain erupted at the sight of her. Her beauty reminded him that he'd blown the best chance at happiness he'd ever known. He wanted to throw himself at her. Undignified, clinging, grasping. After the last forty-eight hours, he wanted to inhale her.

But he couldn't.

Not yet.

She graced him with a smile. "Hello."

The bright red *ON AIR* sign cast a rosy glow on her cheeks.

"Are you Clara Wheaton? The investor?" Dana Novak was certainly quick on the uptake.

"I am." Clara pushed her hair off her face.

Josh didn't know in that moment if he wanted to laugh or cry. Clara's soda-can metaphor finally made sense. The emotion inside him had nowhere to go, so it all lodged behind his rib cage.

"Excellent. Shall we pull up a chair?" Dana signaled to a young woman watching them behind a large window. "Ladies and gentlemen, we've got a surprise guest for you today."

"What are you doing here?" Josh stared at her. He couldn't make sense of her presence. Half of him believed that if he blinked too long she'd disappear. She obviously didn't want people to know about her involvement with Shameless, so why had she shown up during a live interview? Whatever her reasons, he preferred any room with her to one without her.

Dana's assistant ushered Clara closer to the microphone and manhandled Josh back into his own chair.

"I came to tell you something," Clara said, her mouth inches from the mic.

"You want to tell me something now? While hundreds of people are listening?"

"Thousands," Dana corrected.

"Yes." Clara gulped. "I know I said what happened between us was just sex."

Josh's eyes shot around the room at their spectators. He had zero clue what was happening or whether it was good. Still, the word *sex* on Clara's lips was enough to make him half-hard.

Naomi sat up straighter in her chair. *There goes that secret.*

Dana steepled her hands. He could tell from her face that she thought this interview had gotten a whole lot more interesting.

Clara continued. "But our relationship is so much more than that. I came to tell you, and apparently a bunch of strangers listening, that I'm in love with you."

Josh's heartbeat slammed in his ears. He bit his tongue, tasting pennies.

"I'm sorry I was too scared to accept it before. I always thought love was supposed to make you itchy. A crawling-out-of-your-skin kind of obsession. I thought love was synonymous with pining and longing. That it had to hurt."

Josh could read between the lines. She meant, *I thought love looked like Everett.* Man, he fucking hated that guy.

Clara took a deep breath and tilted his chin until he looked directly at her, instead of at his own balled fists. "But love isn't like that. At least not for me. Loving you is like sinking into a warm bath after a lifetime of feeling cold down to my bones."

Josh's chest rose and fell as he tried to gather enough oxygen to process this revelation.

Clara reached for his hand. "It's having someone see me, past the artifice and the posturing, and decide I'm more than enough."

He closed his eyes and ran the tip of his nose against the back of her hand, savoring her words and the petal-softness of her skin.

Clara's voice gathered strength. "My love for you isn't an addiction. Being with you doesn't provide some warped sense of validation for my life. You were never a fling I had to get out of my system. Our love feels like . . . freedom. The kind people give their lives for."

Josh's vision went hazy. He couldn't process this turn of events.

Clara must have misinterpreted his silence because she brought her mouth closer to the mic. "Although I want to be very clear that the sex is unbelievable. Better than it looks on screen. Seriously. You have no idea."

Naomi cleared her throat.

"Right. Sorry. Josh, the reason Shameless exists is because you encouraged me to stop apologizing for what I want and what I deserve. Checklists, guidelines, terrible driving, and all. You're everything I never knew I needed, but I can't imagine my life without you, and frankly, I don't want to."

He sat, stupefied at his good fortune. In a thousand lifetimes, he'd never get enough of Clara. Of her optimism and her nerve. Of her desperate kisses and faith that people were worth fighting for.

Naomi narrowed her eyes at him. "Better get a move on. If you don't kiss her soon, I will."

Josh shook out of his stupor and stood, pulling Clara out of her chair.

He wanted her at that moment more than he'd ever wanted anything in his life. He held her face in both of his hands. "Great speech."

"Thanks." She dipped her thumb into his dimple. "Went a little astray with the sex bit at the end."

"You found your way back." He brought his mouth to hers and Clara wrapped her arms around his neck. His world righted on its axis as their lips met in a tender press. He wasn't sure he deserved her, but he sure as hell wasn't going to let anyone take her away.

Josh had never imagined he'd get to have this kind of softness with Clara.

Dana clapped her hands. "So does this mean we'll be seeing the two of you in future tutorials for Shameless?"

Clara froze in his arms, her eyes uncertain. "I suppose we could do like a kissing tutorial? Fully clothed kissing. Ooh, set to R&B slow jams."

"We're gonna need a lot more rehearsal time before she's ready for an audience. In fact, we should go practice. Right now." His eyes never left

Clara's. "Naomi can take it from here." Josh's cheeks hurt from smiling so hard. "Please excuse us."

He practically dragged Clara out of the studio and into the hallway. "I'm so sorry for the way I acted," he said as soon as the door closed behind them. "I was a complete asshole. I want you to know I—"

Clara eyed the elevator before grabbing the front of his shirt and dragging him into an out-of-the-way stairwell. As the door slammed behind him, she ran her fingers through his hair and molded her curves against his hollows. "Tell me later," she whispered in his ear.

Josh needed no further urging. He grabbed her ass and lifted her off the ground so she could wind her legs around his waist before pushing her against the wall and sucking hot kisses into her neck below her ear.

Clara moaned with abandon.

"Are we really doing this? Here?" If this day was a dream, he never wanted to wake up.

She rolled her hips against him. "Think you can handle it?"

Josh laughed against her lips. "Sweetheart, I've still got plenty of moves you've never seen."

He balanced her ass on the stairwell running against the wall. "This is a nice dress," he said as he shoved the fabric above her waist. With impatient fingers, he shifted her underwear to the side. "God, Clara. You've got the perfect pussy," he said when he found her soaked and ready for him.

Clara clenched her thighs around his hips, whimpering as she bit into his shoulder. "I love you. I love you so much."

Josh swore like she'd said something filthy and bucked his hips against her. "If I come in my pants from the sound of your voice and some dry-humping, I'm going to lose all my street cred."

Clara laughed low in her throat as she closed her eyes and tipped back her head. "Then what are you waiting for?"

Josh didn't miss a beat. He dug into his pocket for a condom. *Thank goodness old habits die hard.* He ripped open the foil packet with his teeth and slid it on. "This is really unbelievable. Like I know it's happening because you're here and you look amazing but—"

"Josh?" Clara's ragged breaths came out in pants.

"Yes?"

She reached forward and grabbed his ass, lining up their hips until he sank into her.

As her tight heat surrounded him, he lowered his head to her shoulder with a tortured groan. "Right."

With his hands behind each of her knees, he tilted the angle of her pelvis so that the head of his cock rubbed her G-spot. He might not be able to make her come twice in a stairwell, but he could sure as hell try.

Josh found himself embarrassingly close as he listened to her whimper and mewl. Her hands dug into his shoulder blades as he inched her thigh higher against his hip and felt her tremble around him. Clara bit down where his neck met his shoulder as she found her pleasure.

"You're incredible." He could spend hours watching her bite her lip and squirm as she came.

Clara moved her hands to his nape, pulling his mouth to hers. "How the hell is being with you *better* than an entire summer's worth of fantasizing?"

Each word conjured a new, magnificent image in his brain until he panted at the edge of infinity. Both starving and sated. His definition of happiness expanded to encompass this perfect, wild moment.

Josh sank his fingertips into the silky skin of her thighs and gritted his teeth to keep from screaming as his own orgasm rocked him. He brought his sweaty forehead to rest against hers. "I can't believe you're real." He slid out of her and helped her down from the railing.

She hastily handed him a handful of tissues from her purse. "Sex in public is as good as I thought, but the aftermath is decidedly less glamorous."

Josh laughed as he cleaned himself off and tucked everything back into his jeans.

Clara's purse started ringing.

"It's Jill," she said, looking at the caller ID flashing on the screen.

"You might need to answer that."

"Hello?" Clara said, bending to bring the device to her ear. Her cheeks had gone red as bricks.

"You've gotta get down here," Josh heard Jill say in the loud, terse tone of someone trying not to panic. "I'm at my office and Toni Granger just showed up asking to speak with you."

Clara stared at Josh and licked her bottom lip. "Now?" Her eyes shot wide. "Okay. Okay. I'll be there as soon as I can."

After a quick stop at the restroom to freshen up, they made their way to the parking lot.

"Come on. I'll drive," Josh said, taking her hand in his.

Clara stopped short. "Actually, I've got a car here."

He swept his eyes across the parking lot. "What? Where did you get a car?"

"Well, it's kind of a funny story . . ."

chapter thirty-seven

♡ ♡ ♡

JOSH TOOK THE news of her spontaneous road trip with remarkable aplomb, all things considered.

"Do I love that you ran back to that dude the first chance you got? No." Josh broke into a grin. "But at the same time, I love the visual of you demanding that chump's keys to make a beeline back to me."

Butterflies beat their wings inside Clara's stomach. She'd gone from one emotional roller coaster to the next, and now Toni wanted to see her?

Josh squeezed her hand as they stood outside Jill's office. "What's going on in that beautiful brain?"

"I'm a little nervous." A lot nervous. "I had all that adrenaline pumping in my veins back at the studio, lots of endorphins, but now I have to face the consequences of my actions."

"Do you regret it?" His voice came out unnaturally neutral.

"Absolutely not. If other people don't like it, they can take a hike."

Josh shook his head. "We gotta get you a millennial phrase book or something. Phrases like that are why telemarketers are always trying to sell you osteoporosis medication."

He hesitated when they reached Jill's door. "Maybe I should wait out here."

Clara pressed her lips to his cheek. "Please come with me. Whatever happens. I'd like to introduce you to my aunt."

He squared his jaw. "Lead the way."

"Good morning," Clara said, taking Josh's hand as they walked into the conference room where Jill and the DA waited. "I apologize for keeping you waiting."

"That's not a problem." Toni Granger rose to her impressive height. "I understand you probably weren't expecting to hear from me."

The DA turned to Josh. "Nice to see you again, Josh."

Clara took an involuntary step backward.

Josh stared at the ceiling with his hands crossed behind his back. Goose bumps erupted across Clara's skin.

"You can imagine my surprise," Toni said, "when I stepped out on my front porch this morning to collect the paper and found this vaguely familiar young man on my doorstep."

Toni put a hand on Josh's shoulder. "When I asked him what exactly he thought he was doing, he told me that he had some valuable information to share with me. Information relevant to my campaign. He handed me a thumb drive and graciously said he would wait outside in case I had any questions."

Clara shot Josh a look that said, *What the hell?* He had some serious explaining to do.

"Now I will admit my first instinct was to kick his ass for trespassing on private property, but something in his eyes made me decide to listen to him."

Josh threw up his hands. "I want to clarify that the situation was urgent. I didn't want to waste valuable time waiting for your office to open. You should make it harder to find your address on the Internet if you don't want to receive visits from concerned constituents."

"I'm glad you found me," the DA said before holding out a small drive to Clara. "Josh has collected a huge amount of incriminating information on the Black Hat corporation and H. D. Pruitt."

Josh stepped directly into Clara's slightly blurry vision. "I've been gathering a bunch of emails and text messages documenting Black Hat's shady behavior for a few weeks now. The cast and crew found out what I was up to—I'm not exactly known for my stealth, as you know—and they volunteered stories of their own. Toni says we've got evidence of almost thirty violations of labor and employment laws. Stu even uncovered production footage we can use in court."

"What?" Clara's mind raced in a thousand directions. "Why didn't you tell me?"

"I wasn't sure if I could go through with it, and I knew if I told you I would have to. I needed a reason that was bigger than my fear. As soon as you left, I knew I had one."

The DA smiled through closed lips. "He also volunteered to serve my office as a witness on behalf of the adult entertainment industry. He said he thought if he aligned himself with my efforts, it would help the community see that I wasn't—what were the exact words you used?"

Josh blushed. "Just another asshole politician using sex workers as a soapbox."

"He seemed concerned I might not act on the evidence he offered, so he politely reminded me that in my campaign platform I promised that when I fight for equality, I don't forget the marginalized or stigmatized. I can only imagine he got that information from you. He also handed me a copy of a position paper I wrote five years ago." The DA's normally steely gaze softened. "Do you want to tell her the rest?"

Josh took both of Clara's hands in his. "I asked Toni to consider allowing you back on the campaign team. I told her you knew how to turn things around. You did it for me, and if she gave you another chance, you would do the same for her."

Clara fanned herself. "May I sit down?"

Josh helped her to a chair.

"Are you sure about this?" She couldn't believe the risk the DA was willing to take.

Toni turned to her aunt. "You're in charge of my PR. Do you think bringing a case against Black Hat would be enough to own the election news cycle?"

"Let's see. It's got sex. Money. Power." Jill ticked off the words on her fingers and smiled. "Yeah. That should work."

"Well, Clara, what do you say? You up for it?" Toni smirked.

Clara turned to her aunt. Jill was one of the strongest and best women she knew. She'd taken a chance on Clara, no questions asked, even after everything the Wheatons had put her through. Jill had held on to her convictions for an admirably long time. Had fought for them not with weapons but with stalwart silence, accepting her family's shunning with more grace than they deserved. She'd paid for her choices, for her freedom, and the soft lines around her eyes marked the duration of her sentence.

Jill had taught her a lot this summer, but Clara didn't want to turn into her. The Wheatons had weathered countless scandals. It was time they learned how to forgive themselves. "I'll come back. But you have to come home with me to Greenwich for Christmas."

Her aunt's eyebrows shot up.

"We can face the music together. Two black sheep returned to the flock." Clara held her breath as she waited for an answer. She was determined that her family wouldn't shut the door on her, but it would be easier if she had Jill at her side. The Wheatons should be proud of both of them. Neither had done something a little PR couldn't fix.

"I'm in." Jill wrapped Clara in a hug. "Proud of you," she whispered in her ear.

"We might not be able to keep your name out of the opposition's mouth entirely," Toni said as they pulled apart. "We're going to need to get started immediately, and none of it will be easy. Even with the right evidence, Pruitt will hire the best defense attorney money can buy. He'll outspend us in every way, including public relations."

"Then let's get to work." Jill winked as she ushered Toni out of the conference room.

As soon as they were alone, Clara turned to Josh. "I can't believe you did this." A lawsuit was more than taunting Pruitt. Much more than Shameless's tiny, quiet rebellion. Going to trial, drawing the spotlight, it all jeopardized his role within the adult entertainment community. Based on what he'd told her before, many people in the industry would see him as an opportunist at best and a traitor at worst.

Growing up, Clara watched her parents make a lot of sacrifices out of love for their children, but never before had a man done anything like this out of love for her. Did she really deserve it?

So much of Josh felt too good to be true. After three months of telling herself, *That's not for you. Those eyes, those hands, that mouth, that kindness, that humor. None of it belongs to you and don't you dare kid yourself.* Even hearing the story from one of the most authoritative people she'd ever met felt surreal.

"I didn't do it for you," Josh said.

Clara's shoulders sank. "Oh."

"But I was able to do it because of you."

He traced the curve of her cheek with the back of his hand. When Josh touched her he completed a circuit, so that electricity poured back and forth between their bodies, making every inch of her more alive.

"All of this feels big," he said. "Not just how I love you, and not just Shameless, but this chance with Toni to help people I care about on a larger scale." He spoke with his hands, the movement generating enthusiasm behind his words like propellers on a boat. "I never thought I would make a positive impact. If doing this, testifying and stuff, if that creates a safer work environment for sex workers, if it protects the industry from men like Pruitt, I don't see that as abandoning porn, or turning traitor. This case would benefit everyone in this business who's ever gotten taken for a ride."

Josh rubbed the back of his neck. "And okay, maybe it is a little bit for you, Clara. But I don't mind. Because when you left two nights ago, I realized I'd do anything in my power to show you how much you mean to me."

Pain flashed in his eyes again. "I was stupid and scared. So sure you would reject me that I pushed you away. I wanted to point to you as proof of my own inferiority. I let society's opinion of my worth declare me unqualified, before you got the chance. I thought if I could start by helping you get your job back that maybe you'd at least let me talk to you about the rest of it, the 'loving you' part."

He pulled a folded sheet of loose-leaf paper out of his pocket. "I took the liberty of making a list of pros and cons."

"You did?" Clara stared at the document. "That's so romantic."

"There are a lot of terrifying women in my life right now, but I don't care," Josh said. "Because when I look at you, Clara, it's like a rabid beast inside me sits back on its haunches and sighs, *Finally*. But I want to make sure you're cool with this. All of it. Before we go any further, have you spoken to your family?"

Clara closed her eyes. This question, among so many other wonderful things about this moment, showed her that Josh had listened, that he cared.

"No. Not yet. But I think somehow it's going to be okay. It'll be painful, don't get me wrong, but I'm getting a lot more comfortable with discomfort. You were right. I've used my family as an excuse to avoid things that scared me, even good things, for too long. I'm done asking for permission. I'm choosing my own life. They'll forgive me eventually. I won't take no for an answer."

"Damn. This has been a big day," Josh said with a panty-dropping grin. "How you feeling?"

"Grateful." Clara perched on her tiptoes and wrapped her arms around his neck. "Thank you. You know, I don't think I would have been content as a silent partner of Shameless in the end. I think I would have read the press coverage and watched the subscribers roll in and seethed with jealousy. I care about it too much. I do want to help Toni win reelection and take down Pruitt, but I think when the campaign's over I might focus full-time on the site for a while, burn through a little more of my trust fund."

His hands traveled from her hair down past her waist to flirt with the hem of her dress. The brush of his knuckles against the outside of her thighs was enough to send a bolt of desire down her spine.

When she spoke, her words came out a little breathless. "It's not every day you get to topple a porn empire."

chapter thirty-eight

♡ ♡ ♡

TWO YEARS LATER . . .

"YOU'RE BURNING THE turkey," Clara whispered in his ear. She lowered the oven temperature significantly but pushed up on her tiptoes to place a kiss on his cheek to soften the blow.

"Your dad said he likes a 'golden brown bird with crispy skin.'" Josh knuckled sheepishly at his cheekbone.

"Looks plenty crispy to me." She pressed her hands over his shoulders, urging his rumpled button-down to lie flat. "I've never seen you this nervous."

"This is the first time the Wheaton and Conners families are having Thanksgiving under one roof. Not to mention a few stray interlopers." He turned back to the oven. "I'm striving for excellence."

Clara tugged on the bow of the gingham apron tied around his hips. "Yes, well, your mother said if you don't go out there and introduce her to Toni, she will have no choice but to show the DA your embarrassing baby pictures. I wouldn't chance it. She brought an entire album. I know because she took me through it within five minutes of her arrival."

"I told her that Toni hates small talk." Josh grumbled. "She only stopped by to drop off a dish of her famous yams."

"It almost upsetting that she manages to be good at so many different things," Clara said. After the Granger campaign had won reelection, Clara had stepped down from the PR firm to work full-time on Shameless, but Toni had remained a constant in their lives.

During the battle against Black Hat, the DA had declared Josh one of the best witnesses she'd ever worked with, calling him her secret weapon to unlocking what many had called a next-to-impossible victory. On the day the guilty verdict came in against Pruitt and his empire, cementing Toni's place in public service history, the attorney had invited Josh to train as an expert witness so he could continue to represent the interests of the adult entertainment community on behalf of her office.

He'd taken her up on the offer and continued to advocate for reform within the industry, in addition to his responsibilities for Shameless.

Naomi strolled in from the den. The smoke detector chose that moment to start wailing.

"There's a joke on the tip of my tongue about how you two sure know how to heat up a room." The redhead grabbed a chair and stood on it to wave a dish towel at the incessant siren. "I'm used to putting out your fires at work every day, Connecticut, but when I accepted your offer to come over for a holiday meal, I didn't know I'd have to battle a literal blaze."

"What can I say, when you fall in love with the hottest man in the world, you learn to accept the threat of occasional combustion." Clara gazed adoringly at Josh until her business partner made an exaggerated retching sound.

"If you don't can it with that mushy crap I'll have no choice but to sleep with your brother," Naomi said, her tone serious.

Clara gasped. "You wouldn't try to sleep with Oliver."

Despite the astonishing success of their website, which now had almost thirty full-time employees, the two women still loved to test each other's boundaries.

"Oh, honey." Naomi batted her eyelashes and dismounted the chair, having vanquished the alarm. "I wouldn't have to try." She sauntered back to rejoin the party.

"I've gotta get out there." Clara moved to follow as her mother rushed into the kitchen.

"Your brother spilled Cabernet all over the society pages." She held up a sheet of soggy newspaper. Red wine bled into the headline *Roommates Turned Business Partners Say "I Do": Wheaton to Wed Conners.*

"Oh, don't worry," Josh said, winking at Clara as he moved to fetch a replacement. "We've got that one laminated."

Crisis averted, Clara guided her mother back to the living room. She returned to find her fiancé fiddling with an electric lighter. "I thought I could brûlée the yams," he said in explanation. "Give 'em a little extra pizzazz."

"Let's not tempt fate," she said, removing the apparatus from his hands. "I don't know what's gotten into you."

"Haven't you ever done something stupid to impress someone you liked?" Josh wrapped his arms around her and pulled her in for a lingering kiss.

acknowledgments
♡ ♡ ♡

I always thought I'd write a book. I just never expected anyone to read it. The brilliant surprise of realizing I was wrong would not have been possible, or as sweet, without the following people:

My agent, Jessica Watterson. Thank you for being incredibly good at selling books, but also for nailing a lot of other jobs including coach, cheerleader, and part-time therapist, which do not appear on your résumé but could if you wanted to add them. I will be forever grateful for your cool head. Thank you for backing this book out of the gate, and for finding it the best home.

My editor, Kristine Swartz. You have always made me feel like this story was both different and special, and you have guided us (me and the book both) to live up to that potential through your skill and empathy.

Jessica Brock, Jessica Mangicaro, and everyone at Berkley who helped this story reach readers. You all are the best in the business, and I'm still pinching myself that I get to work with your exceptional team.

Heather Van Fleet and Lana Sloane. The two of you changed my life when you decided to mentor me and this book. You were the first people to take my writing seriously. Your fingerprints remain across these pages. I love you. Thank you.

The Pitch Wars organization, past and present. This community has given me the greatest gift, in both craft and friendship. I can never repay you, but I plan to keep trying.

My entire Pitch Wars mentee class, but especially the motley crew on Slack. You are my found family. Thank you for sharing every step of this wild journey with me. I would not have made it here without you.

My brilliant critique partner, Lyssa Smith. I don't know what I would have done if we hadn't found each other. I'm keeping you forever.

Lane Rodgers. Thank you for lending your subject matter expertise to this book in the most thoughtful way imaginable. Your support for this story and its goal of promoting the adult film industry positively and accurately means so much.

My debut sister-in-arms, Denise Williams. I don't know what I would have done without being able to share this experience with you. I'm very grateful we've had each other's backs at every turn.

The ARWA chapter, especially Liz Locke and Nadine Latief. Thank you for making a home for me in Austin and making me feel like my dreams weren't just dreams.

The founders and community of All the Kissing. You've created something so special for the romance genre. Thank you for letting me be a part of it.

My hometown friends, with a special shout-out to my early readers, Emily and Ilona, who believed in this story and its potential, and to Quinn, who doesn't care about rom-coms and still listened to me talk about this one nonstop for years. Your faith in me has filled me up on so many days, both good and bad. I love you all so much.

My best roommate, Jess DiFrancesco. Thank you for being the first person to read this book. I would not have had it any other way.

Meryl Wilsner and Ruby Barrett. What can I say? Some days you're my heartbeat. Some days you're my deep sigh. You're my tears of laughter and strife. You're in my words. Thank you for your friendship.

My family (immediate and extended). Thank you for your endless enthusiasm for my writing, especially because I provided you with such limited information about the contents of this book and constantly insisted that you could not/should not read it. Every time you celebrated my progress or showed interest in my work, you made all the difference.

My dad. You instilled and cultivated my love of reading from an early age. You turned bookstores into my favorite places in the world. You once promised to always buy me books and have never appeared to regret that decision—despite many years of my abusing that kindness in my quest to read every one with a pink cover. (Here's another book with a pink cover you had to buy. Sorry. I love you.)

My mom. You're the hardest-working person I know, and in so many ways, you shaped who I am as a woman. You helped make me brave enough to be a writer, and specifically the writer of this book—of which I am so proud.

Micah Benson. The dedication is already super mushy, so I'm going to make this pretty practical. Thank you for picking up my slack, for reading every page of this book in multiple drafts (often while I sat across from you staring), for believing in me even when I don't believe in myself. Thank you for celebrating this story in your art (especially when I didn't explicitly make you do it), and for admitting that I am, on specific occasions, funny. I love you. I love you. I love you.

The Roommate

♡ ♡ ♡

ROSIE DANAN

questions for discussion
♡ ♡ ♡

1. At the beginning of the book, both Clara and Josh have built their lives around other people's expectations (in Josh's case, the lack of them). Which of their internalized societal roles was hardest to unlearn?

2. *The Roommate* flips several genre tropes on their heads—the boy next door, Everett, becomes a lazy antagonist instead of the love interest, and Naomi, the "jealous ex-girlfriend," becomes a partner and confidant. How would this story have been different if either one of those tropes hadn't been subverted?

3. Clara tells Josh that her past partners have let her down in the bedroom, and that "it seemed more efficient" to handle the situation herself. Why do you think she felt that way?

4. Early in the book, Clara believes certain negative stigmas about porn and adult performers that she works through by examining her own bias and getting to know Josh, Naomi, and other industry professionals.

Did you find yourself examining any of your own ideas about porn or adult performers as you read the novel? How can we break down the stigma against sex work and make the world safer for and more accepting of sex workers?

5. While going into business together brings Josh and Clara closer, it also presents a barrier to their entering into a romantic relationship. Do you think starting Shameless ultimately helped or hindered their love story?

6. Clara and her aunt Jill have several parallels—they both followed their hearts to social notoriety and escaped to L.A. with next to no plan. But while Jill cuts all ties with the Wheaton family after receiving their censure, Clara refuses to let them push her away. Why doesn't Clara also abandon the Wheatons in the wake of her own scandal?

7. Do you think Josh and Clara would have gotten together if his contract dispute hadn't led him to stop performing while they were roommates?

8. After moving across the country in pursuit of unrequited love, Clara asks Josh, "Haven't you ever done something stupid to impress someone you liked?" Well, have you? And perhaps more importantly, was it worth it?

9. Josh and Clara go from being roommates to being engaged in the epilogue. What do you think changed when they started living together as romantic partners?

Photo by Micah Benson

ROSIE DANAN writes steamy, bighearted books about the trials and triumphs of modern love. When not writing, she enjoys jogging slowly to fast music, petting other people's dogs, and competing against herself in rounds of *Chopped* using the miscellaneous ingredients occupying her fridge. As an American expat living in London, Rosie regularly finds herself borrowing slang that doesn't belong to her.

CONNECT ONLINE

RosieDanan.com

🐦 RosieDanan

📷 RosieDanan

Ready to find
your next great read?

Let us help.

Visit prh.com/nextread

Penguin
Random
House